THE FAR SIDE OF GRASS

Tale of the Mapogo lions

Enzo Malavart

This is a work of fiction. Names, characters, places, and incidents either are the product of the author's imagination or are used fictitiously. Any resemblance to actual persons or lions, living or dead, events, or locales is entirely coincidental.

Cover design and illustration by Jeff Brown Graphics.

First edition in 2021

ISBN 978-2-9580327-0-8 (E-Book)

ISBN 978-2-9580327-1-5 (Paperback)

"A friend loveth at all times; And a brother is born for adversity"
– Human saying.

"Come on, bro, trust me. When have I ever steered you wrong?"
–T., male lion of the Mapogo coalition

PROLOGUE

THE OLD MALE

How is he both stumbling and scampering?

The old male stumbled out of the bush and scampered up the hill with short, wary strides.

Unsure of his surroundings, he kept his belly low and let the newly grown grass, heavy with morning dew, cling to his damp mane and hide his presence. The green blades wrapped themselves around his ankles and came apart with soft ripping sounds.

He was nearing the top of the hill when a snag from a thornbush caught in his mane and snapped with a loud *crack*. He cursed softly and stopped mid-stride. The vegetation all around him was lush and impenetrable, but he knew better than to assume it to be empty. This was claimed land. Hostile. Everywhere he went, he was an intruder. Had been for a long time. His muscles tensed as he prepared to flee.

He rotated his ears slowly and counted a hundred heartbeats, then another hundred. He sniffed the air and let his palate sift through the smells.

Lions have muscular legs.

Nothing.

He let out a sigh of relief and leaped out of the wet lank. His stiff joints groaned and burned under the effort, but his slender legs ate the remainder of the slope swiftly. Panting heavily, he staggered up the top and sat down on the greasy mud, his burning heart ready to pounce out of his all too visible ribcage. With every painful inhalation, he could feel his diaphragm dig deep inside his emaciated frame.

And to think that it had been a short ascent.

He swallowed down a need to growl and focused his attention on catching his breath. The surrounding atmosphere was stifling. He kept his jaws ajar to cool himself down and absentmindedly rubbed his tongue against the inside of his yellow fangs. A thin rivulet of saliva dribbled down the black of his lower lip and sunk into the sodden earth at his paws.

Ahead and below, the awakening savannah glinted and steamed under the fierce blaze of the rising sun, promise of a beautiful, if slightly vaporous, day to come. For a brief instant he thought about lying down and do absolutely nothing, the way he had on so many similar mornings. He had to consciously chase the thought away.

No rest for wary cats. He could not afford the risk.

He closed his eyes and proceeded to clean the inside of his numb paws with his tongue. He went at it slowly and meticulously, almost lovingly, the way he had done his entire life. *A lion needs his paws clean and free of thorns,* a voice droned inside his head. *Any infection can prove fatal.* At his age, and given his advanced state of starvation, this sounded more like a bad joke than proper advice. But there was comfort in old habits. It helped keep the dark thoughts at bay.

A gaping void was awaiting him in the near future, he could feel it in his guts. How long did he have left? A full season? A moon? Probably less. Sometimes, in the dead of night, he would lay still on his flank with his eyes wide open and his mind would leap out of his control. *There is a patch of land somewhere*, the inside voice would point out with almost cheerful hilarity, *an insignificant stretch of mud, probably not very far from here, upon which you will lay down to rest for the last time. You know how it works, old mane. You've seen it happen enough times.*

Yes, he had. And whenever he thought back on it in the black of night, a small, pitiful whimper would escape his throat and his insides would tie themselves into a knot so tight, it made the starvation feel like a mild stomachache in comparison. The fear alone was almost enough to strike him utterly and completely mad, as if his mind were trying to violently break away from his reality by screaming 'Not me!' over and over again at the top of his lungs.

During daytime, as much as possible, he tried to stay away from those projections. Focus on the present. Concrete tasks helped. Nothing he could do to escape the void, but taking care of his paws? Now that was a problem he could solve.

Far out in the distance, the muffled grunt of a buffalo cursing angrily against the cloud of parasites hovering around his head pierced through the mist.

The old male leapt up instinctively. He knew that kind of voice. He could have recognized the deep, impetuous call anywhere. An old Dagga Boy, a lone bull who had walked away from the pressure of his herd and elected to wander through the remainder of his life alone and in peace. The memories of a hundred previous hunts surged in front of the old male's eyes as his stomach tightened with irrepressible desire. Without thinking, he turned around to face the empty underbrush behind him and almost called out loudly: "Let's go, boys, there is meat for the taking today!"

He stopped himself at the last instant. He could not afford to advertise his presence like that, not in his weakened state. Besides, none of his brothers were in any position to hear him anymore.

He rotated back toward the misty savannah and pondered whether to go down and try to wrestle the Dagga on his own. He had done it before, after all, back when he was in his prime. But things had changed. He looked down at his front legs and shook his head. He hadn't even begun the chase and already they were quivering weakly. They felt empty, out of juice.

Who was he kidding? He would never be equal to the task, not by a long leap. This was the golden sun honest truth of the matter and there was no way around it. Slightly disgusted, he lowered himself back on a spot of flattened grass and tuned the buffalo out.

Ain't that a beautiful con'drum?! That strong bull will tear ya part ‘cause ya're too weak. But the less ya eat, the weaker ya get. Soon, ‘ven a newborn calf will be too much woark for ya to handle.

The old male jerked his head back up and scoured the vegetation behind him a second time. The voice had sounded eerily like his younger brother, but he could not tell whether it had come out of the bush or from inside his head. Once again, he resisted an urge to call out loud.

Ah, ya're losing it, oald mane! Quiet's getting to ya. We were never meant to live like shadows.

The comment triggered a sad, derisive snort out of his battle-scarred, grey muzzle. Wherever it might be coming from – and he was fairly certain that it was not the thornbushes speaking – the imitation was spot on. For the first time in a long, long while, he realized how he missed those snarling growls and barely articulated sentences that had defined the constantly angry, smaller lion.

And to think that there had been a time when he would have given just about anything to shut him up.

The memories all seemed too surreal, so out of touch with his current reality, he could barely believe that they had happened at all.

And yet….

The mist evaporated and the full glare of the sun washed over his face. The Dagga Boy went through another burst of angry grunts but he paid him no mind. As his gaze turned inward, his pupils shrunk to two dark pebbles lost in a lake of haunted yellow grass.

Amid the grass, a story.

ONE

ROMPS AND WILD TUMBLES

Skoro leaped forward and landed awkwardly on short, unsteady legs. He had aimed to pin the slim tail with his paws but fell well short of his target. Quick as a snake, the mongoose wheeled in place and raised herself on her hind legs, her tiny open jaws vibrating fiercely in front of his muzzle, close enough to bite his whiskers off. A succession of strident rattles fired off in bursts of three washed over his rhinarium.

His first instinct almost led him to back down and run for the protection of the pride. To his immortal shame, he would have done it too, had he not discerned an unmistakable quiver of terror betraying the mongoose's jarring threats. The small predator was full of it, he realized.

Human slang

A small growl of pleasure escaped his throat.

A growl is an aggressive sound, not one of pleasure.

He swiped at her head with his front paw and pushed forward. The mongoose scampered off to the left.

"Leon!" he screamed joyously as he jumped in hot pursuit. "She's coming toward you, Leon! Don't let her escape!"

His twin brother sprung out of the yellow grass where he had been hiding and cut the quarry off. Skoro hurried to close the distance and together the two cubs set to work harassing their target from both sides. Unable to turn her back on either of them without risking a sudden attack that would pin her down for good, the mongoose tried to fight on two fronts and kept them at bay by lunging for their muzzles.

They pressed forward together.

They worked as a team and soon had a system all worked out. Every time the mongoose made a move toward one of them, the attacked cub would jerk his head back as fast as he could while his brother, momentarily freed of all dangers, would use the opening to push toward the exposed flank and force the mongoose back into a defensive stance. Then they would advance again and repeat the process.

This was all very dangerous, of course – although the mongoose's teeth were fairly small, Skoro was quite sure that a full bit on the muzzle would still prove extremely painful – but it was also extremely exciting.

Out of the corner of his eyes, he noticed Shaka and Dreadlocks going round on a flanking maneuver. Soon they would have her completely trapped, he realized with no small amount of pride. Truth be told, he could not quite believe that the whole thing had worked out so well. This was the first time any of them had been involved in anything resembling a hunt, after all, and Skoro had been the one organizing the whole show.

Like a proper lion ambush! he thought cheerfully while avoiding yet another lunge by swatting at the tiny head. In his mind, the mongoose was not a mongoose at all but a mighty buffalo, an angry boulder of twitching muscles four times as heavy as any of them. They had to put him down no matter the risks, for the pride.

After one last lunge, the mongoose suddenly lost her fighting spirit and tried to make a run for it. Dreadlocks groaned and pounced forward. His claws bared, he aimed for the hindquarters, the way he had seen their mothers do on real hunts. The two carnivores went sprawling in the loose dirt and their mad wrestling kicked up a brown cloud that hovered in the air and clung to their furs.

The angry rattling and spitting reached a new furious intensity that cowed the other cubs in place.

After much twisting and confused swiping, the more experienced mongoose finally managed to wriggle free of Dreadlocks' clumsy embrace with only one last claw of his front paw still tangled in her fur. Out of breath, the young cub laid himself down on his flank with his trapped forelimb awkwardly extended in front of him, unsure of what to do next.

The mongoose snarled and spat and then… she lunged for his muzzle.

Skoro recoiled. A moment ago, it had seemed to him that they had her dead to rights. The hunt was won. Now, in a curious reversal of the situation that was as sudden as it was unexpected, Dreadlocks was the one furiously trying to extricate himself from a fight he wanted no part of.

"Get her off of me!" the cub groaned anxiously.

Skoro stepped forward and gingerly swatted at the blurry ball of striped fur while making sure to keep his eyes and whiskers as far back as possible.

The stalking and trapping of the prey had all been carefully planned; the killing, not so much. Now, he had no idea how to put an end to this mess.

Not needed

It doesn't really matter anyway, he tried to convince himself in-between dodges. As long as they had her trapped, they could take their time to think of a way to bring her down. They would figure something out.

Bring her down?? One bite would kill her!

But something wasn't quite right. Something was missing. An annoying whiny voice his subconscious had expected to hear throughout the hunt. He looked around and suddenly realized that there was still a big gap between him and Shaka. The circle was incomplete.

"T!" he yelled. "What are you doing?! Come over here!"

A tiny head popped out of the grass. Wet amber eyes glanced at him in fear.

? only

By the grass, he hasn't moved at all. He's still exactly where I placed him at the beginning of the hunt.

Lions don't know what letters are. This is not something they'd ever call each other.

Prodded forward by his brother's angry calls, T. reluctantly trotted toward the fight with short, hesitant steps. Perhaps sensing a change in the group's dynamic, the mongoose locked her eyes on the newly arrived cub and immediately tore herself free of Dreadlocks' last claw.

Skoro tried one last desperate lunge, but it was already too late. "Grab her, T.! Grab her!"

The mongoose charged the younger cub. The rattles came out once more, louder than ever, and T. yelped in fear before jumping to the side. Fast as lightning, the mongoose brushed past him and dove under the cover of a nearby bush.

"You let her go!" hollered Skoro as he watched the last of the mongoose's slim tail disappear. "We had her cornered and you let her go. You botched the whole thing!"

"I'm sorry, Skoro. I just… I thought you guys didn't need me. I didn't want to get in the way."

"But why did you jump to the side like that? All you had to do was stand your ground! How hard can that be?"

The smaller cub lowered his head. "You don't understand," he whimpered. "She was like a monster. She almost *bit* me. On the muzzle!"

A low growl escaped Skoro's throat, like something out of a much older cat's belly. His brother's fear was so intense, he was reeking of it. The bitter smell clung to the roof of his palate and triggered an instinctive aggressive reaction. He leaped forward and easily overturned the much lighter cub. T. did not fight back and for a mad instant he thought about going for the throat.

Leonides ruefully shouldered him to the side at the last moment. "He's not worth it."

Skoro nodded curtly and took a couple of deep breaths to calm himself down. His heart was pounding inside his chest, demanding blood.

In front of him, T. was now shaking all over, petrified. With his ears flattened and his eyes fixed on the dirt, he seemed to have turned into something of an inanimate object.

It was both perplexing and maddening at the same time. As if the cowardly cub had suddenly decided that by ignoring the world around him, he could somehow make it all disappear.

"Only seven cubs out of twenty survive," Skoro spat in contempt, "and this worm is one of them. Riddle me that."

Dreadlocks shambled back to the group and casually lay down between Skoro and T. "Looks like T has proven himself quite the utter Tit again," he sniggered loudly while licking at his own blood coming out of a cut on his muzzle. He swallowed it down with a puzzled look that seemed more appreciative than worried.

The remark made them laugh.

"Don't say that!" T whined. "Don't call me that!" He could not muster any real anger in his voice, only fear and despair.

Skoro turned to his brothers and began to intone a familiar song.

Who is this lion who can't eat meat?
Who can't stand on his own four feet?
Why, of course, it's the Tit!
Who is this lion, so full of ticks,
His mother won't even lick?
Why, of course, it's the Tit!

"Stop it!"

They laughed and raised their voices. Out of the corner of his eyes, Skoro caught a glance of Shaka observing them from a distance, quietly.

Doesn't matter, he decided even as they reached the chorus and joyously screamed at the top of their lungs:

DEAD MEAT, WORM MEAT,
THE TIT'S GONNA BE DEAD MEAT!
DEAD MEAT, WORM MEAT,
THE TIT RUNS ON COLD FEET!

More braying laughter concluded the end of the song.

"Hey, Tit, is it true that one day you were so hungry for milk, you went for one of the Boys dangling parts?"

"No. Of course not–"

"It's true too!" Skoro exclaimed with a knowing side glance aimed at Dreadlocks. "I saw it happen. He went straight for Mak Senior's crotch. Such a roar, the Sabi Sands had never heard before."

"That never happened!" the young cub yelled, shocked by the boldness of his brother's lie.

"Better hide all your bits when the Tit is on the prowl," Leonides snickered.

"Well, it doesn't matter anyway," Skoro concluded. "It's not like any one of them is your real father anyway."

That joke actually stopped the laughter cold. Skoro bit his tongue and swallowed down a curse.

Everyone in the Eyrefield pride knew the rumor. Some of the females had wandered off one day when the Sunset Boys, the five dominant males of the pride, were out on far patrol. At around the same time, coincidentally, some calling roars had been heard in the middle of the night. The wandering females had been quick enough to return before any of the Boys could notice their absence but, soon after, both T. and Shaka's mothers had given birth to their own respective litter. Nobody could prove anything; nobody wanted to talk about it. It was one thing to know the story and find it funny, but quite another thing altogether to actually utter it out loud. Because if those words were to ever reach the ears of the bigger boys, and if said Big Boys were to suddenly put it in their thick skull that they wanted to believe it… Even Skoro knew that this was no joking matter.

T. glared at the three of them in shock. Behind the fear, Skoro could see that he was truly hurt. From the point of view of the younger cub, the joke had probably been no joke at all but a very real death threat; a casual reminder of just how precarious his standing among the pride was, and how easily any cat could seal his fate with little more than a handful of words whispered in the wrong ears.

Slightly nonplussed by his own cruelty and the sudden, devastating effect his words had had on the younger cub, he felt an unexpected and sickening spike of shame constrict his throat, as if there was something down there that he could not quite swallow. He thought about apologizing to the runt. Give him a rough but friendly head rub followed by the good old I-am-going-to-sit-on-you-because-I-like-you trick. That would break the tension and alleviate T.'s fear. Make him feel part of the group again. Skoro would then assure him that he had misspoken. That, of course, he would never really betray his life in such a way. This was, after all, the golden sun honest truth of the matter. No shame in admitting it.

He almost went for it, caught himself at the last instant.

There was another, more important factor he needed to consider. Regardless of whether he truly regretted his remark, an apology was a statement of weakness.

And this, he could not afford. Not in front of his brothers. Not in front of Leonides.

Besides, he tried to rationalize to his own conscience, *at the end of the day, once everything else has been said and done, the truth remains that T.* is *a Tit.*

Clumsy, cowardly, and constantly nagging, barely a lion at all. A rat had more backbone. And a cat does not apologize to a rat. Ever. By the grass, no.

With cold, deadpan eyes full of contempt that betrayed nothing of his inner dilemma, Skoro returned his brother's glare and stood his ground. Just as he had expected, T. lowered his gaze first and, after one last pitiful whimper, turned tail before slinking into the bush in the opposite direction taken by the mongoose.

"T! Wait up," Shaka cried out. The cub stopped and turned to face the trio. "Smart bunch of cats y'all are! What has he ever done to you to deserve this, anyway? By the grass, he's your brother too!"

Skoro drew himself up. That second spike of shame was almost too much for him to bear. Shaka was not T. He enjoyed a certain standing among the other cubs. A reputation for composure and calm courage that could not be ignored so easily. Feeling his heart sink, he clenched his jaws tight and fired up a healthy dose of not-so-righteous anger. "Run on along," he growled with a confidence he was far from feeling, "the Tit needs his mummy to protect him."

At least Dreadlocks and Leonides were still standing by his side. Right or wrong, they were presenting a united front, and that was all that mattered. It helped dilute the guilt.

After one last reproachful glance, Shaka whirled toward the grass and leaped after his younger brother.

TWO

THE VELD

They half-wrestled, half-sauntered their way back to the Eyrefield and found the eight huntresses of the pride sprawled lazily on a patch of cool dirt under the canopy of a large acacia tree. Their sisters, one young cub slightly older than them and one sub-adult, were also present, snuggled comfortably against the warm bellies of the bigger cats.

Dreadlocks let the twins lead the way and hung back to yawn and feel the air. Despite his young age, he had already learned to be mindful of the underlying current of tension coursing through the pride on any given day. Big cats' tempers had a way of flaring up without warning in the savannah heat, and a painful paw was quickly caught.

Not today, he was happy to smell. Today, the pride was lazy and relaxed, secure in the stability of things.

As he hurried to catch up with the twins, he noticed that only one of the Sunset Boys was in attendance. That did not worry him much. More likely than not, the others were simply out on patrol somewhere and would not come back until after sundown, secure as they were in the knowledge that one of their own was watching over the pride in their absence. He let his eyes drift toward the rough direction of the strong scent and caught a glimpse of a golden mane peeking through the grass at the edge of the circle of shade.

He smiled internally. Out of all the Sunset Boys, Blondie was by far the easiest one to live with, if a bit passive and careless at times. A steady rumble informed him that the lazy cat was already fast asleep. Probably had been ever since his last feed.

He broke into a small trot, full of energy, and found Skoro and Leonides assaulting Sifit's rump as if it were an enormous buffalo they had to bring down. Seemingly unperturbed, the old lioness remained immobile and kept her eyes closed while panting steadily through her half-opened jaws to cool herself down; from where he was standing, Dreadlocks could see her tongue pulse with every one of her fast exhales. The light spittle of her breath peppered the ground at her paws.

As soon as the twins reached the top of her rump and nipped at her vertebra, she casually dragged her tail across the ground in a seemingly random pattern.

Dreadlocks swallowed down a chuckle and sat on his haunches to better observe.

The old trick worked as expected. The tassel of black hair at the end of her tail looked irresistibly like a mouse. Upon seeing it move, the twins immediately lost interest in the rump and jumped down to chase after this new quarry. After a couple of near misses, Leonides finally caught it and proceeded to tear at it with all the strength of his tiny jaws. Encouraged by his brothers' success, Skoro leaped at his mother's flank and sunk his teeth into her thick fur. He was rewarded by a fake grunt of pain and squealed in delight.

Next to this loud pandemonium, Dreadlocks' sister, Fer, was still sleeping soundly with her white belly pointed toward the sky and her limbs sprawled out on either side of her body, so still as to look almost dead.

Dreadlocks felt a slight pang in his heart. Her peacefulness and utter lack of concern for the dangers of the outer world was a touching sight. A testament to the pride's success. And an intolerable affront to the younger cubs' mayhem.

Such disdainful bliss could not be abided.

He shimmied forward and worked on his stalking prowl one delicate step at a time. His posture was good, he judged, lined up from the tip of his muzzle to the tip of his tail, but he had to constantly remind himself to keep his belly lower. Once close enough – he could almost touch her with his whiskers – he pounced. She awoke with a jolt and angrily whirled toward him. A steady stream of high-pitched obscenities escaped her throat. Uncowed, he pressed his attack and the two of them romped around for a bit while the rest of the pride looked on, unperturbed.

Sifit yawned and put an end to the games with one brusque swat of her tail that sent the twins scampering away. She stood and stretched her spine in one single fluid movement, then, without warning, padded over to Dreadlocks' and Fer's spot.

As he watched her approach, Dreadlocks sucked in his breath, feeling the familiar mix of fear, awe, and bitter envy invade his heart.

Although heavily built, with a thick neck, broad muzzle, powerful chest, and paws as big as his head, she moved with an effortless, graceful gait that betrayed nothing of the explosive strength lying dormant underneath her tawny-white coat. It was like a dance she had mastered, he reflected. A quiet poise, halfway between a relax stroll and a purposeful stalk, sustained in place, it seemed, by the constant ripples of her upper body muscles moving fluidly along the lines of her large frame.

She came closer and the sun caught on the half-dozen thin scars disfiguring her muzzle. For all her gracefulness, she clearly was no soft-fur, sleek cheetah with brittle legs. At her age, she had been through the cutting grass her fair share of times, and then some. On her left hip, she bore the dark impact mark of a buffalo's horn. A chunk of the upper left thigh was still missing – torn out by the violence of the assault – and the resulting black crater seemed to eat at her like some blood-curdling, overgrown parasite.

Dreadlocks felt a brief shudder travel down his spine. The sight was daunting. With every new step, the parasite appeared to vibrate and come alive, as if eager to expand. It gave the huntress a disquieting aura that went beyond her simple physical abilities, as though her strength of will had been carved into her powerful body for all to see. It made him feel weak and inadequate in comparison, unprepared for the trials that lay ahead.

She stopped and let her gaze fall on him. He clenched his jaws tight and shuffled his front paws on the ground. There was something lost inside the faded yellow of those eyes, some bleached pain, cold and unbending, that made him want to scream inside. As though he were guilty of some unfathomable crime only she could see.

Skoro and Leonides joined him and took position by his flanks.

She ran her pupils over the three of them, wrinkled her muzzle, glanced at the grass behind them. "Where are your brothers?" she said. "The two youngest."

It took all of Dreadlocks' strength of will to resist the temptation to just make a run for it. He would never even reach the end of the circle of shade, he knew. Her immense legs would gobble up the ground behind him faster than a lion could scream 'Not me!', and then… Well, then, she might just gobble *him* up.

He stole a glance at the twins. He had to admit, the three of them had been a bit rough on the younger cub, especially Skoro. To utter the deadly rumor out loud to his whiskers like that…This was taking things too far. As usual, his brother had gotten carried away.

But then again, the Tit had proven himself the equal to his nickname. Why couldn't the insecure worm ever do anything right? Just stand your ground and act like a lion for once in your life. How hard can that be? Every cub knows that, win or lose, it doesn't really matter. Just act the part, take the blows, and stop making a big fuss out of every little spike in the dirt.

He shook his head. It was T.'s fault if they had acted like that, he was quite sure of it. The younger cub had invited the attack by being weak and insecure.

The awkward silence stretched on without end but Dreadlocks did not break. Neither did the twins, he was glad to see. Instinctively, they had gathered closer to one another.

Sifit sighed and dropped the matter. Her pensive tongue darted to her muzzle, then to her fangs. "Follow me," she snapped. "You too, Fer. There is something you cubs need to see."

They strode toward the edge of the canopy and stopped at the limit of the circle of shade.

"What do you see?" she asked.

"Grass."

"And?"

"More grass," sniggered Leonides. "Always more grass everywhere."

The eyes of condemnation fell on him from up high and he promptly choked on his own wits. Skoro's tail swiped him on the rump and the word "dumbcat" – more spat out than really spoken – floated in the air for a brief instant. Dreadlocks could not tell for sure who was responsible but, had he been asked to venture an opinion, he would have said that this was no male's voice.

"Look at those trees out in the distance," Sifit insisted. "What do you see?"

"They're green," Dreadlocks declared triumphantly, certain to have found the right answer. As soon as he heard the words spoken out loud, however, he realized just how dumb they sounded.

Sifit bowed her head and closed her eyes briefly, as though physically hurt by his remark, the sheer stupidity of it. "Yes, a tree is often green when the rains are in," she allowed with a groan, then softer, almost conciliant: "I need you to look beyond the obvious. Just like a cat can be many different things – a lion, a leopard, a cheetah – a tree is never just a tree. It can be an acacia or a baobab, a thornbush or a bushwillow. You need to be able to recognize which is which and draw the right conclusions. The same goes for the rest of the veld."

"The veld? What's that?"

"The veld is everything around you. Everything that doesn't have a beating heart. The grass and the trees, the rivers, the water holes, even the clouds above. That's the veld. And you must learn to make it your own. Now, who here can tell me what's a predator gaze?"

Dreadlocks almost blurted out that it was the gaze of a predator. Luckily, he caught himself at the last instant.

"A predator gaze," Fer recited dutifully next to him, her little voice rising clear and true above the silence of the sunbaked grass, "is a gaze that assesses the landscape, selects the prey, calculates the distance. It is a gaze that *sees*. It commands over the body and the mind. It is cold, it is patient, and, most of all, it is relentless."

She was rewarded by a nod and an affectionate nudge on the muzzle.

"Yes, very good. Don't forget that last part, boys. Relentless. As a predator, a hunter, you never stop assessing the world around you. For instance, those trees. What kind are they?"

"Knob-thorn acacias," Skoro said immediately. "Same as the one behind us."

"That's right. And what can you tell me about them? Not acacias in general, the ones you see now."

Dreadlocks squinted his eyes and leaned forward in a posture he hoped looked poised and lethal. He cleared his mind and tried to see the trees. To *really* see them, the way a predator would. The thin trunks shimmered and danced in the heat haze, their green canopies bobbing ever so faintly at the very top like the heads of small mushrooms. "They've been browsed upon," he blurted out suddenly. "All the leaves below a certain height are gone."

Sifit turned and looked at him with appraising eyes that made him feel like maybe he would be a lion one day. "Correct," she said, her voice still flat, "and what animal browses like that?"

"A giraffe?"

"Yes. Whenever you see knob-thorns with that peculiar mushroom-shaped canopy – or sometimes more flat-top – you can assume that a giraffe has been nearby. Then, if you're hungry and you have enough cats with you, it's just a matter of figuring out how long ago he or she fed, and whether it's worth trying to follow the tracks."

"Is it how you track them down, then? By looking for the trees first?"

Sifit allowed an amused snarl to flash briefly on her muzzle. "That's one way to find them, yes. There are others, of course, depending on the local landscape. That's what I mean by relentless. To look for this kind of things needs to become a second nature. You never go about a hunt without a plan and just hope to stumble upon your prey. That's a sure way to waste your strength and starve. No, you search for clues first. You assess the veld. Most of you are already quite comfortable using your muzzles and palates to sift through local smells. That's good, but that's not enough. You need to learn how to use your eyes and power of deduction as well."

She turned around and ambled back toward the thin trunk of their own acacia. On the dry bark, the knobs covering the tree looked to Dreadlocks' eyes like fat little toes with a single curved claw pointing downward. His gaze followed them all the way to a deep groove cut out of the trunk above their head, like a wound still glistening with fresh sap.

"Who can tell me what this is?"

"A leopard's claw mark?" ventured Skoro. He knew how the spotted cats liked to climb such trees.

"No, too big. Much too big."

"A rhino?"

"Too high."

"Elephant," whispered Fer. "That's the mark of an elephant's tusk."

"Correct. Elephants like to rub their ivory on the bark of those trees – to alleviate an ache, we think. Now, this one is long gone, I checked before we came, but the day you're on your own, that's something you might want to check before you choose a tree under which to rest, lest you find yourself looking up at the wrong kind of trunk and end up dying a trampled death."

Dreadlocks nodded his head slowly and took a second glance at the innocent-looking groove that had been gouged out of the solid wood like a claw-mark through soft mud. He felt ill at ease all of a sudden. Until now, he had never thought anyone could learn so much just by looking at a tree. It wasn't all just boring grass, then. So much depth to this new world. This veld. So much ground to cover. He swallowed loudly and wondered whether he would ever be the equal to the task.

Sifit suddenly pricked her ears and trotted back to the edge of the circle of shade. "Aha!" she exclaimed. "Perfect. One more thing we can learn today."

Without another word, she pounced forward, out of the circle of shade, and cut a narrow swath through the stiff yellow grass in front of her.

After a brief glance at one another, the cubs hastened to follow in her footsteps while keeping their eyes dutifully locked on her guiding tail, intent on not being outpaced by the giant strides.

Gnats jumped in front of Dreadlocks and bounced off his fur. The sharp, jagged end of broken stubs pricked the underside of his paws. Behind him, he could feel the tip of his short tail caress Fer's muzzle lightly. She groaned and sidestepped away.

At one point, they heard a hissing somewhere out to their right. Skoro made a move to go and investigate but Leonides ruefully pushed him back on track. "Not the right time, brother," he whispered.

Although he was too proud to ever admit it out loud, Dreadlocks wholeheartedly agreed with that decision. The dry lank pressing on either side of their little procession was taller than he was. Impenetrable. This was no place to go venturing away from Sifit.

After a hundred strides or so – he had forgotten to count – the grass suddenly relinquished its embrace. He stopped on the edge of the dry lank and found himself staring at some weird, twin-rutted narrow lane of hard-packed dirt that seemed to cut through the savannah from one horizon to the next, as far as his eyes could see. The abrupt change was dizzying and somewhat ominous, as if some enormous grazer had purposefully ripped out the vegetation along this particular stretch of land and never allowed it to grow back.

He was about to ask Sifit to make sense of this new landscape when Fer bumped into his rump and sent him toppling down tail over muzzle into the nearest rut. She laughed heartily and jumped after him. A heartbeat later, the twins jumped down as well and they all joyously piled up on top of each other.

Sifit paid them no mind. She stepped over the rut and casually laid herself down in the middle of the barren soil. While pushing back against one of Skoro's paws, Dreadlocks followed her gaze, and froze.

The responsible grazer was [fixing them.] — Fixing them? Makes no sense.

As big as a rhino, he thought immediately, but the overall shape was wrong. Way wrong. Filled with impossible straight lines and sharp angles unlike anything Dreadlocks had ever seen before, as if the beast were missing something vital, a fleshy rotundity common to all living things. In fact, as it stood there, completely immobile, it reminded him vaguely of those assemblages of hard bones that he had seen sticking out of carcasses once the meat had been removed. Except, of course, that this was no inanimate dead carrion. A foreign growl could be heard coming out of the beast's body. Low-pitched and not very loud, its constant flatness, unbroken by the need to breathe, was off-putting, alien.

A succession of small, high-pitched squeals and coos punctuated by strange clickety-click chirps arose. Dreadlocks raised his gaze and realized with cold terror that the beast's back was covered with beings roughly half the size of a normal lion, like birds on a buffalo.

The four cubs looked at each other, perplexed.

"Where do we go?" Fer breathed out. "Forward or back?"

"Forward. We have to go to Sifit."

"Are you crazy? That thing will see us."

"It's already seeing us! Look at the white eyes at the front of the muzzle."

"Those are not eyes, brother."

"Then what?"

Fer only shook her head, at a loss for words. For once, her intrepid courage seemed to have found its match.

Leonides groaned and let loose a single loud curse, like a battle-cry, then lunged forward and out of the rut.

"Leon!" Skoro called out.

Before Dreadlocks had time to stop him, he had already clambered up the crumbly bluff. He stopped for a brief instant in front of the beast, paralyzed, then rushed after Leonides on stiff legs that seemed to move of their own volition, as if the cub were tethered to his twin by an invisible bound he could not severe.

Fer turned and looked at Dreadlocks.

"Don't," he blurted out.

"For the Eyrefield," she whispered, her eyes gleaming. She let out a mad chuckle and jumped out in the open.

Dreadlocks swallowed down a whimper. He could not stay behind. Not alone. He looked back at the cover of the grass. One leap and he would be safe. Hidden. The unblinking white eyes were looking at him, he knew they were. The beast had let the others go just to trick him. He was the one it was waiting for. As soon as he moved out of the rut, it would pounce.

The others were already halfway toward Sifit.

Shit, shit, shiiiiitt.

He closed his eyes and launched himself forward into the void.

The beast's cold gaze bore into his turned back. Unable to contain himself, he stopped and whirled in place, fully expecting to find the hulking mass bearing down upon him at full speed like some enormous, horrifying bird of prey.

Instead, he found that the beast had not moved a muscle. It looked dead. Maybe it was. Maybe it had never been alive to begin with.

He breathed out a sigh of relief and hurried to catch up with the others. They gathered close together and crossed the remainder of the open ground in a tight formation, flank bumping against flank, as fast as their short legs could carry them.

Once safely hidden behind Sifit's body, Dreadlocks allowed himself to relax and tried to feign a careless attitude. He made a poor show of it; the tantalizing cover of the tall grass was still pulling at the corners of his eyes.

"What is that thing?" asked Skoro, his front paws on Sifit's neck.

"We call them rumblers, because of their constant low-growl. The mammals on top are a separate species. We call them bipeds."

"They smell wrong," said Leonides.

That was true. The stench was worse than anything Dreadlocks had ever encountered. Thick and greasy, it clung to the back of his throat and the roof of his palate like some sticky coating of pungent sap blotting out all other smells. He thought he might actually throw up from it.

"Are they dangerous?" he asked meekly.

"No. They come and go from time to time, but they never do anything. They don't graze, they don't hunt, they don't drink. They're just…there, I guess. That's the strangest part about these things, they don't really interact with the rest of the veld. They're apart. And nobody really knows where they come from. Sometimes, they'll follow you around for a bit and maybe even come pretty close, but don't be alarmed, they're no threat."

"Can they be eaten?" asked Fer.

"Anything can be eaten if you're hungry enough. Given the smell, however, I sure would not recommend trying out one of these guys unless you absolutely have to. As a rule, just leave them alone and they'll do the same."

On this, Sifit rose and ambled back toward the grass. The lesson was over.

Perhaps triggered by her decision to move – who could really tell with such strange creatures? – the rumbler suddenly lurched forward.

The cubs whirled in place and Dreadlocks almost yelped out in fear, but Sifit did not so much as twitch a muscle. After a single short leap, as promised, the enormous muzzle settled back down on its constant low growl, as seemingly inert and dead as a dry stump bleached by the summer sun. More squeals and chirps rose out of the bipeds on its back. Sifit ignored them and plunged into the grass with Fer and the twins in tow.

Dreadlocks stayed behind, alone.

In his mind, he was the reason why the monster did not dare come closer.

Already, he could picture himself assaulting the giant's rear, his claws digging deep furrows through the strange, glinting skin, his furious roar sending the half-crazed bipeds scattering every which way with hysterical cries of terror.

"I'm not afraid of you," he declared, a little too loudly.

The rumbler did not react.

A cloud passed overhead. Slanted rays of sunlight caught on the beast's muzzle and the two large eyes twinkled under the shadow for a brief instant. "We'll see about that, little cub," the cold, cheerless glimmer seemed to say. "Oh yes. We'll just see about that."

Dreadlocks bit back a whimper and hastened to melt himself back into the grass.

THREE

THE WEIGHT OF A PAW

T. did not see the low branch until well after it was too late. He attempted an awkward, precipitous leap, tripped, fell flat on his muzzle. Ankle and ego bruising, he picked himself up with a small grunt of pain and tried to walk away. Some unyielding thing clung to his left leg and stopped him cold. He looked down and felt his heart sink.

His claw. One of his claws was caught in the bark!

He jerked back and pulled with all his strength. The branch swayed back and forth and refused to break. The traitorous claw was firmly lodged inside a thin crack in the wood. He was stuck.

His insides squeezed themselves into a tight ball underneath his speeding heart. Cold panic barreled through his veins as a thousand dark hypotheticals assaulted his mind. What if the branch never let go?

What if a hyena shows up right this instant? What if the pride moves on without him and he can never find them again?

Already, he could picture himself lying dead on this spot, never to move again. Here rots the Tit, killed by a branch. Number of cats surprised: zero.

"Let goooo," he mumbled with a small, plaintive voice that only added more grief to his inner shame. "Let go, please."

He tried to double back but only succeeded in twisting the claw sideways. His pulling turned frantic. Nobody would come to help him, he knew. He was lost in the underbrush alone. Always alone. Panting hard, he placed his right leg against the branch and, once again, pushed as hard as he could. The branch swayed and cracked but did not give up. His trapped limb was growing cold and numb. The tip of his stuck toe was on fire. He began to wonder if he would have to rip it off and abandon the claw. He did not think that he could face that kind of pain.

Where's his mother? Even if she's dead, the other females would take care of him.

"Just relax your toe."

He rotated so fast, he almost sprained his ankle in the process. To his immense relief, Shaka ambled out of the vegetation.

"Stop pulling," his brother advised him. "Relax your muscles, push your paw toward the wood, and retract the claw."

Of course. It was so simple, he could not understand how he had not thought of it immediately. So many things that came naturally to the other cubs always felt so hard and difficult to him. He did as instructed and the claw unhooked itself smoothly.

The receding adrenalin left him on the verge of a nervous breakdown. He licked his foot to resume the blood-flow, then took a couple of shaky steps toward Shaka.

He stopped abruptly.

He wanted to give his brother the biggest, most sincere head rub in the history of the Sabi Sands, but was scared of the potential reaction. What if Shaka recoiled in disgust at the prospect of the Tit touching him? That, he felt, would be too much to bear after everything else that had happened today.

Shaka shook his head and chuckled warmly, as if reading his thoughts, then took a couple of easy strides forward and absent-mindedly smashed through that invisible barrier of personal space that always means so much to a lion.

Lions have NO personal boundaries when dealing with pride members – they're all over each other all the time.

T. braced himself for the oncoming attack.

To his astonishment, Shaka did not try to wrestle him down but simply snuggled up to his chest before lying down.

Something warm and luminous exploded inside T.'s belly; his legs grew weak and threatened to collapse. He hastened to follow his brother's lead and laid himself down as well, careful not to break the skin contact. His body shuddered deliciously. After having been touch-starved for so long, the suddenness of the change was overwhelming. It felt as though some new organ had awakened inside his chest and was now tippy-tapping happily to the beat of his glowing heart.

The branch, the mongoose, and the song, along with so many other half-remembered, foggy things, suddenly receded far away from his mind and turned into small, insignificant absurdities lost in the haze of a blazing sun. Slightly baffled – how could such heavy things be blown away so easily like that? – he simply let the feeling course through his veins, vague and unformed as it was, while a deeper, more rational part of himself wondered for a brief instant if this was the way the other cubs felt all the time.

"Where did you go after the mongoose?" asked Shaka, his back now pressed tight against T.'s spine. "I went looking for you, but I lost your tracks in the grass."

T. was grateful that Shaka could not see the torrent of emotions pouring out of his muzzle. "I got turned around while trying to get back to the pride," he lied. "I didn't know what to do, so I sought cover in the underbrush, the way Sifit told us to do if we're ever in danger. You know, hide and wait."

Shaka laughed. T. tensed up, but there was no scorn hidden in his brother's guffaws, only mild amazement at the cub's thought process.

"That's only if the pride is overtaken by new males, T. Right now, everyone is busy being lazy. You would have waited a long time before anyone even think of looking for you." He paused and licked his rhinarium pensively. "It's funny though, I don't understand how I missed you. I'm sure that I checked all the most obvious trails leading back to the Eyre…" He turned abruptly and broke the skin contact. "T? Did you really try to get back to the pride?"

T. winced. He could feel the weight of Shaka's eyes on the nape of his neck, cold and unyielding, and made sure to keep his own gaze fixed on the ground. "I mean, at first I *wanted* to, I really did. But then I thought that maybe it wasn't such a good idea."

"Why not?"

"What if the males know about… you know… the rumor?"

Shaka jumped on his feet. An angry growl escaped his throat. "Skoro should never have made that stupid joke! That furry snake likes to throw his weight around worse than an elephant in rut; one day, I hope that he trips on his own tongue."

T. cowered in place, intently aware of the sudden disappearance of Shaka's body heat. It was as if a cloud had blotted out the sun.

"You can't think like that," his brother sighed. "You can't let them get to you so easily like that. Look at what happened already. One small remark and you were afraid to go back to your own pride. How long do you think you would have survived hidden in the underbrush on your own? One night? Less? No one can survive above grass alone, T. Certainly not a cub without a pride."

Anger and pain flared inside T.'s chest as he rose to face his brother. "But what if it's true?" he said. "What if my father, my real father, *was* a wander-male like they say? A silent cat without pride. What if I have his blood coursing through my veins? The blood of a cowardly, tick-filled, sleezy mane who sidles through the Sabi Sands at night and can't even stand his own ground and fight for what he wants? What does that make *me*?"

Shaka drew his head back, visibly surprised by the sudden outburst. His tail curled behind him but his eyes remained calm. Finally, he shrugged. "It doesn't matter, T. Can't you see it? The rumor doesn't matter in the least. Nui is your mother. Just like all of us, you've been suckled and reared by all the huntresses of the pride, from old Sifit to young Arca, my own mum. You're our brother in milk and hardships, nothing can ever change that. Regardless of what our mothers may or may not have done, you belong here, with us. Don't ever let anyone tell you different."

"What if the Sunset Boys don't see it that way?" T. breathed out.

Shaka nodded his head slowly. "I won't lie to you, it's a possibility. That's something the both of us will have to live with for as long as we are here, something a cat like Skoro will never understand. But you can't let the fear smother you constantly. As a lion, death, the possibility of it, will always be part of the bargain of your life. You just have to accept it."

This was something that T. was convinced in his heart of heart he could not do. "I don't have your courage, Shaka. I can't be like you." He sat back down and looked up at his brother, a feeble light dancing in his eyes. "You remember that time when Mak Senior was enjoying a feed alone? Everybody was dutifully waiting for him to finish, too scared to approach. Even Sifit. But you, you decided that you were hungry. You were about as big as Mak's paw at the time, maybe less, but that didn't deter you. You practically stole the meat right out of his fangs."

T. recounted the event with an awe similar to the way he had felt on the day the pride had witnessed the whole affair. The most amazing thing, at the time, had not been that little Shaka had dared do something not even Sifit would risk, but that the big boy Mak Senior had actually let him proceed without lashing out, as though some kind of invisible link had connected the two cats.

Afterward, Shaka had returned to the group with a bellyful of meat and a crocodile-size snarl etched on his muzzle. While the other cubs had been quick enough to pile up on top of his blood-soaked head and congratulate him on a crazy job well done, T. had remained next to Nui's protective shadow, unable to take his eyes off of Shaka's newfound aura. What he had done that day was not meant to be possible. Not for a cub in a lion pride. If his brother had told him at that exact instant that he could swallow the sun, T. would have believed him.

Cubs do this all the time - males let their young feed even if not the lionesses.

Shaka listened to his brother reenacting the tale and laughed heartily. "I had forgotten all about this," he said with cheerful humility. "Truth is, at the time, I didn't think that I would get away with more than a single bite. I expected to be swatted away quickly and roughly. But I also knew that Mak Senior would never really harm me. I was in no real danger."

"Still a big risk to take, if you ask me."

"But that's the thing about taking chances, T. If you do, more often than not, you will land on your feet. If you never train your courage, however, it will atrophy, same as any other muscles."

T. nodded faintly, unconvinced.

Shaka cut the conversation short and the two cubs spent the rest of the afternoon playing together while progressively making their way back toward the pride. His insecurities now temporarily forgotten, T. grew bolder and tried some romping with his more experienced brother. Shaka went easy on him and even allowed himself to be pinned a couple of times. The younger cub could not remember ever having laughed so much; they were both completely out of breath by the time they rejoined the acacia, and the pride.

With his limbs and ribs hurting deliciously, T. laid himself down next to a big root at the base of the tree. Shaka winked at him and went looking for a morsel of meat.

"I'll bring you some if you want," he said.

T. only had time to acquiesce briefly before falling into a deep, untroubled sleep.

He awoke to the sound of a roar.

Night had fallen and the hulking mass of the acacia was now shrouded in darkness, with only the soft, silvery light of a full moon piercing through its tall branches. The air felt cool and dry on his fur, a relief after the heat of the day. He yawned and took stock of the pride's smell. They had moved on, but not very far. With the oppressive glare of the sun now gone, the cats were more active; he could hear and smell some of the huntresses getting ready for a night raid under Sifit's leadership.

All the Boys were back as well, he realized. Scar Nose was the one doing most of the roaring to keep potential intruders at bay; from time to time, Blondie would add his own shorter bellows to his brother's support.

Maybe he's trying to make amend for his laziness of the day.

He giggled softly. Under normal circumstances, such a rebellious comment would have horrified him and send him down a spiral of shame and unbearable anguish at the idea of being found out. Now, he only felt cocky and amused by his own wits, such as they were.

His belly growled. He stood up and trotted toward the pride. He would find Shaka and play a little, he decided, and then wait for the huntresses to call for the feed. He was not yet ready to pull the kind of stunt his older brother had in the past, but he would try to get a bellyful nonetheless.

A heavy breathing came out of the darkness next to him. He froze as a new strong scent suddenly invaded his throat and scorched his palate. The grass to his left parted ways and a huge silhouette ambled out with rolling shoulders. He clenched his jaws and suppressed a whimper.

Broken Nose.

There was no mistaking the chilling shape of that bent muzzle, or the way half of his black rhinarium seemed to have been cut away and placed above the other half. Under the faint light of the moon, the thin scar was glistening silvery-white.

The big lion had yet to notice him. He held his breath and hunched down as low as he could.

He won't see you, his racing mind tried to reassure him. *You're far too small and unworthy of his gaze. He's just passing through.*

After licking something on the ground and briefly sniffing the air, Broken Nose abruptly turned toward him. Two murderous eyes bore through his forehead and he felt himself shrink down a size.

"Ya' see' yarself a' hyena som'ere, cub?" The big lion's voice came out hoarse and laborious, stuffed, as though every mangled word was a fight for a breath.

With his own throat choked tight, T. only managed a brief negative shake of the head he hoped with all his heart would not be seen as an affront by the old male. To his relief, Broken Nose only nodded.

"Betta' watch' out, cub. A' thought a' smelt me som' of them dirta' filtha' hunchbac' roamin' aroun' this side o' gra'. Tol' Blondie and Sca' Nose a'much. Them big-bellied lazy-mane been roa'in' nonstop eva' since."

He laughed softly at his own comment, then fell quiet.

To T.'s dismay, he took a step toward him, then another; the enormous mane blotted out the moon and stars above. T. squirmed in place but did not dare move. He was suddenly keenly aware of how alone and defenseless he truly was. Even though the rest of the pride was a mere few leaps away, for all intents and purposes they might as well be on the other side of the Sabi Sands. It was just him and Broken Nose right now.

"Wha' oane ya're anyway, cub? Ya're Nui's ball o' fur? The runt?"

Once again, T could only nod stiffly.

"Ho' coam ya ain't dead yet, cub? All pride says ya' weak. Say ya doan't git it in ya. So, ho' coam you ain't given' up an' goan' dea' yet?"

This time, T. had no answer. Broken Nose lowered his head and he felt the lion's long whiskers grate against the back of his neck.

The hoarse, mumbling voice turned to frost. "A' heard me soam' voices in the gra' say ya ain't oane o' ours, cub. Ya an' tha' other ball o' fur, the cocky oane. A' heard me soam' voices in the gra' say Nui an' Arca went sniffin' out oane day wit' tails uprigh' and hips swingin', lookin' foar soam' lean tangled-mane somewhe'. Came ba' with full bellies, bu' not o' meat. Tha' true, cub? Ya soam' other mane's furball?"

He poked him lightly with his paw.

Behind the seemingly playful gesture, T. could feel the enormous strength of the limb resting down on his spine. His bladder emptied itself and all his recently found courage went trickling down his legs. Gone was the warmth of Shaka's good words, reduced to nothingness. The poison had regained its grip on his entrails. After a brief interlude – a dream, really – he had awakened back into the real world. A world where the Tit stands alone in darkness and fear rules. It was as if the whole thing had never happened at all.

He sniffled loudly and tried to regain some of his composure. More than anything else, he wanted to be back by his mother's side, safe and surrounded by all the huntresses of the pride. He would have given anything to be allowed to seek shelter behind those strong legs of hers again.

Broken Nose poked him some more. "Where's ya' brotha, then? Arca's youngest. The bol' oane."

A part of T.'s mind leapt at the opportunity presenting itself. Guilty relief surged through him.

Yes, he would point those murderous eyes in Shaka's direction. Give up everything he had heard about Arca's roll in the far grass – as Skoro liked to put it – and confirm everything Broken Nose might have heard. All the rumors and dirty jokes and mean comments. If necessary, he would make stuff up.

It's Shaka you want, he thought with abject cheer. *He's the one that don't belong. His mother is the traitor. Not me, not me.*

He said nothing.

To his own, quiet amazement, he realized that he could not betray his brother like that. Not Shaka. The memory of the luminous thing exploding inside his belly was still too fresh in his mind. Despite the threatening weight of the enormous paw pressing down on it, his back still remembered how it had shuddered happily under his brother's friendly touch, the delicious warmth of camaraderie. Now there was something in his spine that refused to give in, something harder than his fear.

He raised his little head and returned Broken Nose's stare. His eyes were supplicant, but he kept quiet.

Broken Nose jerked his head back and quietly pondered the unexpected reaction. "Ya sure are weird oane, cub. Bu' maybe ya ain't from the fa' side o' gra' after oal." He chewed on it some more. His tongue darted to his horrifying scar, then back to his fangs. "Coul' be ya're even oane o' mine. Coul' be."

On this, the pressure of the paw vanished, as quickly as it had come, and after a brief rustle in the grass, the stars returned. Only the smell of the big lion lingered, like a cloud foreshadowing his roaming presence.

Eve' when A'm noat here, A'm still here, cub – Ya see?

T. broke into a gallop and rushed toward the pride. He needed to find Shaka and tell him everything that had happened. Shaka would know what to do, what to say. Most important of all, he would listen.

Yes, Shaka would understand.

FOUR

A LION'S DUE

Shaka sat up brusquely, a puzzled look on his face. Broken Nose was shambling back toward the pride with something grey inside his jaws. Something heavy. He squinted against the haze and tried to make sense of the bundle of fur he could see dangling limply in front of the big forelimbs.

A female hyena, he finally realized. How peculiar. The big male was holding her by the nape of the neck and the strange duo made for a sight that was both touching and deeply unsettling to Shaka's eyes, like some weird lioness tenderly carrying a misshapen, grotesque cub who should have died a long time ago.

As they came into better focus, he noticed how the hyena's belly was pumping hard and fast in the stifling air. Her gasping jaws seemed to be stuck in the half-open position, like a fish. After every rocking step, her black lips would bump against the lion's enormous muzzle and leave a froth mark on his left whiskers. She did not make a sound, but her eyes were frantic. Shaka could see the round pupils bouncing off the edges of her orbits, wide and terror-stricken. The rest of her was slack and dead.

Broken Nose reached the gathered pride and let the hyena fall at his paws. "Gathe'round boys," he barked. "Learnin' time." As he lay down to catch his breath, he made sure to keep a heavy paw on his quarry's flank.

Skoro, Leonides, and Dreadlocks lunged forward in unison with swinging tails and barely contained anticipation.

Bunch of eager cats, Shaka snorted internally. *Always ready to jump in without a thought in their heads.*

A part of him could not help but admire his brothers' boldness. Their courage was of a kind that required a complete lack of forethought or calculation. Squeeze everything tight and just go for it, deal with the consequences later. Coarse and rash as it may appear – not to mention, at times, plain dumb – he had to admit that there was a sort of undeniable, lionlike nobility to it. The virtue behind the action, the mad leap that gets things done, one way or the other.

He let them take the lead and turned around. T. bumped into his flank and looked at him with wide, interrogative eyes.

The younger lion's confidence had grown somewhat over the last few seasons, but it was still very much a work in progress. Ever since that afternoon with the mongoose – so long ago now that the memory was fuzzy in Shaka's head, as if half-dreamed – the two of them had become pretty much inseparable. This suited him fine. His younger brother's tendency to see him as higher than the sun was flattering, if somewhat misplaced, and T.'s reserved demeanor usually made for much better company than the other rowdy cats. As exhilarating as the constant snarling and boasting of the band was in small doses, it could also grow quite tiring. With T., it was different. Even though the young lion never said much and could appear at times a bit placid – withdrawn, even – he always seemed to genuinely enjoy listening to what Shaka had to say, a most rare quality among young males always keen on competition.

But there had been setbacks. The shy cub's misplaced confidence could sometimes come out in sudden bursts and lead him to try out shockingly dangerous things. Like that one time when he had pondered facing a herd of elephants all on his own and Shaka had had to use his sternest objections and threats of broken friendship to dissuade him; or that other time when he had found him poking at a sunbathing crocodile's gaping jaws while screaming, his voice high and cheerful: "Look Shaka, he's not even doing anything. It's like he's dead!"

Even more puzzling were T.'s wild mood swings. After every bout of heart-stopping recklessness, the fever would pass, T.'s courage would leak out of him, all at once, and, perhaps embarrassed by his own behavior, the young lion would grow catatonic and refuse to speak to anyone, sometimes for several days in a row.

This was maddening. As if his brother were constantly oscillating in-between two extremes and could not keep his courage down to a normal, steady level.

The nightmares probably had something to do with it, Shaka reflected. He knew that the Sunset Boys still inspired holy terror on T. Sometimes, when his brother was asleep and the dominant males were roaring in the night, he could hear pitiful whimpers come out of the young lion's throat, and see his legs thrash frenetically in front of him, trying to run away. "Not the spine," he would mutter faintly, "please, not the spine." Shaka would then try his best to calm him down without waking him up, but no amount of shared body heat or soothing words ever seemed to be enough to stop the shaking. When one thought about it – and Shaka had done *a lot* of thinking about it – that fact alone was quite scary. As though his brother had fallen so far inside his own mind, he was no longer connected to the world of the physical. Come dawn, Shaka would find him shambling around in the grass without purpose, timorous and quiet again, his head cast down and his whiskers drooping, an empty shell of a lion.

Broken Nose growled something ominous behind him. Shaka turned back around and realized that the big male was waiting for them. He gave T. a reassuring nudge – at least today the young lion seemed to be in a fairly normal mood – and they both took their place on the right side of the assembled semi-circle.

"Ya cubs ain't cubs no moare," groaned Broken Nose. "Ya enjoy mea' good enou', time ya learn abou' killin'."

"Long overdue," whispered Skoro. "We're practically all grown already." He stole a glance at T. "Well, most of us anyway."

Leonides sniggered and bumped into his flank.

Shaka cringed internally but did not bother with a counter. He could see that T. was far too captivated by the gasping hyena to pay his annoying brother any mind.

He had to give the cocky sub-adult his due, though: the five of them could hardly be considered cubs anymore. They had grown. Gone were the careless days of cuteness, tawny patches, and awkward, short limbs. Thanks to a steady diet of meat provided by the huntresses of the pride, the innocent fluff of their childhood had melted away and ceded place to lean bodies perched atop slightly awkward, gangly legs. 'Slightly-too-long,' Blondie liked to call them, although it was sometimes hard to tell whether he meant their limbs or their reaction times. Their heads had broadened, their muzzles grown longer. A set of thick muscles now lined their young jaws, powerful enough to bite through bones – this Shaka knew from personal experience: he had tried it on an old buffalo carcass when no one was looking.

One thing was still cruelly missing, however: their manes. With the exception of a few scant patches here and there, their scalps and bellies remained barren, like lionesses. And even though they could now face the old males at eye level, none of them, not even Skoro, were stupid enough to believe that they could rival with their bulks. To stand tall on newfound legs was one thing; to bring a powerful shoulder to bear in a fight, something else entirely.

"This, the throa'," Broken Nose continued, his muzzle pointed toward the hyena's neck. "Ya kill by stranglin'. No need fo' lot's o' efforts, sav' yar strengt' whenever ya can, always. Just clamp doawn and thr'ttle the gigglin' bastar'."

"Not too many giggles left in this one," remarked Dreadlocks, and leaned forward, curious.

Shaka followed his lead. With every weak exhale of the hyena, he could feel a fading warmth hit the tip of his muzzle. Her eyes were glazed – whether by shock or fear, he could not tell – and her moist nose was granulated with dirt. Behind her rump, he could see her tail quivering weakly.

He drew his head back. Her overall lack of reaction was the real gut-wrenching part, he decided. The cold, disquieting part. It all seemed too clean, unreal. Here a living thing – another predator, no less – was being killed in front of him, and the whole affair seemed like a formality, as if all parties involved had already come to a polite agreement on how to play their part. That seemed wrong, somehow. Unnatural.

Careful to keep his expression neutral and unconcerned so as to reveal nothing of his inner discomfort, he stepped back and wrestled with the thought.

How could someone die so easily like that? Give it all up without so much as a groan of protest? Of course, this was only a hyena, but still… Could he himself ever reach such a state of exhaustion – or was it terror? – that would force him to resign himself to the unacceptable? The idea went against his very nature and made him want to scream in revolt.

He sucked in his breath quietly. This made no sense. Why did the hyena's end have such an effect on him?

Because he could sympathize with her fear, he realized. He felt pity for the poor thing. And guilt. To be yanked out of your daily life so suddenly like that and dragged, alone, to the place of your enemies to be killed as an exhibit… This was no fate he could wish on any prowler, whether friend or foe. Absurdly, he wondered what her plans may have been for the rest of the day.

"When ya bite," continued Broken Nose, "ya search fo' a feelin' of th' win'pipe. I's a bit like squ'shin' a grass stal' hidd'n' in th' neck. When ya git it goad, shal' feel like th' victim's hart's pumpin' straigh' inside yar jaw. Then, ya squeeze."

He went on to demonstrate. He grabbed the hyena by the throat, his movements smooth and deliberate, almost delicate, and applied the pressure. She did not fight back. After a brief pause, her body was overcome by a few hard shudders, then she lay still.

"An' that's i'. No' much to i', if ya know wha' yar doin'. On biggar grazers, like buffaloes, i' ya can't fin' the win'pipe 'nside the throa', ya kin always smothe' 'em by holdin' th' muzzle shu' insi' yar mout'. Make sure ya cover the nostril too an' he'll suffoca' 'n no time."

All five sub-adults gazed at the hyena's corpse, riveted. Shaka poked it with the tip of one paw. She did not appear so much different from moments ago. Just unresponsive. It was weird to think that after such a simple thing as a bit of pressure on the neck, the deed was done. She would never move again.

By the grass, I make more of a racket every time I go to sleep.

"I's importan' t' noat," Broken Nose added, almost as an afterthought, "th' bite don't nee' be overly stroang. Wha' matter most's th' pressure. Once ya fin' th' pipe, pressure needs be constan'. If you let go, 'ven fo' a heartbeat, 'prey will catch its win'. Wit' a hyena, i's okay, ya kin go agin. Bu' if i's a big bull buffalo yar trying t'wr'stle down, he'll fight ba'. O' worse, call fo' help. That's 'ow cats get dead. So ya kee' tha' pressure constan' no matter wha', ya hear? A' don't care i' ya're gettin' gored an' ya can see yar own insides dangle in the gra' in front o' ya. Ya don't le' go. Ever." He took a deep breath. "Ya hear me cubs?"

They all acquiesced somberly. Shaka was quite sure that none of them really did, but they were all too smart to say anything.

T. sniffed at the hyena's belly. Her udders were already cold and stiff. He licked them gingerly and caught a few drops of milk on his muzzle. Shaka cringed at the slightly obscene spectacle.

"She was a mother," T. said with a soft, bewildered voice.

Broken Nose's eyes shone coldly. "Aye, two pups A' saw. Couldn't kill 'em outright on account o' th' mum A' ha' t'bring back. No matter. They'll be dead soon enou'. Three dea' in oane bite. No' ba', fo' a' old mane."

"So do we eat her now?" asked T.

"Ya kin if ya wan', cub. Me, A' ain't desperate enou' fo' that kind o' nasty taste."

"So why kill her in the first place?" asked Shaka.

Broken Nose rotated his head slowly and, for quite a long while, stared at Shaka as if he were not a lion at all but some kind of weird herbivore in disguise. A hare, maybe. Or an aardvark. Finally, he shrugged. "I's fun."

Skoro, Leonides, and Dreadlocks all acquiesced eagerly, but Shaka was not convinced. That seemed too gratuitous, unbecoming of their strength. Unlionlike.

"Hyenas are a pest," Mak Senior chimed in from inside the circle of shade where he had been observing quietly. He rose and went to give his brother a rough head rub. "If you let them gang up on your pride, they can become a threat to your cubs. They're good hunters too, so that's less meat for you. Although, if your quick enough, you can follow their whoops and cries and steal their kills. Save yourself the trouble of a hunt. Same goes for leopards, as long as you don't mind a bit of tree-climbing."

He stole a glance at his brother with a knowing half-snarl.

"Aye," acquiesced Broken Nose, "leopar' an' hyenas kin be push' 'round easy enoug'. Cheeta' too. Weak cats, th'whol'lot'o'em."

"But isn't that…dishonorable? As lions, aren't we supposed to hunt for our meat?"

"Argh. No such thing as turnin' doawn a free meal when ya're on yar own on the far side o' gra', cub." Faced with their blank stares, Broken Nose sighed and made sure to articulate his next words carefully: "A lion's due is what he takes, no more, no less. Ya understand me, cub? Ya see something ya wan', ya take it. Is tha' simple. Kill fo' it, i' ya have to. Hyena turns her back on ya? Ya kill. Leopar' o' cheetah try 'stand up t'ya? Ya kill. Some piece o' mea' on hooves not paying attention? Ya kill first, ea' later when ya're hungry."

Dreadlocks laughed at this. Unable to refrain himself, he fell into a poor imitation of Broken Nose's speech and demeanor as he pranced around the hyena's carcass to his brothers' delight. "Anything that moves, ya kill! You hear me *cubs*? Hyena, leopards, cheetahs… As long as it's not a lion, ya kill, kill, kill." He concluded his little spectacle by pretending to ravage the hyena's tail.

The sub-adults laughed heartily and even Mak Senior chuckled briefly, but Broken Nose's eyes remained cold. His glare fell on the brash young cat and silenced him. "Soam lions, ya kill too, cub. This, ya'll learn soon enough."

The guffaws died down. An uncomfortable silence settled in.

On an impulse, Broken Nose whirled toward Sifit. The head huntress had been observing the killing from under the canopy of the tree as well, an expression of slight disgust etched on her muzzle. The rest of the pride was sprawled lazily at her feet.

"Nex' buffalo raid, when?"

"Tomorrow morning. Shortly after break of mist."

Broken Nose nodded appreciatively as if some grand plan of his had just come together at last. "Morrow's good," he declared. "Morrow, th' youn' oanes coam too. They learn."

The huntress kept her stance stiff, her demeanor cold and unyielding. "They're too young," she said slowly. "The herd is thirsty and more restless than usual. It will be a difficult bring down."

“Goo’. Mo’ weigh’ and paws fo’ ya if they coam.”

“It’s too dangerous. They don’t have the experience yet. They need to start with something smaller. A gnu, maybe.” Her eyes fell on T.who was still playing with the hyena’s udder. “Or a small bird.”

Broken Nose shook his head and took a half-step forward.

Sifit growled and planted her forelegs squarely in front of the bigger male, ready to drive her point through the stubborn lion’s thick skull by force if necessary. She was holding her head high, but Shaka noticed that her neck was very stiff, and she could not keep her back paws from fidgeting under her restless tail.

The rest of the pride immediately scrambled to her support.

Caught off guard by the sudden rise of cats’ tempers, Mak Senior cursed and hurried to his brother’s side. At the last instant, he smartly kept himself away from Sifit so as not to give the impression that the two males were ganging up on her.

He doesn’t want to start anything that doesn’t need be started, Shaka realized with some small measure of relief.

The five sub-adults watched the stand-off unfold uneasily, unsure whether they ought to join a side or not. Shaka could feel T.’s tense body bump against his left flank, as tight as a springbok’s hindquarters and ready to pronk.

Broken Nose, for his part, did not share in the rising tension. After a cursory glance at the small line of gathered lionesses, he expectorated roughly in a manner resembling a laugh and casually returned Sifit’s stare. “Agh! Ain’t nothin’ ever been easy ’bout bein’ lion, horn-tickler. Ya an’ yar smash’ hip shoul’ knoaw this bette’ tha’nyone. Best those cubs learn fas’ whil’ they kin. Unli’ yar girls, they woan’t ha’ a pride to hide behin’ f’revar.”

On this, he shoved his way forward, past Sifit and through the huntresses’ group. “T’morrow, they coam,” he bit out from over his shoulder as he disappeared in the tall grass.

A few heartbeats later, they heard his short, mangled roars roll down from the top of a nearby hill.

A sullen silence settled in the wake of his departure.

“I’ll come too if needed,” offered Mak Senior, almost as an apology. “Give you girls some more weight for the final take-down.”

Sifit nodded her head curtly. The big male returned to his lazy spot and the rest of the pride began to relax again.

"He's right, you know," said Skoro. "It's about time we are bloodied. You've already taught us everything there is to know about hunting. What more is there for us to learn anyway?"

Sifit looked at him with something resembling deep pity. Or was it disgust? Shaka could not tell for sure, but he did not like that expression on her muzzle much. This day was turning out not at all like what he had anticipated. Things were becoming all too real way too fast.

This is what the hyena must have thought too.

"To know a thing in your mind is nothing," Sifit spat. "We are beings of action. Muscle memory is everything. Only once your body has done a thing, been molded by it, scarred from it, then you can say that you know that thing. Not before."

"Well, we *have* done some hunting already," Dreadlocks tried to argue. "Mongooses and pangolins and such… A porcupine, once." He choked on his words and fell quiet.

"Is it that bad, then?" asked Shaka. "A buffalo hunt?"

In his mind, the horrendous scar on the huntress's hip had already grown to absurd proportions.

"No," Sifit said with a sad, derisive groan that sent shudders traveling down the length of his spine. "It's worse."

FIVE

A LINE OF FLESH

This was madness. Pure madness.

T, lowered his belly as close to the ground as physically possible and pondered whether to start digging himself a burrow. Forget lions, he wished he could be a snake right now, a subterranean creature hidden from the sight of the world.

The herd slowly ground its way across the savannah all around him, each buffalo a mountain of twitching muscles in its own right. Through his paws and guts, he could feel the relentless trundling of the placid hooves hitting the hard-packed dirt, some of them a mere snake-width away from his whiskers. Soft grunts rose out of satiated throats here and there, punctuated by the relentless sound of grass being ripped and crunched and swallowed and chewed again. The smell of shit and rancid, wet cud hit his muzzle in sickening waves he could taste all the way to the far end of his throat. He retched and tried to push it away from his mind.

He raised his gaze slightly, careful not to move his head too much from his prone position, and noticed the thick clouds of flies hovering around the wet eyes and nostrils in a three-dimensional dance that was as old as grass itself. Above the flies, the two ubiquitous sharp horns.

Fused at the top of the scalp in a keratin boss thick enough to crush a lion's skull, their smooth, murderous curves jutted out and upward on either side of the enormous head in a way that made T.'s scrotum want to crawl back inside his belly. Already, he could feel his inner thighs being torn open.

Did anyone really expect them to assault *that?*

His mind scampered back to his original thought like some gazelle caught in the middle of a deadly drought hastening toward the shelter of the one and only water hole she's familiar with: this was, quite simply, madness.

Nui had led them too close. Way too close. What was she thinking? The grass was tall, but not nearly tall enough. They could not remain hidden forever. Soon, they would be discovered. And then the sun only knew what would happen.

A set of heavy hooves split the dry dirt next to his shoulder, close enough for him to reach out and touch the tight tendons lining the enormous dark calf. He held his breath and wondered at the odds of the buffalo reaching down to graze on him. Maybe he could convince the dumb beast that he was not a lion at all but some weirdly-shaped lump of dry grass.

"Well, boys, we're truly in the thick of it now," giggled Skoro, nervously. T. saw him turn his head as he looked down the line of his brothers. His black pupils were big enough to cover the entirety of the yellow in his eyes.

"It's alright," Shaka breathed out. "As long as they don't snort, it means that they don't know we're here. Sifit told me as much this morning."

"Cut the chatter down the line," low-growled Nui, far ahead.

Earlier in the morning, Sifit had detached her to lead a small squad of three huntresses. "I'll rattle them, you four will be the choosing fangs," the old cat had decreed. Nui had simply bowed her head and unleashed a half-snarl that seemed to drip blood, but the three chosen younger lionesses had not been so reserved. Beaming with pride, their eyes gleaming with excitement, they had bumped into her flanks affectuously and, after a few nervous dark chuckles, unleashed a torrent of, as far as T. was concerned, incredibly coarse jokes.

“That’s one foursome those big guys won’t like.”

“It’s alright, I’ll give them a good kiss on the muzzle.”

“Then we enter ‘em, head, chest and all.”

“Right up the hip.”

“Careful they don’t spill themselves early all over you, eh?”

“Nah, I don’t mind getting a bit wet.”

“So long as *I* do the licking.”

“Grazer, grazer beware, the grasp of the pussies whose fangs are bare.”

Sifit had rolled her eyes and snorted with good humor at the girls’ salacious remarks, then her gaze had fallen on T. and his brothers, and her muzzle had frozen. “You’ll take the boys under your shadow too,” she had groaned. “Teach them what it’s like as best you can.”

That had cut the banter short. Two of the younger huntresses had attempted to raise an objection but Nui had silenced them with a single twist of her head. Her jaws clenched tight, she had simply acquiesced and walked away. Her only words to T. and his brothers right before leaving the pride had been: “Keep quiet, follow the girls, and don’t do anything stupid.”

Now stuck in the middle of the herd, T. was not about to argue with her. He had no idea what the overall plan was – nobody had told him anything, of course – but the one thing he knew for sure was that he wanted to get through the day alive and in one piece.

Next to Nui, Fer turned around and briefly stared at them. Although slightly smaller than them, she had already been on more than a few hunts. In her eyes, T. could feel the scorn she felt for the rowdy bunch of lubberly amateurs trailing her hunting unit.

She needs us here like those buffaloes need more flies in their eyes.

He flattened himself some more and tried to shut the ever-closing noise of the encircling hooves out of his mind.

Half-seen through the green grass, a yellow blur leaped out from under the cover of a brambly bush and streaked its way toward the opposite end of the herd at unfathomable speed. T. only had time to catch a glimpse of the dark spot on the blur's left hip before things unraveled suddenly.

The unease travelled through the twitching muscles of the herd like ripples through a pond. Legs grew stiff, heavy heads jerked themselves up, searching. All of a sudden, an avalanche of frightened snorts rose out of a hundred different throats. One deep heartbeat later, the ground began to shake all around the tiny island of the lion's isolated squad.

"Shit, shit, shit," groaned T., his heart pumping wild against the roof of his mouth.

"It's on!" Leonides shrieked somewhere behind him. "Sun blaze almighty, it's fucking on!"

The tremors slammed into T.'s ribs and jostled his stomach and guts. A pair of hooves cut into the dirt in front of his muzzle, hard enough to crush his skull; he felt his whiskers bend under the warm leathery skin. A cloud of dirt washed over his face. He coughed and closed his eyes. A heartbeat later, the pressure of the leg disappeared. When he opened his eyes again, he noticed the deep footprint left behind, like an unspoken threat.

Shaka ogled him with wide, incredulous eyes. A huge snarl slowly uncovered his fangs. "A hair's length away from death, brother. Literally!"

For some unknown, crazy reason, his brother seemed to find this whole debacle hilarious.

T., however, was not amused. His patience was running thin. Why, in the sweet name of soft grass, wasn't anyone ordering a full retreat already?

The kicked-up dirt clung to his wet nose and formed a crust. He sneezed and tried to blink the stuff out of his eyes. All of his claws protracted spasmodically and dug shallow furrows in the ground in front of him. Feeling the panic gain on him, he tried to look to Nui for guidance.

Untouched by the overall chaos, the four females seemed to have found some cold-blooded, reptilian courage. If anything, they looked more relaxed now than they had during the morning's long crawl and ensuing wait. Nui's eyes, especially, were as hard as old fangs, her piercing gaze calmly gauging each individual buffalo passing her by, waiting for the right one to strike. The other three huntresses had turned themselves into extensions of the elder lioness's body.

"Wait..." whispered Nui, her voice sharp and strangely audible above the cacophony. "Wait...Wait...Now! Go!"

She exploded out of her crouched position and hurtled through the herd in a straight line.

"EYREFIIIIEEEELLLLDDDD!!!!!" roared Fer, and pounced forward, fused to her hip.

Her high-pitched juvenile voice cut clear and true through the overall cacophony of the stampede and fired the young males' spirit. The adrenalin whip lashed at T.'s brain and unleashed his legs. Before he had time to process what was happening to him, he found himself running as fast as he could behind the huntresses. Out of the corners of his eyes, he noticed Shaka and Skoro overtaking him gradually.

"Eyrefield!!!!" Fer kept screaming ahead of him. "Eyrefield pride!!"

A young buffalo calf impacted T.'s flank at full speed and knocked the wind out of his lungs. As they both went sprawling in the grass, their eyes locked for an instant and T. had time to notice the absolute terror that was pouring out of the herbivore's pupils.

You and me both, he thought with a crazy chuckle.

He picked himself up, slowly – his ribs and left shoulder were on fire – and stopped short of the calf trashing madly in front of him. As soon as the calf found his legs, he bolted and disappeared into the mass of his peers. T. watched him go and realized that he hadn't even tried to bring him down. The thought had quite simply not occurred to him.

He turned his attention back to the others. He was trailing far behind the squad now. Shaka's tail had turned into a flicker of yellow lost behind a thick cloud of brown dirt. Groaning faintly, he leaped forward and tried to catch up.

Nui had chosen a good-sized female for her kill. T. saw it all happen ahead of him in a flash. Upon reaching proper range, the lioness leaped forward with her claws bared and impacted the left hindquarter of her running target. Carried by her velocity, the rest of her body swung wildly around the buffalo's backside and she almost lost her grip and overshot. She clawed at her prize's skin and used her jaws to

Human term

clamp down on the top of the tail, near the coccyx. Once safely anchored, she let her body go limp and used her weight to hamper the grazer's run.

The buffalo cow was strong, Nui failed to break her gallop entirely but she did manage to slow her down considerably. The other three huntresses joined her and together they added their own weight to the buffalo's backside. This time the grazer stopped completely, but she did not buckle.

"Blood, meat, gore and glory!" roared Dreadlocks as he blew past his brothers and assaulted the titanic mass. Human term

His claws failed to pierce through the thick leather and he almost fell back down. He persevered and after some wild kicking and skidding, somehow managed to find himself perched on top of the buffalo's back. Confused by this unforeseen turn of event, he clamped his jaws down on the top of the grazer's neck. They were not quite large or powerful enough to have any effect on the massive muscles, but he kept gnawing nonetheless.

The twins entered the fray together and decided to go for the throat. The experienced buffalo noticed them lunge at her out of the corner of her eyes and swung around at the last instant. They both missed wildly and went tumbling claws over fangs in the grass.

T. looked to his right and saw that Shaka had found a precarious grip on the buffalo's left hind leg, right next to Nui who was still holding onto the base of the thick tail with her jaws. The appendage was halfway ripped and warm blood was streaming down the buffalo's thighs and into the lioness's eyes and muzzle, blinding her.

Everything was happening so fast, T.'s mind was struggling to keep up with the chain of events.

Suddenly, he realized that he had yet to contribute a single useful thing to the hunt. This was the mongoose happening all over again. Ashamed of his dire lack of fighting spirit, he tried a half-hearted leap at the buffalo's front leg. He hit the powerful limb clumsily but still found a good grip on the shoulder. His curved claws pierced through the thick leather and wrapped themselves around the edge of the shoulder-blade.

Tight! Like a python, he thought proudly.

The buffalo uttered a deep bellow and shook him off as easily as one might a fly.

He hit the ground on his back and rolled to the side. The sun disappeared. A swinging udder knocked him on the head. The murdering hooves trampled the ground all around him, searching for his spine. He curled into a ball and shrieked amid a cloud of kicked up dirt, waiting to die.

The cow moved a few paces to the right.

As the dust settled and the sun returned, he opened a tentative eye and tried to get a feeling of his limbs and tail. He was still miraculously unscathed, he realized. He picked himself up and looked around. Shaka and Fer both had lost their grips as well and were standing next to him. That helped sooth his ego a bit.

"She's a fighter that one," Fer breathed out while looking for a new spot to assault.

T. could have sworn that she was enjoying herself.

With only three huntresses remaining on her backside – and a useless, bewildered Dreadlocks doing his best to ride the thunder – the buffalo cow began to whirl in place with increasing speed to shake the rest of her attackers off.

"Sh'omebody get sh'the sh'throat!" growled Nui, and pulled down on the tail with all her might.

Before anyone had time to comply, Sifit materialized out of the grass and stopped the buffalo cold. She grabbed the head behind the ears with her front paws and lowered the massive muzzle down toward the ground. Then, in one smooth movement, she bent her spine and wrapped her hind legs around the thick neck. Her whole body now hanging upside down, she tried to close her jaws around the muzzle.

The buffalo cows stomped her front legs and swung her head from left to right while grunting fiercely. Sifit's fangs sliced through the battered muzzle, now little more than an indistinct mass of slippery, gooey flesh, but found no proper grip on the bone underneath. She growled a curse and tried again. Then again. And again. To no avail. Thin strips of flesh fell at the feet of the buffalo. She snorted through nostrils that were not really there anymore and, perhaps heartened by the realization that she could still breathe freely, redoubled her effort.

Just when Sifit seemed ready to give up, Mak Senior joined the hunt at a light camper and casually assaulted the rear. This time, the added weight of the big male was too much for the grazer's stamina. Her rump buckled but she managed to keep her forelegs stiffly extended in front of her. Seeing an opportunity, Skoro and Leonides rammed themselves at full speed against her left flank in hope of toppling her. She held fast and they stumbled away in zigzag, dazed and dispirited.

A precarious equilibrium settled as exhaustion crept in on everyone. No one was giving up – least of all the buffalo cow – but the fight's intensity had bled out and was replaced by a sort of rigid, precarious calm that was half shock and half stubbornness.

Sifit stopped her assault and just hung under the throat while trying not to choke on the blood pouring freely all over her face. Behind the massive head, Dreadlocks lay sprawled atop the slanted back like some lazy cat on a warm rock, his limbs hanging loose on either side of the round flanks, his jaws firmly shut around a single fold of skin. Shaka tried a half-hearted nip at the rump next to where Mak Senior was holding steady, but found no grip and promptly gave up. Among Nui's squad, only the elder lioness and Fer were still hanging onto their quarry by the skin of their teeth. The other two had relinquished their grips and gone to lie down next to the twins, gasping for air. T. could hardly blame them. He had done precious little to assault the buffalo himself, and already he could feel his own heart threaten to explode inside his chest.

But the buffalo cow still had some wind in her. Her calls for help grew more frantic, more fast-paced. With every long exhale, she kept letting out a loud, desperate grunt that jarred T. down to his bones.

"Shu' her up," growled Mak Senior, a mouthful of leather stuck in-between his fangs. "Shomeone shu' he' sh'he fu' up *now*!"

To Sifit's credit, she did her very best. Her claws tore through the leather and her legs lost their grip, but she held onto both sides of the massive head with her front limbs and managed to keep the muzzle down to her level with the sheer strength of her shoulders and core muscles. Her mouth finally closed itself around the cow's muzzle and the shut-out grunts dwindled down to muffled whispers before disappearing completely as the cow began to asphyxiate.

T. sighed deeply and allowed himself to relax. He wasn't entirely sure why, but never had renewed silence tasted so sweet to his ears. He looked around and realized that he wasn't the only one feeling that way. The same release of tension was traveling through all the members of the hunting party.

Suddenly, Sifit's fangs tore through the flesh and glanced off the bone once more. The buffalo cow wretched herself free of the death trap and sucked in her breath in one long, wet inhale. A heartbeat later, her calling grunts pierced through the silence of the savannah again, louder than ever.

T. felt a cold chill run down the length of his spine. Pushed by some dark premonition, he turned around… and froze.

He had assumed that the herd would scatter across the plain after the initial attack. The way those big grazers had run, he had expected them to reach the other side of the Sabi Sands by nightfall. Now he realized that the herd had stopped running and coalesced back together as soon as the lions had assaulted the female.

He watched with growing apprehension as the unnerved buffaloes kept glaring at them.

At first, most grazers seemed hesitant to move. They snorted loudly, swung their horns at invisible targets, bumped into one another to reassure themselves, but did not take a step forward. They had escaped the assault safely, they seemed to say. Why should they concern themselves with the fate of someone else? Then, a handful of braver individuals began to walk back toward the lions. Their steps were short and timid, their gaze askance – as if pretending to do something else – and they had to stop frequently to grunt and give each other courage and fire up their spirit, but they kept coming steadily, nonetheless. To T.'s wide eyes, they looked like the first drops of rain falling out of some ominous dark clouds.

More grazers trickled to their side, one pair of horns after the next. They began to coalesce into small groups. Those groups swelled up, one big dumb beast at a time, and joined others to form bigger groups, the way drops of water do when they meet on a smooth leaf. Soon, it sounded as though a thunderstorm was marching back toward the trapped female; a tall line of dense, dark flesh overturning the grass underneath its innumerable hooves.

T. took a step back and whirled in place, thinking that maybe he could run away in the opposite direction. No such luck. Everywhere he looked, the herd was now less than a single leap away from them. They were encircled.

Mak Senior cursed loudly and relinquished his grip on the trapped cow. As soon as she felt the weight disappear, she stood herself up and unleashed the last of her remaining strength. The tail ripped itself off and Nui collapsed on her haunches with the appendage still dangling inside her jaws like some fat, obscene snake. Fer instantly realized her predicament and hurried to let go of her grip. The kicking back hooves grazed her head and she scattered away with a short, high-pitched yelp. Dreadlocks went flying through the air but was fortunate enough to land on his feet, unhurt.

Only Sifit stubbornly clung to her grip. Desperate, she tried one last leap for the throat. She missed and collected a sharp hoof to the sternum for her efforts. Gasping for air, she picked herself up and limped to the side as fast as she could. The buffalo cow did not try to charge her. After one last victorious grunt, she turned around and ran for the protection of the herd, a mist of red blood flying off the stump of her tail after every step.

Mak Senior rushed to the front of the nearest buffalo line.

"Get back!" he roared at the top of his lungs. "I'll kill you! I'll kill you all! GET BACK!"

The line stopped. The lion's roars were such that some of the younger individuals could not help but turn themselves around again. Some confusion ensued, and the equilibrium tittered for a few long heartbeats.

Then, a single buffalo, a young male, took a step forward with his horns lowered. Mak Senior had no choice but to quickly jump out of the way. The last of the circle collapsed.

"What do we do?!" screamed Shaka next to T. as a forest of legs suddenly engulfed them and the sight of the adults disappeared. "T., what do we do?!"

For once, T. had the perfect idea. "Run!" he yelled. "Run, run, run."

He eyed an opening in between two large bulls as big and round as boulders and went straight for it. His idea of a burrow did not seem so absurd anymore, but they would never have the time to dig. No, they needed a tree. Climb up high and wait for all this madness to blow over.

Angry hooves clobbered the ground around him, searching. He could feel the hot, rotten-grass smell of the grazers' breaths on his fur. Sticky saliva and nervous, liquid excrements dribbled down on his head and spine. Some of it trickled inside his mouth; he closed one eye and spat it out. A heavy helmet of fused horns pounded the ground to his left and almost impaled him. Too shocked to be afraid, the putrid taste of dejection on his tongue suddenly forgotten, he jumped to the side and broke into a run. He could see a small sliver of open sky not far from him. With just a bit of luck, they could make it.

"T.!" screamed Shaka behind him. "They got me, T.!"

He froze and whirled in place. His brother was prostrated on the ground, curled up behind a forest of moving legs. A small pool of fresh blood could be seen seeping into the dirt next him.

His scream caught in his throat.

Not Shaka! Blazingsunalmightyplease, not Shaka.

He ran back as fast as he could. A thin leg abruptly came down and he had to sidestep at the last instant. He growled and lashed out at the leathery pillar with all his strength. His claws tore through the thin layer of skin and tendons and, to his satisfaction, he saw the murderous limb being jerked back as if bitten by some blood-sucking insect. More legs immediately followed in its wake, like a sudden downpour. The hard keratin of the sharp hooves grazed his fur, missing his spine by the thinnest of margins. His anger forgotten, he turned himself into something of a liquid cat and focused his attention on weaving himself a path forward.

He reached Shaka and gave him a rough head rub, hard enough to jostle the young lion up. "Wake up, Shaka. Wake up!"

His brother opened a meek eye caked with dirt and grime. "You smell like shit," he groaned.

A huge, nervous guffaw barreled through T.'s chest and squeezed his lungs tight. Unable to suppress it, he let it all out in his brother's face. Despite the dire situation, he felt relief coursing through his veins. Shaka was alive, that was all that mattered.

"You've looked better too," he finally said.

Shaka did not share in the laughter. "T.," he whined, his eyes glazed with shock, "I think they've killed me."

T. swallowed a curse and took a quick glance at the pool of blood. To his immense relief, he saw that the hips and back legs were unscathed. "It's only the tip of your tail. You gonna be fine."

"Is it gone?! Did they cut off my tail?!"

"No, just broken it. It will heal."

At an angle, most like.

"What about my balls? Are they alright? T., *I can't feel my balls!*"

"Trust me, that's only the fear talking. Your balls are fine. Yours legs too. But we need to go now, Shaka. Or we'll both die."

A shy, pitiful smile marred the muzzle of his older brother. "I – I don't know if I can stand, T. I don't think that I have ever been this afraid in my entire life."

I have.

This was the golden sun honest truth of it, he realized with surprise. As a cub, he had spent most of his days suffering from the dual poison of fear and low self-worth pumping inside him. Always fretting about what might come next, always agonizing over potential shadows to the point of making himself sick with terror. But now that he was trapped in the middle of it, he actually found the fear to be somewhat less than what he had felt on those long dark nights of wrestling alone with his thoughts. The panic was lurking close, yes, but part of his mind was also strangely calm and rational, like some cold-blooded crocodile hanging tight in the middle of a raging river.

He pushed Shaka back on his feet. "Just follow my mane," he said with a cheeky half-snarl.

They retraced their steps back toward the opening he had glimpsed. After a few stomach-churning dead-ends, he finally felt the slope rise gently underneath his paws and they emerged out of the herd on top of a low hill.

He stopped for an instant and allowed himself a deep breath of fresh air as he savored the beauty of the blue sky above. All around them, the savannah was boiling with furious grazers searching for cats to kill. The cloud of kicked-up dirt was thick enough to blot out any potential openings leading out of the encircling herd. Their only chance was to find an elevated shelter the buffaloes could not reach. Fast.

"There," T. decided while pointing at a skinny fever tree rising in a slant out of the top of the hill.

They hugged the trunk and used their claws to pull themselves up. The young tree bled freely and sticky sap covered their face, paws, and belly fur. Their whiskers turned into one solid mess of glued hair dangling uselessly on either side of their muzzle. Without them, T. felt exposed, vulnerable to unseen branches on either side of his head. Still, he kept climbing, one careful claw at a time.

"We have to fan out," he said once they had reached a certain height. "Those boughs are too slim for both our weight."

Shaka nodded and settled down on a solid fork about a giraffe's height above the hill. T went a bit higher and clung to a couple of branches near the top. He could feel the thin, green wood bend and sway under his weight. He stretched his limbs out as much as he dared and tried to spread his weight evenly.

The world below was a raging river of black backs and horned heads. A big bull looked up and caught sight of him. After a loud, indignant grunt, he pushed his way up the hill and began to assault the base of the trunks with his neck extended as far as he could reach. More grazers followed his example and the whole tree began to sway back and forth. The cacophony of grunts was deafening.

With his heart heaving up and down inside his chest, T hung as tight as he could and tried to focus his attention on the horizon.

"Is it gonna hold?! T, is the trunk gonna hold!?"

"Yes!" he screamed, far from certain that he was believing what he was saying. He looked away and scanned the savannah, wondering where the others might be.

A lone, tawny figure caught his eye.

Nui.

The lioness had failed to make good her escape and was now stuck on flat ground with the herd surrounding her on all sides. He watched as she roared and lashed out at the wall of lowered horns steadily closing-in on her, the terror in her voice unmistakable even at a distance.

"What's going on?!" screamed Shaka. "T, what do you see?"

"Don't look. Whatever you do, don't look."

Even though every fiber of his body was urging him to follow his own advice, he found that he could not do so. His eyes were not his anymore.

Transfixed, he saw how the lioness growled and stood her ground while trying to force the grazers back. Then, once the buffaloes were close enough to touch her, he saw how she soiled herself and frenetically bolted from one side of the encroaching circle to the other.

The circle collapsed and his mother disappeared from sight.

For all of three heartbeats, it looked as though nothing was going to happen. Then, he saw her body being propelled straight up in

Human term

the air, higher than a giraffe's head. Amazingly, she did three full cartwheels before falling back down on the awaiting horns.

Except, of course, that this was not possible.

Because full-grown lions don't do cartwheels up in the air like that. Everybody knows this. This had to be some kind of a mistake. An illusion of the haze.

He closed his eyes, opened them up again.

Nui's broken body bobbed atop the grazers' back for a brief instant.

Then, she sunk. sank

SIX

THE DARK-MANED

A lioness would never be so dismissive of her young, or any of the pride's. They're extremely protective.

"Take them if you want," she groaned coarsely in-between two greasy bites. "Eat them, for all I care. They are more trouble than they are worth anyway. Whatever you do, be quick about it. Things are hard enough on the pride right now, I don't need you to add to the turmoil."

On this, she walked away and, after one last disdainful snarl, turned her attention back to the sunbaked carcass twisting above ground under the eager pulls of the five lionesses. An old hyena kill, he judged, maybe a gnu. Hard to tell with only a few white bones connected to a thick hide left.

Not needed

Well, so much for greetings, he reflected bitterly.

Clearly they were busy, but still.... After all this time, no small talks, head rubs or friendly snuggle of any kind? Any other cat, such a long exile would have been enough to mellow things a bit, let bygones be bygones. Not with that old gnarly root of a female. Don't

The mane appears first on the chest, not the belly. It's rare ever for adults to grow manes on the belly.

count on it. In her voice, he had felt the frost of that fateful morning all over again.

He bit back a wisecrack – he didn't need the trouble – and followed the huntress' advice. He found them dozing on the parched yellow grass out in the open, far away from everyone else. Still unnoticed, he stopped and gauged them from afar.

Three sub-adults with golden belly-manes, cocky muscles rippling underneath a healthy coat of tawny fur, and only the faintest hints of dark hairs growing out of their naked scalps. He watched them as they stirred and wrestled playfully. They were callow and boisterous in their attacks, rigid and unsteady in their defensive stances. At times, they seemed to retreat when there was no ground for it while many of their cocky offensive stratagems bordered on the ludicrous. On occasion, one of the young cats would find himself sprawled on his back, surrounded by a cloud of dust with his four paws trashing frenetically and uselessly in the empty air. Now forced to try and fend off his two encircling brothers with his head upside down, he would growl and curse continuously and – at least for an overly long amount of time that was almost too painful for Makhulu to witness – do nothing to change the fact that his belly and crotch were exposed wide for all creatures to see and gnaw at.

Clearly these were not experienced, muzzle-scarred lions. And yet there was something deeply hopeful in the way they behaved, like a wildfire rising ever higher after the first drops of rain have begun to fall. As the sizzling increases, you can tell that the end is near, but the flames keep on burning anyway, secure in their naïve belief that they can weather the storm, that they can endure anything, the glorious fools.

Makhulu sat down on his haunches and drank in the rare beauty of youthful over-confidence as of yet uncut by the sharp edge of grass.

From a strictly physical standpoint, the Eyrefield had every reason to be proud. Those cats were well-fed and well-raised. Despite her cold, dismissive attitude toward the young males, Sifit had clearly outdone herself once again.

The oppressive heat cut their banter short. Panting heavily, they restored peace with a few deep snuggles and head rubs before sauntering away from the scuffed-up dirt with their tails held high.

They didn't move very far. As he watched them settle down again on open ground without a care in the world, as if they owned the very spot on which they lay, Makhulu felt a pang in his heart. The physical resemblance with his younger self was so striking, it was almost painful to see, as if he were looking at a reflection of his own past.

With one big exception, of course.

He forced the thought away from his mind. This was cold blood spilled on the far side of grass, no point in reopening old wounds now. He rose from his hideout and trotted forward.

They caught sight of his approach and immediately hopped to on wary legs, ready to burst into a run at the first sign of a roar. He made sure to maintain a respectful, unthreatening distance before sitting down on his haunches again. They did not relax completely, but that was alright.

"Who are you?" growled one of them. His belly-mane was slightly less golden than his brothers, more brown-red.

"The name's Makhulu," he said, his voice flat and neutral.

"You're Split Rock or Shaw?" another sub immediately asked from behind brown-red. Although he did not share his brother's red hue, he looked exactly the same age. A twin, if the females were to be believed. He seemed even more nervous than the other two.

"Neither. I am a son of the Sunsets, same as you. I was born to another pride but the Eyrefield took me in when I was roughly the same size you are now."

"When?"

"Before you were born."

"Why?"

"The Boys needed an extra mane to deal with the arrival of the three Mlowathi males."

He had not done any real fighting at the time. Mostly, he remembered the whole thing as a succession of confused raids and night roars. That, and a lot of pissing around to show dominance.

The three subs looked at each other in surprise. He could see the suspicion in their eyes. "If the Eyrefield took you in, where have you been all this time?"

"Away. I was cast out shortly after you guys were born."

Once the Mlowathis had mysteriously died off and were not a threat to the pride any longer, of course.

"Alone?"

"Yes."

"So you're a wander-male now," the second twin blurted out as if revealing some hidden, shameful secret he had suspected all along.

The third sub glared at his brother and shoved him aside. Although younger than the other two, he was already as big as any of them. He stepped forward. "What my brother is trying to ask, poorly, is: how have you been able to survive all on your own without a pride?"

"I made do."

Just barely.

"Makhulu, eh?" interjected brown-red. "As in a junior to Mak Senior?"

"Yes, he gave me the name along with everything else."

An awkward silence fell on the group.

"I guess you should know, then," the third sub mumbled.

"Know what?"

"Mak Senior's dead. Buffalo hunt gone wrong."

Makhulu closed his eyes. He had heard the rumors on his way to the pride, of course, but had not dared give them too much credit. Deep down, he was not really surprised. It did not really matter anyway. As far as he was concerned, Mak Senior had died a long time ago, on a chilly dawn filled with curses and roars, hot breaths steaming in the cold air, and the deafening silence of a cowardly lion averting his gaze.

Farewell, lazy mane. Leopards across the Sabi Sands are sleeping sounder now that you are gone.

"So, who is left?" he asked the sub-adults.

The way they all looked at the ground, hesitant to answer, told him all he needed to know. This was no fluke of bad luck. Things were going bad for the Sunset coalition. Really bad. Not daring to express his hope out loud, he waited patiently for the names to drop. At least the foreign urine he had smelled on his way here suddenly made a lot more sense.

"Only Broken Nose," brown-red finally said.

Makhulu swallowed down a growl of disappointment. Of course, the one cat in the whole veld he wanted dead the most had to be the last one standing.

As if on cue, the hated roar suddenly broke through the surrounding silence and washed over the sunbaked plain. A bolt of fear travelled through Makhulu’s spine, all the way to his neither region, and he had to repress a need to jump on his legs and start running. Just like that, he was a young belly-mane all over again.

I‘ ya ‘ver loak at ‘er like tha’ ‘gain, A’ll break yar spine, cub. A’ll spill ya wet all ‘ver this here dir’, watch me if A’ doan’t!’

He forced the inner voice out of his mind and listened attentively. The roar had changed. The formerly aggressive bellows that used to pierce right through you and melt your insides into water had grown flat and empty. They ricocheted off his skin like mere tantrum grunts. The pace was much faster too, he noticed with no small amount of glee. Broken Nose’s abdomen could not sustain the strain of the push any longer.

Still, the old male seemed determined to squeeze the bellows out relentlessly, one push after the other, as if nothing had changed. Under the fake bravado, one could easily discern the desperation. As if he knew full well that he was trying to compensate for something he had lost and was secretly hoping that no one would come and call him out on his bluff.

“He just got his face mauled by the two Split Rock males,” the younger sub explained. “He barely escaped with his life. Everyone in the pride says that his next fight will be his last. He doesn’t even have any teeth left.”

A toothless Broken Nose, what a sight that must be.

For half a heartbeat, Makhulu was tempted to go up that hill and settle an old score at last. “What happened to the others?” he asked instead. He did not want to antagonize the sub-adults so soon.

The young males shrugged. Although they insisted on putting up a cool facade of indifference, Makhulu could see in their eyes that they were terrified by the abrupt turn of events. He could understand the conflicted feelings. For better or worse, those big males had constituted the bedrock of the young cats’ lives ever since their birth. Despite all the fear and resentment, maybe even hate, a part of them still idolized those rough manes who had allowed them to grow and thrive amid a stable pride. To them, they represented everything a male lion was supposed to be. And to witness them fade away so rapidly like that, as if they had never existed in the first place, could not be easy.

Such a small gap between hate and love, he reflected while taking a long hard look at his own fading resentment, *an all too easy leap for a lion.*

One of the twins cleared his throat. "Both Scars, Scar-Nose and Scar-Eye, disappeared in the night over the course of the last rainy season. We believe that they were picked off, either by the two Split Rocks or the Shaws. Blondie just went to sleep and never woke up. That was a moon ago."

"And now the whole pride is rotting away," moaned the second twin. "Foreign males roam our land freely and steal our kills, and the females do nothing to stop them. Just two dawns ago Dreadlocks almost got mauled to death by one of the Split Rock for trying to defend a gnu. A gnu we had brought down ourselves! Nobody seems to care. The pride is constantly split into smaller groups spread out across the savannah, and nobody knows where anyone is anymore. The Eyrefield has no center. It's chaos."

Well, that's a transition for you, Makhulu thought while nodding his understanding to the younger cat. Chaos, confusion, and blood. The pride was in for a rough season indeed.

"So, which one of you his Dreadlocks, then?" he asked, eager to change the subject.

The younger sub laughed lightly and bowed his head. "That be me. When I was a cub, I liked to roll in the mud and grass to pretend that I had a mane. Those idiots came up with the nickname, and it stuck."

They all laughed.

"I'm Leonides," said brown-red.

"A good name for a lion."

"This one is my twin, Skoro."

"Some lions call me Pretty Boy."

"No they don't," groaned Dreadlocks. "Nobody in the entirety of the whole of the Sabi Sands as ever called you that. And no one ever will."

Skoro leaped forward to avenge the insult and Dreadlocks met the assault head-on. After stealing a glance at Makhulu, Leonides hurried to jump in and the rambunctious trio wrestled its way through the short grass, each cat switching sides on a whim as he saw fit.

Although he very much wanted to, Makhulu refrained from joining them. He knew that he was too big for them, it would not be fair.

"So you three are the only subs left in the pride?" he asked once their flash of temper had finally petered out. "The word across the wind spoke of five young males born to the Eyrefield, but that was probably before the downfall of the Sunset Boys and the arrival of the foreign males."

"The word across the wind is accurate," said Leonides as he sat back down slightly out of breath, "we are still five."

"Well, more like four and a half, really."

"Shaka and T. are our two younger brothers," Dreadlocks explained. "They still spend a lot of time with the females."

"T.?" asked Makhulu, nonplussed. "What kind of a name is that?"

A short, awkward silence followed his remark.

"Well, it's kind of our fault, really," said Leonides. "We used to call him 'The Tit' when he was a cub."

"On account of the fact that it took him forever to be weaned," Skoro hurried to add with a snigger.

"Now that he's all grown up, sort of, we just call him T. for short. Nobody can remember his given name anyway. Not even him."

"And it's not like his mother is still around to correct us."

More sniggers came tumbling down Skoro's throat.

"It's a weird name," said Dreadlocks, "but it fits him, you'll see for yourself soon enough. Shaka is alright, a proper steady cat, but ever since that buffalo hunt that took his mother, T. has been different. He was never much of a lion to begin with, but now… I don't know. It's like he's grown even more quiet, somehow. Retreated inside his head or something. Whenever he looks at you, you can practically see his thoughts grinding their way across his mind like so many buffaloes living behind his eyes."

"Kind of creepy," Leonides concluded with a shrug.

Unsure of what to make of this, Makhulu simply nodded and laid himself down on the grass. After a short heartbeat of hesitation, the three subs hastened to join him and they frittered the rest of the afternoon away together by swapping stories and coarse jokes.

Skoro, Makhulu learned quickly, had a prodigious mind for this kind of thing.

SEVEN

THE BEAST WITH HORNS

The cacophony of uninterrupted gravelly grunts, gasps, and muffled curses had a strange, baffling quality to it, almost like a spectacle. T. stopped briefly at the foot of the hill and listened. Above it all, he could discern the laborious breathing coming out in wet, angry chuffs, every wheezy inhalation threatening to close the windpipe in its wake.

He had developed a soft paw over the course of the last few moons; he knew that, should he want to, he could easily sneak up on the helpless wretch. He thought better of it and ascended the hill slowly in the open. Once at the top, he sat down on his haunches at a respectful distance and introduced himself with a soft growl.

Broken Nose jerked his head up and frantically pulled on his front legs to drag himself across the loose dirt. After much scuffing, he finally managed to rotate and face him.

T. winced. He could not decide what was more heart-wrenching: the painfully slow way with which the big male had moved, or the putrid stench emanating from his fangless, sagging jowls. The flesh on his backside had melted away, revealing the sharp bones of the hips underneath; his back legs were splayed at an angle from his body, with his paws immobile and blue; his mane, although still as dark as night, had lost most of its depth and was now plastered flat against his fur, making his upper body appear grotesquely thin compared to his head.

The worst was the face. The front of his muzzle was now a dark ruin of lacerated flesh and old puncture wounds overseeing a battered grey tip. The black rhinarium had swollen to absurd proportions and the cleft in its middle had turned into a blood-curdling crater. At the top of the brow, a bite wound was still bleeding freely and thin red streaks could be seen trickling down the side of the left eye, through the dirty fur and out the dripping corner of the lower black lips.

T. took it all in with clenched jaws and dead, uncompassionate eyes. The irony was not lost on him. Now more than ever, Broken Nose was living up to his famed name, courtesy of the Split Rock males.

The mangled muzzle brought forth to his mind the images of a young zebra whose snout he had witnessed being ripped almost clean off by a crocodile. After having endured the murderous barrel-roll without so much as a cry or complaint, the poor dumb thing had agonized for a long time while the reptiles consumed him slowly, still stubbornly alive despite the fact that his chewed-out muzzle now ended at the level of his eyes. T. could still remember watching the whole show unfold from the safety of the opposite bank, dumbstruck and fascinated by the horror of the spectacle, a queasy feeling running through his stomach even as his saliva filled his mouth. The bones had cracked under the abrupt tearing and twisting of the flesh. Some weird spongy matter had gushed out in a rosy torrent and foamed briefly above the rapids before being swept away. But no screams from the zebra, oddly enough. That had marked him the most. No screams. Never any scream.

Another beautiful day above grass, my fellow cats. Next up, the amazing cartwheeling lion! But first, let's watch this old male die in his own shit.

"Ya' c'm'ere t'g'wk? O' fini' me o'?"

T. almost strained his ears trying to decipher the gooey sentence. The chewed-out words were also half-choked, as if there were something viscous clinging to the inside of the big throat, something the old male could not quite spit out no matter how hard he tried.

Broken Nose drew himself up and tried to stare the younger lion down, but his searching gaze failed to lock on T.'s mind the way it used to. The scouring glare was now shaky and askew, feeble; the yellow in the eyes, usually so fiery and dreadful, had turned cold and viscous, like sap mixed with piss. He was keeping his pupils far too wide for the mid-day sun, as if convinced that it was still the middle of the night. As a result, the reflective tapetum inside his eyes had turned leathery and his over-exposed retinas were milky white. They harmlessly glanced off T.'s shoulder and landed on the dirt to his left.

"A' kn'w y' h're! A' c'n st'll sm'll y', y' li'l sh't! Y' came h're t' figh', o' wha'?"

T. took a soft step forward. He was now close enough to reach out and touch the whiskers of the old brute, and smell the pain hidden underneath the stench. For the first time in his life, he was not afraid of Broken Nose.

Rather than cheering his heart, that realization took him by surprise and scared him more than the tyrant's gaze ever could. There was something ominous lurking behind it. Something…ugly. He swallowed down a need to scream and tried to wrestle with the idea. He failed to sink his claws in fast enough and the thought made good its escape back to his unconscious. Untroubled – he was used to his own thoughts running freely inside his head by now – he let it go and simply kept staring at that pitiful thing that had once been the most fearsome creature of his world.

Too weak to keep his half-stance up any longer, Broken Nose laid his head back down in-between his front paws. A small pool of blood and saliva formed underneath his muzzle and turned the dirt into mud. As it clung to his wet rhinarium, some of the mud entered a small cut inside the swollen crater.

Can't be good for the bloodstream, that.

"Ya' g'n' go an' l've wi' tha' n'w slee' dar' m'ne, th'n?"

"Perhaps," T. said, his voice stiff and slightly dismissive. He was still staring at the mud coating the inside of the fresh cut, thinking that maybe he should scoop it out.

He had met Makhulu only the day before and was not quite sure what to think of the older son of the pride just yet. After a long exile, the cat had come back just when the Sunset Boys were either dead or dying. That could not be a coincidence. And with all those new males roaming around with their tails held high, it was hard to know who to trust.

He had to admit, though, there was something almost majestic shining out of this elder brother of theirs. Something calm and powerful far beyond what even Shaka or Dreadlocks could project. Just like a big tusker calmly trundling across the plain one heavy step at a time, secure in his own size and strength, Makhulu did not seem to know the meaning of the word fear. Whenever he thought about it, that made T. want to scream. The strength and vigor of youth, he could understand, but not the tall demeanor and arrogant self-confidence. Self-assured cats were fools. Sooner or later, they always ended up doing cartwheels in the air. Grass ruled all. To be smart was to be a shadow.

But, of course, Shaka could speak of little else these days, and already the other three had gone on a few hunts with Perfect Mane and were now affectuously calling him 'Big Mak'. If T. didn't know better, he would have sworn that they were in heat.

He had heard the whispers too. Talks of leaving the pride and striking out as a coalition of their own. Nobody had consulted him, of course – it was Shaka they wanted – but he had heard. He didn't know how to feel about that either. Were they betraying the pride by leaving? Should they stay and try to keep the other males at bay? Was that even possible for a bunch of young belly-manes like them? Would they not just be getting in the way of the pride's well-being? What course of action was the least selfish? Should he care at all?

The prospect of leaving the safety of the pride made him want to scream and hurl himself straight out of his mind. The idea that Shaka – *his* Shaka – might choose Makhulu over him and leave him behind, alone, was too frightening to even contemplate.

It's natural for adolescent males to leave – they go of their own accord or are driven out by the pride males. They cannot stay and breed with their mothers and sisters!

“F’ckin’ Ma’,” Broken Nose kept on ranting with his eyes now closed. “A’ shal’ ha’ kill’ h’m ‘lon’ ti’ ‘go. ‘n ya. A’ shal’ ha’ kill’ all y’ ungr’tf’l c’ts ‘lon’ ti’ ‘go!”

T. swallowed down a soft giggle. Buried deep somewhere inside that wreck of mangled flesh, some small ambers of the old Broken Nose’s temper were still burning bright after all. He wished more of it would flare up. He wished the old male would try to swat at him brusquely, chase after him, call him a waste of meat, a worthless ball of fur, an unfortunate spillover out of some dirty wander-mane’s loins. Anything to make him feel like the old days were not done and gone, long spilled into the dirt like that stupid pool of saliva and blood which was – by the grass! – still growing.

Instead, Broken Nose fell into a rib-splitting coughing fit that left him panting hard and wincing in pain.

T. sighed and began to trot away. He had seen enough horror for one day, this was one death he did not wish to witness. As he made his way down the hill’s gentle slope, he heard Broken Nose scream one last time. With the added distance, the words sounded more confused and feverish than ever. “Kill ya cub! Ya‘ear? Killya! Yakillkillya. Kill! Cub! Kill!” Then, oddly clear and audible, almost cheerful: “Blondie? What are you doing here?”

T. broke into a run. The downward slope turned into a flat plain. He raced across stiff stubs of yellow grass that stabbed his paws. He sped up. His legs were barely touching the ground. The wind of his own speed ruffled his nascent belly-mane but did not cool him down. The air was stifling, oppressing. He felt his ribcage pumping hard to sustain his effort. His cramping muscles caught on fire. The pain was bittersweet. It almost chased everything else away. Almost.

His front legs stopped in front of a thornbush. He could go no further. Panting hard, he screamed something unintelligible. His spine felt cold all of a sudden, exposed, as if his fur and skin had been peeled off his back. His whole body shivered. The world danced in front of his eyes. He was about to lie down when, astonished, he felt his belly contract spasmodically, and his first roar traveled through his slender frame like hot, gaseous bile. His eyes rolled inward and he let it all out with a shudder.

The throaty bellow, little more than a loud grunt, filled the emptiness of the savannah.

He hawked and caught his breath. This was ridiculous. Why did he have to care about Broken Nose's death so much? His whole life, he had done his best to steer clear of those dead eyes that seemed to wash over you as if you were not even there at all, as if you were a thing already spent and rotting under the sun, not worth a single thought. Oh, how he had hated that flat, creepy, dismissive, I-see-right-through-you stare. Had had nightmares about it. The kind you wake up from with your heart still racing inside your chest and your mind scrambling to assess what is real and what is not.

So now that the tyrant was about to become little more than a whiff of ripe air blown across the grass, why could he find no comfort in the prospect of being free at last? In fact, he was more terrified than ever. Why?

His roar turned into a whimper. He paced back and forth, his belly heavy and low as if laden with rocks. A thousand thoughts swirled freely inside his mind like lions doing abject cartwheels in the air. They were laughing gleefully the mad bastards, oblivious to the horns awaiting below.

You worry too much, why don't you join us?

Yeah, we're having so much fun!

As long as you don't land, you'll be fine!

But of course, everyone lands sooner or later. Those cats were already dead and they didn't even know it. Their faces were crawling with worms.

He closed his eyes. The fear had never been so intense, so physically overwhelming. He was sick from it. Retching.

Who's this lion, who can't stand on his own four feet? Why, of course, it's the Tit! Who's this lion, so full of ticks, his mother won't even lick? Why, of course, it's the Tit! Cold feet! Cold feet! The Tit runs on cold feet! COLD FEET! COLD FEET! THE TIT IS DEAD MEAT!!

A strident cry snapped him out of his agony. He jolted and whirled in place.

Hidden underneath the thornbush, a female baboon he had not noticed before was staring at him. Perched on her back, a small ball of darker fur with large pinkish ears and tiny, stringy arms was clinging to her flanks with all its might. The female baboon had nowhere to go, he realized instantly, she was stuck between the underbrush and T.'s much bigger body. Her cry had been a last-resort warning.

He's big enough now that a baboon is no threat.

Not wanting to start anything by mistake, he slowly stepped away.

As soon as she saw him backtracking, the female baboon bristled her fur on either side of her face and let out a burst of fierce hoots rising in crescendo. Two prominent canines flashed behind her peeled lips.

"Please don't," T. gasped.

The baboon charged.

He swallowed down a growl and ran away. The baboon chased after him with loud whoops and lunged at his tail while, on her back, the ball of fur held tightly onto her fur and screamed hysterically as if riding his own mother into battle. The high-pitched screeching rattled T.'s nerves. He could already feel those ignominious, weirdly articulated black paws grabbing a hold of his fur. The thought made his skin crawl.

Fortunately for him, apart from a few bushes here there, this was mostly open ground. He was much bigger than the baboon, he could run away easily. Find the safety of the pride. Find Shaka. Let him deal with this mess.

No.

His legs stopped of their own volition. Without thinking, he swiveled in place in one smooth movement and faced his attacker. Taken aback, the baboon froze a half leap away from him and he heard her last whoop dying a strangled death inside her throat.

He saw it. In her eyes. Fear. More than that, terror. As clear and bright as the sun above. Sweet, juicy fear. The baboon was terrified, of *him.* The sudden realization was as unexpected as it was delicious. Intoxicating. His brain raced to follow all the implications suddenly branching out of his mind like some mad, feverish tree breaking free of a muddy river.

Fear, much like a buffalo, was a beast with two ends. One end, the front end, had horns. That's where you don't want to be, the receiving end of fear, where he had lived most of his life. But there was a second end. A hindquarter end! You could jump on it and be in control. As long as you don't let go, you are fine, the front end can't reach you. As long as you are the one who is feared, *you do not have to be afraid yourself!*

When you walk out on a moonless night so dark even your cat's eyes cannot pierce through the pitch-black darkness and all you can hear are strange creaking and muffled grunts all around you, you can either squirm in fear and crawl into a hole and wait for the sun to rise with your heart inside your throat, or you can realize that the darkness is hiding you just as much as it is hiding them. Take two steps inside yourself, calm your breathing down and turn your mind around, you *are* the thing that roams.

Such a small change, this other side of fear. A difference of attitude, really, nothing more. T. felt as though he had stepped into a different world. A darker world. In it, he was feeling so much lighter. The stones in his stomach were gone, they had never existed in the first place. The veld, this vast and cruel expanse of grass he had subconsciously dreaded his whole life, had opened itself up to him at last. He was treading on flat terrain. Not a hill anywhere in sight. And no shadows.

A lion's due is what he takes. No more, no less.

The inside of his mouth filled with saliva. He hunched his shoulders instinctively and lowered his belly to the ground. Three quick steps gingerly taken, as fast as lightning, and he was on top of the baboon. She tried to run away but he toppled her down with a rough slap of his left paw. Her baby went rolling in the short grass and screamed bloody murder, his small face covered with dirt. That made him giggle.

She bit him.

He drew himself back and frowned his muzzle. He could see blood – *his* blood! – trickling out of two small cuts in his right paw. The pain, he realized, was nothing. Barely a sting. He was still holding firmly onto the good side of fear, this was no time to let go.

He growled and feasted on the terror he could see oozing out of her dilated pupils.

No tree foar ya, littl' girl. Not today. Shudda run when ya'd th' chance.

With her baby now prostrated on the ground behind him, she could not escape. And despite all her posturing, she could not fight him either, not really. She was tethered to his mercy.

He played with her for a little while, grabbed her and threw her in the air. She did not do full cartwheels, not quite, but close enough. At some point he let her get close to her helpless ball of fur, only to fall back on her at the last moment and toss her aside as if she were nothing. By the grass, it felt good. She *was* nothing. His chest and shoulder muscles were bulging like never before. For the first time in his life, he was feeling strong. In control. Invincible. He kept the cruel back and forth going for as long as possible, savoring it a little bit more after every new swipe.

Eventually, the female baboon slowed down, exhausted. He stopped and took a long, hard look at her. She was bleeding from a hundred different cuts. A chunk of her tail was missing. In some places, her fur had been completely ripped off and large patches of raw, rosy flesh could be seen gleaming faintly, oozing out some kind of sticky, light-yellow fluid he had never seen before. Not blood.

He went to poke her one more time but she barely responded. Her movements had turned sluggish, catatonic. Had he really done all of that? It was hard to believe. It seemed that no time had passed at all. He was barely breathing hard himself.

He looked up and gasped. The sun had plummeted and was now low enough to graze the flat canopy of faraway trees.

He was suddenly reminded of that hyena Broken Nose had brought back for their benefits what seemed like a lifetime ago. She had been a mother too, he remembered. Two pups she had left behind. The baboon was different in that regard. Unlike the hyena, she was not giving up on her young. Even though she was dying, she was still trying to crawl forward to reach him, somehow. She had spirit.

Rage and hatred overcame him.

Growling, he leaped forward and grabbed her by the neck. Underneath all the fake fluff, her skin was as thin as an acacia leaf.

He could feel the small vertebras scratch the roof and bottom of his mouth. So fragile, like twigs. He squeezed, ever so slightly, and savored the tiny cracks popping against his tongue. The baboon went limp. He dropped her and stepped back to better admire his work. A small, involuntary spirt of saliva gushed out of his muzzle and impaled itself on the stiffened fur. He gazed at it, hypnotized. He could see each individual droplet slide down the length of the dirty hairs.

She's not wiping it off. She can't. I did that. And the neck. Sun blaze almighty, I did that too.

He licked his muzzle. He was not hungry. This was different, far more potent. If only he could put words on how he felt. As usual, the thought remained unformed, ethereal. He shrugged it off and roared. To his immense satisfaction, it came out more forcefully this time, not some half-choked grunts but a series of proper bellows pumped out of his throat by the powerful contraction of his belly.

He laughed. He was a lion at last.

Behind him, the baby baboon, shocked beyond fear, began to cry in seizures. The irritating sound hammered at his eardrums. He turned and locked his predator gaze on the tiny, wrinkly face.

The ball of fur went quiet.

A half-snarl rose on his muzzle as he stepped forward.

EIGHT

THE LEAP

Shaka stopped and frowned his muzzle at the unusual sight. Had he not been able to see it with his own two eyes, close enough to literally put his whiskers on it, he would not have believed it.

"You guys managed to take him down on your own?"

"That's right!" crowed Skoro from atop the huge promontory of grey skin. "Enough meat to last us days, and we did it all ourselves." He lay down and growled softly. With his distended belly grotesquely sprawled out on either side of his flanks and his left forelimb nonchalantly dangling off the huge carcass, he had all the appearance of a satiated leopard taking a nap on top of his favorite branch.

If he swallows down another bite, Shaka thought, *he's going to explode.*

Soft rips and cracks of bones sprinkled with intermittent sharp curses reached his ears from the other side of the carcass. Skoro might be done, but it sounded like Dreadlocks and Leonides were still going at it happily.

"How did you do it?" he asked, genuinely impressed.

Somewhat reluctantly, Skoro pointed at the rhino's front right leg. Shaka noticed the jagged end of a broken bone piercing through the thick skin.

"We ran him down until he tripped and broke his leg. After that, it was relatively easy, actually. Turns out, rhinos are not very flexible. Once down, they can't reach their own belly."

So simple and yet so ingenuous. Although Skoro's few words made it sound almost like a dull affair – he ran, he tripped, we ate – Shaka knew better. More than anything else, he admired the sheer audacity of the task. At some point during the day, his brothers – those very same brothers he had witnessed running circles around Sifit's wrath – had looked at this seemingly indomitable hulking mass of grey armored leather and decided to go for it.

The gall of those cats!

Secretly, Shaka wished that he had been there with them. Not for the meat, but the story. This was the very definition of lionlike. The kind of glorious thing you could genuinely be proud of and talk about long after your meal has been digested: "Remember that one time when we were young and brought down a rhino? What a day that was!"

Still, he doubted that his brothers had seen things in the same light. Maybe Dreadlocks – he had a similar flare for this kind of thing – but not the twins. Those two had only joined for the meat, he was quite sure of it. Something was still missing.

"A buffalo, I can understand," he said with his head cranked up toward Skoro. "We sure have learned how to deal with them. But that thing? It's huge! Why even risk it?"

"The bigger the prey, the bigger the reward," a soft voice declared behind him.

Makhulu slowly ambled out of the grass. After having greeted both Shaka and T. with a brotherly head rub, he pointed his muzzle toward the dead rhino. "In my experience, going after big games always makes a lot more sense. With an antelope or a warthog, the risk of injury might be less, but you still need to expand a lot of energy. Those nervous little creatures are good at pronking and running zigzags all over the place. More often than not, they'll leave you panting hard in their dust with your belly growling. Even when you manage to catch one, it's still a measly meal barely worth the effort. Unless you are very skilled, it's a losing strategy. This is how a roaming lion starves. But if you have the strength and the numbers required to take down a bigger prey, say a Dagga Boy, an adult giraffe or, like here, a rhino, for the same amount of effort you put in you will reap a far greater reward. Enough meat to feed you for several days, as Skoro pointed out."

"What about the increased risk though? A buffalo's horns and hoofs are one thing to dance with but a giraffe is a whole other beast altogether. With a single kick she can leave you writhing in pain in her wake with your body bended in all sorts of wrong ways. There is no getting back up on your feet after that. As for that monstrosity over there… By the grass, I don't even want to imagine what would happen to me if I were to ever find myself on the wrong side of that horn. It's hard to enjoy a bellyful of meat if your spine is broken in half, Makhulu."

"As a lion, death, the possibility of it, will always be part of the bargain of your life," T. grunted softly next to him. "You just have to accept it."

"That's the spirit," approved Makhulu, oblivious of the thick irony surrounding the smaller lion's remark.

Shaka stole a glance at his brother but T. kept his gaze on the rhino. Already, he was licking his muzzle in anticipation of the meal.

"You're right, Shaka," continued Makhulu. "Bigger game means greater risks, but that's also the secret to success. That's why I led the others after the rhino today. I wanted to show you guys, all of you, what we are capable of as long as we keep together."

Here we go, Shaka thought.

He sat down on his haunches. Ever since Makhulu's arrival and Broken Nose's death, he had known that this moment was coming, awaited it with impatience and excitement, even. Dreaded it too, if he was being honest. Instinctively, he knew that this was a pivotal moment in his life. He still wasn't sure what he would decide.

Dreadlocks and Leonides, both half-covered in fresh blood, came from around the other side of the rhino and sat down to the left of Makhulu. Skoro skidded his way down and took position on his right.

"I have been to the figurative far side of grass," the dark-maned said, his voice steady and grave, "and I can tell you, this is no easy stroll under the sun. A lone lion out there, it's really not much of anything at all. You think you're strong and can carry yourself, but it's the silence that really gets you. The silence and the big emptiness of the veld that doesn't care. Always running only one step ahead of your own hunger, never able to stop even for a moment, never at rest. It drains you. From the inside." His voice trailed off. He sucked in his breath and kept his eyes downcast, reminiscent.

It's like he's ashamed, Shaka realized suddenly. *Ashamed to ask.*

"The truth is," the dark-maned continued after clearing his throat, "we're social cats. Our real strength is in each other. Now, you all know the current state of the Eyrefield, and you already know what I am going to ask. Me, I can't stay, but as sub-adults you all have a choice to make. You can either try to stick with the females, live comfortably in their shadows and bend yourselves to the authority of whichever coalition eventually takes over, hoping that they will be merciful, or you can come with me. Together, we can form a coalition of our own. Six lions. We'll be a force to be reckoned with throughout the whole of the Sabi Sands."

He concluded his little speech with a curt nod of his head before abruptly stepping away, as if trying to put some distance between himself and the implications of his words.

Shaka felt his chest fill with love. He could have hugged the big mane right there on the spot. By his own admission, it was pretty clear that Makhulu did not think that he could survive another exile on his own. The big male needed them. And yet, he was not being pushy. Now that he had said what he had come to say, he was waiting for them to make up their own mind freely. As far as Shaka was concerned, although he had not grown up with them and shared in the same hardships, on this day, at this very instant, by respecting their right to make their own decision, he had earned his place as one of them. A brother.

Still, that did not make his proposal any less daunting.

Dreadlocks broke the silence first. "Go to the far side of grass on our own, eh? No females to help us hunt? Nothing but our wits and our strength?"

"And your ever-cheerful attitude," added Makhulu, his eyes gleaming.

Dreadlocks groaned and cleared his throat, then bowed his head. "Yeah, alright," he said. "Fuck it, after all, why not? I guess when you look at it from here, it's a far and foreign place, but once you stand on it, it's just another boring patch of dirt." He went to give Makhulu a head rub before seating down next to him. "We'll make it our own."

"But wouldn't that.... I mean, with all due respect, wouldn't that make us wander-males?" asked Skoro. "You know, since we wouldn't belong to an actual pride anymore and all that..."

"For a while, maybe."

That did not convince the skittish cat. "I don't know, Mak. I just… It seems kind of a big jump in the dark. It's too soon. We don't even have proper manes yet. And the rainy season is coming. All the grazers will scatter. Shit, I don't know… Leon, what do you think?"

"I think that I'm in. And so are you." He went to sit by Dreadlocks' side.

After glowering at his twin for a few heartbeats, Skoro simply nodded his head stiffly and quietly joined him.

Four sets of yellow eyes fell on Shaka who felt his insides shrink. No more delaying the leap. Either you're a lion, or you're not. He turned toward T. for reassurance.

Amazingly, his brother seemed completely indifferent to the choice ahead of him. "I'm with you no matter what," he simply said with a bored shrug.

So be it.

"We'll need a name," he said, his voice slightly blank. "For our coalition, I mean."

A happy little growl escaped Makhulu's throat, like a cub who had found his way to the carcass at last. "I know just the one," he said.

NINE

THE WANDERING ISLAND

They crested the top of the rocky ridgeline and came upon a smooth, vertical drop that seemed to disappear under their paws. While the others groaned at their misfortune and fanned out to look for a way down, Leonides stopped to bask in the beauty of the green valley stretching out and away as far as his eyes could see. The wind was stronger near the ledge and the constant drizzle was hitting him at a sharp angle, almost horizontally. Already drenched from paws to ears, his muzzle dripping steadily, he squeezed his eyes into two narrow slits and savored the fresh taste of the rain on his tongue and rhinarium.

So much land everywhere. Under the grey light of the overcast day, the landscape seemed strangely still and peaceful, as if the whole world were holding its breath for his viewing pleasure. He had never thought that the veld could be so big, so enormously immense.

Makhulu was still putting on a show of leading them in one specific direction, but in truth he knew that they were completely lost.

Every new dawn he was convinced that they would soon reach the end of it, the absolute farthest side of grass, the place with no horizon. Dreadlocks loved to joke that it was all only dirt. Surely, there had to be a finite amount of it. Surely, at some point, the ground would have to cry out in despair and say: "Stop it, you've won! I have nothing more to give."

But even after an endless succession of days and nights spent walking until their paws felt numb, they were still breaking new ground with every new stride. It was enough to make a proud lion feel like a mouse, as if the Sabi Sands had swallowed them whole.

Skoro padded over to him and lightly bumped into his flank before casually seating by his side. "You alright?"

"Yeah. All this roaming around makes me feel a bit small, that's all. Not you?"

His twin shrugged. With his chin's hair dripping and his nascent mane plastered against his chest, he seemed to have shrunk down a size. Leonides cringed as he wondered for a brief instant if he looked just as disheveled. Now, *that* would be a small tragedy. A proper lion ought to look the part, always. Not like some badly-wrung pelt hastily thrown over a slender frame.

"Maybe a little," said Skoro, "but I love it." Despite his poor appearance, his gaze was burning bright, almost feverishly. "I wasn't so sure that I would when we left. I thought that maybe we had made a huge mistake. But I do. By the grass, I do."

"But we're lost, Skoro. We're completely lost. I can't even remember the time when we last saw a familiar feature. Right now, I don't think that I could find my way back to the Eyrefield if my life depended on it."

"Nor I. So what? Just let go of things. Embrace the wilderness. To be lost is to be free. No more Sifit to order us around, no more pride to tie us down. Best of all, no more social order to worry about. We can go anywhere we like, hunt anything we want."

"No more pride means no more safety. Without them, we're castaways without a shred of land to call our own. Drifters in the grass."

“Nah, that’s not true. As long as we’re together, anywhere we stand is land we own. Don’t forget that you’re a Mapogo now, a coalition lion. We’re an island of ourselves.”

Leonides scoffed at the idea. The name was still foreign to his ears. It seemed so pretentious. Coalition lion! Yeah, right. Quite the pompous title for a loose bunch of meandering, raggedy rough cats lost in a never-ending cycle of foreign landscape they could not escape. Of course, he did not express his opinion out loud.

“‘Anywhere we stand is land we own’, he repeated instead. “You really believe that? It sounds like one of Broken Nose’s rants.”

Skoro chuckled. “That’s right, *cub*! Listen to what I have to say, *cub*. I know these things, *cub*. Hmm, oh yes, hmm. Loak at me. I’m the baddest, shabbiest, ugliest, stinkiest cat the Sabi Sands ever seen. I have an entire beehive stuck inside my head and more scars than brains, but that’s all goad, cause I got guts. That’s right, *cub*. Lion’s guts, buffalo’s guts, zebra’s guts, I got it all. Every time I toalk, it sounds like a hyena’s living inside my throat; the bloady scavenger keeps stealing the vowels out of my words! When I croass a river, the water would rather part ways on its oawn rather than touch the filth on my face. The day I reached the far side o’ grass, it moved away froam me, scared.”

Leonides burst out laughing and collapsed on his back with all his limbs shaking spasmodically in the air. Skoro had fluffed his mane up and clumps of damp hair were sticking out of his head and chest every which way. With his shoulders hunched in his best impression of the late male, he began to run circles around his brother’s helpless body while cheering him up with more delicious nonsense.

Eventually, the guffaws ran their course. Feeling much better now, Leonides picked himself up, out of breath and ribs bruising, and went to give Skoro a nudge. “You think we’ll ever see it? The actual far side of grass?”

Skoro sighed, his face suddenly grave. “The dirt has to end somewhere, I guess, but I seriously doubt that it’s anywhere near here. As far as I can tell, the far side has always been more of a figure of speech than anything else.”

“What a feeling that must be, though! To know that you’ve seen it all at last, tasted it all, conquered it all. To be able to look at any place amid the grass, any place at all, and say: 'I know this spot, I've been there before.' No lion has ever been able to make such a claim."

"We'll be the firsts, then," said Skoro, his eyes sparkling brighter than ever. "We'll go to the absolute farthest place any lion can go, take a good gander at it, and come back to our respective prides and say, all jaded and pretentious: 'The end of the world? Yeah, been there. Same old dirt everywhere. Nice place to take a piss, though.'"

More laughter greeted his remarks.

"I'd like that," Leonides finally whispered, more to himself than Skoro. "I'd like that a lot."

From far away, they heard Shaka's shouting. The lion had found a way down.

Skoro rose and gave Leonides' muzzle a light nudge before trotting away at a vigorous pace. "Let's go, brother!" he exclaimed. "We've got a few more horizons to punch through today."

Down in the misty valley, tall stalks of fat reeds stuck to their damp fur and tickled their underbellies. Tiny leaves came undone and turned into itchy smudges splattered over their belly-mane, making them appear like weird, green-spotted leopards. Intermittent sneezes punctuated by the occasional curse or rough expectorations of a throat clearing soon erupted up and down the line as irritating seed plumes and gnats assaulted their nasal cavity.

Leonides didn't mind. The weak grasp of the shoulder-high vegetation did not hinder their progress much and he enjoyed the lazy pace Makhulu was leading them with. He let his curious gaze wander and stopped here and there to take a whiff of the ground or play with the tiny frogs jumping out of the spongy mud underneath his paws.

Bouncing from one throat to the next, soft, high-pitched coos helped them keep contact with one another amid the dense foliage. The back and forth was reassuring and Leonides happily added his own voice to the chorus of calls. As a rule, every time he did, Skoro's peculiar double-tap would immediately answer him from the back of the line, promptly followed by T.'s own weird gurgle that always sounded so much like some poor duck being strangled. Makhulu's front coo, ever clear and forceful, would usually come on the heels of the dead duck, and then Shaka's and Dreadlocks' short bursts would rival against one another to get the last word out. This was their own little private song, as effortless and immutable as the passing of the seasons.

Here comes the mighty Mapogos, chirruping like birds.

A thin shadow cut through the ambient greyness and caused his pupils to dilate. He looked up and saw the kinky tip of Shaka's tail dangling above his whiskers. Feeling giddy, he gave it a quick nimble and was rewarded with a surprised grunt and a sudden shuffling of paws. He hastily lowered his head and pretended to be absorbed by the beauty of a moist stick. To his immense surprise – and some measure of disappointment – Shaka looked at him but did not press the matter further. Soon the bended tail had resumed its place above his head, still waving insolently within reach of his muzzle after every one of the lion's steps.

He went for another yank.

The black tassel dodged his attack at the last instant and casually slapped him across the rhinarium. Stung, he jerked his head back and swallowed down an angry growl. It was his fault; he should have known better than to try the same trick twice.

In front of him, the cheeky lion was still feigning ignorance. He licked his muzzle and let out a soft coo. Shaka answered him, then the whole band went through the song one more time.

Eventually, they came to a river.

"That's the Sand River," declared Makhulu. "It marks the end of the Mala Mala. The Londolozi lies on the other side, full of buffaloes and opportunities."

"Doesn't look too sandy to me," observed Dreadlocks.

Stabbed and churned by a now constant downpour of rain that looked to Leonides' eyes like solid, white-blue quills out of a porcupine's back, the swollen river was lashing out at the flat shores encompassing it, its usually placid surface now transformed into a convulsed and impenetrable brownish current.

"We need to cross," Makhulu insisted.

Skoro abruptly raised his head. "Here? You can't be serious."

"What about crocodiles?" inquired Leonides.

"They don't like rapids," T. said softly. "They prefer calmer waters."

"What do you know about it? What if we get nabbed by a crazy one who likes to do barrel-rolls on his own where the current is strong?"

"He's right," said Dreadlocks. "I once heard of a big male lion who got snatched like this. He went for a drink at a river, probably thinking that the big thing floating in front of him was just some weird log, and *whoof!* He was never seen again."

"That's why I stay away from filthy river water," said Skoro. "Always get my fluids from my meat. That way I know where it's been, thank you very much."

"Who told you that story?" Shaka asked Dreadlocks.

"A lioness from the Eyrefield. Etoke. She heard it from some other cat."

"Etoke? Isn't she the one who walked right up to that wounded Styx female by mistake once?"

"Yeah, I remember!" Leonides exclaimed. "Dumb cat didn't even realize the Styx female was from a different pride until she flat out refused to return her head rub."

He laughed at the memory.

It had been a beautiful chaos, with huntresses from both sides suddenly running around everywhere and lashing out at each other without really knowing why something had been started, only that it was on, and Leonides and his brothers caught by surprise in the middle of the mess, perplexed as to why cats' tempers had to boil over so suddenly like that. They had shined that day, though, and help push the intruding pride all the way back to the edge of the dry shrubs. His sister Fer had been positively blazing with rage and had nearly killed one of the younger Styx in the fight. Shaka and Dreadlocks had had to intervene to disentangle her from her screaming, claw-raked victim and Leonides could still remember watching the poor thing bolt past him amid a mist of her own blood like some crazed gazelle escaping the grip of a pack of wild dogs.

His inner smile broadened as he tried to imagine what his head-strong sister might be doing at this exact instant. He could easily picture her crouched low amid the grass in the middle of yet another herd, waiting for Sifit's signal to pounce, her cold predator gaze mercilessly scanning for weaklings, selecting. He wondered if he would ever see her again and, if so, whether he would be able to recognize her. She had been fully grown by the time they had left and probably would not change much anymore, but what about him? Would he ever forget her appearance? Let himself turn into a stranger? At what point could he be considered a foreigner to the Eyrefield anyway? A wander-male? Had he already crossed that point?

His thoughts meandered and he found himself wondering if she would ever let a male cover her and give her cubs of her own. The idea disturbed him deeply; he pushed it away from his mind, preferring to bring back the happy memory of that casual little fight under the sun, back when the Styx had crossed the line.

Afterward, Sifit had severely chastised the inattentive Etoke for wasting the pride's energy and the young males had snickered at her misfortune while bringing their own adrenalin down with much snuggling and mutual grooming. Fer had joined them and helped lick their scratches and they had welcomed her like another brother, a first since the beginning of their adolescence, and a last. For reasons Leonides was not entirely certain he could fully explain, they had quietly grown apart and never spent time together after that day.

"Yeah, Etoke wasn't exactly the most reliable of cat," Shaka concluded, cutting his reverie short.

"That doesn't necessarily mean that the crocodile story isn't true."

"Don't worry, if you see a log swimming against the current towards you, you don't need to swim faster than it, only faster than Leonides."

"That's not funny!"

T. sniggered and went to give him a couple of scornful taps on the muzzle. He low-growled and ruefully pushed him away.

"Alright, alright, cut it out," bellowed Makhulu. "We'll find a safer place to cross."

They didn't have to look for long. A few paces upstream, they found a narrower bend where the banks were spottily bridged by a few dark, glistening rocks sticking out against the onslaught of the rapids.

Leonides cursed under his breath. The crossing promised to be perilous.

Before anyone had time to voice their objections, Makhulu deftly leaped forward and gracefully landed on the first promontory. Using his momentum to preserve his balance, he pushed on without stopping, his paws barely grazing the rocky surfaces, and was soon all the way across. His now ill-defined silhouette turned around and looked at them through the curtain of rain, interrogative.

Leonides hurried to follow in the wake of the dark-maned lest his courage betrayed him first. He leaped and splayed his limbs to get traction on the smooth, slippery stone. His front paws skidded to the left and he was almost thrown into the water. He groaned and instinctively threw his tail to the side to balance his tilt out before awkwardly jumping toward the next rock, a much smaller cone-shaped peak. He managed to land on it with rigid limbs, somehow, but then froze. The promontory was too small for him, he was forced to adopt an anthill stance with all his toes awkwardly stepping over each other and his own claws scratching at his skin. His body began to rock back and forth. His tail swung madly from side to side. Cold water lapped at his ankles. He looked down and his gaze fell on the dark rapids coursing all around him. His heart jumped inside his throat. He was losing his grip. Cursing loudly, he half-leapt half-fell toward his next target and forced himself to keep going without stopping. He did miss the very last stone but at this point the water was only thigh-deep and he managed to splash his way to the shore with clenched jaws. Makhulu chuckled and greeted him with a head rub.

Dreadlocks soon followed behind him, then Shaka and T.

"Fucking shit!"

Leonides jolted and turned around just in time to see the last of his twin's body disappear under the raging water. "Skoro!" he screamed.

Shaka cursed under his breath and jumped back into the water. Makhulu followed in his wake and the two lions waded into the current with their heads raised high until the water overflew above their shoulders. Unable to go any further, they called out Skoro's name and fumbled blindly with their extended paws.

Pacing back and forth on the shore, Leonides tried to scan the surface as best he could. The rain was getting in his eyes. The choppy surface had turned into a mass of impenetrable brown greyness.

"I can't see him!" he screamed in despair. "Dread, you see anything?"

His brother had already run to the river's bend in hope of catching a glimpse of Skoro's body before the unfortunate lion was swept into the much larger downstream channel.

"Nothing!" he yelled back.

"There!"

Skoro's head exploded out of the water and floated for a brief instant before sinking back down again, replaced by his forelimbs frenetically batting against the current.

After being swept downstream almost all the way to the bend, he reached a spot where he could stand and, after some more sloshing around, managed to gingerly trot out of the river with small, uneasy steps.

"I'm alright," he declared, his voice small. "Just a little tumble. I'm good." He curled up and hawked. A yellow liquid gushed out of his muzzle and seeped into the moist ground at his paws, leaving a few white bits of half-digested meat stranded behind.

They all rushed to meet him.

"Seriously, I'm fine," he insisted, laughing faintly even as they piled up on top of him.

After much cursing and teasing, they finally broke it off.

"Did you see any crocodiles?" T. asked, deadpan.

Skoro groaned and tried to swipe at him. T. dodged easily and ran away. Leonides watched his twin give chase, he laughed good-heartedly with the rest of the band.

Eventually, they turned themselves back toward the grass.

TEN

OF GIRAFFES AND BAOBABS

The strident squeals of the piglet cut through the peace and quiet of the savannah, all the way to his defenseless eardrums. Skoro clenched his jaws tight and shuffled his head around in the dirt before pressing a heavy paw against his folded ear so as to shut the noise out. It did not work.

By the grass, this was no kind of day for such loud exuberances. Ever since dawn, the heat had soared and exploded bright over the parched savannah, washing it clean of all activity. After some half-hearted meandering, the little band had finally come to its senses and settled down on an open spot, eager to enjoy yet another vacuous afternoon frittered away in yawns, mutual grooming, and, most important of all, sleep – or so Skoro had naïvely hoped.

More screams came and went, like a pack of relentless wild dogs on the prowl. He was nearing the point of complete despair when, suddenly, one final outburst was cut short mid-shriek. He braced himself for a new wave; when it never came, his wariness slowly melted away. The summer sun hammered at his skull and shone red through his closed eyelids, its cleansing, all-encompassing heat pushing his mind down toward a well-deserved slumber. He smiled internally and allowed himself to drift away at last, his drowsy mind eagerly lapping every single drop of blessed silence up like some fine buffalo blood.

The cacophony returned, more strident than ever. A jolt traveled through Skoro's body. His adrenalin spiked and his surprised muscles twitched. Now fully awake and ready to bite, he heaved himself up on numb forelegs.

Oblivious to his brother's suffering, T. was having great fun throwing his small quarry up in the air and watching it do a full turn begore landing heavily on broken legs. Skoro watched in disbelief as the smaller lion hastened to grab the piglet by the back of the neck again and used his lips to clamp down softly without breaking the skin, like some mad lioness taking care of a deformed cub. After shaking the piglet slowly, almost affectuously, he repeated the maneuver a couple of times.

"Just finish him already," snarled Skoro.

"Or at least shut him up first," Leonides' voice growled sleepily somewhere to Skoro's left, his body half-hidden behind the stiff dry lank. "It's the middle of the afternoon, for grass' sake! Some lions would like to sleep."

"Besides, it's bad for the meat," added Makhulu.

"Nah, it's always better if you play with them a little before the kill. That's why it's called 'Game'."

"Such a small prey, all the fear toxins are going to ruin the taste."

T. shrugged. "I don't mind the taste of fear."

"Well, whatever you do, do it quietly," snapped Skoro.

To his surprise, T. held his gaze for a few heartbeats. A soft growl escaped his throat.

Skoro drew himself up and answered in kind, his rising anger suddenly ready to boil over.

The smaller lion sighed and promptly lowered his eyes back down. After one last half-swallowed groan of protest, he sulkily grabbed the piglet by the throat, this time with fangs flashing. A wet gurgle strangled the nerve-rattling squeals, then a soft crunch concluded the remarkably bloodless affair.

Peace and quiet resumed their hold over the veld at last. Skoro flopped back down and snuggled up to his twin, eager for the sunrays bathing his muzzle to drag him all the way to the land of unconscious bliss at last.

This was not meant to be. As T. proceeded to gnaw his way through the tiny rump, his raspy tongue eagerly peeling the skin off the young meat, Skoro's ears twitched again, this time tickled by that particularly delicious spongy sound of juicy flesh being masticated. His mouth filled with saliva. His stomach rumbled. A bite or two out of that soft, stringy meat would not go unnoticed, it seemed to say. After all, it had been a while since they had last brought a buffalo down. A long, long while.

He sighed, licked his muzzle, stood himself up. After stretching briefly, he nonchalantly padded over to his younger brother's side, his eyes fixed on the horizon, his meandering course a zigzag of deceit.

The little show did not fool anyone. At his approach, T. immediately covered his possession with his front paws and wrinkled his muzzle to reveal his fangs.

Human slang

His position now hopelessly exposed, Skoro stopped and tried to adjust his strategy. "Say, T., my dear loving bro, my pal in blood and hardship, my everything, you wouldn't spare a leg for a fellow hungry cat, would you?"

"Get back! I caught that one myself. It's mine!"

"Oh, come on! Just a little leg for your big bro. Pleeeease."

T. snatched the piglet up and scampered away. Once far enough, he let it back down and resumed his meal with twitchy, wary eyes bouncing off his brothers in quick succession, as if trying to freeze them in place with the sheer strength of his gaze. "A lion's due's wha' he takes," he muttered in between two hasty gulps, "no mo', no less."

Skoro ground his fangs and rolled his eyes. "You're not *him*!" he said. "Stop trying to sound like you are."

"He's not wrong, though," Shaka chimed in, slightly amused. "He's the one who killed the piglet. By right the meat belongs to him. This is the golden sun honest truth of it."

"Maybe so," retorted Skoro, "but I'm *hungry*."

He jumped on the smaller lion. Ever gullible, T. immediately let go of his prize and lashed at his head. Quick as a snake, he dodged the attack and grabbed a hold of the piglet's right foreleg. Realizing his mistake, T. ushered out a desperate whimper and fell back on his quarry. An intense tug-of-war ensued, punctuated by a long litany of angry snarls and muffled curses. The piglet's thin spine and ligaments finally gave up with a fat ripping sound, like green grass being torn from the ground, and a drizzle of blood splattered the dirt. Skoro capered back to his twin with the bigger half of the piglet firmly lodged inside his jaws.

"You cheated!" T. hollered out while twisting in place back and forth, not sure if he ought to try to recover his stolen goods or keep guard of his last remaining half. "You didn't even try to fight me."

"I call that one the sneaky-snaky-snack-snatcher," said Skoro. "Neat move, hey?"

"Yeah, rolls off the tongue like gnu's fat off your fangs," snickered Shaka.

Skoro paid him no mind. "When you're on the defensive like that," he continued for T.'s benefit, "don't ever go after the player. Always keep your eyes on: 'The Game'."

"Well, I call that being a dirty thief too scared to hold his ground like a proper cat. I've seen hyenas with more honor than you!"

"There is a valuable lesson to be learned here, little kitten. Had you spared me a leg in the first place, you wouldn't have lost half your prize. You see, you need to be more of a team player. We're supposed to be a coalition after all. Sharing is caring."

Leonides raised a saliva-soaked muzzle. "Can I have some then?"

"Get lost," Skoro growled back, slightly annoyed to see his own hypocrisy exposed so quickly like that.

The others laughed heartily and good-naturedly, but not T. After having returned to the pitiful wreck of his former quarry, he forced a disquieting fake bray out of his throat and resumed his meal with peevish eyes gleaming darkly.

A somber atmosphere settled over the awkward silence. Skoro shrugged and focused his own attention on the piglet.

Not a whole lot of meat to warrant such a big fuss anyway. Barely a few bites off the bone.

T. was overreacting, as usual.

He lapped the flesh up quickly and then cracked the thin ribs in order to suck the marrow out – a delicacy he had picked up from watching hyenas eat – but his appetite was mostly gone and he only went through the motions out of spite for his brother's temperamental behavior.

Makhulu stood himself up and went to give T. a forceful head rub. Stiff as wood, the smaller cat did not return his affection, but did not shy away from it either.

"Don't take it so hard," said the big male, his voice soft and guttural. "They mean you no harm, they're just joking around."

"You worry too much," Leonides hurried to add. "That's why you can't grow a proper mane. The stress his eating at your skin."

Probably true enough, Skoro reflected, slightly saddened by the younger lion's unfortunate fate.

Over the last few moons, they all had noticed with no small amount of glee and pride how their respective manes had begun to come into their own. This had naturally led to a chaotic whirlwind of endless back-and-forth taunting, snide comments, and surprise gnawing aimed at: "checking the depth and density, bro." The whole thing had turned into a bit of an obsession, to say the truth. Something as simple as a slight change of shade was now celebrated like the growth of young grass after a long drought. Density was a prickly subject best avoided, as hard to judge as the depth of thornbushes, it was always hotly contested. By contrast, the growth of a single new black hair was see as akin to the rise of a baobab; with its shadow spreading far and wide across the parched savannah of the lucky lion's mane, its simple, undeniable presence would eclipse all other topic of conversation for days on end as its length and hue and position and slightest bend were hotly debated ad nauseam by all parties.

Words had ascended to new meanings. Adjectives such as 'tawny', 'thin', and 'light' were now considered insults of the gravest variety. 'Barren' was a declaration of war. To pluck someone's hair, even by mistake, a capital crime. 'Dark' had turned into something of a philosophical concept, an ideal looming large inside everyone's mind, as ethereal and out of reach as the far horizon – except, of course, for Makhulu whose thick, lush mane, it was unanimously agreed, had come to define the very word.

Amid this feverish atmosphere, their loud and boisterous banters had often escaped the closed circle of their little procession. Once, Leonides had even gone so far as to ask a passing leopard to be the arbiter of a long-lasting dispute regarding shades of brown between him and Dreadlocks. “An impartial decision from a keen-eyed cat”, the self-conscious lion had argued while trotting toward the dumbstruck stranger. At his approach, however, the spotted cat had only snarled fiercely before scampering up a tree, an unfortunate reaction which Dreadlocks had immediately decreed to be the irremediable proof that Leonides was far too ugly to even approach another living thing, let alone hope to rival with his own lush mane. Leonides’ cold voice had retorted that he would not leave this spot until the climbing coward had finally given him an answer, with his fangs working the bastard’s windpipe through his very throat if need be. Seated on their haunches, they had laughed at his anger and joyously watched him fail to climb the tree, the claws of his overly broad paws uselessly scratching the dry bark off the trunk in a cascading shower of thin shavings.

Skoro chuckled internally as he savored the memories.

Under all this youthful posturing and light-heartedness, he still had his own doubts. The thickness and coarseness of the long hairs provided a welcome protection against blood-sucking insects, thornbushes, and sharp blades of grass, true enough, but he was still finding the added weight heavy and somewhat awkward to carry, unsettling. On occasion, he would catch himself shaking his head and furiously scratching at his trapped neck with his back leg as if subconsciously trying to wriggle himself free of this tantalizing trap in which he was being ensconced. A full mane was the mark of a full lion, and he wasn’t at all convinced that this was a burden he was ready to bear yet.

At least, there was no arguing with the dashing new look.

While none of them could yet boast the intimidating, rich darkness of Makhulu’s hair, they were all undeniably growing in size and depth. And color. The mane on their belly had turned bark-brown while, around their head, a golden crown was beginning to form, its lighter shade contrasting sharply with the darkness encroaching their neck.

Of course T. was different, as usual. His mane was still in two separate pieces: a brindled belly-mane at the front and a thin strip of coarse hair sticking rigidly out of the top of his head and neck like a zebra's encolure. On either side of the strip it looked as though his golden forehead was overflowing out of his temples along the sides of his barren scalp like some fierce, unhindered torrent bent on tearing everything down in its path. As a result, without a proper upper mane to nestle them, his ears looked bigger than they really were. This, compounded by the sharp, almost cheetah-like beauty of his slender face's well–delineated features, plagued him with the strange, intemporal look of a cat without age, like some overgrown cub forcefully dragged through the cutting grass before his time, his juvenile mane already growing as scarce as an old cat's mangled coat, his lean body, although in reality as sprite and healthy as the others, seemingly already spent beyond its strength and ready to collapse.

Maybe Leonides was right, Skoro reflected. Maybe it was the stress. And maybe they were partly responsible too, what with the jokes and all.

He stomped his paws and shook himself out of his reverie. So what if T.'s mane was as split and misshapen as his personality? The grass was tough all around, this was no hair off his own scalp.

The half piglet had turned into a small pile of brittle bones strewn across a patch of greasy trampled grass in front of him. He stepped away, stretched his legs, froze.

Out on the horizon, a strange, asymmetrical creature was galumphing its way through the heat haze, its course a gross approximation of a straight line. Despite a constant flurry of jerks, stops, and half-heard muffled curses aimed at righting itself, it seemed as though it could not resist veering toward the left slowly, as if pulled by some invisible force. A broad streak of flattened grass could be seen behind it, betraying its tribulations as far back as a distant cluster of trees.

Shaka saw it as well and wrinkled his muzzle. "What the f–"

"It's Dreadlocks," said Leonides. "He's dragging something."

Leonides was right. The broad-chested cat was now close enough that they could see him panting heavily, a weary wet snarl etched on his gaping muzzle. He stopped and let go of his awkward burden to gather his breath. Then, grunting, he straddled it one last time and heaved it up inside his jaws, his powerful shoulders bulging under the effort. His body became a blur anchored down by the point of his fangs as he alternated between hard yanks and forceful shoves. Slowly, relentlessly, he managed to worry the huge carcass through the hindering grip of the dense grass one heavy step at a time.

They witnessed him disappear down a shallow ravine, the back end of his prize still visible on the opposite bluff, then trudge back up painfully before finally crossing the remaining distance with one last, heart-bursting, all-or-nothing awkward camper.

They hastened to greet him with a flurry of head rubs. When his turn came, Skoro felt tangled knots of caked blood scrape against his fur. Next to him, Shaka and Leonides were already ogling the prize their brother had brought back, too shocked to talk.

"Here you go boys," Dreadlock puffed out triumphantly. "Plenty of meat for the taking."

The juvenile male giraffe looked back at Skoro with white, empty eyes, his notoriously longue tongue, now limp and granulated with dirt, dangling off his dislocated mandible. In the corner of the mouth, one could still see the green smudges of his last meal. The body was fresh, killed this morning at the latest, and partially eaten at the under-belly.

That's weird.

While the others fell over themselves to congratulate their brother on a job well down, Skoro went to give the gaping wound a sniff. "How did you kill him all on your own?" he asked. He could see lumps of dark hair coating the sticky side of the wound. A rib had been gnawed through and through.

Dreadlocks shrugged. "I didn't. Found him already dead, begging to be taken."

Makhulu jerked his head up. "Stole him, you mean."

"Is there a difference?"

T and Leonides chuckled approvingly, eager to sink their teeth in, but Makhulu shut them up. "Dread," he said, his voice suddenly soft and insistent. "Who did you steal this magnificent giraffe from?"

Dreadlocks shrugged again, this time with stiffer shoulders. "I don't know. It's not like I waited to ask for permission or anything. Some careless bunch of cats, I guess. They can't have been overly concerned with the meat since they left it completely unguarded. But don't worry, I was careful not to be followed."

Upon hearing this, as if choreographed, they all looked back in unison at the wide streak of flattened grass that still betrayed the broad-chested lion's path for all creatures with eyes to see.

Then, they heard the roars.

"Oh shit!" yelped Leonides as he jumped away from the carcass, his hunger suddenly forgotten.

"Well done, Dread," Shaka hissed sarcastically. "Even for you, that's a big one."

Dreadlocks glanced at the horizon then back at his giraffe and tilted his head in a way that seemed more puzzled than contrite, as if he were failing to make the connection. "But I was careful not to be seen.... I swear I was!"

They all ignored him.

T. closed his eyes and rotated his ears slowly. A calm expression etched on his muzzle, he seemed to drink-in the growing roars with the approving look of a fine connoisseur. "Three males," he declared. "Maybe four. Less than half a horizon away, I would say."

"Full grown and dark-maned," added Skoro.

"How do you know?"

He pointed at the black hairs inside the wound that were marking the giraffe as clearly and decisively as the acidic smell of fresh piss on a tree.

"Oh shit, oh shit, oh shit," repeated Leonides as he retreated further toward the long grass.

"What do we do?" Shaka asked Makhulu.

"We run," T. said. "We have to." There was no fear or trepidation in his voice, only a bitter resignation that seemed to verge on boredom.

Makhulu considered the issue for all of a heartbeat before bowing his head. Another bout of roars echoed in the distance, this time much closer. "He's right, we run."

He did not need to say it twice. As soon as they heard the words, they darted into the tall grass and scattered as quickly and nimbly as meerkats caught under a growing shadow.

All of them except Dreadlocks.

Skoro whirled in place and witnessed the bewildering spectacle of his brother gorging himself on the carcass as fast as he could, his body already half-turned toward the cover of the lank, his nervous back legs furiously scuffing the ground beneath his paws, eager to make their escape.

"We still have time!" The gluttonous oaf growled as Skoro doubled back and ruefully shouldered him away from the giraffe. "It's good meat!"

"Yes, it is. You want to die for it?"

A new burst of roars jolted their heart, close enough to shake their diaphragm. The rising staccato of heavy paws trampling through dry stalks whipped their adrenalin up. Skoro raised his head, his throat suddenly dry. Four lines of swaying grass were hurtling toward him at impossible speed, like giant mambas.

"Ok, let's go," Dreadlocks breathed out.

They bolted and melted themselves under the cover of the dense vegetation. With their spines lowered and their legs working double time to take short, rapid steps as fast they could, they seemed to skitter like insects. Dreadlocks' preposterous belly – swollen to the point of looking pregnant – kept swinging into Skoro's flank. He stole a glance backward and saw that it was digging a shallow rut in the loose dirt as well. Swallowing down a curse, he adopted a meandering course he hoped would prove harder to follow.

Grass slapped his whiskers and cut into his rhinarium. Gnats filled his nostrils and invaded his throat. Soon, he was gasping for a breath. Behind him, he could feel Dreadlocks' blood-laden spittle pepper his rump. The big cat's wet lungs sounded as though he were drowning in his own fluids; unable to continue any longer, he stopped abruptly. Skoro doubled back and, for a brief instant, wondered if they would have to fight the big males two against four. The thought made his insides crawl under his chest and he almost bolted but caught himself at the last instant. In front of him, Dreadlocks' eyes rolled inward and he shuddered and hawked a couple of times before finally regurgitating the stolen content of his stomach.

"What a waste," he moaned with forlorn eyes aimed at the chunky puddle of red goo. For half a heartbeat, he seemed to seriously consider lapping it all back up.

Skoro groaned and pushed him onward.

At dusk, they reunited with the others by the side of a shallow stream. Empty of all strength, his paws raw and numb, Skoro collapsed next to Leonides. His twin turned around and affectuously nibbled his ear.

Dreadlocks giggled briefly and went to wash his muzzle in the cool water. After much snorting and blowing, he shook himself dry in the middle of the group, casually splattering everyone's fur in the process, and declared triumphantly: "Nice bit of fun that was. Got my heart going for sure."

"You guys fought?" asked Shaka, slightly worried that he might have missed something glorious.

"Nah, we ran like the wind, same as you."

"Just not as fast, I guess," said T.

A chorus of snide comments and sharp jokes greeted his remark.

Skoro closed his eyes and pushed the voices away. All in all, he had to admit, they had gotten off easy.

And yes, now that he was safely away, he supposed that he could see the fun in it. Already he could picture himself reenacting the story over and over again by the side of a nice buffalo, his brothers laughing easily at the shared memory. He wondered briefly why it was that all the best memories always seemed to come from the crazy experiences that felt so awful when lived in the present, then he thought about nothing at all.

As his muscles relaxed, his limp body shuddered deliciously under the snuggles of his twin. The happy blood coursed inside him through and through. His head grew as light as a feather.

The falling night found him dreaming of a giraffe chasing him through an impenetrable mane made of thornbushes and baobabs.

ELEVEN

LOW AND QUIET

Dreadlocks groped his way forward with soft, hesitant paws that seemed to hug the ground after every caressing step. He crouched low and smelled a cluster of moist leaves. A root left an acidic taste on his tongue; he let it bathe his mouth and shuddered with mild pleasure as he swallowed the sharp flavor down. His whiskers vibrated and extended wide at the end of his muzzle. Alert to the slightest touch, he delicately rocked his head from side to side and took a couple more careful strides forward, slinking through the dense canopy of the brush as quietly as possible.

In the pitch-black darkness of the overcast night, his cat's eyes could see nothing at all. Moving blindly by the paws and whiskers, his advance excruciatingly slow and meticulous, he cheered himself up by picturing himself a snake sidling with grace and fluidity through the vegetation, his cold, smooth body untouched by the gripping embrace of the creepers that littered the ground.

A thin branch cracked. A cluster of thorns grated his right shoulder and clawed at his mane. He froze and gently felt his way forward with his front left paw. A dense brambly bush was standing in his way. He groped for a way through then, finding none, tried to backtrack slowly. His paws caught in a vine. He cursed under his breath. All this sneaking around was growing on his nerves. He was a lion after all, not a mouse.

He clenched his jaws and ruefully shouldered his way through the thornbush with an angry grunt. The dry, thin boughs crackled loudly in his wake. Torn tendrils overturned the earth with a fat ripping sound. Two full leaps and he was free. Almost. One last thorny tongue was still wrapped around his rump. He whirled in place and lashed out at it furiously.

"Some silky cat you are," hissed Skoro somewhere to his left.

Leonides bumped into him. "This is claimed land," he growled under his breath. "*Lion* claimed. You want to kill us all?"

Dreadlocks shoved him back and let loose a brief roar. "Let them come, whoever they are. What are we, rats?"

"You don't know what you're talking about."

He snorted but kept his mouth shut. Best swallow down his bile rather than start something he might regret later. Half of it was his empty stomach growling anyway, he knew. It had been days and days since any of them had enjoyed a proper relaxed meal.

Hunting wasn't the issue he reflected bitterly as he resumed his painfully slow advance, his lowered belly rustling softly against unseen leaves and creeping roots. In fact, they had become quite proficient at bringing down buffaloes and even big old Dagga Boys were no longer safe from them. While Makhulu had refined the art of navigating the front horns and pin the head down into the ground with a mix of skill and power that would have made even old Sifit envious, the rest of them had become experts at assaulting the rear and use their combined weight to stop the boulder cold and topple him down. T. especially, of all cats, had grown into a fierce, relentless hunter. Once his claws were sunk in he was like an angry tick. Nothing could shake him off.

One dawn not so long ago a particular hunt had gone unusually wrong. Leonides had missed his leap, Shaka had caught an early kick that had left him writhing in pain, useless, and, after a seemingly promising tackle, Makhulu's claws had slipped on the caked mud that covered the bull's muzzle. The Dagga, seeing his chance, had buckled madly and broken into a thundering gallop across the flat, green plain. Skoro and Dreadlocks had been quick enough to judge the situation desperate and let go of their grip, but not T. Under the bewildered gaze of a few ostriches nervously bobbing their heads at the insanity of their world, the younger lion had stubbornly clung to the underside of the bull's throat and let himself being dragged around like some weightless cub, the claws of his stubborn back legs digging six parallel grooves in the soft soil. After catching their breath – Shaka had needed a bit longer than usual – they had followed the tracks through no less than two water holes before finally finding the Dagga Boy on his knees and snorting blood, too exhausted to move a single step further, a massive lion-shaped ball of mud still growing out of the base of his neck like some tumorous excrescence. Once they had secured the kill, the tumor had blinked its yellow eyes and mumbled: "Took you guys long enough", before passing out with its jaws still shut tight.

comma inside quotes

No, hunting was not the issue. The issue was that this supposedly big, empty veld wasn't so empty after all. The Sabi Sands, it turned out, were crawling with lions of all sizes and ages. A cat could not spill blood anywhere in peace without soon having to contend with some opportunistic dark-maned rushing-in to steal his meat. As a result, despite their hunting successes, they were still mostly living off hasty gulps swallowed down in-between desperate runs. Half the time Dreadlocks was forced to regurgitate the content of his stomach just to keep up with his brothers. Talk about a losing strategy! To give up on a stolen giraffe was one thing, he could understand the logic, but to be forced to abandon his own kill still mostly untouched… To go through all this trouble and know that you almost certainly won't have time to get a taste of those delicious shanks, or the chewy brisket, or the sweet, sweet flesh of the inner thighs… By the grass, this wasn't right!

And even when other lions were nowhere in sight, hyenas and wild dogs and vultures could always be counted on to come in and spoil the pleasure. Even a hippopotamus, once. The enormous boulder had

Lions do not regurgitate at will the way canines can. They vomit, an involuntary action, when forced by their own bodies – they do not choose to do it.

exploded out of a nearby swamp and snatched Dreadlocks' prize before disappearing back under the murky water as quickly as he had come. Dreadlocks still had a hard time swallowing down that one.

A good culling, that was what the Sabi Sands really needed. Bigger herds and less cats to contend with. More space for everyone to roam and hunt freely. Was that really too much to ask for?

He blindly bumped into yet another thornbush and felt a sharp branch stab at the corner of his right eye, almost straight into his pupil. He jerked his head back violently and had to physically bite his tongue to refrain himself from exploding.

"You alright?" whispered Makhulu next to him, close enough that he could feel his breath on his fur.

Dreadlocks swallowed down a long litany of bitter curses. "Yes," he finally said, his voice tense. "No. I don't know. Where are your taking us, Mak? I'm tired, I can't see anything, and I'm starving."

He felt some stiff whiskers graze his face and assumed that the dark-maned had just nodded his head. "Follow me," he said.

Dreadlocks had to admit, the big lion had quite the soft paw. And he knew how to navigate the night by ears and smells far better than the rest of them. He led them out of the brush and onto a sloping valley of recently burned grass. Small lumps of charcoal twisted and cracked underneath Dreadlocks' paws. Cold ash plastered his ankles. The acrid smell was overwhelming but not entirely disagreeable. The clouds parted ways and the modest glint of the crescent moon unveiled the desolate landscape to their reflective tapetums. With liquid eyes shining blue-green, Makhulu brought them to the burnt remains of a young antelope.

"That's all I could find," he said, almost as an excuse.

Dreadlocks bent down to get a whiff of the blackened carcass before abruptly pulling back. "No," he mumbled. "By the grass, no."

Leonides shrugged and lapped some of the cooked flesh off the stiff upper thigh. "Meat is meat," he declared, his muzzle covered in black ash.

Skoro tried a tentative bite but had to spit it out before he could swallow it down.

"This is ridiculous," Dreadlocks whispered angrily. "We can't live like this anymore. We're too big to be beggars."

"I know," said Makhulu, and lowered his head. "I'm sorry, I looked everywhere."

Dreadlocks sighed. He had never meant for the older lion to take their current dire situation as a personal failure. He swallowed down his anger and snuggled up to the seated cat who was not so much bigger than him any longer. Their manes linked. Dreadlocks gently pushed his head sideway and felt Makhulu return the gesture. "Don't be too hard on yourself. You know me, my stomach's always louder than my mind. I know you're doing your best. We all do."

A few long heartbeats elapsed in silence. He could feel Makhulu's breathing push against his flank, too fast, as if the big lion were gearing himself up for something he did not want to say.

"I'm scared, Dread," he finally whispered back, careful not to let the twins hear him.

"Scared? Of what?"

"Of where I must take us next. I'm scared some of us won't make it through. It's my fault you don't have a pride any longer. I've taken your safety and comfort away. And know I'm afraid that I must offer you death."

Dreadlocks thought that he knew what his brother was alluding to but kept quiet. Some things were best left unsaid, especially on such a night as this one, when true darkness roamed.

"Your fault?" he said instead, his tone purposefully cheerful. "How can any of this be your fault? You saved us, Mak. Without you we would have been chased away by the Shaws or the Split Rocks or some other coalition. Left to eke out a living for ourselves on the margins of the Eyrefield. I don't even want to know what would have happened to us then. At least with you, we were able to leave of our own volition, with steady legs and our heads raised high. That's what you truly gave us, Mak: a fighting chance and the freedom to choose our own hardships. If that's not what Shaka calls lionlike, I don't know what is." He marked a pause to let Makhulu appreciate the truth of his words. He had not meant to fall into such a speech but now that he was out and running he felt that he had to say that last part out loud, for his own sake if not his brother's. "They'll follow you no matter your decision. You know that right? I'll follow you. Through starvation, pain, and blood, all the way to the end of grass if needs be."

Makhulu swallowed loudly. "You don't speak much Dread, but when you do, you do it well."

They laughed. A comfortable silence settled in-between them and together they watched the sliver of the moon play hide and seek with the crumbling clouds like a small tilapia swimming in a stream under the shadows of hungry storks. The dark birds eventually took flight and the bended fish resumed its slow, lazy swim amid a placid river of purple stars.

"All of them, you think?" Makhulu asked with a soft, amused voice. "Even T?"

"Well Shaka will follow you no matter what, that much is certain. T will follow Shaka. Same difference."

"Speaking of those manes," Makhulu said loudly while standing up, "where are they?"

Dreadlocks looked around and suddenly realized that his younger brothers had yet to emerge out of the brush with the rest of them. That did not surprise him much; nor was he really concerned. Those cats were known to spend a lot of time together, sometimes pretty far away from the rest of the coalition.

"We must have lost them in the forest."

"Should we call?" asked Leonides. He had stepped away from the carcass and was now trying to clean the black ash out of his muzzle. He was hesitant to lick it off and instead proceeded to swipe it on his mane. Large black streaks soon marred the deep burnt-sienna hue of his chest.

Dreadlocks turned toward Makhulu. The dark-maned averted his gaze. They both knew that a call in the night risked bringing all sorts of undesirable cats down upon them. And in the confused darkness there was always the accrued danger of one of them being set upon, alone.

As the twins looked to their elder brother for guidance, Dreadlocks rushed to his rescue. "Shaka knows how to take care of himself," he pointed out, "and T is with him. They'll be fine. It's not the first time they go wandering out on their own."

Makhulu nodded his head, relieved. "We'll call for them at sunrise."

The twins accepted his decision without much concern.

After one last disdainful look at what remained of the burnt antelope, they left the black open slopes and moved through a small wood recently made sparse by the same forest fire. The flames had reduced the low creepers to a pile of soft, white ash that clouded their steps but most of the thin trees were still standing, their cracked and blackened trunks untouched above the level of Dreadlocks' shoulders. In some places the fire's tongue had licked only one side of the trunks and left the other half completely unscathed. Here a there, a particular tree had been unjustly singled out and reduced to a standing pile of dead charcoal.

At dawn, they found a water hole already claimed by a small herd of elephants. They approached the opposite side gingerly and openly, so as to communicate their peaceful intentions plainly, and quenched their thirst under the wary gaze of the pachyderms. Dreadlocks noticed a young calf chasing after a flock of ducks on the outskirt of the group. With his short, awkward legs galloping at full speed under his round body and his trunk swinging happily from side to side, his large ears flaring, his mind completely oblivious to the dangers of the world, the calf reminded him of a lion cub. He smiled internally at the comparison and licked his dripping muzzle.

The calf's mother caught his gaze and misinterpreted his intentions.

Trumpeting her outrage, she exploded out of the water and charged them, her thunderous pace shaking the ground under their paws and sending tremors all the way up to their diaphragms. They groaned and made a quick run for it while laughing blithely and arrogantly as they crested the safety of a low hill.

Dreadlocks shot a glance backward. The elephant cow had already given up her chase and rushed to the rescue of her calf who was now toppled halfway down inside the water hole, a steady stream of tiny bubbles escaping his inexperienced trunk.

They traipsed down the hill and took a couple of random turns in the grass. True to his word, Makhulu began to call for Shaka and T.

Still trotting at a light camper with his lower black lips peeled back, he streamlined himself and forced his abdomen to pump a quick succession of short, steaming bellows out. Froth gathered at the corner of his mouth and a shower of warm spittle splattered the dry dirt in front of him. Suddenly, he stopped and lay down. With his eyes now closed, he began to elongate his exhales.

Dreadlocks sat down on his haunches to better enjoy the spectacle. Skoro and Leonides joined him.

Makhulu's tail spasmodically swiped the grass behind him. His powerful muscles bulged underneath the tawny coat of his flanks. His ears flattened themselves against the top of his mane. He sucked in a big gulp of air and held it tight inside his taut belly. His abdomen contracted for a brief instant, suspended in the effort, and his gathered roar rolled around inside his throat like wet gravel tumbling down raging rapids. Then he let it explode out, all at once, in one long, deafening, vibrating bellow that washed over their eardrums, throbbed inside their chests, and warmed the inside of their bellies. Before the first roar had died down, he was already gathering the next one in. He lined a good half dozen bellows out, one after the next, before returning to a short-burst tempo for a little while. Then he went back to the long, vibrant exhales again.

They watched in awe.

There was something primal in that display. Something pure. Makhulu seemed to thoroughly enjoy the effort, find strength in it. Beyond the already impressive show of might and stamina – it seemed that the very grass around them was shaking now – what cheered Dreadlocks' heart the most was the sheer naïve joy he could see etched on his brothers' muzzle. Ever grave and soft-spoken, so even-tempered as to appear untouched by any kind of lion emotion, Makhulu was finally allowing himself to let some of his raw character loose.

He's pushing through it. This isn't really about Shaka or T. Those roars are aimed at his own heart. He's trying to prove something to himself.

In a way, he looked a young cub again, proud and filled to the palate with self-confidence, ready to take on the whole of the Sabi Sands by himself.

He finally stopped to catch his breath. "That was a good pump," he said meekly while licking his muzzle, as if ashamed.

Dreadlocks noticed that he was not panting really hard.

A short burst echoed across the savannah. Perhaps due to the added distance, the answering roars sounded like mere chuffs to Dreadlocks' ringing ears, but he could distinctly make out the deep baritone pushes that were priming each bellow, clean and precise in their execution, almost calculated, somehow.

"That's Shaka alright," he said.

The two younger lions sauntered out of the underbrush.

"No need to overdo it like that with the calls," snickered T. "We didn't go that far."

"Someone needed to hear those roars," Dreadlocks replied with a side glance aimed at Makhulu.

"Did you guys find any meat?" Leonides asked.

"Yessss. But we ate it all without you."

"You're joking, right?"

T. chuckled and Shaka admonished him gently. "No joy. You?"

"Only a small herd of elephant by the water hole," said Dreadlocks. "One of them is a terrible mother, far too overprotective."

T. stretched his spine and licked his muzzle in that slow, ostentatious way that always made Dreadlocks want to hurl himself at his throat. A worrisome, feverish gleam flashed in the smaller lion's eyes. "Elephants, eh? Shall we give that a try? The six of us together, I'm sure that we could bring one down."

"Yeah, let's totally do that," Skoro retorted cheerfully while cleaning his paws. "You go first, I'll be right behind you."

"A full horizon behind, to be precise," Leonides hissed happily like some kind of puffed up snake, an adder maybe.

"Think of the meat!" T. exclaimed. "We'd eat like fat hyenas for the rest of the moon!"

"By the grass, he's actually serious," snorted Leonides.

T. turned to Shaka for support; Dreadlocks could see that he was working himself up to his own idea. "What do you think? Isn't that something you would call brave? Lionlike?"

Shaka shuffled his paws in the dirt as he pondered an acceptable way to phrase his answer. "You're aiming a bit too high," he finally said. "This one is beyond us."

"It's completely crazy is what it is," Leonides groaned.

"I am *not* baring my fangs anywhere near an elephant in broad daylight," Skoro declared categorically while looking at Makhulu, as if suddenly worried that the proposal might be taken seriously by the elder cat.

Makhulu looked at T. for a short while, grinding his fangs, then nodded his head curtly. “We’ll leave the elephants alone. Too dangerous. Besides we shouldn’t tarry in the area, other lions might come.”

“I’ve seen recent marks of short grass being pulled out,” Shaka offered as a way out. “Could be nothing, could be gnus.”

“Now that’s more our speed.”

They all agreed and before their younger brother had time to voice a dissent, fell in line behind Shaka who led the way.

“Y’all a bunch of cowardly cats wit’ shaky legs and empty guts,” T. called out behind them. “The Mapogos will never amount to anything if we don’t learn to stand our ground!”

They ignored him and pushed on, confident that he would soon catch up to them. When he failed to do so, Makhulu doubled back and went to give him a friendly head rub.

“One day soon, brother,” he said. “One day soon.”

TWELVE

MAPOGOS

He teetered his way back to the gathered group with weary, half-closed eyes. His paws were made of numb mud; his shoulders, two rocks grinding painfully against his stiff neck. His forelegs crossed in front of his chest and he stumbled sideways for a brief instant before righting himself. He reached their scents and collapsed heavily on the ground, panting wet through half-closed jaws. The light rays of dawn shone through a nearby tree and caressed his fur. He licked his muzzle and savored the tickling of the warmth over his fresh wounds.

"Makhulu, you alright?"

"By the grass, he's bleeding."

"Where have you been?"

"Who did that to you?"

The blurry shapes danced in front of him as if seen through a heat-haze. His brothers' voices sounded dim and distant, like the chirps of annoying birds trying to poke through something that did not belong to them. Something sacred. He shut them out.

They can't understand.

He was still in the middle of it. Closer, in fact. He could feel the shadow on his spine.

Four heavy paws pounded the hard-packed dirt. Hot breaths washed over his muzzle; he shuddered as he tasted the foreign stench on his palate all over again. The glare of two rage-crazed eyes bore through his mind. His hind legs groaned and strained under the effort as he scrambled to meet the challenge steadfast. His chest absorbed invisible blows with muscles made of wood. Cutting fangs glanced over his muzzle and he ran a loving tongue over the fresh, itching cuts. And to think that, at the time, it had all felt so surreally remote, impersonal. Even as his body had carried him through the motions, he had been surprised by the cold rationality of his own mind. *I need to get my adrenalin up, get some fear into me,* he had reflected at some point early in the fight, almost amused. *Otherwise I'm never getting out of this one.*

His mind slowly went through the sequence of movements again, savoring every leap and dodge, every explosive lunge and bite. He saw, in slow motion, where his adversary had erred and how he had been able to overcome him, amazingly. He winced as he felt the roots of his fangs burn all over again when his memory brought forth the soft crunch of punctured bone and the sudden wild whimpers that had accompanied it – more surprised than hurt, it had seemed. A strange kinship blossomed in his heart with this foreign cat he had fought, his early hatred mixed with a poignant surge of respect. Together they had shared something unique.

"Makhulu!" snapped Shaka, his commanding voice cutting through the fog. "What happened to your lower right canine?"

"Huh?"

He ran his tongue across the fang and felt a jagged stub where it used to stand. Stupidly, he looked down and scanned the dirt in front of him. "I must have left it inside the other male," he mumbled.

"*What?*"

He looked up and sighed, still dazed. Four of his brothers were gathered in a close semi-circle in front of him, expecting answers he could not give. No matter how hard he tried, he could not bring himself to put words on the events. To voice them out loud would be wrong, he felt. Sacrilegious. How could such deep, inner feelings ever hope to survive the light of day? Or the excruciating tearing of his brothers' cross-examination? Once laid bare, they would rot and fade away, become mundane. Worse, if shared, they would not really be his any longer.

But the stares were insistent.

Begrudgingly, he went through his explanation as quickly and cursorily as possible. "I went after the Nhlanguleni male last night. Since the Ottawa pride had just run away from us, I knew that he would be close-by. I was hoping I could lure him into a fight. I was right."

Dreadlocks growled softly, impressed. "You took on a full-grown dark-maned on your own? Are you crazy?"

Makhulu spat blood and raised himself up. His tongue was still getting accustomed to his loss, but his mind was clear. With his adrenalin receding away, the last of the tingling dizziness leaked out of him. He bid it goodbye quietly as one might an old friend.

"This is something I had to do alone."

"Did you kill him?" whispered T. Slightly withdrawn from the group, he had been the only one not pestering him with questions.

Makhulu cocked his head and hesitated as he thought back on the events that had concluded the fight. "No," he finally decided. "The Nhlanguleni limped away. He probably went back to the Ottawa. I don't think he'll die."

"Then we best go after him and finish him off. What do you say?"

They fanned out and followed the scent as best they could, their weaving paths criss-crossing above the short grass, ready to converge at the first sign of trouble. Ahead of the group, Makhulu trotted at a brisk pace, no longer concerned by the noise of his own steps. He could not wait to find the other lion again. Settle things once and for all. He hoped the Nhlanguleni had had time to recuperate. His muscles were aching for a good fight.

They found his corpse on the third dawn by the side of a shallow stream.

"Looks like you did kill him after all," sniggered Skoro. "The big cat was just too dumb to realize."

Makhulu brushed past him without a word. The Nhlanguleni was laying still on his left flank with his black lips dry and his belly deflated. The right side of his face had puffed out grotesquely and turned purple, shutting out his eye. His jaws were frozen open in one last snarl of agony, as if still trying to bite.

Or use his palate to better smell his own stench.

Shaka went to give the carcass a light poke. The desiccated body moved rigidly in one block. "That wound must have hurt like burning grass," he mused. "He went to the stream to alleviate the pain. Then, he died."

T. sniffed the putrid flesh of the bloated cheekbone. With his tongue, he jiggled something white embedded deep inside the swollen wreck, all the way through the bone. "Mak, I think I've found your canine," he laughed. "Want it back?"

Makhulu ignored him. He was having a hard time contemplating what was left of this lion who had charged him so bravely a few nights ago, his dark mane billowing in the wind of his own speed, every breath a promise of death to come, full of pride and vigor, a master of his life.

"He looks smaller now," he let out blankly, stupidly. There was really nothing else to say.

T. looked at him with cold, appreciative eyes and nodded his head gravely as if to say that the two of them were suddenly sharing some deep inner truth no one else could see. Makhulu returned the gaze and shrugged.

It's called death. It deflates even proud lions. Big fucking deal.

With a growl, he tore himself away from the sight of his own work.

"What do we do now?" Dreadlocks asked the group, his deep, vibrant voice suddenly fat with expectations.

Makhulu turned around and took the time to ascertain the hardness of his brothers' will.

Shaka, seated on his haunches, returned his gaze with calm resolve; next to him Dreadlocks was pacing back and forth, his restless eyes burning bright with hunger, his powerful shoulder bulging; Skoro and Leonides stepped around the carcass and gathered close to one another with Leonides' head pressed tight against Skoro's mane, as they looked back at him, they licked their muzzle in unison and tightened their jaws; T. laid a casual paw on the Nhlanguleni and unleashed a ferocious, almost amused half-snarl, in his eyes, a cold flame danced.

By the grass, he was proud of those cats. Not a single shaky leg to be found in the whole lot of them. That was almost enough to undermine his own self-confidence. How could he be worthy of them? How could he lead?

He pushed the doubts away. "Now," he said, his throat laden with gravel, "we break the Ottawa girls."

They crossed the stream and ventured into the unknown savannah at a brisk, unhindered trot, their shadows stretching tall under the light of the fast-rising sun. They came upon a twin-rutted lane of dirt and followed it for a little while before crossing back into the low grass. Speeding up, Makhulu roared at the top of his lungs and savored the slight burning of his legs' muscles. Five powerful bellows immediately echoed on his heels and travelled through his guts, jolting him to his core. Taken aback, he groaned his pleasure and hastened to push out another vibrant chuff. His brothers backed him up with all their strength.

They fell into this new song without concertation or second thought. It gave them the courage they needed to chase away the fear, as though they had control over the very air and the grass beneath. Makhulu had never felt so free in his entire life.

He stumbled upon a cold leftover of the Nhlanguleni's odor at the base of a tree. The hated smell triggered something deep inside him. All of a sudden, his bladder felt ready to burst. He lifted a leg and ceded to his body's urge. His steaming gush erased the last of the defeated male. His brothers followed his lead and soon the whole area was scuffed and marked with the Mapogo scent. As they pushed forward, they made sure to stop and repeat the process on a regular basis. All these things were new to them but their body knew what to do far better than their intellect. They let their instinct take control.

At dusk, they caught a first glimpse of one of the Ottawa lionesses.

"Over by the ridge!" cried Leonides.

The female bounced and scurried away. They leaped after her with joyous whoops and coarse catcalls, their jaws overflowing with saliva as if they were hunting a pronking antelope.

They lost her trail in a cluster of thornbushes.

The following dawn, two more females scampered at their approach. One of them was holding a cub inside her jaws. Putting their hunting skills to the task, they attempted to trap them with a flurry of roar, fake charges, flanking maneuvers, and much confused backtracking. The smart cats still gave them the slip.

"What are they playin' at?" grumbled Dreadlocks, and collapsed heavily. He was panting hard under the heat of the mid-morning sun, his broad chest seemingly ready to burst. "Their male is dead, why don't they give up already?"

"They're worried about their cubs," Shaka breathed out. "They'll try to move them around and evade us for as long as they can."

"Not so easy hunting hunters, eh?" said Leonides, cheerfully. "Those cats sure know how to move."

"And with their knowledge of the land they can hide their young just about anywhere they like and run circles around us until we're spent."

"They'll tire firs'," T. groaned, his anger and exhaustion seeping through his manner of speech. "They go'to eat a' soam point. Soon' o' later, they'll *have* t' face us."

After three more days of lung–bursting chases and failed ambushes, the younger lion was finally proven right.

They rounded a small grove and faced the standing Ottawa pride on an undulating plain of low, green grass. The three huntresses bared their fangs and crouched low at their approach, their powerful shoulders protruding out of the line of their back, ready to explode.

No cubs in sight Makhulu noted.

Suddenly, a big rumbler rudely wobbled its way through some dry bushes and came to an abrupt halt a half-dozen leaps away from them, the bipeds on its back unusually still and quiet for once.

They paid it no mind.

The air grew heavy.

"They won't submit, will they?" Skoro hissed through clenched jaws.

"Not without a fight."

An anonymous growl escaped the line somewhere to Makhulu's left, some kind of mumbled threat that made no literal sense. A signal.

All tempers broke loose.

He leaped at the closest female and overturned her with the sheer momentum of his bulk. She spat and lashed at his muzzle before slipping out from under his grasp in a whirlwind of scuffed up dirt and overturned grass. He charged her head-on and she backtracked with the speed of a mamba, her forepaws furiously lunging at his muzzle like lightning strikes plowing through yellow grass. He brushed the pain aside, pushed through her inner circle, sent one heavy paw slamming against her ribs. She screamed and bit at his right eye before leaping up in the air, her fur electric. — lions don't know what 'electric' is.

They covered the distance to the rumbler in a handful of mad heartbeats. Her scrambled retreat sent her sliding over the square snout of the obnoxious beast, her claws skidding loudly over the hard, unnatural flat skin. Carried forward by his own momentum and rage, Makhulu leaped over the rumbler's head and felt something blunt impact his right shoulder. He crashed on the ground and tasted dirt on his tongue. He coughed and angrily spat it out.

"Get the fuck out of the way!" he bit out from over his numb limb. The dumb oaf did not react but the bipeds squealed loudly. He turned his back on them.

The lioness scurried back to her sisters. To his left, Makhulu saw a second huntress standing up to T's and Shaka's assaults, shoulders hunched and head cocked low almost all the way to the ground. Shaka tried a flanking maneuver but only collected a flurry of kicks for his effort and was forced to retreat hastily with a shocked yelp. Seated on his haunches, he bent over and licked at a red gash blossoming over the white of his belly. T screamed his brother's name and let loose a torrent of obscenities before leaping forward with distended, crazed pupils, the gurgle of an indignant roar dying a strangled death inside his throat. The huntress dug in and tried to withstand his assault. He raised himself on his forelegs and slapped her on the side of the head, hard enough to send her rolling across the grass.

She came to a tumbling stop next to where the third sister was being cornered by Skoro, Leonides, and Dreadlocks' triangle. Whirling in place with the ferocity of a stuck honey badger fighting for her life, she was keeping the encircling males at bay by lunging at their muzzles faster than their eyes could follow.

Makhulu's own lioness rushed to her sister's rescue and leaped on Leonides' back as if he were a buffalo she had to bring down. The bigger male screamed in pain and surprise and swiveled in place to meet his attacker. The third huntress, no longer cornered, rushed Dreadlocks and bit down on his front paw before pulling back with all her strength, hard enough to topple him down and risk breaking his limb.

Makhulu charged with a deafening roar and body-slammed her at full speed. Their intertwined bodies tumbled head over paws down a light slope. She shrieked and squirmed and unleashed a storm of claws, her muzzle searching for the underside of his throat. He used both his front paws to bash her head against the solid dirt, hard enough to daze her but not to kill, he hoped. She began to relent.

Before he had time to pin her down for good, the second female, still teetering slightly from T.'s slap, rammed herself against his thick mane.

"Get back!" she roared at the tops of her lungs, her fangs biting at his ear, her front claws raking his chest as if she were digging herself a burrow. "Get back, you fuckinpieceoshitmurdermane! Get back! Get back!"

He buckled and jumped to the side. His claws found a grip on her fur and he used the full force of his massive bulk to topple her down and crush her under his belly. Her squeezed-out lungs emptied themselves brusquely and he felt the short burst of her wind ruffle his mane.

The feisty cat did not relent.

"Fuck you let's go!" she screamed while biting large chunks of hair off his mane, her eyes blazing, a steady river of blood now streaming out of the corner of her mouth. "That all you got, cub-killer?! I ain't scared of you! Ottawa! OTTAWA PRIDE! LET'S FUCKING GO RIGHT NOW!!!"

Makhulu groaned in pain and almost lunged for her windpipe. He held himself back at the last instant. As he struggled to figure out a way to shut her up without killing her, the second sister jumped on his spine. Her fangs grated against his vertebra and one back paw mercilessly ground his tail into the dirt. Caught in-between two pair of jaws he could not shake off, he roared his despair at the top of his lungs, ready to kill.

Shaka and Leonides rushed to his rescue and slapped the assaulting lioness off his back. In the ensuing confusion, the pinned huntress tore herself free of his embrace and wriggled back on her feet.

After having taken a couple of steps back, she spat a large ball of slimy hair out and flashed her bloodied fangs at him. "Had enough, big cat?"

A shadow fell on her. T. used the slope of the low hill to dive from above like some horrifying bird of prey with four wings. He missed wildly and Makhulu had to jerk his head back to dodge the bared claws. The younger lion flopped on the ground, hard, and rolled around in the overturned grass, his limp body seemingly devoid of bones. He picked himself up without a word.

"You alright?" asked Makhulu.

"Yeah, jus' scratches."

After a quick head rub, they both assaulted the huntress together.

Exhausted and breathing wet, her cramped shoulders seemingly locked in place, she met their attacks head-on with clenched jaws, cold eyes, and stiff limbs. From the other side of the low hill, Makhulu could hear Dreadlocks and Skoro still trying to deal with their own unbowed lioness. Behind him, the last huntress was screaming like a stuck warthog despite Leonides' slightly dismayed injunctions to: "Let it go! By the grass, just let it go, please!"

The madness boiled over and reached a paroxysm of confusion, pain, and roars. Then, just when Makhulu was beginning to think that they would never see the end of it, the whole thing abruptly died down in a manner typical of cats' fights.

Gasping for air, drained to the bone of the very last drop of energy, their bitter temper spent at last, the three lionesses abdicated their precarious position and slowly limped their way back to a nearby tree. They had poured their hearts and rage and desperation into that last stand, but no matter how hard they fought, they could not hope to break the combined bulk of the six much bigger males. They closed their eyes in shame and collapsed under the shade of the canopy.

With his right eye now swollen and every single muscle of his body sore, Makhulu slowly staggered up to them and lowered his head toward the center lioness, the elder one who had called him a cub-killer. After one last hesitant jerk, she returned his head rub with a soft, wary growl and a stiff neck that seemed to melt under his contact.

He sighed and allowed himself to relax. Feeling giddy, he brushed over the other two lionesses in a similar fashion, savoring the healthy wetness at the tip of their battered muzzles and the slight bending of his whiskers against their disarmed fangs.

He turned around toward his brother, took two steps, whirled back.

"How many cubs?" he asked bluntly.

The two younger lionesses shuddered and glared at him in shock but the elder female only closed her eyes wearily. She let her neck go limp and appeared to retreat inside herself. He kept his shadow on her and calmly waited with the patience of a vulture who knows that his due is soon to drop. He could almost taste the carrion in his mouth.

"Eleven," she finally confessed, her jaws quivering against her chest as if ready to bite her own heart out. "Eleven cubs."

He nodded curtly and went to re-join his brothers. He found them snuggled up in one big pile at the top of a low hill that overlooked the undulating plains they had just conquered. Out on the horizon, the last of the rumbler's gleaming rear could be seen disappearing behind a dust cloud of its own making.

"By the grass, those wild pussies fought harder than any male," sniggered Dreadlocks. As he wrinkled his muzzle, the folded skin tore at the sides of a deep gash above his nostrils.

"Is that it then?" asked Shaka. "We won?"

"Yes, but one matter remains."

"The cubs," Skoro said somberly.

"Yes, the cubs. The Ottawa girls won't fight us any longer, but they won't give up on their young ones either. As long as they live, they will try to sneak out and hide them and feed them behind our back."

Leonides shrugged. "So what? The little balls of fur are hardly a threat to us right now. We'll have plenty of time to chase them away once they are grown."

"That's not the only concern, brother."

Makhulu nodded slowly, his head cast down. The taste of carrion had turned to ash inside his mouth. "As long as they are caring for their young ones, the females won't be in estrus."

"And it could be entire seasons before the last of them is finally weaned," added Shaka.

"Yes, that's true too."

"Are we really discussing this?" Dreadlocks said, all traces of hilarity suddenly gone from his muzzle.

"What are you guys talking about?" said Leonides, clueless. "What does that even mean: 'Won't be in estrus'?"

Skoro rolled his eyes. "It means that as long as the little ones live, we're not getting any."

A guilty silence settled over the group as they all contemplated that horrendous possibility.

T. shook his head and let out a rough laugh before strolling to the forefront of his brothers' line. "The cubs die," he said, his tone suffering no objections.

The 'issue' is that they could easily be ousted by new males before they can sire their own, if they wait for the cubs to be weaned. The average tenure of males with a pride is only two years.

THIRTEEN

THREE LITTLE CUBS

Eleven little cubs, hiding in the grass,
"But where could they be?" the big lion asks.
Down low he searches, up high he inspects,
And atop a tree, a tawny fruit starts to shake.
"Hang on tight little kitten,
Onto that thick, dry vine!
Beware you be smitten,
By those yellow eyes of mine."
The cub sways and turns to a blur.
"Do your worse," he screams, "my conscience is pure!"
But green plants are treacherous by nature,
And when the tall grass calls in her due with tempting allure,
The weaker vine dares not endure.
Crack! That ripe fruit will not mature.

Ten little cubs, hiding in the grass,
"But where could they be?" the big lion asks.

Actually, there were only three left. T. stretched his cramped neck and slowly blinked his tired eyes twice. The clumsy little song had been beleaguering him ever since dawn, chaffing his intellect one relentless repetition after the next, its awkward, off-beat verses clinging to his thoughts like sap trickling down a tree. He was suffering from lack of sleep, he knew. Three consecutive dawns he had witnessed without taking a single break and still the feverish song remained deaf to the protests of his exhausted body. It was as if two deep ruts had been dug inside his brain for his mind to follow relentlessly.

The strain on his legs, paws, and shoulders was bittersweet.

He capered around a tall anthill and let his muzzle sweep the ground next to the crumbling edifice like a warthog in search of roots. His gaze stumbled upon a two-way procession of busy ants and he stopped to watch, captivated. The disciplined little insects were carrying all sorts of seeds, sticks, and dead preys back to their massive colony. Some of them reminded him of Dreadlocks in their greediness and he chuckled as he watched their tiny, indomitable legs frantically pull at burdens far heavier than they were, their serrated mandibles clamped down on their prize like a lion's jaw, refusing to let go. In the opposite line, free ants were hastening toward the great beyond with boiling fervor. He tried to follow their line of march but lost them under a shrub a couple of steps away.

Such different lives, his slightly delirious mind reflected.

Every instant of every day spent standing in line, waiting for permission. Every step regimented by the collective good. He tried to count the ants but his attention span was not sharp enough and he kept stumbling at around one hundred or so. He wondered if the ants were more numerous than the buffaloes. Probably. More numerous than the stars in the sky? Than grass itself?

He shook his head. Who could know such things? To live with five brothers was hard enough, but this? He could not imagine it.

He gave the procession a quick lick and rejoice at the ensuing chaos he had created.

Something to get your adrenalin flowing, little ones. You'll thank me later.

He sauntered off and cut through the easy meadows with long, carefree strides.

Nothing like the pleasure of being a free cat on the prowl. There would be blood today, he could smell it. Only three cubs left scattered across the whole of the Ottawa's territory. Today, he would find one.

Three little cubs, hiding in the grass.
"But where could they be?" the big lion asks...

His brothers were out for blood as well, he knew. In fact, just last night, Leonides had caught one. Pure luck of course. The stupid ball of fur had squealed in fear at his approach even though he wasn't really looking and would almost certainly have missed him had the cub remained quiet. Another two had fallen to Makhulu the previous afternoon but the remaining five had been his. For once, he was ahead of the competition.

He had a knack for it, he had discovered. His brothers were going at it as if they were chasing full grown lions, thundering through the grass at full speed while roaring at the top of their lungs in hope of triggering a fleeing reaction, a mindless bolt out of the foliage. T. knew better. He could still remember, all too well, the pressure of the paw on his spine, and the disquieting coldness inside the stomach that made you want to dive and hide under the grass so deep you actually become the dirt. He knew intimately the incredible strength of will that often came with such stupefaction, the survival instinct that takes over control of the body and turns it into wood, forcing the panic at bay. He only had to close his eyes and he was that cub again.

No, those last few kittens would not run mindlessly away from him. He would have to dig them out, one by one.

He reached a dense patch of lush, shoulder-high lank and stopped to slowly scan the border with his muzzle. Sure enough, he quickly stumbled upon the fading remnants of a moist puddle. He grimaced and used the roof of his palate to distill the cold scent.

A cub had stopped there shortly after dawn. The sunbaked dirt was too hard-packed for the lightweight to have left any paw prints, but it didn't take a master hunter to understand what must have been going on inside that little head of his once confronted with the towering stems of grass.

He tasted what was left of the moistness where the cub had emptied his bladder. The piss still had that sharp, acidic smell to it. Fear piss.

That brave little sucker went in, didn't he?

He licked his muzzle and examined the dense lake of green grass slowly waving in the wind in front of him like the soft fur of a civet. There was a precious golden treasure hidden in the depth of those rippling stalks, he was sure of it. But where?

To his right was a large fallen trunk. Too obvious. Further away, almost to the horizon, the dark shape of a thornbush could be seen cutting a jagged silhouette out of the lower blue sky. Too far. Without any visual reference, the cub would never have been able to navigate his way through the encroaching tall grass. Could he have jumped on the trunk and then blindly struck an approximate course? Probably not. Too risky. With the sun already high in the sky, he would have been in a great hurry, the poison coursing through his veins screaming at him to find some cover and lie low. To the left, nothing. No bushes, no trees, only a large stretch of impenetrable lank as seemingly innocent and devoid of depth as the cold water of a dark pound. No large lion could hope to hide in there without leaving a streak of destruction in his path, but what about a careful cub whose paws have been turned into feathers by terror?

With a tiny growl of satisfaction, T. ventured in. He kept his head low and strived to see the encroaching vegetation through the eyes of his quarry. As expected, the patch of grass was not as candid as one might think; upon closer inspection, its secrets were revealed. The small cat had done a good job of weaving himself a smooth path without leaving much of a trail behind, like a fish swimming through a pond, but bended stalks could still be found here and there and a rough course could be approximated.

T. followed it with all the speed of a lazy mollusk while savoring the taste of every stone he licked along the way, every dent in the dirt he sniffed. He loved the crawling pace of this kind of stealthy prowl. The ineluctability of it. However slow his progress might be, he knew that his victory was as inexorable as the setting of the sun. In a way, the wait was actually more exciting than the reward.

This was not the mindless hard charge aimed at a buffalo, the fast springing of the trap and the mad contest of brawl where shoulders were strained and fangs ripped off. No, this was a battle of wits. One had to be smart and methodical to succeed. Relentless. Above all, one had to be able to understand the inner workings of fear. Feel the poison coursing through one's veins and see the veld through the eyes of the cub himself: a vast expanse of hostile grass where every shadow is a promise of death to come.

He came upon a small broken stick with a single tawny hair caught underneath the half-peeled bark. He stopped and scanned the scene. He could make out the shallow prints where the cub had frozen in place, his tiny claws protracting in fear. He chuckled. The treacherous stick had probably sounded like a lightning strike in the oppressing silence. He smelled the hair. The scent was fresh. It had taken the little one the better part of the morning to reach this spot. He could not be far now.

He raised his head and realized that he was almost at the edge of the lank. The cub could not have known that. He would have stumbled out of the protection of the tall grass and scurried back inside immediately, not daring to try and cross the naked plain in broad daylight. Afterward, he would have steered further right in hope of sinking deeper into the green lake.

He lowered his head back down and adjusted his course accordingly. He had no doubt that the cub was aware of his presence by now. Somewhere near, two large ears were probably rotating slowly, following his every move, and two little shoulders were quivering quietly. A young brain, sick with fear, was scrambling for an idea, a trick, anything to get away from this moment, to stop the setting of the sun.

He found another spot where the scent was still warm but then erred in his judgment for the next mark. The smart little bugger had gone through the effort of throwing-in some random sharp turns to confuse him. He backtracked slowly and drew a shrinking circle around the area where he knew in his guts the cub had to be.

Suddenly, without warning, the tall grass parted ways one last time and quietly surrendered its hidden treasure. T. stopped abruptly.

He could scarcely believe that he had actually pulled it off. Such a small cub hidden across such a large territory. One could think the odds impossible. But no.Not to a properly motivated lion.

Most of his brothers tended to scoff at this, especially Dreadlocks and Shaka. They did not have the patience for it, the inner cold drive. They could only find worth in the most obvious of things, the feats of strength and speed accomplished under the sun. In a way, he pitied them. They would never experience the sheer pleasure of seeing those long nights and days of hard tracking being rewarded at last when the grass itself gives up its prize quietly, like a reluctant offering. This was almost better than the actual killing.

Almost.

"Please," the cub whined, petrified. "Pleeeease."

T. licked his muzzle and fell on him without a word.

Afterward, he scampered back to the Ottawa pride with one half of the cub's body dangling merrily inside his jaws, its wild swinging punctuating every one of his springing steps. The small head was lodged in-between his lips and gums like a small fruit ready to pop. He could feel the jagged edge of the last remaining ear tickle his whiskers. The small carcass was almost completely drained of blood and the end of the severed backbone could be seen protruding out of the mangled meat like a tiny white worm.

His stomach growled. Saliva overflew his mouth. He dropped the carcass and snagged a few bites off the chest with his raspy tongue. Then he picked it back up again. - Lions only eat their own kind if starving.

He knew exactly where he wanted to go. Who he wanted to see.

He reached the Ottawa lioness by mid-afternoon. Ever since that day when she had stood up to both him and Mak with a frenzy of lashes and a cursing mouth that would have put a crocodile to shame, they had taken to calling her Defiant. He lowered his prize in front of her and feigned ignorance while gnawing at the stub of the vertebra. He could still remember how easily she had dodged his leap and how cruelly she had sniggered when he had gone sprawling in the dirt like some helpless cheetah after a wrong turn.

He offered her a bite out of the carcass. She drew herself up and kept perfectly still.

"Oh, I'm sorry. Was this one yours?"

Her cold glare glanced over his fur, almost as delicious as the meat of her cub.

"Smart thing you did, staying away. Without you to lead me to him, it was a long track. The little guy was very careful. You would have been proud. Proper stealthy cat. Not much of a fighter, though. In the end, he squealed."

Still, no reaction. That stoic cat had some hard bark wrapped around her temper, he had to give her that. In her empty, deadpan eyes he could feel all the scorn she was refusing to express out loud. But there was something else pulsing at the edge of those pupils. Shock. That gladdened him.

"Don't worry. I'll put another one inside you soon enough."

She moved forward and for half a heartbeat he was convinced that he had finally pushed her over the edge. His shoulders tensed and his eyes lit up as he prepared himself for the dance. To his dismay, upon reaching him, she simply lowered her muzzle toward the remains of her cub and took a single sniff, as if to make sure.

Or perhaps say goodbye, he thought, puzzled.

Her gaze glanced over his face and looked past him – through him! – as if he didn't exist. Finally, she walked away.

He sat back down and watched her tawny silhouette recede at a lazy pace.

He brushed it off. She could pretend all she wanted, he knew that he had hurt her beyond words. Broke her, even. Maybe.

He turned his attention back to the pitiful brown thing that had once been a cub and lapped some more flesh off the small, bird-like bones. The cold, saliva-soaked fur tasted like something out of a swamp. A thin strip of white tendon clung to his fangs.

Shaka ambled toward him.

"That makes nine," said T. "Two to go."

"Nope. Skoro and Makhulu both got one today as well."

T groaned. "It's all over then?"

"For this pride, yes. What's the final tally?"

"Skoro and Leonides: one, Makhulu: three, me: six."

Shaka chuckled and nibbled his ear. "Well done brother. Well done indeed." He watched T masticate. "Hey, you share a bite?"

"Help yourself."

They feasted in silence and soon only the skull remained along with a few scattered bones and hair. Shaka licked his muzzle and wiped the blood and grease off his fur. "I really don't know what it is about this flesh," he observed, "but I love the taste."

T. soft-growled his approval. "Nothing like the sweet taste of life cut short melting on your tongue."

"Well, well, well, I didn't know that my own brother was such a poet. You've traveled a long way since we were cubs, T. I'm proud of you."

Only two steps really.

He still beamed internally at the compliment.

"I still don't understand why it doesn't feel the same when I kill a calf, though," Shaka pondered. "Or a piglet."

"With a lion, you can relate to what it is that you're taking. A grazer is a mindless beast, little more than a walking tree. His life is dull and not worth much. For that reason, it is cheaply taken. But those cubs are different. It wasn't too long ago when you were one of them. You know their hopes and dreams. And because you know exactly the worth of the life that was awaiting them, it feels all the better on the tongue when you snatch it all away from them and swallow it down."

Shaka tilted his head and worked his way through the explanation. "That was surprisingly insightful," he allowed, "but in this case why don't more lions do it? I don't think that I have ever heard of any of the Sunset Boys eating another cat. Killing, yes, of course, but eating? Not even Broken Nose would do it." His misgivings shone briefly inside his eyes. All of a sudden, he seemed to regret ever having partook of the cub. "Once the word on the wind gets out, the other cats will call us monsters," he whispered.

T. made a gesture to dismiss his brother's concerns. "To be monstrous is to be free, Shaka. Once you've crossed that river and know that the other cats will never forgive you for it, that's when you can truly live your life without compromise. The only thing you have to worry about then is fear, but there are ways to deal with that particular beast."

Hang on to the hindquarter side and never let go.

"Most lions are cowards," he concluded, "even the strong ones. They are afraid of other cats' reactions so they put limits on themselves so as to be better accepted by their peers and hope that they will be protected in return. It's a fool's bargain."

Shaka lapped the argument up eagerly. "I guess there is a sort of crude, lionlike nobility to it. As a way to send a message across the grass if nothing else. 'Behold who we are and what we dare! We do not fear you!'"

T. laughed softly. "I don't know about lionlike, Shaka. You're the one who always worry about that sort of thing. Me, I eat the cubs because they taste good. I take what I want when I can and I don't ask for permission or forgiveness. If you ask me, that's the only way to be any kind of lion in this world."

Shaka accepted his explanation without another word. T. could see that he was not entirely convinced but he did not push the point further. They lay down and slept for a little while.

At dusk, Shaka noticed Makhulu and Skoro walking side by side on a far crest. He called out to them with a few short bellows and soon the four brothers were reunited.

Makhulu's right cheekbone was still slightly swollen, courtesy of Defiant's paw. The vertical claw-mark underneath his right orbit seemed to eat at his eye from below, forcing it into a permanent, stoic squint that marked his face for all cats to recognize. T. had taken to calling it his lazy eye. The effect was quite impressive, as if the big lion had been cut by the grass itself.

"Nice work," the dark-maned approved while prodding the tiny, mud-caked head with his enormous paw. The skull toppled to the side and revealed a set of clenched white teeth that seemed to grin at the four males from beyond death. "Your doing, T.?"

"It didn't take much to kill him. Just a few shakes, that's all." He kept his voice cool and matter-of-factly, betraying nothing of the warmth growing inside him.

"Still, those smart kittens were not so easy to find. You got six of them in record time. That's impressive."

Makhulu went to give him a forceful head rub. Feeling his insides melt, T. quickly looked away to hide his beaming pride. He knew that he was doing a poor job of appearing unaffected, but somehow that didn't matter much.

"Everyone behold: T., the mighty cub killer!" sniggered Skoro. "Good thing for you that they don't fight as hard as a mongoose, eh? How does it feel to kill helpless members of your own kind?"

The coldness returned. "What are you talking about? You've got the same blood on your muzzle."

To his surprise, Skoro only chuckled. "That I do, little brother. That I do."

He went to give him a short head rub himself before snuggling up to him with the bulk of his weight comfortably resting on T.'s right flank. Shaka pushed from the other side and T. found himself being smothered in-between two large manes of light-brown hair. He didn't mind.

"It had to be done," Makhulu proclaimed softly, more to himself than the others. "However distasteful it might have been, it had to be done. We would never have secured our hold onto that pride otherwise. At least now, thanks to T., we don't have to drag it out any longer. Better a quick, clean sweep for the lionesses to come to terms with the new reality. Now we can focus on mending our bounds with them."

"Out with the young ones, in with the old cats. Is that it?"

"Exactly."

"We should go on a hunt," said Shaka. "The six of us with the three lionesses. That way we can show them what we have to offer to their pride, the sheer amount of weight we can bring to bear on a single take down. Once they feel secure in the fact that they won't grow hungry, it will be easier for them to move on."

"Yesssss," exclaimed Skoro. "I haven't had a proper bellyful since before I became a pride lion. All this business of death is exhausting."

"Speaking of the six of us," said T., "where are Dreadlocks and Leonides?"

Skoro laughed merrily. "Leonides is still on the prowl, if you can actually believe it. Dumb cat doesn't know it's all over already. I think Dreadlocks went on patrol to figure out the size of the Ottawa's territory."

"He's probably fallen asleep under a tree somewhere," said Shaka. "Either that, or he's busy munching on someone else's kill."

"Probably."

"Is it really over then?" asked T. "We've taken over our pride and that's the end of it?"

"No," Makhulu replied, a poor imitation of T.'s own half-snarl flashing bright under his hard lazy eye. "This is not the end. Not by a long leap."

FOURTEEN

THE CONDEMNATION OF TRIUMPH

“Oh no by all means, please, feel free to finish. Don’t let us interrupt.”

The big male leaped up and unmounted his mate so fast, Shaka had time to see the wet pink of his penis flash briefly in front of his eyes before it shrunk back inside its sheath like a small, terrified turtle. The Styx lioness groaned in pain and arched her back under his clumsy trampling. He found his footing and took a couple of hasty steps to the side as if to distance himself from her and hide his guilt.

“Now that was rude, brother,” cackled Skoro as he ambled out of the scrub on the opposite side of the small glade, “you cut him mid-thrust.”

The big male twisted sharply toward him, then wheeled back, contemplating his escape. Three sets of yellow eyes cut his hopes short. With cool, murderous poise, as quiet and motionless as grey elephants unveiled by the tearing of the mist, Leonides, Makhulu and Dreadlocks slowly materialized out of the foliage.

The Styx lioness squealed in fear and scatted through the low wood. In the wake of her departure, T. made his late entrance on Shaka's left.

The seriousness of his situation finally dawned on the big male. "You guys move quiet," he groaned. "I didn't hear you sneak up on me." He seemed more disgusted by his own failure than really afraid.

"You were a busy cat," Makhulu pointed out.

The golden-maned turned to face the elder Mapogo. "You. I know you. I heard you roar in the distance. You're the one they call Makhulu."

"Indeed. You should have run when you had the chance."

The trapped cat made a dismissive gesture as if to say that the matter was not worth the consideration. His flitting glance bounced off Dreadlocks and the twins before settling on Shaka's forehead. The pupils glided down the length of his body, all the way to the bended end of his tail, and Shaka had to swallow a need to squirm.

"You're the one they call Kinky Tail, aren't you?"

Shaka's tail curled unconsciously as his anger surged. Suddenly keenly aware of the presence of his fangs, an acute desire to puncture bone overfilled his mouth and dribbled down his chin. "Not to my face they don't," he finally said while striving to keep his temper in check. An ominous tongue darted to his muzzle.

The big male clenched his jaws shut and took a half-step back. "You cats are the Mapogos," he declared peremptorily, as if handing out some sort of irrevocable judgment. "The cannibals."

"Our reputation precedes us," whispered T.

Dreadlocks stepped forward. "We know that you're one of two Nkuhuma males. Where is the other one?"

"I don't know. What difference does it make?"

"None," agreed Skoro. "Do you have a name, though?"

"Blondie."

Shaka jerked his head back in surprise.

"How dare you?" hissed Leonides. "How dare you use that name?! *His* name?!"

Skoro low-growled and prepared himself to pounce.

Puzzlement washed over the Nkuhuma's face as he bared his fangs and wheeled in place to meet his assailants' anger. "It's just my name!" he barked defensively. "That's always been my name!"

Makhulu's easy laughter cut through their rising temper and stopped Skoro in his tracks. "Just about any cat with a golden mane calls himself Blondie these days," he said, amused. "We lions are lacking in imagination. But please do tell me: if you're ruling over the Nkuhuma pride, how come we find you here with a Styx female?"

Blondie shrugged. "She was wandering around in estrus with her tail raised high, looking for any male to cover her. What else was I supposed to do?"

"Those lionesses really have no respect for any pride's territory," remarked Leonides.

"I seem to remember a couple of Eyrefield girls pulling a similar stunt," Skoro quipped with his eyes on T.

The smaller lion bowed his head and greeted the sally good-naturedly. "Poor Blondie!" he said while taking a couple of ominous steps forward. "Blinded by pussy, he trips over a Styx and sees himself carried to his death."

"On a river of his own blood," added Shaka, his own throaty voice laden with frost. He matched his brother's advance and eagerly drank in the sheer terror he saw blossoming on the big male's face.

"Go on then!" screamed Blondie. "I won't die so easily."

"Yeah, that's what Vulolo said too," whispered Makhulu.

"And Dzunani," added Skoro.

"To say nothing of the fucking entirety of the Ximunvanyane Pride," snarled T.

Blondie roared. The circle collapsed.

Jostled from side to side by the eagerness of his brothers, Shaka shouldered his way forward and lunged at the lower spine. The targeted backside slid out of his reach and he only managed to grab a hold of the tail inside his jaws. He pulled on the appendage as hard as he could, his curved claws furiously raking the damp dirt underneath his paws, and felt his fangs pierce through the sleek fur. Something cracked sharply underneath his palate.

How's that for a kink!

A sudden outburst of frenetic roars erupted in front of him. Through a cloud of kicked up leaves and dirt, he caught a glimpse of

Dreadlocks going toe to toe against Blondie's jaws and forelegs. Closer to him, both T. and Leonides had found a tenuous grip on the lion's flanks and were now working on opening him up from the sides. Skoro assaulted the right hind leg and tried to break the femur by biting through the thick bone while twisting madly like some weird crocodile straining to do a barrel-roll.

With his head raised high, Makhulu coolly trotted around the whole lot of them. After gingerly bypassing Dreadlocks' fury, he casually stepped over T.'s ferocious gnawing and pounced on Blondie's backside. One lightning-fast bite on the spine and he darted away.

Blondie roared once more. "Dozie!" he shrieked plaintively. "Dozie, I'm getting killed over here! Help me! Help me!"

A galloping commotion suddenly rose out of the scrub behind them. Shaka let go of the tail and turned around just in time to see a second, smaller lion leap into the glade and assault Skoro's back.

"Oh no, you don't!" he bellowed, not realizing that the words had escaped his throat out loud.

T. reacted first. He leaped over Blondie's prostrated body and impacted the newcomer's chest at full speed, thus forcing him to relinquish his grip on Skoro who hastily crawled out of the way, slightly dazed. Dreadlocks and Makhulu peeled themselves off Blondie's front to support their younger brother. Shaka and Leonides hastened to join them.

Everything turned into a blur. Shaka unleashed a fury of scuffs, lashes, and bites on the lion's chest and muzzle without concern for his own safety. Something briefly clawed at his rhinarium but he brushed it off as one might a fly. On either side of him, he could feel Leonides and T. doing the exact same thing. Badly mauled beyond recognition in the span of a single, half-swallowed roar, the newcomer promptly turned tail and disappeared under the scrub.

Breathing heavily, his front paws two blocks of numb wood, Shaka teetered back to the center of the glade. His muscles seized up under the strain of the adrenalin and he felt his claws retracting and protracting spasmodically. His heart was thundering for blood. T. went to comfort him, but he pushed him away. "Not now, brother. Not now."

He glanced around the clearing. Blondie was nowhere to be seen.

"FUCK!" screamed Leonides, his spittle spraying the overturned ground where the big lion had stood moments ago.

"He disappeared," Dreadlocks muttered wetly, in shock. He limped around the glade with his left forelimb painfully folded against his chest. "How did he... Where did he.... Right here. He was right here." He collapsed abruptly and sat down on his haunches. Fresh blood spurted out of a gash in the middle of his forehead and streamed down the middle of his battered muzzle, into his nostrils.

Something cold dropped inside Shaka's guts. He hastened to his brother's side and gave him a quick head rub before licking some of the grime off his rhinarium. "Easy there," he said, his voice soft. "You okay big guy?"

Dreadlocks groaned and rammed his head against Shaka's mane with friendly vigor. "Don't worry, I'll be alright. This is not the way I die."

"Maybe next time don't assault the front like that," said Skoro. "You should know by now that's where all the teeth are."

"Fine. Next time you can take my place."

Leonides angrily swiped at a cluster of wet leaves. "I can't believe that coward gave us the slip like that! By the grass, we had him dead to rights! What do we do now?"

"I punctured his spine," Makhulu reminded him calmly. "He won't go far."

"So which one do we track down?" asked T. He was glancing at the spot where the second lion had emerged out of the low forest.

"The bigger one," Leonides groaned, exasperated. "We track down the bigger one."

The meandering trail was not hard to follow. The injured lion's painful shamble had flattened the spongy green grass and left streaks of brown blood in its wake. Nuggets of soft scats littered the way as well. They nursed their wounds and followed the trail at a relaxed pace even Dreadlocks could sustain despite his wound. They almost lost the scent at the bed of a shallow river but then caught sight of the deep grooves where Blondie had struggled to overcome the slippery rise of the opposite bluff, slightly downstream.

Shaka took a closer look and noticed a peculiar dragging mark gently brushing over the smudges of the strained paw prints, as if some weird snake were locked on the lion's trail as well. "He's lost the control of one of his legs," he said out loud.

"The right hind leg," Makhulu agreed next to him. "I must have cut through some nerves in his spine."

"Even on three legs he's still moving faster than Dreadlocks," laughed Leonides.

An outburst of angry, unintelligible curses answered him in the distance.

They caught up to him in the middle of the night, an antelope's pronk away from the Chitwa Chitwa lake. The moisture emanating out of the nearby body of water hung heavy in the cool air and tickled their noses. Exhausted beyond his ability to feel pain, Blondie was now crawling mindlessly forward with the sole help of his forelegs. On his back, Shaka noticed Makhulu's fresh bite glistening darkly under the silvery moon. Streaks of gleaming black blood were covering his rump. As they closed-in on him from behind, they heard a faint mumble coming out of his throat, like a soft and pitiful high-pitched droning wail that seemed to pull him forward by the muzzle.

Inside the wail, words: "Just need a tiny bit o' water. That's it. Water. Stupid legs are cramped up, is all. All I need is a bit o' water. And rest. One night. Just one night. I'll be better. I'll find my legs. It's okay, I still have time… Still have time…. Just need my legs. If I have my legs, I'm good. No worries at all…." He winced in pain and stopped briefly, his eyes closed. "Justneedmyfuckinglegstoworkagain."

Shaka stepped in front of him.

"No!" shrieked Blondie. He drew himself up on his forelegs and desperately tried to turn himself around. "No! Please wait! Just wait. We can work this out. Wait! Wait!"

They easily overturned the paralyzed lower half and fell on him from behind.

Shaka found a good grip on the loose flap of white skin connecting the right leg to the hip and worked to open it up with vicious jerks of the muzzle. Once that was done, he worried his way through the thick layer of muscles. Grease and blood marred the fur underneath his eyes. To his left, Makhulu ripped the lower belly open, while, to his right, Leonides went after the scrotum. Something wet and grey gushed out of the glistening wound and spilled all over the grass. T.

recoiled in disgust after having mistakenly bitten through the lower colon.

Shaka let go of his grip. Straddling the overturned hips, he sucked in the steam fuming out of the gaping wound with big, eager gulps and savored the rich taste of the lion's inners perspiring on his palate. A blood frenzy overcame him. Roaring at the top of his lungs, he burrowed through the mass of red goo with the savagery of a rabid honey badger and furiously scattered the remaining intestines to the side. His fangs closed-in on something bitter. The liver. He ripped it out. The chunk of dark, spongy meat dangled in front of him and splashed against his mane. T. swooped-in to grab the opposite end and together they shared the still-warm organ in a few wild bites.

Somewhere far away, near where Blondie's head was supposed to lie, they could still hear his screams. "Stop it," he begged. "Please…we can work something out."

Shaka laughed. The high-pitched, desperate pleas seemed like a good joke on the doomed lion's part, if somewhat absurd.

He dove into the gaping wound. T.'s eager head rammed against his right ear and almost shoved him to the side. He adjusted his stance and happily pushed back. Somewhere behind him, he could feel his wagging tail swipe at another cat's muzzle. Dreadlocks, maybe.

None of them actually noticed the moment when Blondie finally died. As they were consuming him from the rear, away from his fangs, it seemed a small matter. At dawn, nothing was left of the big lion but a large chunk of mane and a few scattered bones.

They moved off the spot of their killing and briefly stopped by the lake to quench their thirst and relax their strained bodies.

His bloodlust now spent, Shaka was feeling numb, almost in shock. He teetered to the water's edge and caught a glimpse of his reflection undulating under the ripples of his brothers' lapping. He froze in awe and disbelief. Covered in grime from head to claws, battered down and disheveled, every muscle sore to the point of sluggish torpor, he seemed an apparition out of some lioness' belly, a giant cub still sleek with birth-fluids opening his eyes to the harshness of the world for the very first time.

The Nkuhuma's screams echoed inside his head. *Wait! We can work something out. Wait!*

He groaned and recoiled from the accusing lake. This was nothing new, the confused feelings were always hard to shake after a fight. They were conquerors, they were murderers; triumphant under the rising sun, the shadow of their guilt already stretched far and wide across the grass; in their chest, a wild beating heart engorged with life, in their throat, a lingering taste of death.

His brothers were feeling the same way, he knew. Already he could hear their temper swerving madly between cheerful giddiness and somber disquiet. Skoro, especially, could not stop himself from babbling. "Did you see this? Did you see that? And when he did that? By the grass, what a fight! Did you see? Did you see?" Next to him, Makhulu and Leonides were humoring him patiently. Yes, they had, in fact, seen it. Indeed, they had been right there, by his side, the whole time. Hadn't he notice? Skoro paid them no mind and let his tongue pronk freely in all directions, his monologue of rhetorical questions punctuated only by the smallest breaks required for the curt, one-worded replies his brothers indulged him with. They knew he needed it.

Shaka laid himself down to better enjoy his brother's senseless observations with T.'s head comfortably snuggled against his distended belly. Somewhere to his right, Dreadlocks was already snoring faintly.

After a short, rejuvenating nap, he opened a drowsy eye and realized that the gazelle trapped inside Skoro's head had finally exhausted itself. The savannah had fallen still and quiet again, sunbaked.

He decided to wash the grime off his body. The thick layer of caked blood covering his head and chest was like solid mud, he could actually feel the crust weighing down on his mane. He cleaned his front paws first, one deep, thorough lick of his raspy tongue after the next, then moved to the sorry mess of tangled knots that was his chest. The lumps of greasy hair pricked at his skin but he persevered with the tenacity of old habit. Once his lower front had returned to its usual, lush darkness he turned to T. for the areas he could not reach.

His brother had already concluded his own scrubbing and was patiently waiting for him to finish. At his invitation, the younger lion stepped forward and proceeded to lovingly lick the blood off his muzzle and back of his head with a practiced, darting tongue. Shaka snuggled up to him and progressively rotated his head so as to better guide his efforts. As he did so, he shuddered deliciously and closed his eyes to better enjoy the warmth of his brother's care.

His mind turned fuzzy, languorous. His neck went limp and he let himself being rocked by T.'s thorough scrubbing like a soft leaf on the wind. One full horizon away from his consciousness, wrapped in the heat-haze of his bliss, he could feel the rest of his sprawled-out body relax and melt under the heat of the morning sun.

They took turn grooming each other slowly, amorously. Long after the last of the blood and ticks had been scrubbed off, they kept going at it with joyful reciprocity. The reality of each other's existence, the undeniable physical presence of it, was all that truly mattered. It diluted the taste of death on their tongue and dispelled their misgivings. Under the onslaught of head rubs and brotherly love, the misty shadows lurking in the back of their mind proved themselves empty, vaporous. Just like the wind, they had no true hold on them. Just like blood, they could be washed off. They were proud cats, alive and healthy under the bright light of the sun. Everything else was just noise.

Shaka noticed T.'s deep snoring and stopped his licking. After one last head rub, he stood himself up, stretched his spine with a satisfied sigh, and turned to take stoke of his brothers. Makhulu was gazing at the lake, lost in his thoughts. Dreadlocks was nursing his wounded leg. Next to him, the twins were sleeping with their back pressed tight against each other and their swollen belly heaving up and down in unison, the same way they had since they were cubs. With their front paws casually laid over their whiskers, they looked much younger than they really were, almost innocent.

Dreadlocks raised his head and gazed back at him with a puzzled look. Not for the first time, Shaka noticed the long locks of dark hair dangling underneath his broad chest.

That's when it struck him: *Dreadlocks has become a lion.*

They all had. In the course of their relentless run after yet another pride, incredibly, adulthood had snuck up on them in discreet increments, as imperceptible as the growing of the grass, as undeniable as the change of the season.

Their gaze had grown more placid and self-assured, drained of the last of that sparkling, sub-adult awe that had defined their spirit ever since the day they had first stepped outside of the Eyrefield, as if the world were a bit duller now, tamed. Their demeanor had cooled accordingly and become more poised, less prompt to wild, playful outbursts that wasted energy for no reason. Their shoulders were stockier, their gait stiffer. With every new step, their padding forepaws seemed to softly slap the ground underneath them, as if quietly forcing it into submission. Most obvious of all, their mane. While Dreadlocks' disheveled tufts were unique to him, they all had developed an impenetrable dark thickness over their chest and neck, like a dense wood keeping the light of the sun away from the cool, moist ground.

That last realization stabbed him in the heart with the viciousness of a gazelle's horn. He felt it twist. He looked down at T. in disbelief, hoping against all hopes that at least one of them might have been spared. No such luck. The younger cat's forehead and temples were still hopelessly barren but the dark of his chest had grown just as much as any of them. It was now connected to the black zebra mane by a plain of long, golden hair that covered the sides of his neck. The golden crown around his face was thinner, less obvious, but undeniable nonetheless.

Just like the rest of them, his cub brother had fallen prey to adulthood.

"You look like you've seen a dead cat," whispered T. His eyes, still glazed with sleep, were wide open.

Shaka chuckled softly and went to nibble his ear. "I think I have, big cat. I think I have."

The sun began the second half of its arc. One by one, his brothers went through the slow process of rousing themselves. After much stretching and several relapses, they finally moved off the lake at a lazy, meandering pace and struck a course toward the general direction of the Nkuhuma's pride.

"Those girls are going to make us chase them, won't they?" groaned Dreadlocks. He was still limping noticeably.

"Worse than that," said Makhulu. "They still have a male to rally to. That Dozie cat fellow. If we don't deal with him one way or the other, the females will never surrender."

"With the cubs in tow they should be moving fairly slowly," Shaka said.

"Well then let's go boys!" T. exclaimed gaily as he pranced forward. "There are lions for the taking today!"

At dusk they fanned out in pairs: the twins on one side, Makhulu and Dreadlocks on another, and T. and Shaka together in the middle. They used the cool air of the coming night to pick the pace up. No doubt the Dozie male could hear them coming, but that was also part of the plan. Strike fear in his heart. Turn him into a brainless shrew. Force him to make a mistake.

Night came.

"Once we take over the Nkuhuma, how many prides do you think that will be?" T. whispered next to Shaka. His tail was raised high under the bright moon, his short steps light on the soft cushion of silver grass. In the quiet of the night, Shaka could hear his easy breathing coming out at a fast, excited pace.

He considered the question with interest. So many things had happened in the span of a few seasons, it was hard to keep track of it all. The memories were blurred inside his head. "Well, let's see. The Ottawa was the first. Then the Ravenscourt, although they didn't fare very well. The Sand River pride after that, I think. Oh and, of course, the Tsalala too."

"Ah yesss, Rocky. I had forgotten all about that big old gnarly cat. He was so infuriated when we showed up on his territory, for a brief instant I thought that he might actually drop dead just from seeing us. Almost wanted to tell him to keep breathing."

"He did fight, though."

"If you want to call it that. Didn't taste too good afterward. Too much stress I guess."

"Not everyone can melt under your tongue, T."

His brother groaned happily at the quip. They rounded a small cluster of bushes and stopped to scuff the ground and leave their mark on the glistening leaves. Then they pushed forward.

"Should we count the Ximunvanyane pride as well?" asked T.

"Not much point, is there?"

The infuriating memories were still gnawing at Shaka's guts. Long after the death of their cubs, to the Mapogos shocked dismay, those girls had persevered in their refusal to submit, well beyond the point of reason.

The coalition had tried everything to get through to them. By the grass, they truly had. Swallowing down their pride, they had done their best to cajole them and sooth the lioness' wrath by promising them everything and anything, from first pick at buffalo meat and litters after litters of strong, healthy cubs, to full control over the whole of the Sabi Sands and the sun above. When that had failed, slightly disgusted, they had groaned and let the fangs show behind the soothing tongue. T. had unleashed his full repertoire of curses and threats of deaths to come – some sentences, even Shaka had been shocked to hear – and together they had endeavored to beat the females into submission. To no avail. After the death of the first lioness – an accident – the whole affair had quickly devolved into an endless bitter guerrilla of snarls, chases, ambushes, and retreats the big males had been unable to stomp down. As if they were trying to grasp water with their paws. In the end, they had been forced to make an example out of the girls and whittle them down, one by one.

Shaka shook his head and tried to push the sordid murders out of his mind. He wasn't quite sure whether he ought to feel ashamed or angry. As a coalition, it had been their first real failure.

But not the last.

He closed his eyes. One particularly surreal scene he could still remember all too vividly. The deep growl of a rumbler fixing them in the dead of night with its dual, out-of-worldly beam of lights washing bright over their reflective tapetum, blinding. The frantic grunts of the trapped female – for the life of him, Shaka could not remember her name or her pride – who had refused to share her impala. Skoro casually munching on her back leg with mild curiosity, as if trying to ascertain what the limb was, and T. holding her by the back of the neck, whispering: "It's gonna be alright," over and over again even as he throttled the life out of her.

What a waste.

"You think it's gonna be the same with the Nkuhuma girls?" he asked, slightly uneased.

T. shrugged. "First we need to kill their last male, or at least drive him off. Then a few of them might still try to fight us to protect the cubs. It's always the same."

"I just hope the whole thing doesn't turn into another bloodbath. I'm sick and tired of it. Between the old standing males, the cubs, the defiant females, and the odd braindead wander-male, I honestly can't get a good grasp of the number of cats we've killed."

T. chuckled lightly as if Shaka had cracked another good joke. "Me neither, brother. Me neither."

"So when does it end?"

"What do you mean?"

"When do we decide that we have enough?"

T. stopped in his track and glared at his brother with non-plussed eyes. "It never ends, Shaka. It's like hunting buffaloes. You might be satiated one day and think that you're done with the killing, but just wait a few dawns and you find yourself on the prowl again with your stomach growling."

"Killing lions is different."

"No, it's not. There will always be more prides for the taking, more males stepping up to us. It's endless, like swimming across a river with no shores. If you stop, you sink."

"But then what happens when things go the other way? What happens when we meet a coalition we cannot defeat?"

"A bunch of cats who can stand up to the six of us? Not likely."

"So we'll always be on top then? No matter the passing of the seasons, we'll always be swimming the river?"

"Of course. Why not?"

Shaka fell quiet as he pondered his brother's answer. It seemed too easy. And yet, he could find no flaw in his reasoning. As long as they could hunt, they would remain strong. As long as they were strong, they were untouchable. T. was right, it was hard to imagine any lion overcoming the united front of the six of them, not when they had been able to kill the likes of Blondie so easily. The loop was self-feeding. Like a wildfire, their spread seemed unstoppable.

"I just don't see much point to it anymore," he whispered.

"In what?"

"In getting more territory, more prides. I mean, how much can six lions really need? I look around and I know that all this grass is supposedly mine because I've pissed on a tree somewhere nearby, but it's not like I can step on all of it at once. No matter the size of the territory, I can still only experience the veld four paws at a time. How is that any different from the time when we were wander-males? To tell you the truth, the more I think about it, the more I feel like I don't really own much of anything at all."

"You're looking at it wrong. It's not the owning of the prides and territories that matters, only the taking of them."

"What do you mean?"

"Consider our situation right now: chasing after yet another pride. Do we need it? Are the Nkuhuma lionesses and their territory going to bring us anything that we don't already have? Of course not. But then what do we do? Do we not take it? Do we let Dozie live and escape with his pride so that he can tell everyone how he beat the Mapogos? Are you really willing to let that happen? To restrain yourself in such a way?"

"I-I don't know. All this killing, it can't just be about the ego, can it?"

"No, not the ego. Something deeper. Simpler. We do these things for the same reason that we do everything else, from ascending a new hill to killing a litter of wild dogs: because it's right there. And because not to do them would be, as you so often say, unlionlike."

Maybe T. had a point. While Shaka could see little worth in claiming yet another pride, he had to admit that he was wroth to let them go. They were so close after all.

He shook his head. Maybe it was best not to dwell on these things which had no answers. Go with the flow of the river, see where it takes you.

T. nudged him on the shoulder and scampered ahead. Shaka pounced forward and baited him into a mindless race across the night. The younger lion giggled and happily obliged.

At sunrise they regrouped with the others to share their findings and decide on a new course to follow. A succession of dawns came and went in a blink. Their progress stalled.

"The problem with grass is that there is so much of it," said Dreadlocks one morning, utterly dispirited after yet another failed chase.

"That Dozie is giving them wings," grumbled Makhulu. "We should have killed him when we had the chance."

Their only true advantage were the cubs. Despite their mothers' help, the younger ones could not keep up with the merciless pressure the Mapogos were inflicting upon the fleeing pride. One by one, those left behind were discovered and promptly dispatched. A few they ate, more out of spite than anything else. Perhaps not so surprisingly, this did not dampen the lionesses' resolve to protect the last of their litter.

As the chase wore on, their ties loosened and they fanned out to better appreciate this new, lush territory they had conquered. A drier season came, carried by a cool, gentle breeze that chased the stifling morning steam away. The grass turned yellow and sparse. In the trees, the incessant trills of the woodland kingfishers, no longer nesting, became more sporadic, almost shy.

Soon, Shaka knew, they would have to turn back and reassert their control over those lands they had neglected. Already they had been gone too long.

One dawn, the desperate bleating of a waterbuck being torn apart caught their ears. By the time they regrouped and reached the still warm carcass, the females had already scattered. They gorged themselves on the free meat and followed the scent. Much to their surprise, they stumbled upon one of the lionesses. She was limping badly, unable to run away, but she still whirled and snarled at their approach in a well-known, defiant manner that had by now grown quite dull to Shaka's eyes.

"Enough," he hissed. "It's over. You're trapped and you're alone. This is pointless." tail

But the female was not listening. She backed away slowly with her tails tucked between her legs and lashed out at Skoro's muzzle. Leonides and Dreadlocks swung around her and cut off her retreat, forcing her to seat down on her haunches in a desperate attempt to protect her most vulnerable parts. sit

"Where are the others?" growled Makhulu. "Where is Dozie? Tell us and we can spare your life. The Nkuhuma will thrive under our protection."

More lashings and snarls.

"She won't cooperate," spat Dreadlocks. Just like Shaka, he sounded dispirited and bone-tired. "No matter what we say, she won't give up her kin."

"Right."

T. peeled to the side and strode out of the female's field of vision before abruptly cutting into her personal space with three quick steps. He pounced and clamped his jaws on the back of her neck. Her fury exploded all at once but he adroitly wrestled her to the ground and pinned her down with his hind legs wrapped around her mid-section and one heavy paw pressed on the side of her muzzle. He was used to the exercise by now and went through the movements as if they were a well-rehearsed choreography.

The lioness' panting turned wheezy, then quiet. Her eyes glazed. In her agony, her back legs were still quivering slightly, as if trying to fend off an imaginary enemy.

This was more than Shaka could stomach. He wheeled and tore himself away from the spectacle. Then, on an impulse, he turned back around and shoved his face against the lioness' gasping muzzle. A thin rivulet of blood was already trickling out of the side of her mouth. Close as he was, he could not feel the wind of her breath.

"Why?!" he screamed. "Why do you make us do this?! What's the point of throwing your life away like this?! We've got you beat. Just bend already! Who do you girls think you are?!"

A few hard spasms overcame her as she tried to raise her head. T. groaned and adjusted his grip on her windpipe. A faint gurgle escaped the female's throat.

"Nkuhuma…Nkuhuma Pride!"

Then, she died.

Shaka backed away, his limbs stiff. A series of furious roar overcame him. He shook his head and closed his eyes.

Dreadlocks bumped into him. "You alright?"

"I don't know. Killing males and foreign cubs is one thing, but this… This is the Ximunvanyane all over again. By the grass, it feels like such a waste!"

"Some cats you can't reason with," Makhulu said. "It is what it is."

Leonides came back from having scanned the area. "The tracks disappear into the Manyaleti. The scats are cold, those cats have long scattered."

"Dozie?"

"Yeah he was with them. Cubs too, I think. Half a dozen at least, probably more."

"We should go right now," said T. "If we hurry we can still catch up with some of the young ones by nightfall."

Nobody moved.

"Frankly," Dreadlocks groaned, "I've had enough of this running around in circle nonsense."

"Me too," said Skoro. "Besides, we need to worry about the other prides. We have a lot of ground to patrol now, we can't just stay up here and play games indefinitely."

T. was still straddling the lioness' body. He leaned forward to sniff her udder, caught some cold milk on his rhinarium, raised his head back up again. "So we let them get away, then?"

"Not really," said Leonides, "we've already pushed them off their territory. That ought to be enough."

"That Dozie cat played his position well, we've got to give him that," said Skoro. "He wins this one. Sort of."

"What if he comes back here after we've left?"

Dreadlocks shrugged. "Then we come back as well. And settle things once and for all."

That answer seemed to satisfy the younger lion.

"We'll stop by what remains of the waterbuck," Makhulu decreed. "Then we make for the Londolozi."

Before leaving, Shaka stole one last glance at the dead lioness whose body had already grown stiff and lukewarm. On her muzzle, the ticks and fleas that had inhabited her fur and benefited from her warmth her entire life were gathering in groups, eager to depart and start searching for a new host.

A small dark laugh escaped his lungs.

When you sink, he reflected, *you sink alone*.

FIFTEEN

A LION'S HONOR

"I'm not asking for much. Just back me up on this one!"

"Forget it, we're not calling you Pretty Boy. You're nowhere near sleek enough for that, what with your big dumb head and broad, ugly muzzle. Besides, you're my twin. You have no right to call yourself pretty if I don't."

"I might be your twin but I don't look anything like you. I have a much nicer streak of dark hair up on my forehead, you can't deny that."

"Shaka's got an even better one, I don't hear him going on and on about it."

"Alright. How about 'The Ghost' then? I'll call myself 'The Ghost' and you'll be 'The Darkness'. Together, we'll be the Ghost and–"

"In your dreams."

"What's a ghost?" Shaka asked softly from the other side of the small cluster of thornbushes under which they had sought relief from the afternoon sun.

"A ghost? That's like the idea of a perfect stalker. A cross between a silky cat moving on feather-paws and a shadow. If you ever see a lion crawling through the woods so quietly that he seems to be gliding above the ground, that's a ghost."

"Put another way: the complete opposite of Skoro."

They all laughed.

"Why do you want to have a nickname so bad anyway?" said T. The younger lion was sprawled out on the grass next to Shaka. "What's wrong with Skoro?"

"Nothing wrong with the name per say, but a nickname is a title. It tells a story about the cat who wears it, who he is, what he's done. You hear his roar, someone whispers the nickname, and already you know that this lion has been around long enough for others to take notice of him. A picture takes shape in your head, influenced by the monikers the cat has received. Enlarged by your imagination, it runs loose. You haven't even laid eyes on the cat yet, and already you're shuddering in fear."

"You're overthinking this way too much, brother."

"Yeah? Name a single one of the Sunset Boys by their cub name. Go on, I'll wait."

A short silence ensued.

"Well…Mak Senior must have been called Makhulu at some point in his youth, I guess," Leonides offered weakly. "Until our own Mak came along and claimed the name for himself, that is." The answer was somewhat less than satisfying, he knew, but he needed to deny his twin the pleasure of being right.

Skoro groaned his scorn. "Fine. But what about the others? Blondie got his name after his golden mane, Scar-Nose and Scar-Eye after the fights that marked them. And Broken Nose! By the grass, you tell me that's not a name to send shivers down the spine of even the sturdiest cat."

"Fair point, but not all monikers are so great," countered T. "Some of them are like an itch you can't get rid of, a stain on your personality. Every time you hear the name it saps your inner strength and brings you back to unwanted memories that remind you of how the world truly sees you, regardless of how you see yourself."

Leonides raised his head in surprise and squinted his eyes toward the back of the lion's mane he could see pressed tight against the sparse green foliage separating them. "You know that we don't mean anything by it anymore, right? It's just how we're used to call you now. That's all."

A soft growl, between laughter and self-contempt. "I know, I know. Some itch you learn to love. With time, they become bittersweet."

"Besides," said Shaka, "'T.' is not so bad, as far as names go. It's got a good, sharp sound to it, like a fang puncturing a bone. And because it's so uncommon, cats can't help but wonder who in their right mind would choose such a nickname. It creates an aura around you, like you're some sort of creature shrouded in mystery."

"An uncommon name for an uncommon lion," concluded Leonides, affectuously.

"You guys are poets. Truly, I am touched."

"T. has a point, though," Skoro pressed on. "If I'm not careful I'll end up with a stupid nickname I did not choose. Something moronic like 'Kinky Tail', or worse 'Dreadlocks'."

The broad-chested cat raised a drowsy head out of the tall grass and turned his muzzle in the group's direction. "Somebody called?"

"Yeah. Skoro said your name is dumb."

"Oh."

Dreadlocks yawned and seemed to ponder whether the slight was worth getting up for. After having decided against it, he let his head fall back down and lay so still as to look dead, with his eyes closed and his four paws cradling his big belly in a self-soothing hug reminiscent of a young cub's innocence. A careless vulture could have been fooled, were it not for the heaving of his distended flanks and the occasional darting tongue licking his muzzle. After a few deep breaths that bordered on snores, his slurred voice lazily boomed out of the lank again. "Is the little kitten still ranting about his appearance then?"

"You can call me whatever you like," spat Skoro. "At least my name doesn't infer that my mane sweeps the dirt every time I take a step."

"I don't need no fancy nickname to help me, Skoro. I prefer my enemies to be contempt and overconfident. Easier to catch them that way. Then, when I charge, they learn why my name starts with 'Dread'."

A chorus of laughter and groans of ascent rose over the savannah.

"Good one," said T. "By the grass, that was a good one."

Besieged on all sides by his brother's mirth, Skoro stood himself up, stretched, and attempted a couple of lackadaisical steps away from the bushes' shadow. The sun glare seemed to hit him like something physical. He scuffed the ground half-heartedly and collapsed back down a lion's length away from where he had started while pushing out a satiated sigh, as though he had achieved something of great import.

"Besides, you're missing the bigger picture," Shaka said after a short while. He seemed to have given the topic a lot of thought.

"Please do tell," Skoro grumbled with all the trust of a meerkat answering the call of an eagle.

"Skoro, Shaka, T., Dreadlocks, Leonides, those names don't matter. Not even Makhulu's. What matter is the coalition. Whenever one of us roars, all the other cats know that the Mapogos are nearby. They don't care to know which one. Why would they? They know that the *coalition* is here, and that is more than enough to send them looking for another horizon."

"Most of the time anyway," sniggered T.

They shared another laugh, this time all together, and a contented silence ensued as they reveled in the bliss of each other's company and a belly full of meat. They had a whole afternoon of chewing quips and munching words ahead of them, they knew. No point in rushing anything. Leonides shuffled his head around in the loose dirt and breathed-in deep the clean scent of the dry grass grating against his muzzle. He growled happily. What more could a lion ask for?

Not far from them, the grunts and groans of the Ottawa females fighting over what was left of the buffalo they had brought down – and the brothers had shamelessly appropriated – dribbled through his light slumber. One sound he savored above the others: the crackling of brittle bones under their powerful jaws, like dry wood caught in a wildfire, or the first heavy drops of rain impacting the hard-packed dirt after a long drought. As he kept listening, he noticed short, insistent yelps punctuating the girls' deeper rumbles. He smiled internally. Makhulu's cubs.

"Anyone knows where the big guy is these days?" he asked.

"I heard his roar last night," T. answered. "Sounded like it was coming from beyond the Londolozi, almost all the way to the Sand River. He'll be on far patrol for another few dawns, at least."

"That Big Mak sure loves his patrols," mumbled Shaka, half-asleep.

"And his lionesses," added Dreadlocks. "Since we've taken over, he has covered just about every girl who has surrendered to us. All the cubs are his, more likely than not."

Leonides' ears pricked up. There was a hard, bitter edge in the lion's tone that did not sit well with him. "What are you saying?" he asked as he raised his head.

Dreadlocks shrugged. "Nothing new, I guess. Only what everybody is thinking. Shaka pointed out that the coalition matters more than the individuals, that we all share the name 'Mapogo' equally. That may be, but as far as the litters are concerned, Makhulu got himself the lion's share."

"That's true," T. remarked, somewhat forlornly. "It will be a looooong time before any of those girls are in estrus again."

"That was his right, though," Leonides pointed out, suddenly up and alert. "He is the dominant male."

Dreadlocks stood and stretched his spine with a groan before pacing back and forth in front of the small cluster of thornbushes, his tail restless. He seemed to have some difficulty expressing his opinion out loud, as though he could not follow the river of his own thoughts. "Is he still?" he finally blurted out after coming to an abrupt halt. "Back when he was the only true dark-maned, you would have been right. Absolutely. The lionesses instinctively turned to him for protection and I don't blame them, nor him for accepting their favors. The night he killed that Nhlanguleni male, in single combat no less, he stood as tall as the sky above, and we were all living under his shadow. But not anymore. We've all been through the same cutting grass, spilled the same blood, earned the same scars. And we all carry the same darkness on the chest to show for it."

"Dreadlocks is right," Skoro decided brusquely; in his voice, Leonides could discern the sharpness of the recently converted. He roused himself and shook the sleep out of his mane. "Makhulu can't expect us to behave like little ducklings marching behind his tail forever. If we're all Mapogos, we all stand on the same line, as equals."

Leonides rose and took a couple of steps back, uneased by the way his brothers' cat tempers were flaring up so suddenly. Gone were the light-hearted piques and the drowsiness. Despite their swinging bellies, a new hunger gleamed in their eyes. Already they seemed ready to go on the prowl. But where?

A rustle reached him from the other side of the thornbushes. T. and Shaka rounded the brambly island and strolled to the side of Dreadlocks and Skoro.

"We'll express our concerns to Mak when he comes back," said Shaka. "Next time we take over a pride, he'll know that he can't expect us to just stand aside."

Skoro nodded, seemingly content, but Dreadlocks shook his head.

"How long will it be before we go on the path again? Already our territory his huge, with dozens of huntresses to protect and more borders than we can cover even if we were to walk for a moon straight without rest. And that's without considering the odd braindead wander-males we have to fight off every now and then. Given the sheer amount of energy required to keep all of this mess under control, it will be a long, long time before we can claim any new pride."

"So what do you want the Big Mak to do about it?" Leonides groaned in frustration. "Even if he agrees to share the lionesses he has already covered, it's like T. said: it will be a long while before any of them are in estrus again."

"There is a simple remedy for that," whispered the younger lion.

Leonides jerked his head back, dumbstruck. "You did not say that," he breathed out. "By the grass, you did *not* say that!"

His alarm turned into a full-blown panic howling inside his chest. Starving for support, he let his gaze bounce from one brother to the next. None of them appeared overly concerned by T.'s proposal. In fact, he realized with a shock verging on despair, Dreadlocks and Skoro both seemed to have reach a similar conclusion on their own. Shaka held his gaze for a few heartbeats and then lowered his head and shuffled his paws, his mane seemingly wilting under the intensity of his glare. “I don’t see any other way,” he mumbled weakly in lieu of an apology.

“You’re mad,” Leonides spat, his voice quivering. “All of you. You’ve lost your grip on reality. Makhulu will never agree to this!”

“That’s why we won’t be asking his permission,” T. said softly, almost rationally. “We’ll do what we have to do, like proper standing lions, and present him with the facts when he comes back.”

“I guess that’s one way of saying that you’ll do it as long as he’s very fucking far away from you.”

“You stand to benefit from this as well. Can’t you see that?”

“T., he’s your *brother*!” roared Leonides, glad to see that he had found a good grip on his vocal cords at last. He wasn’t entirely certain that the flash of temper was a good way to go about it, but he couldn’t really help it either.

Undeterred, the younger lion stood his ground and let leap his own temper. “Yes, he’s my brother! And I love him. I would die for him! But I’m sorry, that love does not extend to his spawns. Not when it gets in the way of my own interest.”

“You would end his lineage forever then? Really you would do that? Murder our own brother’s cubs as if you’re some kind of vicious wander-male sneaking past our defenses?”

A cold growl escaped T.’s throat. For half a heartbeat Leonides thought that he might lunge for his spine. He adjusted his stance instinctively and prepared himself for the dance. At the last instant, the impetuous lion reconsidered his course of action and clenched his jaws tight, hard enough that Leonides heard the fangs grind wetly against the gums.

“Somebody talks some sense into this fool, please,” grumbled T., and turned his back on him.

Dreadlocks stepped in. “Nobody is sneaking anywhere. And we’re not talking about ending his lineage either. Makhulu is not his cubs. Once the playing field is more…leveled, he’ll have plenty of occasions to start anew.”

“Check your thinking big cat, you’re a few fangs short of a full rack.”

"What do you mean?"

"They're his cubs, Dread. *His own cubs!*"

"Ah, he'll get over it. Cubs die all the time. Sometimes it's predators, sometimes it's hunger, sometimes it's just bad luck. Nothing anyone can do about it, that's just the way it is. That's why we make a lot of them to begin with. Makhulu will understand."

"He will kill you for this, that's what he'll do. All of you. He will never accept that you have betrayed him like that."

Dreadlocks drew himself up with a puzzled look. For the first time since this insanity had begun, he seemed to grasp all the implications lurking behind his proposal, what Makhulu's reaction might be once he found out, where it could lead them. After careful consideration, he lowered his muzzle back to Leonides' level. His easy bravado had disappeared but something infinitely harder had taken its place. Something Leonides did not think his brother had in him. "If that's the way it must be," he proclaimed, each one of his words dripping out of his dark lips like poison, "then so be it. If Makhulu can't let it go and insists on laying it down on the grass, we'll pick it up. *I'll* pick it up."

"Really? Just like that? You're going to kill your big brother and then happily move on with your life as if nothing has happened at all? You can do that, eh?"

Dreadlocks glared at him and stepped away. For all his obvious misgivings, the hardness had not left his eyes.

He'll go through with it. By the grass, he'll jump right in without a thought in his head and when Makhulu finds out and confronts him, he won't have a choice at all. It will be his life on the line.

Desperate, he whirled toward Shaka. "What about you? You agree with them? When Makhulu finds out what you all have done, you're ready to kill him too?"

"Leonides…"

"No! I want to hear you say it. I want to hear you say that you'll sink your fangs in his spine and wait for the crack. I want to hear you say that you'll listen coldly to his pleading – *your own brother's pleading!* – even as you ravage his midsection and spill him wet all over the dirt. Go on, I'll wait. You're all so tough all of a sudden. Proper steady cats. So say it. Tell me how killing Makhulu is something that you can live with. Something…what's that word you always use? Lionlike. Yeah, look me in the eye and tell me that this is *lionlike*!"

"Leonides, it won't come to that."

"How can you be so sure?"

"Well, for one, it would be the five of us against him alone," T. interjected. "He would have to be insane to fight us."

"You, shut up," Leonides hissed through closed fangs. His heart raged inside his chest, ready to pounce.

T. felt it. Suddenly silenced, he sat down on his haunches so fast it seemed that the movement had been involuntary, as if some nerves in his spine had been cut. That cheered Leonides a little. His brother had a fierce demeanor about him, but he was not exactly a push over himself either. He turned his attention back to Shaka. "You were saying?"

hearts

"Makhulu will see reason. He will understand our position. It's not fair for him to have backed us against this rock in the first place. He knows that we love him with all our heart, but he can't expect us to deny ourselves either. Something has to give. And at the end of the day, once everything else has been roared and done, he needs us just as much as we need him. More, even. If not his brotherly love, his survival instinct will stay his paws."

Leonides swallowed down, dejected. The worst of it was that Shaka's argument actually made sense. As usual, the sensible lion was right. Their current situation was not fair.

Who was betraying who?

The idea that it might be Makhulu's fault, that the dark-maned had proven himself overly greedy and thus forced their move, was enough to turn his stomach inside out. He felt his temper wane even as his own guilt surged.

Just like his brothers, he could feel it roil inside him, this urge in his midsection, like a burning itch underneath his guts. No point in denying it. It felt like a pain that was almost the exact opposite of an empty stomach. An irrational need to explode and spread himself. Try as he might, he could not repress it.

Had he remained far smaller than Makhulu, he suspected that the situation would have been different. Defiance being an absolute impossibility, a death sentence, the need would have been stomped by his unconscious. But things were not so easy any longer. He had grown in size and strength to the point that he was now able to look Makhulu in the eyes. They all had. Consequently, their inner fortitude, their strength of will, had grown weaker.

He ground his fangs in self-disgust. Was this the true depth of their loyalty then? A shallow puddle all too eager to evaporate as soon as it suited their self-interest? How easy it is to call oneself virtuous so long as one is weak. Was there no way for a strong lion to stand in this world without stepping on another cat's throat?

Fear took hold of him. He felt his heart lurch inside his chest as though he were standing near the edge of a cliff. Even if they could somehow find a way to abate Makhulu's wrath without killing him, how could their coalition ever hope to survive afterward? How could they ever hold each other's gaze again and mend the bounds?

Moaning, he tried one last pitiful appeal. "What about the lionesses?"

"What about them?"

"They'll never understand. We're not foreign males taking over. They've already submitted to us. Put their trust in us. As far as they are concerned, we're all one coalition. It doesn't make any sense for us to kill our own cubs."

"Well, this coalition is different. They'll just have to get used to it."

"We'll be the most hated cats in the whole of the Sabi Sands. Not just feared lions. Not just cannibals. Monsters! *Aberrations*."

"Let'em hate," T. declared as he brushed past him. "We're an island of ourselves, we owe them nothing."

Dreadlocks followed in his younger brother's paw prints. "If any of the girls wants to voice her concerns," he said gruffly, "she knows where to find us."

Shaka averted his gaze and sidestepped around Leonides as if he were a crocodile. Once free, he broke into a camper and hastened to catch up with the others.

Only Skoro remained. He had been silent throughout most of the exchange.

"You're going with them?" asked Leonides, his voice laden with tremors he could not suppress.

His twin nodded quietly. "You know I have to. And so do you."

"No, I don't. I want no part of this."

"Really? You're going to let them get their fangs dirty on their own, deal with Makhulu's reaction on their own, and then, when the deed is done and the lionesses are in estrus again, you're going to have the fortitude *not* to go for it? Or are you so much of a coward that you are willing to reap the benefits of your brothers' killing without having spilled your own share of the blood?"

"I–I don't know. There has to be another way, Skoro. A better way."

"There isn't. This is it. The course has been plotted; the quarries have been chosen. Your brothers need you. *I* need you. Either you're a Mapogo or you're not. Where do you stand?"

Leonides fidgeted in place. He could feel an abject calm creeping up inside his heart, an emptiness that argued against resistance. "You know," he whispered in lieu of an answer, "when we talked about going to the far side of grass and back, I didn't picture it quite like this."

"We promised ourselves that we would go there, Leon, but no one ever said anything about it being a pretty path. Remember the old cat's saying: 'Ain't nothin' ever been easy 'bout–'"

"Don't! Please. Don't quote him. Not know."

"Listen," Skoro sighed, "you don't have to be at the forefront of this. The way I know him, T. will ferret the little ones out faster than anyone of us can spit. With me, Dreadlocks, and Shaka to help him, we'll have more than enough fangs. All you have to do is keep the lionesses off our back. Maybe deal with a young one or two, if they stumble in your direction. That's it."

"What if I just can't? Physically, I mean. What if I can't do it?"

"You've killed cubs before. This is not so different."

"Not like this I haven't. Theses ones are not just some foreign furballs out of some unknown male's loins. They're Makhulu's cubs. I've watched them grow. I've seen them play. I know their *names.*"

"So do I. Don't fool yourself, I feel the same way you do. To some degree, I even agree with you. This is just about the worst thing our coalition has ever done since leaving the Eyrefield. But the two of us can't sit it out under the shade and wait for it to happen while we do nothing."

"Why not? If you know this is abject, why do you agree to participate? Where is the honor in that?"

Hurt by the retort, his twin raised his muzzle and let his face sag. His stare turned blank. "I refuse to keep myself clean while my brothers trudge through the mud and shoulder my share of the burden. No matter how distasteful the act, we do it together or not at all. There is no in-between."

"So you'll agree to do something you believe to be vile, something you know perfectly well will haunt you down to your guts afterwards, so long as it means that you've stayed true to your brothers? What kind of sick, peer-pressured honor is that?"

"A lion's honor, I guess. If there even is such a thing. Listen, I'm not Shaka, I don't spend my time wondering if something is lionlike or not. To tell you the truth, I'm not even sure that the word means anything. But this I know: we're not meerkats. We don't get to shy away from the world and hide in a burrow. Whatever happens, we face it out in the open, under the sun. And the only way for us to do that is if we're together. So whatever you might be feeling right now, shut it down. Find your grim spirit and your coldest fang. The sooner we get started, the sooner it's done."

On this, Skoro gave him a quick head rub and plodded past him, his sleek tail gently brushing the length of his flank in the process.

Leonides remained where he was, his head cast down, his stiff legs frozen on the edge of the abyss in front of him, refusing to move. Never had a lion's mane felt so heavy.

With a groan that eerily reminded him of a doomed buffalo's last grunt, he finally found the strength to tear himself away from his spot and whirled toward his twin's disappearing rump.

The first step was the hardest. Once in motion, his paws carried him the rest of the way.

SIXTEEN

THE EQUILIBRIUM OF CHAOS

The morning's twilight shone blue through the fat stalks of waving grass and slowly unveiled the new horizon. Broad lines of powdery, bone-white clouds lit up with the orange fire of coming dawn. In the distance, tall trees stood as dark cutouts against the backdrop of the purple sky.

A small serval gingerly stepped out of the underbrush and gazed upward with a dispirited frown, his fast breathing betraying his hunger and restlessness. Daytime meant the end of the hunt for him; he was nowhere near big enough to stand his ground under the sun. He sat down on his haunches and carefully assessed his surroundings with his oversized ears. Satisfied, he proceeded to clean himself of the night's prowl.

Makhulu watched him with a puzzled, vaguely amused look and wondered for a brief instant if the night had somehow turned his body invisible. He sneered at the cat's boldness and an unfortunate snort escaped his muzzle, little more than a warm rustle. The serval yelped and skittered back under the cover of the scraggle, his tiny paws churning the soft, dew-soaked red-brown sod behind him.

Makhulu bounced and gave chase but lost the trail almost immediately. The smaller cat had slunk underneath the dense vegetation without so much as a single branch betraying his passing. He might as well have tried to catch a hummingbird.

No matter.

He untangled himself from the clinging thorns and angled toward the easier meadows at a brisk camper. Picking up speed, he savored the light caress of grass on his chest and the inviting touch of the open sky on his shoulders. The crisp air nipped at his lungs and a wet chill licked his paws. Chuckling softly, like a cub, he drank in the stillness of the veld stretching in all directions all around him. It seemed as though he were the only living creature in the whole of the Sabi Sands right now.

He reached another cluster of trees and stopped just long enough to leave his scent on the leaves before following a twin-rutted dirt lane for a little while. On a whim, he veered toward a downward sloping meadow. The gravity pulled at his soaked mane and he let himself fall into a tumbling gallop. Sticky wet lank slathered his fur with dew. Thrilled, he licked his nose and tasted the aroma of grass in every droplet of water.

There was a small stream at the bottom of the depression. He leaped over it and used his momentum to scale the opposite bluff. He ran out of speed a third of the way up and had to keep pushing up with forceful, claw-anchored strides that turned his breathing into hard-earned chuffs. Just when he thought that his lungs might give up on him, he crested the rise.

Slightly dizzy, he ambled onto the flat ground, drained but content.

As the deafening beating of his heart slowly died down, a flurry of angry cackles and high-pitched hollers reached his ears. Crouching low, he used the cover of the shoulder-high grass to investigate, unnoticed.

A deeper grumble, faint but continuous, rose as he got closer, underlining the frenzied snarls. He risked a peek.

The giant silhouette of a rumbler towering over the low mist filled his vision. The beast was standing still with the two small suns of its stocky muzzle trained on the source of the cacophony. A dense cloud of gnats could be seen dancing in the vaporous beams of cold, yellow light, while, at the edge of the light, the dark silhouettes of an ill-defined cluster of trees could be vaguely guessed at. Absorbed by the spectacle ahead of them, the bipeds on the rumbler's back remained oblivious to Makhulu's arrival.

The strong smell of buffalo meat reached his muzzle.

He lowered himself some more – so low that he could feel his belly gather dirt – and carefully stalked forward while using the big mass of the rumbler for cover. He was very close now. Had he wanted to, he could have leaped up and snatch one of the unsuspecting bipeds from behind, like a bird. Instead, he rounded the beast's square muzzle in three quick steps and turned his attention toward the carcass ahead. As he crossed the beams of light, the intensity of the glare burned at the corner of his left eye and a collective gasp rose out of the bipeds' throats.

Alerted by the sudden commotion, the hyenas froze in disbelief. Their eyes gleamed in the fake light. Fresh blood dribbled out of their muzzle.

The game was up.

He raised his head and let loose a joyous roar before barging through the hyena's clan like some gruesome apparition out of their worst nightmare. After a brief, half-hearted attempt at standing their ground – for honor's sake, perhaps – the hunters reached into their inner geese instinct and scattered to the four winds with short, outraged yelps. He chased them around the carcass, laughing at their anguish.

Amid the chaos, a half dozen stiffer huntresses attempted to mount an organized defense and gathered close together, flank against flank, in an intimidating display known as the beast-with-many-heads formation. Surprised, Makhulu stopped just long enough to look them over. Large ears held upright. Cocky growls. Defiant eyes. These were high society; a dominant core of experienced killers grouped around the alpha female. Probably the same girls who had brought the aging buffalo down in the first place, he reflected. An impressive feat for their kind. Moving as a single unit with their hackles bristling in unison, they stalked forward and threatened to mob him.

Makhulu felt the adrenalin whip at his heart and growled appreciatively. Were he a younger cat, he might have relented, but unfortunately for the valiant defenders this was not his first turn on the grass. He roared and barreled through them as one might a flock of birds, brushing off the pecking of their fangs even as he overturned the lead female with a cruel swipe of his front paw. She let loose a pitiful whimper and twisted out of his grip before escaping in a cloud of dust, shocked but unscathed except for a few shallow scratches – no real mercy, his forward momentum had betrayed him. The last of the hyenas followed her example and beat a hasty retreat. He sat down to better watch their short tails disappear in the fast-receding twilight. Two clans in total, he judged. Almost thirty individuals. And none of them had so much as stood a chance against him.

Straddling the bloody remains of his stolen prize, he pumped a series of lung-bursting roars out. To keep them running, he told himself. And because it felt good.

A trumpeting bellow answered his challenge, followed by a cavernous, rock-avalanche growl that seemed to come from the depth of the Earth itself. Something in Makhulu's nether region shrunk. Frozen in place, his throat suddenly dry and his whiskers tingling, he slowly rotated his head.

His pupils expanded so fast, they almost popped.

The clusters of trees had moved closer.

Swallowing down an urgent need to grow wings of his own, he willed himself still and focused his gaze. With his eyes no longer hindered by the beams of the rumbler, he was able to make out the shapes more clearly. A herd of elephants. They were looking straight at him.

Once again, his inner instinct argued in favor of flight. He was about to concede when, to his surprise, he found that he could not bring himself to give up the carcass. Not so easily. Not without a fight. This was not his hunger holding him in place – there were plenty of easier, safer ways for him to find meat – but some strange, new inner force. An indomitable spirit, prideful and fiery, for which the idea of turning tail was, quite simply, unthinkable. No matter the threat.

He returned the elephants' gaze.

The matriarch stomped forward and unleashed an ominous grunt that resonated through the deepest recesses of his belly. The rest of the herd followed her lead and the line advanced in unison, their powerful trunks swinging and snaking in front of his muzzle. Undeterred, he scuffed the ground and emptied his bladder all over the dead buffalo.

A shy voice inside his head declared that his stupidity would cost him his life. He silenced it.

The matriarch flared her ears and lifted her head up while casting her eyes down in a domineering gesture that seemed to growl: "I can see you! You small, small thing." The rumbler's lights caught on the white of her ivory and Makhulu instinctively took note of the smooth curve on the right tusk, more worn-down than the left. She was right-pawed like him. Should the attack come, either trunk or tusk, it would swoop down from his left. He prepared himself mentally for the swift leap to the side. right-tusked, in her case

Should it come to that, however, he had no plan for what he would do next. Maybe charge them, he thought. After all if one must die stupid, one might as well go all the way.

The matriarch's resolve weakened. Her trunk went to her right tusk, massaging it, then curled in front of her face in a nervous snake stance. Visible doubt gnawed at her confidence. Angered and confused by the much smaller cat's cold demeanor and lack of fear at her advance, she retreated slowly and melted herself back inside the protective line of grey flesh.

The rest of the herd furiously trumpeted its objection but the indignant bellows had lost their ominous edge. Against all logic, something invisible had shifted in Makhulu's favor. The elephants had lost their footing.

Amazed at his own recklessness, feeling his paws grow numb even as the thunder in his chest rose and raged inside his ribcage, he strode forward, shoulders bulging, his head held high. He roared once more. "I can see you too, you big, big thing! And I am not afraid!"

This was madness, of course. Sweet, delicious madness. The morning sun peeked over the horizon and set his soaked fur ablaze with a thousand pearl-shaped glimmers. An insane chuckle escaped his throat.

This was, quite simply, perfect.

The spectacle proved too much for the pachyderms. Too strange. With short growls that sounded very much like insults, they retreated backward and trundled away. Once far enough, a younger member, little more than a calf, bravely turned around and trumpeted his challenge with his trunk held high. Makhulu laughed and roared back. The calf squealed and ran for the protection of the adults.

He watched them disappear with a pang in his heart. A new kind of chill crept over him. Moments ago, the stand-off had seemed to stretch on excruciatingly without end, each nervous heartbeat possibly his last, an entire lifespan in its own right. Now it was all over. He blinked and tried to wrap his mind around the sequence of events. Pin it down as he might a buffalo just so that he could hold it in front of his eyes and savor it a little while longer. It was no use. The whole thing was just one more memory now. Already the physical sensation had deserted him, replaced by an emptiness that ran bone-deep.

His brothers would never believe him. Not really. They would listen and nod politely, of course, not daring to question him openly, but internally they would be shaking their heads. Even if they did accept his story at face value, they would never be able to understand the true feeling. How *real* it had been.

A sudden spike of loneliness stabbed through his heart. His spirit sunk. His heart settled down. His shoulders sagged. It was all in vain. The coalition, the conquests, the prides, the mind-boggling, gigantic amount of energy spent pushing ever further beyond the horizon. Even the countless murders. All of it a result of his pathetic need to reassure himself that he actually belonged somewhere. That he was not alone. But of course he was. Always had been. Always would be. For all his successes, he was still the same lonely lion who had wandered in exile all those seasons ago.

He turned back toward the carcass and tried a few bites but found no satisfaction in the juicy flesh. Behind him, the clickety-chirps of the rumbler's bipeds rose in intensity. The gigantic beast lurched forward and came to an abrupt stop at an angle from the carcass, the lone biped on its snout bobbing precariously.

He rose and shook his mane before scampering away at a brisk pace to ensure that the rumbler would not follow. He would cut the end of his patrol short, he decided. He desperately needed to feel the touch of another cat.

The sun soared and chased the chill away. He slowed down and panted lightly to cool himself down. As the veld slowly came alive all around him, his spirit rose.

His brothers could never hope to understand the beauty of the moment, true enough, but they would still be sick with jealousy once they heard the tale. Shaka, especially, would eat his own tail and sink into despair at the idea of having missed such a lionlike moment. After some loud antics and denials, the honor-obsessed lion would come back and ask for the story again, his spirit consumed by the awesomeness of the event like a moth by a flame. T. would most likely try to seek refuge behind his usual half-snarl and rigid self-control but he would also train those penetrating eyes of his on Makhulu's face as if he were the only lion who could understand how he felt, which maybe he was. The others would quip and laugh and call him a crazy cat, a proper mad-mane, an absolute unit of a Big Mak. Understanding nothing, they would give worth to everything.

He was well inside the Londolozi now. Somewhere amid the undulating hills, the Ottawa pride and his brothers were waiting for him. He let loose a few calling roars and waited for the reply that would guide him.

Nothing.

He angled toward a tree island in the distance, rounded it, tried again. His bellows sent a family of baboons scrambling for the protection of a tree, but no reply. This was strange. He was quite sure that his roars were carrying far enough. One of the cats, at least, ought to be able to hear him and give him a beacon to zero-in on. Maybe they had left the Londolozi for some reason. Gone on patrol somewhere.

No, there were cubs with the Ottawa, they knew that they had to keep a relatively close watch.

The cubs...

Something just wasn't right. A sense of urgency gripped his vitals. He picked up the pace, his trot now restless, his swerving course more purposeful. He kept his muzzle to the dirt and sucked in the scents so as to build a construct of the events that had transpired over the past few days.

The picture was blurry, incomplete, and layered through time like the colorful stripes of a rocky outcrop. A lonely hyena had crossed the area a few nights ago and left her mark for others to follow, like a scent-road. A jackal had given birth nearby, probably in an underground den somewhere. An antelope had been assaulted, bled to death, then dragged off; he followed the thin grooves left by her hooves and found her skeleton stuck in-between two boughs up in a large acacia tree. The leopard responsible, a male, had left a single soft scat at the base of the trunk no later than this very dawn.

Makhulu growled in anger. None of this was of any interest to him. Trying to scan the whole of the Londolozi haphazardly like this was pointless, he had to come up with a better method.

While he was on far patrol his brothers had been in charge of keeping the Mapogo scent fresh inside the inner territory. No matter what else might have happened, they would never have been so derelict as to neglect such a task, not while they were still inside the Londolozi. If he could find a marked tree, he would at least have some idea of how recent their last passage had been.

Galloping, he rushed from one promising spot to the next, favoring tall trees and lush, green bushes. On the third attempt he struck paydirt. A lion's scent had been sprayed quite liberally at the foot of a thornbush. He recognized the scuff marks on the ground, deeper than necessary. This was T.'s doing, he was quite sure of it. He licked the darker patch of dirt and found it still moist.

Perplexed, he raised his head and pushed out another roar. This time he let his anger show behind the bellows. Unless the young cat had somehow figured out how to fly, he was still in the vicinity. And Makhulu was willing to bet his scrotum under a buffalo's hoof that the others were with him as well. They *had* to be able to hear him.

So why, by the sweet stench of rotten grass, were they not roaring back?

When no answer came, again, he lowered his muzzle and painstakingly scanned the area around the thornbush with the cold resolve of a lion who knows that he is being played and doesn't like it one bit. He uncovered a hint of a pawprint and launched himself in the general direction of his brother's trail, the taste of T.'s scent still lingering on the tip of his tongue.

Munching on dark thoughts, he crested a small ridge and let his gaze scour the savannah ahead. Just when he was about to call again, a new scent wafted to his nostrils, some faint putrefaction mingled with dry grass and lion scat. The taste of freshly-spilled blood tickled his palate.

He broke into a gallop with his muzzle suspended in the breeze, as if reeled-in by some invisible spider line.

He found him – her? it? he could not really tell – prostrated on a patch of rigid, yellow grass with his tiny muzzle covered in brown dirt and his front paws curled against what remained of his chest. A column of industrious ants had already cleared a path all the way to the carcass and were now mingling atop the enormous prize, seemingly lost in the forest of dirty, disheveled hair. A lone vulture sashayed nearby, his head bobbing, his clawed feet shuffling hesitantly. Makhulu growled and the heavy flapping of the bird's departure momentarily filled the air.

Working through his inner daze, he turned his attention back to the small ruin of flesh lying at his feet. The cub's head was resting at an impossible angle. The twisted neck, swollen on one side, seemed poised to overflow his small shoulder. A single puncture wound, bustling with ants, was visible above the right eye. Underneath the torn ribs, the bottom half was gone.

A high-pitched whine escaped his throat, like the constricting of a small animal living inside his chest. He gasped and almost collapsed. After righting himself with some difficulties, he scanned the grass for the other half. That was the only thing that mattered. He had to find it. Put the whole thing back together, somehow. That was his cub who had been murdered. His own cub. He owed it to him.

Her.

It.

The search proved fruitless and he soon found himself standing in front of to the accusing carrion again. The small body moved in one rigid, lifeless block under the stroking of his clumsy paw. His gaze caught on a protruding vertebra where a shallow groove could be discerned, its size an exact match for a lion's fang.

A weight dropped inside his guts and sapped the strength out of his back legs. A pitiful moan emptied his lung. Breathing heavily through taut muscles, he collapsed down on his haunches, like a tree undone by lightning. His jaws clenched.

This…insanity had been done openly, in broad daylight. The cat had not even bothered to cover his tracks afterward. He could see the trail of blood left in the wake of his departure.

"T!" he roared. "T! T! Teeeeeeeeeeeeeeee!!!!!!!"

He straightened himself up and leaped after the trail, still roaring but no longer concerned by the lack of replies. Let him hide and squirm in silence if he wanted to. That would not save him. Nothing could.

A brusque, hoarse bellow barked a reply. He ran it up to the source and found Defiant planted on her haunches near a large acacia, her body halfway outside the circle of shade as though she had failed to notice that the sun had moved.

"Where are they?" he growled.

She tilted her head and let her empty eyes fall on him, her posture stiff, haunted. "Where have you been?" she breathed out. Underneath the shock, he could discern the barely suppressed white-hot rage. Before he could come up with a reply, she sniggered loudly in a way that sounded somewhat less than sane. "Doesn't matter much now anyway. The deed is done. What is it that you guys always say? Cold blood spilled on the far side of grass? Well it is spilled alright, but maybe not nearly as far as you might have liked."

"Why didn't you fight?" he spat, tasting the poison in his words, the injustice of it, not caring.

"Don't you fucking dare," she hissed. "We tried to hold them off with everything we had. And we called for you. *I* called for you. But of course you were nowhere to be seen. Proud, honorable Makhulu! Always venturing out on far patrol to protect us from outsiders! Little does he suspect, while he fights off monsters and shadows, his own brothers are gutting us from the inside." She sucked in her breath then concluded, dejected: "We should never have agreed to surrender to you."

"You didn't have a choice then, and you still don't now. How many cubs did you lose?"

"Why, *Big Mak*, that's a stupid question. When have you ever known your beloved brothers to be anything less than thorough?"

It took a couple of heartbeats for Makhulu to process the cruel sentence. "All of them?" he gasped.

"We tried to hide them as best we could. We really did. But your brother found them all the same. Didn't take him very long either."

"Which one?"

"The cold cat with the stiff spine and the zebra mane. You know the one. The degenerate."

"Where are they now?"

"Why do you care? They're your own brothers, after all. And there's five of them. What are you going to do?"

"Never mind that," he low-growled, "just answer the question."

The truth was, he had no idea what he would do. The rage throbbing inside him, all the way down to the far recesses of his chest, was far too wild for him to think rationally, let alone formulate any kind of plan. All he knew was that he needed to lay eyes on the cats. Confront them. Then he would know.

She pointed her muzzle in the direction of a far away, hazy tree. "They already know you're here."

He left without a word.

The tree grew and turned into a stout, multi-trunked baobab with naked branches that looked like sprawled-out roots. At its base, the five lions were lying down, waiting. Even at a distance he could see that they were restless.

He roared, and they stood up. Not in a jump but with the slow, deliberate movements of those who know that they must set themselves to an unpleasant, dangerous task. The twins took the center while Shaka and Dreadlocks positioned themselves on either side, slightly withdrawn and ready to flank. The memory of Blondie's last moments briefly flashed in front of Makhulu's eyes. He pushed it away.

At his approach, T. slunk halfway behind the trunk.

"You," Makhulu breathed out. "You did this."

T.'s eyes grew wide. Growling, Makhulu shoved a dumbstruck Shaka to the side as if he were a mere hyena and leaped toward the smaller cat. Dreadlocks interposed himself and ruefully shouldered him aside. He landed at the foot of the trunk and wheeled in place with his back to the tree, his fangs bared.

"It wasn't him!" Dreadlocks gasped. "I mean, it wasn't just him. We all did it."

"No, you didn't. Not all of you. No!"

Skoro stepped forward with throbs in his voice. "He's telling you the truth, Mak. We killed your little ones. All of us. We murdered them when you were gone."

Something in the way he said it, whether it was the pitiless, unadorned statement of the monstrous fact or the seemingly genuine sadness that came with it, pierced through Makhulu's heart. Reeling from an invisible blow, he stepped back, temporally defanged. "Why?" he croaked. "How could you... Skoro...Why?!"

The lion choked and averted his gaze. Dreadlocks stepped in his place. "You left us no other choice. You've covered all the girls without leaving any lionesses for us to mate. We've grown too, Mak. We have needs, same as you."

"You have...needs. My cubs are dead, you killed them, because you have *needs*?"

All of a sudden, it was too much for him to bear. Too grotesque. Roaring at the top of his lungs, he lunged forward and lashed at the muzzle of the broad-chested lion he had once called his brother.

Dreadlocks tried to meet his attack head-on but Makhulu was too fast for him. Feinting toward the right, he leaped to the left and sunk his teeth in the back of the lion's mane before overturning him with one strong shove of his front paws. Dreadlocks screamed and kicked frantically, his belly exposed. Skoro instinctively rushed to his defense and tried to assault Makhulu's back but his attack was hesitant, half-hearted. Makhulu easily pushed him off and slapped his muzzle to the side with one almighty paw that sent the shocked lion stumbling away. Leonides cursed and lunged for Makhulu's right ear. He dodged and bit through the clumsy front paw. Leonides howled in pain and backtracked. Out of the corner of his eyes, Makhulu noticed that Dreadlocks was getting back up again. Before the broad-chested cat had time to gather his strength and wits, he body-slammed him at full speed. Dreadlocks groaned and went sprawling through the grass.

Makhulu picked himself up with a numb shoulder and was immediately greeted by Shaka's frontal attack. The smart lion had timed his assault perfectly. His jaws closed around Makhulu's muzzle and his fangs cut through the black of his lips. Pushing through the pain, Makhulu charged ahead and drove Shaka all the way back to the baobab. The lion's back-paws frantically clawed at the trunk in search of a grip on which he could stand and resist but Makhulu's drive was too powerful for him to overcome. After a strange, half-aborted somersault move, he was forced on his back. Makhulu tore himself away from the fangs and bit through the thick of his mane. Then he used his paws to pound Shaka's head into the root-woven dirt. The lion groaned, jumped on his feet, stepped away.

Makhulu let him go and whirled to face T.

"It wasn't just me," hissed the smaller lion. "You really want to do this for a bunch of cubs?" His shoulders were hunched, his legs tense. There was no rage in him, no discernible fear either. Only a bottomless sadness and a hard resolve. Somehow, Makhulu knew, this would be a different kind of fight altogether.

That undid him.

Stumbling like an oaf, panting hard, he took a couple of steps back, dazed. The shoulder that had impacted Dreadlocks was now throbbing with a dull pain. Blood trickled out of the lip Shaka had cut and mingled with his saliva. He spat it out and watched it seep into the brown-red dirt underneath his paws. It looked like cub's blood.

"I trusted you!" he roared suddenly. "All of you! You were my brothers and I loved you. I would have died for any one of you. Ten times over I would have!" The roars devolved into a high-pitched wail. "How could you do this to me? To your own blood?!"

Dreadlocks tried to find something to say, came up short, closed his mouth. The others seemed to wish they could turn themselves invisible.

Makhulu winced in pain and limped away.

The hated tree disappeared behind the horizon. He found himself wandering aimlessly, alone yet again. Never had the veld felt so empty before, so mercilessly silent and cold-hearted. He was feeling unbearably old all of a sudden, stretched beyond his strength, spent. He dropped down on a spot of no particular importance and strived to drive the lonesomeness out of his heart by absorbing himself in the mundane task of cleaning his paws and fur, one slow, methodical, self-soothing stroke of his tongue after the next.

The steady movements rocked his mind and calmed his heart. He collapsed into a fitful sleep.

He awoke at dusk and squinted against the weak glare of the setting sun. Slanted rays of orange light shone on T.’s silhouette standing next to him.

“What do you want?” he growled, suddenly alert.

T. lowered his muzzle in an appeasing gesture. “Jus’ wanna talk, is all. I’ that’s alrigh’ wit’ya.”

Makhulu sucked in his breath and made a conscious effort to remind himself that T.’s mumbling and off-beat accent were both parts of a character that he liked to channel whenever he was nervous. He did not need to ask from which cat he had borrowed the idea.

He yawned to smell the air – the two of them were alone – and licked his muzzle to drive the last of the sleep away. Then he nodded his head curtly.

T. swallowed down his saliva and laid himself down with his flank pressed tight against Makhulu’s belly and his spine ostentatiously exposed. After a few heavy breaths, he found his tongue. “I ain’t gonna deny wha’ we did wasn’t hard. O’ course it was. An’ ya had ‘very right to react the way ya did.”

Wrong way round

Makhulu groaned. His brother’s rough manner of speech was intermittent, as if linked to the wild skipping of his heart.

“But none o’ tha’ change the fac’ that we love you, Mak. Truly, we do. Wha’ we did… Well, however cruel it migh’ seem to ya, wha’ we did wasn’t no slight aim’ at ya. It was strictly abou‘ gettin’ the girls.”

“You’re saying that I shouldn’t take it personally? That killing my cubs was just…what? Another hunt?” He had a hard time keeping his temper in check but he made an effort. “Forget about my feelings. What about yours? I can’t even understand how you guys found it in yourselves to do what you did. You murdered your own kind without batting an eye. What lions even do that? What bottomless abyss did you guys reach into? And how could you possibly do it without hating me at least on some repressed level?”

T. shrugged. In the sinking orange light, his shoulders suddenly appeared taller, his hardened face etched in red stone, with a warm fiery hue wrapped around his mane. Had Makhulu not known better, he would have sworn that, at this moment, his brother was wise.

“You don’t need hatred to kill,” the young lion said, his mumbling forgotten. “It was just the logical thing to do.”

"Logical?"

"We're social killers, Mak. As lions, we crave for each other's company because, unlike the lonely cheetah or the elusive leopard, we can't go without the touch of another cat for very long, not without feeling empty inside. We need the bound. But we're also hunters and killers. Very much so. The taste of blood, the instinct to solve a problem, *any* problem, in the most straightforward and simplest way possible is always there, lurking. Once you've sharpened that instinct and gotten used to bringing grazers down to satiate your stomach, the idea to kill another lion to satisfy another need comes easily. It's just the next step in a logical progression, you know this better than me. Wander-males, lionesses, cubs, it makes no difference. Death is death, a potent tool at any cat's disposal, if somewhat crude. When we killed your young ones, we were not trying to challenge you or upset you in any way. We were not acting out of spite or rage or any kind of emotion either. We were simply trying to solve a difficult situation the most straightforward and definitive way possible. A difficult situation, I should add, however painful it might be for you to hear, that you forced us into."

"That's a nice speech. Did you rehearse it before coming here?"

T. flashed his half-snarl. "You know I did."

"Alright, I'll bite. So where does it end? Foreign males and lionesses, I can understand. I never liked wasting females much but I can't pretend that I had too many qualms about what we did either. Clearly our own cubs are also fair game now. Alright. So what's next? Brothers? Like this morning for instance, would you have killed me?"

The answer came fast, unequivocal: "Yes. Either that or you would have killed me. No hatred, just a problem that needed solving. Still needs solving, actually. That's why I am here. I'd like to see if the both of us can come to some sort of a mutual understanding that would get us out of this rut. I have already discussed it with the others and they have agreed to it on principle, so long as you do too."

"Go on," Makhulu groaned. He was intrigued. Clearly they still wanted him in the coalition, but how could they possibly expect him to come back?

"Alright, here's the idea: from now on we all agree that, as far as killing is concerned, brothers are where we draw the line. Everything else is fair game. Whenever we have a disagreement among ourselves, we fight but we stop short of the spine. Whoever wins the contest on any given day gets what he wants and the other cat must relinquish his claim. That means that you won't be the dominant male any longer."

Makhulu glared at him. He should have known that some sort of catch was coming.

"In truth," T. hurried to add, "there won't be any dominant cat at all. Not in this coalition. Everyone will have a chance to triumph on any given day."

"An equilibrium born out of chaos," Makhulu mused out loud. He was genuinely impressed.

"Exactly. No standing hierarchy. Each new issue is settled on the spot by the two parties pulling in the direction of their own interest until the stronger one prevails and the weaker one relents. Like a hunt, but without the death at the end."

"And you're the one who thought of this?"

T. nodded. "That's the way things work above grass, the only kind of equilibrium worth anything. And the only way this coalition stays together. We won't accept anything less, Mak. If you can't agree to it then I guess we'll all have to go our separate ways."

This was bold, even for T.

Suddenly, it occurred to Makhulu that none of his brothers had offered any kind of apologies for what they had done. And now they were dictating terms to him as if he were the one asking to come back to the group. "You seem overly sure of yourself," he growled, savoring the unease he could see spreading on T.'s face. "What makes you think that I'll let any of you go? Why shouldn't I just finish what I started this morning?"

As T. pondered his reply, his half-snarl made another appearance. He relaxed and snuggled his head against Makhulu's belly. "You're forgetting that I've seen you fight this morning, big cat. You went through the five of them like an elephant charging through a pack of hyenas."

Funny, that.

"My point exactly," he said out loud. "And I can do it again."

"And yet, with all that speed, all that power, you didn't inflict a single spine-bite. Getting sloppy?"

Makhulu clenched his jaws tight and remained quiet.

"You don't want to kill us any more than we want to kill you," T. continued, confident in his own reasoning. "I think that, deep down, you just want to come back to the coalition and put all this mess behind you as bad as we do. You know why we did what we did. You know that we won't apologize for it. But you also know that it had nothing to do with disrespecting you. We all agree that you're still the best of us. So now it's really just your ego getting in the way. You're afraid of what the Ottawa girls might say if you rejoin us."

"Well? What will they say?"

"I haven't got the slightest idea, and I don't care. That's one of the good things about being a lion, you don't have to concern yourself with other cats' opinions too much."

Truly, this was a day for bold cats. Try as he might, Makhulu could not deny that his younger brother had hit the mark. He *did* want to rejoin the Mapogos. The very idea of being alone, again, was more than he could stomach. And now his brothers were showing him a way back he could follow without losing face or accepting defeat. He would not be dominant anymore, true, but he had never really cared about that. The hierarchy had just come to him naturally as an unspoken matter of fact, because he was the elder, stronger, bigger lion. Now he would be one among equals. A peer. He could live with that.

As for the cubs.... Well, there was nothing he could do for them anymore.

He sighed as he realized that his decision had already been made a few heartbeats ago. "Of course," he said, intent on having the last word, "you guys understand that in this new chaotic order of ours, I'll be coming out on top more often than not."

"We would expect nothing less, Big Mak," T. growled happily. "Nothing less."

SEVENTEEN

THE LOST PRIDE

"Nothing? You're sure?"

Skoro squinted his tired eyes and scoured the horizon one last time. The heat haze played tricks on his pupils and turned every fuzzy patch of yellow grass into a resting lion, every waving tree into a walking cat.

Behind him, he could hear Leonides tearing himself a path through the dense underbrush. They had left the leopard hills a half-dozen dawns ago and pushed through what he guessed was now the Ulusaba area, the edge of the territory where the Mapogo roar still ruled. He had never personally trodden on this dirt and was unfamiliar with the new landscape.

"No," he finally said. "I don't think they went that way."

Leonides extricated himself from the grasp of the thorns and carefully sniffed the ground. "Not a scent," he muttered in disbelief. "Not even a hint of a cold trail."

"I'm telling you, we must have missed them further back."

"You think they're hiding from us?"

"It's possible. They clearly don't want to share their kills with us. And they're probably stressed for the male subs as well, so they're being evasive. It won't last."

"I guess maybe we were a bit rough on those belly-manes."

"Don't worry, as soon as they feel threatened by some wandering cat, they'll come crawling right back under the Mapogo shadow. They need us."

Leonides nodded and licked his rhinarium, unconvinced. His gaze swiveled toward the horizon. "A whole pride gone without a trace," he whispered. "Two huntresses and five sub-adults, including three males. That's not exactly like losing a lone cub. You don't think anything could have happened to them, do you?"

"Like what?"

"I don't know. *Something.*"

Skoro shook his head. "We would have heard the roars and calls for help. Those girls are not stupid."

Although, to be fair, one could never be too sure with the Sand River pride. Those were some peculiar cats, strong-headed and prompt to roam. According to rumors, seven members of the pride had already vanished in a similar fashion shortly before the Mapogos' takeover. Skoro was half-convinced that the girls had created the whole tale out of thin air so as to cover the escape of their sisters, but in light of recent events he had to admit that he could not be certain.

"You want to keep pushing?" asked Leonides.

He sighed.

And to think that he had been eager to leave. After countless moons spent patrolling the same territory, the search for the lost pride had offered a much-needed break from his tedious routine. A refreshing challenge which he had embraced with all the energy of a young belly-mane. Without any obvious trail or scent to follow, they had settled on a meandering course toward the general direction of the sunset, their light trot punctuated by a few intermittent calling roars. At first he had not been overly worried about their chances of success and had expected the reply from the wayward cats to come fairly quickly. Even a few begrudged grunts would have been enough. Barring that – some lionesses' stubbornness could verge on stupidity sometimes – he had still been supremely confident in their ability to pick up the noise and scent of one of the lioness' kills. All lions need to eat, and buffaloes don't tend to die quietly.

This had been a dozen dawns ago.

Now, as he stood on yet another foreign hill without the slightest idea on which course they should pursue next, he had to admit that his confidence had gone the way of trickling blood in the loose dirt. His paws were numb, his legs stiff, his mind jaded. Worse, his muzzle ached for the familiar scents of the Londolozi and the Singita. He could feel their absence inside him, like a hole in his chest.

His puzzlement had grown to a level matched only by his frustration. They had called and cajoled, cursed and threatened. Nothing. Not a sound. They had chased after every single carcass rotting under the sun in hope of stumbling upon one of their kills – quite the ordeal, in a land full of hyenas, leopards, and other meat-stealing vermin – only to come up empty. At a loss of idea, they had kept searching mindlessly, to no avail.

The Sand River pride had, quite simply, vanished into thin air.

"We should go back," he finally said. "We've been gone too long."

"And the Sand River girls?"

"We did everything we could. If they don't want to be found, that's fine by me. They can all rot under the grass for all I care." He turned his back on the horizon and made for the thornbush they had just crossed. "You're coming?"

Leonides did not react immediately. His gaze was following a vulture hovering far above the mottled savannah. "I really thought that we would reach it this time," he said. "But there is still so much more to explore."

"Huh?"

"The far side, I mean. I thought that if we pushed far enough through the Ulusaba, we would finally catch a glimpse of the edge. It can't be much further now." There was something of despair and immense regret in his twin's voice, as if he no longer believed his dream to be feasible.

"We can keep looking if you want," Skoro blurted out. "There is nothing tying us back to the others. We don't have to turn back at all."

Even as he said the words, he felt the lassitude in his legs' muscles groan its dissent. But if Leonides wanted to keep exploring he would push ahead with him. He knew he would.

His twin considered the offer for a brief instant. "Nah," he finally said, his eyes downcast. "I'm drained too. We'll try again some other time. No need to rush anything, right?"

"No need at all."

Leonides scuffed the ground, lay down his scent – "For when we want to find our way back here," – and abruptly tore himself away from the tantalizing view. Skoro followed behind his tail.

"It would have been glorious, though," his twin said after a brief silence. They had skirted the thornbush and were trotting over some easy meadows. "Imagine: we find the runaway girls, bring them back to the coalition, and then casually brag about reaching the end of grass to Makhulu and the others around a nice, fat buffalo." He giggled softly. "Think about Shaka's face."

"Poor cat would've shrunk on the spot. Makhulu's elephant story was already hard enough for him to swallow. On this, he would have choked."

They laughed together and Leonides' big, hearty guffaws chased a herd of antelope out of a nearby cluster of trees. Skoro stopped and took the time to appreciate the grace of the slender grazers bouncing away at their approach like so many giant grasshoppers. He was growing hungry, he realized.

"In the end, we didn't even make a dent in it."

"A dent?"

"In the horizon. It hasn't move one bit. If anything, it looked further away on that last hill than when we started."

That was true enough. For reasons Skoro could not explain, the world had felt bigger at the Ulusaba. Indomitable. He told himself that it was only a side effect of being starved and exhausted while treading on new grounds.

"Maybe that's what swallowed the Sand River pride," mused Leonides. "The horizon got them."

Skoro had nothing to reply so he kept quiet.

"You wouldn't have seen his face anyway," he said after a little while, eager to break the river of thought that, he knew, was running wild inside his twin's head.

Leonides gave him an inquisitive look.

"Shaka," he insisted, "even if you had reached the far side of grass and come back to tell the tale, Shaka probably wouldn't have been there to hear it. He and T. are spending all their days with the Tsalala pride now. They even have cubs of their own."

Leonides chuckled. The idea of T. being a father was incongruous enough to chase the gloom out of his spirit. "I guess the feisty cat got tired of losing against the Big Mak all the time. Some distance will do him so good."

Skoro nodded. Ever since the Ottawa cubs affair and the new, mutually agreed-upon order of things, casual fighting among the coalition had become the norm. For food and mating rights, mostly, but also just for the fun of it. In the absence of other rival males to kill this was a good way to let their cat's temper flare out and keep their fighting skills sharp. And since Makhulu was not the dominant male any longer, this was not considered a challenge to his authority. However, as usual, T. had taken things to another level. His attacks were more frequent, less warranted, and almost exclusively aimed at Makhulu. Unfortunately for him, dominant or not, the elder lion still had the overwhelming physical advantage, and T.'s assaults, while brave and relentless, often had all the puzzling appearance of a kitten ramming himself against a tree. Maybe Leonides was right. Maybe it wasn't such a bad idea for their brother to finally put a couple of horizons between him and Mak.

They broke into a canter and raced each other around the trees while searching for the odd leopard or hyena to kill. Their luck failed them but at dusk they stumbled upon a lone Dagga Boy and brought him down with an uncommon, thirsty savagery that betrayed their homesickness. Beyond their hunger, they knew that they also needed to feel the familiar taste of blood on their palate.

They fed on the bull for the better part of three days. Then, on a whim, they trotted out of the Ulusaba and swerved toward the Inyati.

One night, Leonides picked up a scent and immediately scurried away without a word. Skoro only had time to catch a glimpse

some

cubs

palates

Human name

of the tuft of his tail snaking through the grey grass before he disappeared.

"What is it?" he asked in a hushed voice as he leaped after him.

His brother ignored him.

Intrigued, Skoro sniffed the air. Outside of the usual dry smell of grown grass and the occasional nugget of a grazer's dropping, nothing tickled his interest. Their course seemed random, full of abrupt twists and wild swerves, as if they were chasing after a fleeing snake. Leonides' body language was clearly conveying deep focus but after struggling to keep up for what he felt was a sizeable chunk of the night, Skoro had to wonder if his twin was not playing some kind of elaborate prank on him. He was about to call him out on it when, suddenly, Leonides froze and sat down on his haunches, slightly out of breath, his eyes gleaming victoriously under the soft twilight of the dense meadow of stars.

"What do you see?" whispered Skoro.

His twin pointed his muzzle toward the base of a jagged acacia stump. A chorus of short, high-pitched squeals reached their ears. A shaggy shadow briefly flashed in front of the stars before sinking back under the protection of the stump's darkness. It took a moment for Skoro's cat eyes to adjust to the contrast.

It was some kind of hyena, he was sure of it, but it looked different from the spotted intruders he was accustomed to hunt and kill. Smaller, with a long, shaggy fur that pointed every which way on top of stick-thin legs, a shorter neck, and a body held close to the ground in a slightly less slanted posture than usual hyenas. In the tiny, forward-facing eyes, however, Skoro recognized the same jittery instinct that defined all those killers who were condemned to perpetually walk that thin line between being the hunter and the hunted.

They are not hunted!

"Leon," he whispered, "what are we looking at?"

"The Ottawa girls told me about these. They're called brown hyenas. Very hard to find. Always extremely discreet. They roam alone, you see, and can cover great distances for their food."

"The Ottawa lionesses told you this?"

Leonides nodded. "They hunt them for sport when they can. They told me it makes for a more challenging track."

He fell quiet, lost in his observation.

Animals never hunt for sport. Lions kill other predators to reduce competition and protect their young.

"Well this one is not alone at all," remarked Skoro.

At the feet of the hyena, a collection of pups' heads could be seen protruding out of a burrow. Their endless romping was the source of the squeals.

"It's a communal den. That's where all the clan keeps its young."

"The clan? I thought you said they were solitary creatures."

"They are, most of the time. Their society is stretched across the grass and linked via scent-trails they create to find each other when they want to. It's like a giant spider-web they can follow without attracting attention. The Ottawa girls call it 'pasting'. That's how I found the den. Once you know it, the smell is quite easy to recognize. But the spots are few and far between, almost impossible to follow back to the source if you don't know the layout. That's why I had to zigzag so much."

Skoro wasn't sure how he felt about this. He was used to seeing hyenas and leopards as occasional intruders passing through his territory; annoying squatters who had to be chased away on a regular basis like wander-males, or ticks. But this was different. An invisible circuit of organized trails permanently crisscrossing his territory right under his muzzle? This required an answer.

"It makes you wonder," muttered Leonides.

"About what?"

"We think we own the land because we've claimed it, but there is always so much more hidden under the surface of grass. Worlds within worlds within worlds. To them, we must look like elephants. Big things they cannot remove and must learn to evade and live with quietly."

Skoro snorted. His brother was not making any sense. "It will be a cold day under the afternoon sun before any elephant scares me out of my roar or forces me to live like a meerkat inside a hole."

"Still, you can't deny that there is so much more to our territory than we can ever hope to control. What does an ant care for a lion's roar? Our strength has its limits, Skoro, and even the most powerful paw cannot kill what it cannot reach. Those brown hyenas know it. They're perfectly aware that they can't go head-to-head against us. But far from relinquishing their claim to this patch of grass, like any sane cat would, they've adapted their behavior to circumvent our patrols in the most ingenuous way. Kind of like how we've learned to go around a wildfire ourselves."

"Maybe, but as long as we are the ones standing upright under the sun and they're the ones slinking in the shadows, I'd say we're still the superior beings."

Leonides nodded his head tiredly, almost dismissively, and returned his attention to the hyena's den. He seemed to have given up trying to convey his point, as if he had decided that his twin was too dense to understand.

"What are you trying to say?" barked Skoro.

The hyena jumped on her feet, her fur electric. They dropped to the ground and flattened themselves behind a dense bush. She trotted in their direction and stopped a few steps away from their hiding spot. Skoro held his breath, not entirely sure why he felt the need to hide from this smaller predator, doing it anyway, for his brother's sake. Something in the back of his mind immediately informed him that the breeze was working in their favor. But the hyena was close and he had no idea how good her eyesight was in the darkness.

Finally, she seemed to relax. The pups timidly re-emerged out of the burrow and she scampered back to the stump. Leonides sighed in relief.

"I don't know that I have any kind of point, really," he whispered. "Only that our grasp on things might be far more tenuous than what we're inclined to believe. The veld is too complex. T. always talk about life being a river without a shore; he claims that, as long as you keep on swimming, you're fine. Maybe so. But then it's also fair to say that there are crocodiles swimming in the depth of that water, and many other unknown things no lion can predict."

Skoro shrugged, unconvinced. He was a Mapogo lion, a member of a coalition of six, with access to more female than he could count. If that wasn't enough to have a good grasp on things, he didn't know what was. As for crocodiles, he had outgrown his juvenile fear of them a long time ago. Even won a tug of war over a gnu against one of the putrid long-nose once. He knew the strength of his shoulders and was not afraid of any unknown things lurking in the depth of anything.

All of Leonides' rambling about their hold over the savannah being an illusion was nonsense. For proof, they had found the hyena's den. Smart as they may be, an entire generation of the overgrown, disheveled, rat-like killers was now at the mercy of their fangs. Maybe it was time to remind his twin about the virtue of good old-fashion lion action.

"Lions may not have a say in the growth of every single blade of grass in the Sabi Sands," he whispered as he stalked forward, "but they sure know how to get things done when needed. Shall we?"

"No, wait," hissed Leonides. He leaped forward and interposed himself as quietly as possible.

Skoro drew himself up, outraged.

"Better to let them be," Leonides insisted, his hushed voice spitting the words out precipitously. "They're far too rare to kill. Too precious."

"Leon…they're intruders. Vermin."

"They're cunning, resilient, and discreet. Think of all the places where they've roamed, all the things they've seen, far more than any of us can even imagine. They've earned the right to be spared."

"Not if we can find them and catch them, they haven't."

"Skoro please, just trust me on this one alright?"

Unaware of the debate unfolding a single leap away from her neck, the brown hyena laid herself down on her flank. Two pups came to suckle at her tits.

"Wait. You don't actually think that she's better than us, do you? I mean for grass' sake, look at her. She looks like a moving bush with a tiny rat head."

"Looks can be deceiving. In any case, we don't have to always kill kill kill everything we see."

We don't have to, but it sure is more fun that way.

Nevertheless, Skoro was not about to go against Leonides over this. If his twin wanted to spare the scrawny thing's life, so be it. He relented and they watched a little while longer before moving off on feather-paws, as quietly as they had come.

The remainder of their stay in the Inyati proved pleasant. They supplemented their diet of buffalo with gnus and zebras, which they often found grouped together. The zebras having the better eyesight and the gnus the better hearing and sense of smell, Skoro supposed that it made sense for the two species grazers to forge an alliance for better protection. But the cohabitation often looked quite shaky to his eyes, riddled with abrupt jerks of the head and nervous fits and starts. One particular incident, especially, had marked him. While still crouched low far away from the herd, unnoticed, they had witnessed a startled zebra kick a gnu straight into the head for seemingly no other reason than the grazer being, maybe, a little too close to him. The gnu had dropped to the ground without so much as a grunt of protest, like a tree, and the entire herd had scattered in panic, with the assaulting zebra making a show of joining the mad scramble so as to hide his guilt. Scarcely believing their luck, they had pounced on the opportunity and quickly suffocated the dazed antelope. Afterward, Leonides had reflected that it was probably the first time a zebra had participated in a lion's hunt in such a way.

Eventually, they left the Inyati and entered the Singita, the vast chunk of land that bordered the Londolozi. A familiar roar reached their ears.

"That's Dread alright," said Leonides.

"He sounds angry."

They traced the roar back to its source and settled on a low hill. Below and ahead, they found the broad-chested cat trudging in the middle of a shallow puddle roughly three times his size. A dead buffalo could be seen protruding out of the murky water next to him, his swollen flank and one curved horn rising above the brownish surface, the lower half of his belly opened wide and coated with mud. With his limbs extended stiffly toward the edge of the puddle, he looked as though he had been frozen while standing up and then tipped over.

A clan of around thirty hyenas surrounded the big lion and his prize.

Despite Dreadlocks most threatening bellows, growls, and promises of deaths to come, many of the scavengers had already begun feeding on the carcass from the opposite side of the buffalo, where they knew that the big cat could not reach them without first going around the mountain of meat. Others were taunting him from the safety of the firm ground, ready to bolt at the first sign of a leap.

Skoro and Leonides watched as their brother splashed around helplessly for a little while.

"Mine! Mine!" they heard him moan in-between two lunges at the greedy thieves. "Get off of here, it's mine!"

The hyenas evaded his attacks with ease. A few braver huntresses even nipped at his rump. With their bobbing head, short yelps, and playful leaps to the side, they seemed to be having the time of their life.

Dreadlocks, however, was not amused. His first instinct led him to leap inside the buffalo's open belly and grab as many bites as he could as fast as possible. Even from afar, Skoro could distinctly see the grazer's legs twitch back and forth under the tremors of his brother's feverish gnawing. Then Dreadlocks changed his mind and whirled back toward the scavengers swarming his prize on either side of him. They quickly scattered at his approach but made sure to remain tantalizingly close, on the edge of the pool and a mere few steps out of his reach.

Finally, unable to choose between two courses of action, feed or attack, Dreadlocks sagged down on his haunches in the middle of the puddle and watched numbly as more and more of his precious kill disappeared down the gullets of the swarming hyenas. The dark, glistening mud that completely covered his muzzle, legs, and belly seemed to accentuate the gold of his mane.

"My meat," they heard him whimper faintly. "That's my meat you're stealing!"

The sorrow in the big cat's voice went right through Skoro's heart.

"Tell me how cats are the superior beings again," said Leonides.

"That one might be the exception."

Still unaware of their presence, Dreadlocks finally turned his back on his buffalo and slowly heaved himself out of the pool with his tail between his legs, utterly dispirited. The hyenas followed his retreat and nipped at his rear. Twice he wheeled around in anger, but never managed to land a blow. As he reached hard ground, he made for a tree. Skoro noticed that he was limping severely.

"He's hurt his leg," he blurted out. "I've told him a thousand times not to go after a buffalo this size on his own."

"He wants to prove that he's just like the Big Mak," Leonides said, laconic. "That he's just as strong."

"Prove? To whom?"

"Himself, most likely."

Skoro shook his head.

Upon reaching the shade of the canopy, Dreadlocks laid himself down to catch his breath. His tongue absent-mindedly licked his muzzle, out of habit, and immediately recoiled at the taste of mud. Skoro let out a short calling roar. Their eyes crossed. The big cat found his paws again and proceeded to limp his way uphill. Perched on top of their newly-acquired prize, a few hyenas carefully followed his departure with wary eyes. Below them, the carcass was now completely covered by the clan's feeding frenzy.

"You guys could have helped," Dreadlocks complained as he reached them. His eyes were sparkling, there was no real pain in his voice.

Skoro went to greet him with a tentative head rub while doing his absolute best to avoid marring his fur with mud. He failed.

"We didn't want to interfere," said Leonides. "You seemed to have everything so well under control."

"Argh, the filthy bastards are relentless. When there's so many of them it's impossible to drive them off alone, it's like trying to swipe at water."

"Leon seems to think that we should leave them be. That they are better than us."

"I never said that."

Dreadlocks looked at the twins in puzzlement but did not inquire any further.

Skoro turned his attention back toward the puddle. The teeming scavengers had not lost any time; much of the carcass's flesh had already been consumed. With the thick black leather now fully peeled back and the flesh almost completely gone, the white of the bones and connecting tissue seemed to gleam under the warm sun. Far from being done, the boisterous thieves were now overflowing out of the hole and chasing after each other for the last scraps of juicy red.

"You want us to go back down with you and chase them off?" offered Leonides.

Dreadlocks sighed and made a gesture to dismiss the idea. "Under normal circumstances I'd say yes, of course; just for the principle of the thing if nothing else. But right now I can't be bothered. Besides, there really isn't much point getting the carcass back anymore, is there?"

Skoro nodded his head sadly. Hyenas were quite efficient in that regard, it was known. Soon not even the bones would be left. And that was without counting all the other scavengers.

As if on cue, he noticed two white-backed vultures hovering high above the kill. They glided down an invisible shrinking spiral and came into better focus: the rigid, sprawled-out wings; the tiny, seemingly naked head swiveling at the end of the crooked neck; finally, the eyes, fierce and serious, with their dry, no-nonsense pupils rapaciously locked onto their target. The pair landed on firm ground at the edge of the pool and hopped around with bobbing heads and half folded, nervous wings while waiting for an opening into the hyena's clan.

Skoro turned away.

After vigorously shaking himself off of some of the mud and splattering his two brothers in the process – on purpose, Skoro was quite sure – Dreadlocks lay down to clean his paws. "It's a shame really," he said in-between two licks. "That was a beautiful prize. By the grass, you should have seen the fight. He did not go down easily."

"You hurt your leg?"

"Yeah, he hooked me with his left horn. Very nearly flipped me upside down too." He shrugged. "I don't really mind. It's an honest wound. It will heal."

A rumbler suddenly came to life on the opposite side of the water hole, its huge body half hidden by the grass. After lurching forward in fits and starts, it stopped abruptly at the foot of the hill and presented its flank to the lions' gaze. Even at a distance, Skoro had the distinct impression that the bipeds on the back were looking at them.

"Has it been here the whole time?" asked Leonides.

Dreadlocks groaned. "Came right after the hyenas. Sometimes I have to wonder what attracts them. They sure don't seem interested in the meat or the grass."

"The water, maybe?"

"Then why isn't it drinking?"

Leonides had no answer to offer. None of them did. The reason behind the comings and goings of the rumblers were a mystery, a small drop in the never-ending river of unsolvable riddles the grass always seemed so found of producing for their stupefaction. A cat might as well try to figure out the workings of lightning.

Still, it was fun to let the question tickle your brain from time to time.

"I say that the bipeds are actually a part of the rumbler like leaves on a tree," Leonides declared.

"Nah, they move too much. Besides, they have eyes."

"So how come we practically never see them away from the rumbler?"

"Maybe they're scared."

"You're projecting. These are not lions; clearly, they can't feel fear or any other emotion."

Dreadlocks rolled on his back and presented his white belly to the sun. "I don't know about other emotions," he said, "but fear is of the flesh. If their body can produce adrenalin, then they know about the jolt and the poison, same as everyone else."

"What about rage?"

"Yes, that too. At least fear-induced rage, when the body spikes itself up to face a threat. Injustice-rage… I don't know."

"Alright, what about happiness and friendship? What about lust?"

"Or that feeling you get when you finally get rid of that piece of buffalo fat stuck behind your fang?"

Dreadlocks chuckled. "Alright, alright. I'm not saying that they are as emotionally developed as cats. Of course not. Their behavior is clearly not complex enough. But they're not mindless trees either. They must have some sort of personality and basic emotions; we just don't see it because they're so different from us. We can't relate."

Leonides was not convinced. "The smells are too strange. You talked about adrenalin. Fair enough. Did you ever smell it on one of them? Because I haven't."

"Maybe they're just not that afraid of you."

Skoro giggled and Leonides went to swipe his muzzle. He dodged easily and let himself fall next to Dreadlocks.

As though aware of their conversation and worried for the sanctity of its secrets, the rumbler awakened once more and turned itself around in that weird, wide-arc fashion common to its kind. After having emptied the gaseous content of its stomach – the strange smell drifted all the way to them and clung to their palate – the beast clumsily galumphed its way over the uneven terrain with the bipeds on its back swaying absurdly after every bump.

"Speaking of mysteries," said Dreadlocks. "Have you guys found the Sand River pride yet?"

"No," said Leonides. "Nothing. Not even the shadow of a cold trail."

"That's strange. And you checked the Ulusaba, yes?"

"Of course. Up, down, and sideways. No trace of them. You have an idea where they might have gone?"

The broad-chested cat made a casual gesture to dismiss the question. "Maybe," he said, his overturned eyes fixed on the rumbler disappearing behind a tall thicket of trees. "I'm not sure."

Skoro did not try to inquire any further. He was done with the Sand River girls. The last thing he needed was for Dreadlocks to motivate Leonides into yet another erratic wild duck chase. His twin could be such a sucker for that kind of thing.

Fortunately for him, his brother kept his thoughts to himself and they all relaxed and enjoyed a long and blissful quiet afternoon.

At dusk, they moved off the hill.

"Say, any of you has seen the Big Mak recently?" asked Dreadlocks.

EIGHTEEN

THE CUB BENEATH

"Over here!" roared Makhulu.

Dreadlocks snapped his head up and wheeled toward the source of his brother's voice just in time to witness him dive under a low thornbush. The cluster of shrubs throbbed and swayed under his impact. Without missing a beat, Makhulu barreled through the dry scraggle with all the eagerness of a crazed warthog rooting out his food, his enthusiastic, half-breathed grunts betraying his fast progress over the loud crackling of thin branches snapping like so many brittle bones in his wake.

An outraged snarl erupted out of the opposite end of the thornbush. A heartbeat later, the Styx female burst out of her cozy hideout and stood in the open, her fur electric, her neck and shoulders tangled in freshly ripped vines. Dreadlocks froze as she faced him with her head raised high and her chest exposed. The tuft of her tail seemed

Makes no sense, even if lions knew what 'electric' was

to play with the air behind her rump. In her eyes, he could see the mischief shining, like an invitation.

Makhulu exploded out of the foliage and promptly trampled over the delicate moment like the proverbial elephant in rut. The Styx female snarled and bolted in the dense lank to her left. Makhulu leaped after her. Dreadlocks cursed under his breath and rushed after them.

"Shaka, on me!" he yelled, almost as an afterthought.

His brother caught up to him and bumped into his back. "She's in there?"

"Yes. Careful, she's a nimble one."

They judged Makhulu's trajectory and entered the lank on what they hoped was a flanking course. A short scuffle broke out a few leaps ahead of them. They merged with Makhulu's lane and converged on the spot just in time to see the lioness bolt out in front of them again. Leonides and Skoro closed in on her tail from the opposite direction. Leonides leaped forward and attempted a wild tackle. She ducked and his claws harmlessly glanced off her hindquarters. She wheeled about, found herself face to face with an out-of-breath Shaka barreling toward her with all the grace and agility of a blind buffalo, wheeled again and dashed out of the lank toward a cluster of thorn trees, her galloping paws a blur over the flat ground.

"No!" hollered Skoro. "No!"

In a flash, T. rounded the thicket and leaped in front of the lioness. The two cats collided and went rolling in the dirt. The rest of the coalition formed a circle around them.

That second scuffle did not last long. Upon realizing that she was trapped, the Styx female disentangled herself and lay still with her tail twitching nervously behind her flattened body. Dreadlocks noticed that she was gasping for air. That made him feel a little bit better about his own burning lungs.

Once they felt confident enough that she was not going to run away, they all relaxed and sat down on their haunches.

"Well done, T.," Makhulu mumbled. "I thought that you were still with the Tsalala."

Shaka went to give the younger cat a head rub.

"It sounded like you guys needed my help," T. said with a knowing half-snarl. "Good thing I came too. Without me, she would have escaped."

Makhulu frowned. “It’s always a team effort, T.”

“Yeah, but you didn’t even know I was there, did you?”

The dark-maned shrugged and turned his back on the smaller cat. “Do you have a name?” he asked the female.

“Tsavie, from the Styx pride.”

“Well, where is your pride, Tsavie-from-the-Styx?”

“Here and there.”

“Isn’t that the truth,” snorted T. “You girls cover more ground than a bunch of wander-males chased by shadows.”

“You have a sister with two new cubs,” Makhulu said. “Where is she?”

“In her den.”

“Where is that den?”

Tsavie issued an amused grunt and shook her head.

T. growled and stalked forward but Makhulu casually interposed himself and shoved him aside – rather ruefully, Dreadlocks thought. “You are under the protection of the two Shaw males, yes? Where are they?”

The Styx lioness drew her head back, slightly nonplussed. “What do you boys know about the state of things in the Mala Mala right now?”

“We were born there,” said Shaka. “You can assume that we know the area quite a bit.”

Tsavie laughed in his face. “Clearly you don’t. Otherwise, you would have known that only one of the Shaws remains, not two.”

“One? What happened to the other?”

“A crocodile grabbed him.”

“Aha!” Dreadlocks exclaimed. He turned toward Shaka. “I knew that it was possible.”

“Just because it happened to an old Shaw doesn’t mean that it can happen to a real lion. Certainly not a Mapogo.”

“You’re just being a sore loser, it doesn’t fit you.”

Leonides ignored their banter and stepped forward. “If only one of the Shaw brothers remain,” he said, “how come the Split Rock coalition hasn’t killed him already?”

She looked at him with wide, incredulous eyes. “You boys don’t know?”

“Know what?”

"The Split Rocks died a long time ago."

The six brothers sucked in their breath in unison. The Split Rock coalition had ruled over the Eyrefield pride ever since they had left the Mala Mala.

"Tell us what happened," said Makhulu.

"Not much to tell, really. If you recall, the Split Rocks and the Shaws have been at each other's throat for a long long time in the Mala Mala. I believe the Shaw brothers were a coalition of six originally, but other cats whittled their number down when they were still little more than belly-manes. The Split Rocks maybe, although we all suspect that the five Sunset Boys did most of the killing. Back then, they were still the dominant force in the Mala Mala and had full control of the Eyrefield pride."

"Why doesn't that surprise me?" sniggered T.

Dreadlocks wrinkled his muzzle. For the timeline to fit, he would have to have already been born and weaned when those events occurred; and yet, he could not remember witnessing any male-on-male fight at the time, nor his mother ever having to run or hide him in the tall grass. That did not prove much, though. Kept, as they were, far away from the older cats' confidence, safe and secure in their cub's ignorance, they had all grown blissfully unaware of the wild dangers that roamed the periphery of the pride. It suddenly occurred to him that he had never thought to ask what the old males' patrols really entailed. He had always just assumed that the ill-natured cats needed some time alone, away from the females.

He chewed on it some more. A coalition of six young wander-males roaming at the edge of the Sunset Boys' territory would have been worrying news for the old manes, true enough, but as long as they kept to their side of the grass and did not interfere directly with the well-being of the pride – as it seemed they had – the old males had no reason to go out of their way to chase after them. This was what roars were for after all: to act as a deterrent so that an established lion could conserve his strength without having to go chasing after shadows every time a bunch of wide-eyed, over-grown kittens suddenly realized that they had developed some gravel inside their throat.

Well Broken Nose might still have done it just for the sheer pleasure of it. Dreadlocks giggled internally as he tried to picture the old mane stumbling upon the foreign urine for the very first time. The joyous rage suddenly rekindled and flashing bright in the dead, yellow eyes; the murderous snarl disfiguring the mangled muzzle; the half-strangled, indignant roar bursting out of the tight belly, irrepressible. Yes, the Sunset Boys were not exactly a bunch of live-and-let-live kind of cats. Their temper had more than likely played a big role in their decision to go after the Shaws.

Still, Dreadlocks could not help but think that maybe something else had played a role as well. A softer voice hidden deep inside each one of the big males' chest, less boisterous but far more primal. A sense of duty. The old manes would have undoubtedly scoffed at the very idea but there was no denying the fact that the six Shaws would have presented an insurmountable obstacle for the young Mapogos once outside of the pride. Especially during those shaky moons when they were still just a bunch of loose wander-males roaming around without a clue as to the way of things above grass.

Yes, maybe they all owed a little bit more to the Sunset Boys' cold cruelty than they had previously assumed.

Tsavie cleared her throat and brough Dreadlocks' attention back to her. She had no idea who the Sunset Boys were to them and remained unaware of the flow of thoughts her remark had created. "After the one they called Broken Nose died," she said, "and with no worthy males to take the lead, the Eyrefield imploded. The Shaw and Split Rock coalitions quickly collided in their urge to fill the gap. The Split Rocks came up on top, for a while, but the Shaws were able to retreat and take over another pride, the Selatis. Eventually, they came back and managed to either kill or drive off the last of the Split Rock males and take over the Eyrefield entirely. They even killed the dominant female in the process. Then–"

"Wait," Skoro exclaimed, his voice little more than a strangled whimper, "they killed the dominant Eyrefield female?"

"Yes, an old huntress with a scarred hip."

"Why?! Why did they have to kill her?"

"She tried to fight back so the Shaws killed her to make an example." She paused to better enjoy the stunned silence her words had created. Her eyes were gleaming with a sort of heinous, dark joy. "I'm sure you Mapogos can relate," she snickered.

A wave traveled through the coalition. The circle shrunk. Already Dreadlocks could picture himself ripping the smug lioness to shreds, squeeze her windpipe tight and make her choke on her own words.

Again, Makhulu interposed himself. Although no longer the dominant male, nor even the bigger cat, his dark presence was still formidable. Without so much as a soft growl, his tired eye checked their advance. Dreadlocks felt his anger melt as fast as it had come.

"In conclusion," the elder Mapogo said with a soft, emotionless voice, "both the Eyrefield and the Styx prides are under the control of a single Shaw male now. Is that what you are saying?"

"Not quite. A young cat has joined the lone Shaw since the death of his brother. His name is Solo."

"Solo?!" exclaimed T.

"You know him?"

Shaka answered for his brother: "He's a young cat from the Tsalala. T. almost killed him when we took over the pride but he managed to escape. In all honesty I would never have thought that he would be able to survive out in the grass on his own. The belly-mane's as hard as an old root."

"He certainly has that reputation," Tsavie said, "and his mother is a legend on both sides of the Sand River as well."

"His mother?"

"She's nicknamed Tailless," T. said with a sigh. "She's the lead huntress of the Tsalala pride. Cold eyes harder than sharp hooves and a temper to match. A real piece of work. She lost the appendage while fighting off an entire pack of hyena on her own. Not only did she survived, but she managed to save her cub in the process as well. Then when the wound turned warm and putrid, she bit off what remained of the stump herself like it was nothing. Or so the story goes anyway. She doesn't talk about it much."

"Like I said," the Styx female concluded, "a legend."

Leonides tilted his head toward T., surprised. "And now she's under your protection?"

"Believe me, Tailless does not need anyone's protection. But yes, she has submitted herself to us. More or less. Along with the rest of the pride."

Dreadlocks frowned. Something was not making any sense. "How come the Shaw male allowed that Solo cat to join him? Are they blood-related?"

Shaka shook his head. "Not only are they not blood-related, but the two Shaws actually killed all of Solo's siblings when he was just a cub. At the time they were trying to take over the pride, but failed and had to retreat."

"What?!"

"That's true," said T. "At least that's what the Tsalala girls told us. That's why we didn't go after him. Between us, the Split Rocks, and the Shaws, we thought that he had nowhere to go. By all accounts, he should have been dead meat."

Tsavie shrugged. "I don't know anything about that. Only that the young Solo has joined forces with the last Shaw and now they control our pride along with the Eyrefield. They rule the Mala Mala."

"I suppose that the hard circumstances of grass can make for strange fellowships sometimes," Makhulu mused. "Brothers in blood spilled rather than shared." He turned toward the female. "How goes the cohabitation between the Styx and the Eyrefield?"

"It's… Well let's just say that it's a good thing the Mala Mala is so big. Plenty of space for everyone's cat temper to be kept in check, most of the time anyway."

"No wonder the old cat greeted that young mane with an open heart," Skoro laughed. "Forget about rival coalitions, he needs all the help he can get just to keep his girls from killing one another."

"Yes, but how come Solo agreed after what happened to his siblings?"

"Clearly the need for survival must have overridden his desire for revenge."

"What about his honor?"

Makhulu dismissed Shaka's remark. "Not all lions can afford to think like you do."

"Only two males then?" said Leonides. "An old cat way past his prime and a young belly-mane without a single dark hair anywhere on him. Is that what's standing between us and those prides? Or am I missing something?"

The Styx female unleashed a poisonous snarl. "You're missing the prides themselves. The males will never fight you directly, they're too smart for that. And you can't compel them, the Mala Mala is too big. They'll run circles around you until your strength is spent."

"We don't need to compel them," T. growled. "They can run around the Mala Mala until their heart bursts for all I care. As long as we have the girls, they're welcome to the dirt."

She shook her head. "That's my point. As long as a single one of the males still live, my sisters will never give up on their cubs. If you go after them, they'll give you a cat fight like you've never seen before. So will the Eyrefield."

"Great," Dreadlocks groaned, "it's the Nkuhuma pride all over again." The very idea of going back to this kind of nonsense led his leg muscles to cry out in agony. No number of lionesses could be worth that kind of grueling pain.

The others, he was quite happy to see, seemed to share in his opinion. All of them except T. "A cat fight like we've never seen before," the younger lion snarled, "sounds like fun."

Tsavie turned her back on him. She was done with the questioning and she showed it by cleaning her paws.

In an abrupt transition typical of cats' behavior, they all fell quiet and allowed themselves to relax. With the tension of the chase now gone, Dreadlocks felt secure enough to step back and grant the lioness some more room to breathe. Behind her, the twins did the same. She took notice and lay down on her flank so as to communicate her willingness to stay put, at least for the time being. The conversation crumbled into small bits of quips and gossips as various pairs drifted toward different islands of shade. Dreadlocks chose to remain near the female and laid himself down next to her tail before seeing to his own grooming.

They frittered away a sizeable chunk of the afternoon in this manner then, feeling hungry, roused themselves and slowly coalesced back together before going on the prowl. T. found a hippo's footprints and went to scout ahead with Shaka trotting next to him.

"A hippo?" asked Tsavie. They were hanging in the back of the formation. "Really?"

"Yeah," said Dreadlocks. "You know, like a warthog but bigger."

"I know what the obese pigs are," she snapped. "I've tasted a few myself."

"Your kill? Or carrion?"

They're not pigs, or even very closely related to them.

"Carrion, of course." She glanced at him and lowered her voice. "You guys really go after those things when they are alive?"

"Of course," Dreadlocks laughed. "After all, why not? At least they have no horns that we need to worry about."

"What about the giant jaws full of teeth at the front? How do you deal with that?"

"We usually ask a young female to act as our decoy."

"Really?" she said with a grin. "Is this why the Mapogos have such a bad reputation with their lionesses?"

"Maybe."

He did not know why, but this huntress was growing on him. He liked her free spirit and easy-going nature. Just this morning, she had been fleeing for her life while they roared and chased after her through the tall grass as if she were a quarry they wanted to rip to pieces; now she had joined their hunting party and was holding her side of the banter as well as any of his brothers as if it were the most natural thing in the world to do. Talk about not holding grudges.

"Well, I am relieved then," he heard her say, her voice purposefully light and – dared he believe it? – slightly flirtatious. "Here I thought that you and your brothers were cat-killers. Turns out, it's the hippos who should have been blamed all along."

"Exactly." He opened his jaws wide in his best hippopotamus impression and gently nipped at her shoulder. "BWAAH," he boomed, his eyes sparkling from behind his distended jaws.

She screamed in mock outrage and chased after him. Laughing, he dodged and swirled and chased after her tail. A back and forth ensued and they swapped places between hunter and hunted a couple of times. Once she decided that she had been properly avenged – he felt her fangs lightly graze the side of his face – she broke it off and they both fell back on the trail, flank bumping against flank.

They quickened the pace and caught up with Makhulu and the twins seated on their haunches. Shaka and T. were already coming back.

"You found him?" asked Makhulu.

"Her," Shaka said. "And you're not going to like where she is."

The two lions led the hunting party into a tall thicket of wet, dense reeds. The glare of the sun decreased behind the impenetrable cover of the vegetation; they stopped briefly and let their cat's eyes adjust to the sudden half-light. A new world of insects greeted their nostrils and mouth and sprung to life underneath their paws. Dreadlocks angrily flicked his ears and tail but refrained from clearing his throat in the hushed atmosphere.

At a signal from T., they all crouched low and methodically groped their way forward, their light steps taking full advantage of the softness of the spongy mud. Small puddles began to appear underneath the pressure of their paws. They caught a glimpse of sunlight shining through the dense vegetation ahead of them and pressed forward. The water rose and swirled around their ankles. They slowed down and assumed a rigid posture while moving as cautiously as possible, their muscles tense, three points of contact at all times, one leg delicately dipped after the next so as to prevent any unfortunate splashing.

Leonides stumbled and almost lost his footing. He caught himself on Skoro's flank at the last instant, teetered some more, regained his balance. They held their breath and watched his ripples travel ahead of their position. T. turned around and threw him a wilting glare.

One excruciating long prowl later, they reached the edge of the reeds. The stalks parted ways and revealed a small water hole with what Dreadlocks first assumed to be a large, glistening boulder jutting out of the placid water in the middle with a single white stork perched on top. The boulder twisted in place and raised its head. He sucked in his breath and cringed as he felt the ripples of its – her – disturbance lap at his ankles. "By the grass," he whispered, "that's what I call a unit."

"She's practically the size of the hole," Leonides muttered in disbelief.

Tsavie considered the water she was standing in, then stared at him. "Surely you are not going to attack her here."

"What's the matter?" T. sniggered. "Scared o' gettin' wet?"

"There are no reeds growing in the middle of the hole. That means that the water is probably too deep to stand in. If that big lump of lard gets you under her weight, you'll drown."

"I suppose that we could try to scare her out of the hole," whispered Shaka. "But she might not take the bait, in which case we would have lost the benefit of surprise for nothing."

"We should wait for the night," Makhulu said. "At dusk, the temperature will cool and she will move out to graze. In the darkness and on open ground, we'll have the clear advantage."

This triggered a scornful reaction from the younger Mapogo. "I ain't waitin' for no moon's permission to do my killin'," he spat.

"T.," Shaka hissed, as loudly as he dared, "wait!"

But T. ignored him.

Careful not to disturb the water any more than he had to, he delicately waded his way forward. As the water rose and closed around his limbs and licked at his belly, he raised his head higher. Ahead of him, the female hippopotamus still had her back turned to them. Blissfully unaware of their presence, she wallowed around and basked in the coolness of the water covering her tender skin, her nostrils snorting above the waterline, her fuzzy, cone-shaped ears wiggling happily behind her bobbing head.

The crane noticed him first. Her small round pupils fell on the approaching cat and exploded inside their orbits. A brief squawk escaped her sharp beak as she scrambled to take flight. The hippo grunted in surprise and swiveled in place, sending white plumes of sloshing water cascading down her round flanks and washing over the nearby shore in successive waves.

The reeds quivered. T. froze. The hippo dove.

"The fool is going to get himself killed!" Dreadlocks screamed. He could see the wake of the underwater grazer charge toward the smaller lion at unfathomable speed.

But T. had a plan.

He waited for the wake to be almost on him, then waited another agonizing fraction of a heartbeat. The gaping mouth lurched out of the water. He leaped to the side, through the distended jaws, and ducked down under the cover of the water, his back legs kicking wildly behind his rump like some crazed waterfowl. He reemerged near the partially submerged hindquarters. The water was too deep for him to leap but he used his front claws to get a good grip on the skin and pulled himself up by the strength of his shoulders, onto the enormous back.

The hippo roared and swerved madly. In her confusion, she stumbled through the forest of reeds and into shallower waters where the hunting party was hidden.

"He's done it!" exclaimed Shaka, and leaped forward.

Tsavie pounced in his wake. "Styx!" she screamed, momentarily forgetting her current company, "Styx pride!"

Dreadlocks groaned and joined the charge.

"Don't let her go back into the deep end!" Makhulu admonished them. He leaped forward and grabbed a hold of the short tail to anchor the enormous quarry down. The water grazer shrieked and whirled in place. For all his strength, Makhulu was lifted off his feet and flung about as if he were a mere cub. Leonides, Skoro, and Shaka rushed to his support and grabbed onto the rump to add their own weight to the effort, forcing the hippo to stay in the shallows.

Dreadlocks swerved around them and leaped up to join T on the hippo's back. He tried to stand up on all four, but his paws skidded wildly over the slippery sheen of sunscreen produced by the purple skin. He flattened himself down and used his claws for traction as he carefully crawled his way forward. He caught a glimpse of T ahead of him, spread-eagled on top of the hippo's shoulders. The mad cat was nipping at the folds of skin rising in successive waves behind the frantic head. At Dreadlock's approach, he turned himself around and unleashed a snarl that bared his fangs. "That Styx girl is all kinds of crazy," he laughed. "I love it."

Jostled every which way, Dreadlocks tightened his grip, craned his neck, and peered around the massive head.

The Styx female was taunting the hippo with small hops at the edge of her reach. It took a moment for Dreadlocks to understand what she was doing. By making herself into such an obvious, tantalizing target she had become the sole focus of the hippo's rage and redirected her attention away from the deeper end of the pool. She was, in effect, using the hippo's blind temper against herself to help anchor her down.

He shook his head, impressed. This was the kind of mad stunt Shaka was always talking about. Adrenalin-filled gallantry in service of a murderous purpose, with the prospect of a belly full of meat at the end. The very definition of lionlike.

Still, the only thing that prevented the enormous grazer from suddenly lurching forward and killing Tsavie instantly was the strength and determination of the four males hanging onto her rump and tail by the skin of their fangs. And that strength, while considerable, was not inexhaustible. Her position was extremely precarious. They had to act fast.

"Wanna try a kiss-o'-death?" T. asked him, his eyes sparkling.

"Not really."

"Right. The spine then." throat

He crawled toward the rump and used his sprawled-out paws to compensate for the hippo's wild jerks and heaves. To Dreadlocks eyes, he seemed a baboon gingerly moving through the thinnest of green branches in the middle of a storm. The image was somewhat baffling and he hastened to blink it away. This was no time for reveries.

T. reached a point above the hips and stopped. After having adjusted his grip and made sure that his claws were secured, he bared his fangs and began to gnaw.

Dreadlocks joined him.

The acid of the skin's sunscreen ate at his throat and burned his nose. He sneezed and retched and forced himself to swallow it down. His palate now scorched and numb, he pulled at the bared skin. The leather was thicker than a buffalo's and much harder to rip apart, like rubbery sap. Flattened as they were, they could not use their shoulders for leverage, they had to rely solely on their jaws and necks to pull as hard as they could. Dreadlocks' muscles began to burn but he kept at it relentlessly. Once the skin finally gave way, they continued, now tearing away large chunks of red meat they swallowed eagerly.

They went at it with all the eagerness of a couple of starving woodpeckers.

"Aha!" T. finally exclaimed, his muzzle dripping with dark blood. "Here it is."

They lapped the last of the flesh and blood away and revealed the glistening white bone underneath.

"Let's excavate," Dreadlocks grunted.

They tore at the edge of the hole and exposed a second vertebra, then a third.

The hippo's shrieks turned frantic. Crazed by fear and pain, she suddenly backtracked and stepped over Makhulu who groaned and cursed as he lost his grip. The enormous, stubby legs stomped through the shallow water and groped for his prostrated body with murderous fury. The lion's dark mane bobbed to the surface once before disappearing under the white splashes.

"Mak!" Dreadlocks screamed. He twisted in place and leaned over the hippo's flank to catch a glimpse of his brother.

Freed from the weight of the big male, the hippo redoubled her jerks and wild whirling.

Caught off guard, Dreadlocks felt his front paws slip out from under him. He gasped and tried to push himself back up but found no grip on the treacherous rotundity. His back arched, his head tipped over the point of no return, his heart came undone inside his chest and dropped inside his mouth. Blood rushed his brain and dulled his senses. His legs launched themselves into one last heroic attempt at holding him back but his claws only dug deep, useless furrows through the slick skin. A half-sucked breath later, he cleared the curve and went flying over the edge of the hippo's back.

bearings Cold water slapped his face and rushed his lungs. Brown silt swirled up inside his nostrils. The taste of mud and decay invaded his throat. He trashed in the murky darkness and frantically tried to get his bearing. The sun had disappeared behind a brown-green maelstrom of silt and suspended leaves. Without any point of reference, he could not tell which way was the surface. He had a feeling that he was upside down and sinking, but he could not be sure.

He stabilized himself and let loose a thin stream of bubbles. By following their ascent, he managed to get himself upright. He began to swim up.

Short, black stubbles as stiff as reed stems grazed the right side of his mane. He kicked and twisted in place. Unveiled by his stirring, an enormous purple-pink protuberance slowly emerged from behind the curtain of greenish murk, close enough to caress his exposed chest. Two small, unblinking eyes fell on him.

He screamed a breath he could not afford and watched it bubble out of his mouth, along, it seemed, with his heart. The monstrous jaws opened wide and for a brief heartbeat he distinctly saw the white of the ivory rushing toward him.

Something tawny shoved him out of the way. Up became down, then up again. Wild gurgles filled his ears. He choked on a mouthful of water. His flailing back paws found support on something sturdy. Without thinking, he pushed upward as hard as he could.

He breached the surface and washed out into the shallows. Coughing brown water, he gripped a cluster of reeds and took a few wet breaths to calm himself down while enjoying the delicious warmth of the sun shining bright through the droplets covering his eyelids.

He blinked them away.

T. was sprawled next to him, looking like something another cat might have spit out.

"Still alive?" his brother joked.

"Yeah, I think. What happened?"

"The hippo saw you fall and rushed after you. So I jumped."

"You saved me?"

T. shrugged and shook some of the water out of his plastered mane.

Dreadlocks heaved himself up and looked around. The surface of the water hole had recovered its tranquility. "Where is she now?"

T. led him back to the site of the ambush. No more screams could be heard. A deathly heaviness hung in the air. The struggle, although far from over, had ascended to that strange state where blood-loss, shock, and exhaustion make all parties involved seem placid, almost polite.

The hippopotamus had made some progress toward the deep end of the hole but was still only half-submerged and seemed not to have the strength to push further. Tsavie had joined the last three mud-covered Mapogos and was now hanging onto the rump stiffly. They all seemed too tired to do anything else but bite down.

Makhulu limped out of the reeds. "Don't let her reach the deep end," he croaked. "We'll never get her out if she dies down there."

"Won't she float sh'up evensh'tually?" asked Tsavie.

"Nope," Skoro replied, his jaws closed tight around the hippo's tail. "Hippos sh'don't float. She'z oane sh'ton o' sh'pu' muschles, she'll shink righ' sh'down."

Dreadlocks turned toward T. "Should we jump back on her and finish the job?"

"No need, it's done. She'll bleed out soon enough."

"Should have… cut… the brachial… artery," Shaka stammered, out of breath. Unable to get a good grip with his jaws, he was hanging onto the left thigh by the front claws with his back arched backward so as to bring his weight down. His shoulders were quivering under the effort.

"Brachial artery? What's that?"

"The artery…running under…the crook of the… forelegs," the lion gasped with his cheek pressed tight against the hippo's skin. "Fastest way… to bleed…. a pig. Also… keeps you… well away…. from the jaws… while… you… hold it down."

"Sh'at's tru'!" Leonides exclaimed from the other side of the hippo's flank. "I oan'sh sh'aw a sh'leaopar' sh'kill a sh'warthog like sh'that!"

"Well a hippo's not a warthog, is it? But if any of you wants to crawl under her belly and tickle her armpit, be my guest."

None of the lions moved.

Satisfied, T. flashed his half-snarl and made a cocky show of cleaning his paws while his brothers grunted and labored in front of him. "Now put your back into it, boys. I'm getting hungry."

Dreadlocks shook his head and went to find a spot next to Tsavie.

"A'm sh'goin' to sh'kill sh'at pompou'sh'cat," she snarled. "A' sh'wear it by the sh'weet edge o' sharp gra'sh, A' will end 'im."

He chuckled and added his own weight to the hippo's rump.

Eventually, the powerful grazer buckled. Her eyes glazed over, her head grew heavy, her body shuddered. After one last grunt of despair, she laid herself down softly, as if falling asleep with her slanted muzzle half-submerged and her left nostril spuming above the waterline. She was still breathing weakly when they tore her apart.

As usual the whole thing devolved into a feeding frenzy.

Dreadlocks eagerly plunged into the deep cavity of the open flank and angrily snarled at Leonides who was trying to shove him to the side. Somewhere to his right, Tsavie lashed out at Shaka as they both tried to gnaw on the same rib. After failing to squeeze through on one side, Skoro tried the other, unsuccessfully, then simply elected to jump in the middle. He pushed and wormed his way through the dense ball of cats, only to be violently pushed back when they all turned on him.

Overeager as ever, Dreadlocks went too far in his chastising of his brother and ended up finding himself on the outside of the frenzy, with his brother's wagging tail now barring his reentry to the feast.

He was about to grab Leonides by the back of the mane when he noticed T. calmly jumping up to feed on the spine-wound. Makhulu stalked after him and, without warning, shoved him off the carcass.

The noise of the splash cut through the frenetic growls and wild tearing of soft tissues. Covered in blood, they all fell quiet and turned away from the open wound, the meat temporarily forgotten.

"By the grass, what was that for?!" T. exclaimed as he trotted back into the shallows. He seemed more surprised and amused than anything else.

"You don't feed," the dark-maned growled. "At least not until we're all done."

"Mak…that's a huge hippo. There is more than enough meat for everyone to enjoy, and then some."

Makhulu jumped down his promontory of flesh and met T. at eye level. "I don't care. You almost cost us this hunt. You don't get to eat with the rest of us."

"Cost you this hunt?! I was top cat! I am the one who dealt the death-blow!"

"I told you to wait for nightfall when it was safer but you went for it anyway. Your recklessness almost cost me and Dreadlocks our life, to say noth–"

"I *saved* Dreadlocks' life!"

"To say nothing of the hippo who came this close to escaping into the deep end! I'm tired, T. Tired of your antics."

"My antics are my business."

"Not when they have a direct impact on the rest of us, they are not. A *negative* impact."

"I'm the only reason anyone of you is eating right now!"

"From now on–"

"I'm the one who got you that hippo, Mak! Just because you're getting slow and lack confidence, that doesn't mean–"

"SHUT UP!"

T. snapped his head back, his jaws frozen shut.

In the lingering silence, they could distinctly hear Makhulu's laborious breathing striving to contain his temper. "I don't want you anywhere near me when I'm eating. And I don't mean just today. From now on, you don't eat until after I'm done. Ever. I'm dead serious."

"Mak," Shaka chimed in calmly, "you don't get to make this kind of decision anymore."

"Exactly," T. growled. "You're not the dominant cat anymore, you can't tell me when to eat."

Makhulu ground his fangs slowly as he considered the issue. "Fine," he spat, "then I'm challenging you for the carcass."

"You can't lay a challenge for the entirety of that heap of meat."

"I just did."

"That's a full hippo, Mak! You can't keep it all to yourself!"

"I'm not. The others are welcome to it. I'm not challenging you for the sole possession of the carcass, only for the right to deny you the meat."

"You can't do that. Not if there is enough for everyone to go around."

Makhulu shrugged. "I'm doing it. If you're unhappy, we can settle the issue right now, on the spot."

T. snapped his jaws shut. Behind his shocked expression, Dreadlocks could see the pain and rage boiling inside his eyes. For a fleeting instant he seemed to consider attacking Makhulu head-on, but then thought better of it. "You would go out of your way to deny me what's rightfully mine?" he croaked.

"Call it what you want, I'm done with you."

On this, Makhulu turned around and trotted back toward the carcass.

The silence left in the wake of his departure seemed thick enough to tread on. They all looked at their brother and anxiously awaited his reaction.

It never came.

With his paws firmly rooted in the damp soil and his eyes cast down, the younger lion seemed to have been struck by a lethal blow. Dreadlocks noticed the spasmodic contraction of the claws and the way the whole body was swaying in a non-existent breeze, as if T. was in shock and going through some reassuring physical mantra only he could understand. Then his face sagged and he appeared strangely open and vulnerable all of a sudden, almost honest, as if some facade he had secretly held in place his entire adult life had suddenly dropped; underneath it, the fearful, awkward cub his brother had always been was now exposed for all to see.

The noise of Makhulu's mastication reached their ears. With an eagerness that made him feel slightly guilty, Dreadlocks turned his back on T. and hastened to rejoin his elder brother. Tsavie followed in his wake and so did the twins. Shaka, unsurprisingly, stayed behind.

Dreadlocks tore himself a path through the meat. For a short instant he heard Shaka trying to appease their younger brother with soft, reassuring words, then the cacophony of the renewed feeding frenzy drowned the voice out and he pushed the whole affair out of his mind.

They ate their full. Dreadlocks could never get enough hippo meat, it was always such a rare treat. Once ready to burst, he slowly disentangled himself from his grisly work and drifted away from the water hole onto firmer, drier ground, his belly swinging wildly after every step in a way that reminded him of their late quarry.

"When you eat the hippo, you *become* the hippo," he joked to Tsavie who was walking with some difficulty next to him.

She laughed.

Out of the corners of his eyes, he noticed Shaka and T. slinking through the reeds toward the carcass, half crouched so as to keep well away from Makhulu's gaze. As soon as the dark-maned moved off with the twins, they moved-in, as if they were some kind of scavengers who had not participated in the kill. That didn't feel right to Dreadlocks but he kept the thought to himself.

They lay down under the shade of a large acacia tree, away from the others. After allowing herself some time to digest, Tsavie finally decided to turn on the heat. Dreadlocks grinned internally as the eager wagging of her tail on his rump chased his sleep away. Her flirty comments morphed into thinly veiled calls for action. Feeling cheeky, he lay still and played dumb. As a last resort, she trotted around the acacia's trunk and let loose an inviting wet growl deep enough to skin the belly-mane off a young cat. His hind legs shuddered briefly but he managed to stay put. She trotted back, seemingly vexed, and made a show of veering toward the tree island where the twins and Makhulu had chosen to rest.

Dreadlocks instinctively lurched to his paws and cut her off. She chuckled and laid herself down next to him, her tail raised high, her eyes gleaming victoriously.

He gently grabbed the flap of numb skin behind her head and positioned himself on top of her, straddling her hips. She low-growled again, this time in pleasure, and wriggled in-between his legs. Panting hard, he closed his eyes and shuddered under the ecstasy of her smaller body grinding against his mane. She smelled of warm fur, dry dirt, and caked blood.

Her muzzle curled as they both peaked at the same time. She let out another, deeper growl, something halfway between a snarl and a roar, a gnawed at his whiskers. Spent, he tottered away, his legs temporarily weak. She rolled on her back with her eyes half closed.

"That was nice," she giggled.

He bellowed his pride for all to hear.

They went at it another half dozen times in the course of the afternoon, alternating between short walks around the tree to stretch their legs and brief bouts of pleasure. Eventually, Dreadlocks was forced to stop. He lay down for a well-deserved nap.

Tsavie snuggled up to him. "Don't tell the Shaw male I was ever here," she joked.

"You will go back to your pride then?"

"Of course, this is where I belong."

"The Shaw male will kill the cubs."

"He will never know he's not the father."

Dreadlocks sighed. "I suppose his days above grass are numbered anyway. T. and Shaka are pushing for us to cross the Sand River and take over the Mala Mala. When we do, the two males will not be able to resist us. You know what will happen next."

"We fight you off and make you rue the day you ever thought of crossing that river?"

He tapped her on the nose, gently. "You Styx girls are hard fighters, no-one's denying that, but you're not that strong." His muzzle crumpled as he licked his nose. "Will you fight alongside your sisters to protect their cubs?"

"Yes,of course," she said cheerfully, as if it were the funniest thing in the world. "They're my pride, I owe them my fangs and claws in times of hardship, you know how it is." She noticed his concern and went to nibble his ear affectuously. "Who knows," she whispered, "maybe I'll end up being the one who breaks the spine of the mighty Dreadlocks. What a famous girl I would become, my name to be sung all the way to the far side of grass and back."

"Don't joke like that," he growled. "That's not funny."

She smiled and snuggled a little deeper into his mane. He thought about getting up but for all his posturing he found that he could not get angry at her right now. Not really. "I would never hurt you," he said instead, very seriously.

"Huh-huh."

"You don't believe me?"

"In my pride, we have a saying: 'Promises made under the shade never survive the glare of the sun.'"

"You think I will just forget?"

"We're having a good time right now, no need to spoil it. When we meet again, you'll do what's in your nature, and so will I."

He mused on it for a little while. A doubt assailed him. "Did you come here on purpose? To gain our favor in advance in case we take over your pride?"

"If you remember, you mighty Mapogos trapped me."

"Yes but all your sisters had already escaped to the other side of the Sand River by then. Why did you linger?"

"I'm going to have a litter soon," she sighed, "that much cannot be avoided. As far as the old Shaw and the young Solo are concerned, the cubs are theirs. If they prevail, they'll still protect them. If you guys prevail, however… I can always count on the fact that you know the truth."

"So you win no matter what," he said, a bit more harshly than he had intended. "Pretty smart I guess, in its own treacherous, deceitful, and spineless kind of way."

She raised her head and glared at him, her face suddenly hard. "Do you know what it feels like to lose a cub?"

"I… No. I guess not."

"It's like a part of you has been ripped from your chest, as though you've been stabbed by a horn through and through. Only instead of dying you have to keep on going as if nothing has happened, for the sake of the pride, and the fucking fact that you're still a breathing cat standing above grass. So you carry on, one hunt at a time. 'It's alright,' you tell yourself. You can take the pain. You're a lion after all, right? But then, as soon as the memory starts to fade, your body realizes that a few moons have elapsed and the need creeps back on you. You don't want it to, of course, but you don't have a choice, your own guts have betrayed you and you can't stop yourself from scratching that itch any more than you can bite your own heart out to stop it from beating." Her voice failed her. She took a couple of deep breaths to calm herself down and swallowed the lump that had been growing inside her throat. "So you go find a mate," she continued. "Maybe he's the same mane who killed your litter in the first place, maybe not. It doesn't really matter. It's all cold blood spilled on the far side of grass at this point, right? But while he covers you, you can't stop yourself from wondering: is it going to be the same thing all over again? Are you creating lives just so that they can be snuffed out in pain and misery before they even have a chance to truly experience the world? Are you going to be an abject failure again? The doubts, Dreadlocks, I tell you, the doubts are almost enough to drive a lioness insane. That's what we have to live with just about every day of our life." She raised herself up and sat down on her hindquarters, away from him. "So yes, when I see a coalition of six males on the outskirts of my pride's territory, I plan ahead for the welfare of my next litter. If you think that's cowardly and spineless, you can bite me."

Dreadlocks went to give her a tentative head-rub. She avoided him. "I'm not judging you," he said. "All cats do what they have to do. Sometimes I just speak to say words, I don't mean anything by it."

She bowed her head curtly and withdrew inside herself, her eyes fixed on the horizon. Not knowing what else to do, he waited quietly next to her. The awkward silence lingered and stretched over the grass along with their growing shadows.

"So were you just playing hard-to-get when we chased you?"

To his surprise, she laughed. "Of course. One has to be convincing if one wants to play this kind of game. Besides, it's good for the legs."

He groaned and said nothing.

"I'll admit, though," she chuckled, "I did not plan to be dragged into a hippo hunt in the middle of a water hole. You Mapogos are crazy, but you sure know how to show a huntress a good time."

"Yeah, to tell you the truth I don't really know what happened there. That thing between Makhulu and T, it's not always like that. T has always been, well, T but it wasn't right for the Big Mak to blow up at him like he did."

"I personally don't blame him for refusing to put up with your brother's antics. When that cat tackled me he rattled my fangs hard enough to shake them loose. Very nearly cracked my ribs too. I didn't snarl or say anything at the time, but I can assure you that's not something I'm willing to swallow down quietly ever again."

"T. *is* a bit of an acquired taste, I'll give you that. But once you get to know him, he's actually a great lion. Brave and relentless, always eager to help. It's just… I don't know. I think he's getting worse these days. It's like he is trying to outdo Makhulu at every turn for no reason at all."

"You shouldn't worry about it too much. Makhulu is the elder, T. is the youngest. A little bit of tension is to be expected. Quite frankly, I am amazed that the six of you managed to stay together for so long." She fell quiet as her head swiveled toward the water hole. "Speaking of the cat, here he comes."

Dreadlocks lurched on his feet. He had hoped that the two younger lions would elect to return to the Tsalala pride immediately after their feed. This would have made the most sense and no one would have faulted them for it. Instead, he watched them saunter across the stretch of grass as if nothing had happened at all, their muzzle and dark mane coated in fresh blood, their heavy belly swinging after every step.

He cursed under his breath. That T. proved himself stubborn and facetious was no surprise, but Shaka should know better.

Under the canopy of their own tree, Makhulu and the twins roused themselves as well. Dreadlocks watched them with some apprehension as they ambled to the edge of the circle of shade and waited there, their face inscrutable. It was obvious that none of the usual mutual grooming and easing of tension necessary to cool cats' tempers off had taken place. All three lions were still covered in the hippo's blood, with their ragged mane sticking out of their body in glistening red spikes and the tight muscles of their stiff shoulders bulging behind their neck.

Tsavie huddled closer to him. "That's going to be trouble," she said.

Dreadlocks could only nod.

Shaka peeled off to greet Makhulu and the twins, but T. bypassed them without so much as a sideway glance and immediately angled toward Dreadlocks' tree. The broad-chested cat went to greet him but T. ignored his presence.

Without breaking a stride, he attempted to cover Tsavie.

She retreated precipitously and threw her rump against the protection of the trunk. Dreadlocks leaped forward to interpose himself.

"She's taken," he growled.

T ticked and whirled in place. "But I'm the one who tackled her."

"And I'm the one who claimed her."

"I saved your life moments ago, or have you forgotten already?"

"One thing has nothing to do with the other."

"It's not fair! I should have been given a chance to claim her first."

"Yeah, well, you didn't."

"Only because Mak unjustly forced me away."

"Drop it, T," groaned Dreadlocks, his tone peremptory, his voice purposefully booming out of his throat so as to better hide his unease. "You missed your chance. Now she's mine."

He leaned forward and towered over T in an attempt to cow the defiance out of him. His brother mistook his intentions and roared his indignation while lunging at his head. Dreadlocks drew himself up, surprised, and absorbed the blows. Grinding his fangs against the pain – his brother had grown into quite the powerful cat despite his smaller size – he closed his eyes and pushed through the storm of claws raking his muzzle. T lost his footing and went rolling in the grass, his belly exposed, his legs uselessly shredding the air above his groin. Dreadlocks sidestepped him and moved toward the head. T lashed out and his right forepaw cut a deep gash into Dreadlocks' left shoulder. He roared and leaped back, then lunged forward again and delivered a fast bite on the thick of T's mane, away from the vulnerable throat but hard enough to drive his point home. Satisfied, he retreated toward the tree.

T raised himself up, slowly. His lip was bleeding but he was otherwise unhurt. "You're a hard cat to topple down," he said, his voice blank.

Dreadlocks shrugged. It wasn't his first time trading scratches with one of his brothers, of course, but something felt different with this particular scuffle. The way T behaved was more serious, more shifty, as if something long repressed inside his mind was about to burst out. More than anything else, he did not like the glint he could see in the corner of the young cat's eyes; it seemed to shine yellow, like a drop of poison glistening at the end of a snake's fang.

Skoro and Leonides rushed to interpose themselves. Shaka ruefully bumped into T.'s flank and forced him back.

"Alright, boys," Leonides said, his tense voice striving to sound cheerful, "enough is enough, the challenge has been settled."

"Who said that I was done?" T. replied.

"Come on," said Skoro, "Dreadlocks had you by the throat, we all saw it."

"You're beat," Shaka said calmly, "that's the golden sun honest truth of it."

"I have a right to that female! I'm the one who caught her in the first place, not him."

"You have a right to fight for what you want, nothing more," Dreadlocks spat. "You did, and you lost."

Shaka pushed back against his brother's attempts to advance. "Let it go," he hissed. "It's fine. There will be plenty of other opportunities. Just let this one go."

Reluctantly, T. ceded to Shaka's steady pressure and the two of them slowly sidewinded away from the group, all the way to the other side of the acacia's trunk. Once they were out of the circle of shade, Dreadlocks allowed himself to relax. He turned to face Tsavie.

"That was a bit dramatic," he joked.

She nodded and kept quiet. Ever since T.'s arrival, her back claws had been nervously scratching the trunk of the tree behind her. At the sight of the deep gash gouged out of the hard bark, Dreadlocks chuckled and tried to think of something clever to say that would raise her spirit.

Suddenly, her eyes grew wide.

"T., DON'T!"

Shaka's voice reached him a heartbeat too late. Two massive paws slammed down on his rump and locked him in place. A lion's hot breath peppered the small of his back. Ice-cold fear barreled down the length of his exposed spine. With a whiny grunt that was part anger and part sheer terror, he jerked to the side and tried to wriggle free of the murderous embrace. Pain nipped at his back. He twisted his neck vertebrae

and caught a glimpse of T.'s fangs grazing his fur alongside his vertebra. Just when the younger lion was about to adjust his grip and try again, something black impacted his flank. He went sprawling in the grass.

Released from the pressure, Dreadlocks bounced back up, threw his back to the tree, and frantically scanned the grass in search of his attacker.

Roaring and snarling at the top of their lungs, Makhulu and T. tumbled all the way to the limit of the circle of shade amid a brown cloud of kicked-up dust. T. found his feet first and swiped at Makhulu's muzzle with his right forepaw. The elder Mapogo rolled to the side, leaped on his paws, shoved T. down. The claws of T.'s right forepaw remained stuck on his muzzle. Dreadlocks gasped in horror as Makhulu's jaws reached out and delicately grabbed the extended limb with all the grace of a stork plucking a fish out of the river. For a single suspended heartbeat, the two lions appeared locked in position, unsure of what to do. Dreadlocks was about to scream at them to stop when Makhulu suddenly growled and pulled hard toward him.

They all heard the sharp *crack* of his fang piercing through T.'s bone.

T. howled in pain and anguish and exploded out of Makhulu's grasp. His anger suddenly forgotten, he half-ran, half-limped backward, all the way to the protection of his brother's side. Makhulu chased after him but Shaka interposed himself, ready to pounce. The twins jumped into the fray.

"ENOUGH!" roared Dreadlocks.

His outburst cut through the rising storm of snarls and growls and froze everyone in place. Makhulu's distorted face sagged as if he had been physically slapped. He regained his composure and stepped away. Panting hard, his legs shaking, Shaka did the same.

T.'s whimpers broke through the growing silence.

"By the grass," whispered Leonides, "Mak, you almost ripped his paw off."

"He'll heal," the dark-maned spat after a cursory glance at T.'s bleeding forelimb. "In the meantime that'll give him something to chew on."

T. growled and heaved himself up on three legs. The pain etched on his muzzle seemed to go far beyond mere physical hurt.

"Ya…fuckin'…cheat," he gasped in-between two angry sobs. "Ya'd no righ' t' intervene! This wa' 'tween me an' Dread!"

"Cut the Broken Nose act, little kitten," snorted Skoro. "The challenge was already long settled. You're the one who asked for it when you went behind Dreadlocks' back and lunged for the spine. Brothers are where we draw the line, remember?"

"But it's true that Makhulu went too far as well," Shaka retorted. "He could have crippled T. and forever prevent him from being able to hunt. That's the same as killing him."

"But he *asked* for it, Shaka."

Leonides nodded vigorously. "If you choose to go after a buffalo on your own, it's all fine and good, but don't go complaining afterward if you get the horns."

"Are you trying to convince me, or yourself?"

Dreadlocks stepped forward. "Everybody should just calm down. The issue is settled, no one is maimed, not really, so let us all agree to put an end to this before a cat gets truly hurt."

"No," T. barked. "I'm not putting an end to anything. I'm done with you ganging up on me to prevent me from getting what I've earned. It's always been the same, ever since I was a cub. You all think that I can't see it, but I do. You still think of me as the Tit who will swallow everything."

"Come ooooon," moaned Skoro. "That's not true."

T. ignored him. His voice crackled as he fell into a poor imitation of the song they had plagued him with what seemed like a lifetime ago:

The Tit, the Tit,
His scrawny ass don't need no meat!
The Tit, the Tit,
All the lionesses give him the split, faster than you can spit!
The Tit, the Tit,
The four of us all together, we have him beat!

"T…" Dreadlocks interrupted, "I don't know where you're getting all of this, but that's not what happened and you know it."

But his brother was not listening. "*I* am the one who jumped on the hippo first. *I* am the one who tackled the female down. Not you!

Me! So how come you still feel that you have the right to deny me what's mine?"

"Just because you're first does not make it yours! It's always been a team effort, T. Always! That's the way it works in a coalition."

"Not anymore. I'm done with this coalition. I'm leaving."

That actually shocked them into silence. Even Shaka was taken aback.

Even T.

He had let his voice run out faster than he could think – an all-too-common issue with him – but they could see that he was not joking. He did seem to waver for a few heartbeats, unsure, but then he drew himself up and Dreadlocks saw the spark of his resolve flicker in his eyes. Just like that, his brother's mind was made up. In a strange, self-fulfilling loop, to hear the words spoken out loud had given him the confidence to see them through.

"You're leaving?" Skoro blurted out. "Where to?"

"Toward the sunrise. Across the Sand River and back into the Mala Mala. The Eyrefield and the Styx will be mine."

"You really think that you can take on two prides by yourself?" Leonides groaned. "By the grass, you'll be dead before the rise of next dawn."

T. shrugged. Behind his mask of defiance, his fear and sadness were visible for all to see. He swallowed it all down and hardened his countenance. His eyes were downcast, resigned. "Better this than to stay here with you."

"Go then," growled Makhulu, his cold voice mercilessly cutting through what little remained of their coalition like morning frost splitting a cracked rock in two. The fur on his face was a hard mask of frozen yellow grass. Although he did not say it, it was obvious to Dreadlocks' eyes that T.'s abrupt decision had hurt the big male in a far more profound way than any of them could really understand. "You think that you can do better on your own?" he continued, his spleen inside his mouth. "Fine. No one's stopping you. Go be a free cat on the prowl. See how you like life above grass without us to back you up. Without *me*."

T. stood still, his eyes locked on his elder brother.

"GO!" Makhulu bellowed. "But remember, you're the one doing this. This is on you, not us. You hear? Not me! *You* made the decision. Now *you* can live with it. Die by it. I don't care. I don't want to see you ever again!" He turned around, turned back again. A mirthless cackle that was more bite than laugh leaped out of his throat. "If you ever try to come back here again," he growled, "I'll spill you wet all over this here dirt, watch me if I don't."

T. drew himself up. His tongue darted to his nose as he seemed to ponder a reply, some snarky remark he alone had the secret of; eventually, he decided against it. Without a word, he turned his back on them and limped away with his extended tail fluttering behind him in a show of carelessness.

"T. wait!" Shaka called out.

"Don't," said Makhulu. "Shaka, don't follow him. Not this time."

"He'll never survive alone on his own."

"You know that can't be helped," said Leonides. "You can't keep protecting him from himself like that. He's a grown cat and he's made his own choice. Don't let it drag you down under the grass too."

"Maybe it's better that way," Dreadlocks heard himself say despite himself. "Alone, it will be a quick death. That's a mercy."

"You don't believe that. He's still your brother."

"Shaka," Skoro interrupted, "you have to think of the good of the coalition. We have prides to protect. Cubs. We need you here with us."

"And it's not just about the responsibilities," Makhulu added. "Think about your loss of comfort. What your life will be like. If you go with him, you will lose everything you have grown to take for granted: the females, the good hunting grounds, even the safety of a patrolled territory. Everything. You would be starting from scratch with nothing to your mane. Think about it before you do anything rash."

Shaka stared at the ground, his muscles tense, his entire body wobbling back and forth. Their arguments were gaining on him, they could see his resolve wane. On an impulse, he turned to catch a glimpse of his younger brother.

Dreadlocks followed his gaze.

T.'s body had already receded halfway to the horizon, the tawny fur of his rump now lost in a surrounding background of yellow grass. Only the black tuft of his tail was still clearly visible, billowing above the lank.

Shaka wheeled back to face the group. He gave each one of them a quick head-rub, then said: "Dirt and prides are nothing to be owned. The only thing a lion ever truly has, are the things he's done."

On this, he ripped himself away and turned toward the lank.

A heartbeat later, he was gone.

Not needed

NINETEEN

MAD PRONKS AND HARD TICKLES

"Gone?"

"Yeah, gone."

"What do you mean, *gone*?"

"I mean that when I reached the end of the trail and looked at the last four paw prints, there was no lioness standing in them."

T, groaned and went to lap a drink out of the Mlowathi river. The fresh water splashed on his muzzle and helped calm his feverish mind. The last few moons had been restless, to say the least.

"So where did they go?"

Shaka lay down by the side of the gurgling water, his eyes half closed. "The trail is a mess. The whole Styx pride has scattered. I think they've crossed into the Djuma."

"The Shaw male is with them?"

"Probably. That old mane knows his tricks: roar a couple of times and then, boom, scat like the wind. He crossed into the Djuma on his own but as sure as green grass turns yellow, he will reunite with his pride once he's certain that we're not coming after him. And to think that this cat might actually be our father."

"Don't say that. Don't ever say that. We should have trapped and killed him when we had the chance. We shouldn't have run."

"I don't remember you being particularly eager to stand your ground that day."

T. grimaced. "It's the koppies that did it. Those big rocky outcrops gave the lionesses all the cover they needed to ambush us and take us by surprise."

Shaka nodded sadly. "In hindsight, we really should have known better. Those girls are many things but they're not stupid. Still, I can't believe that they actually managed to fight us off like that."

T. leaned forward to take another drink out of the river. His scraped throat was still sore from all his roaring, as though he were spitting gravels every time he spoke. "They played us like a bunch of antelopes," he groaned, feeling his temper rise again. "Us, the most fearsome cats this side of grass, reduced to pronking madly in-between rocks like some skittish grazer."

"Don't let it get to your head, we didn't have a choice. They had the numbers and the terrain. Hadn't we run, one of us would have been mobbed and seriously injured, or worse."

"I know that we didn't have a choice! I was there! I'm the one who called for the retreat, remember? But I can assure you that this is not the end of it. By the grass, give me a clear line of sight and some proper flat ground to flank them and I'll show these girls what a true cat's fight is all about. We'll see how they like their spine once I've pulled it straight down their belly. Let's see those hips bounce then!"

Shaka giggled and shook his head. "Yeah, well, it's too late now. They're gone."

T. took a deep breath and began to clean his paws. He needed the self-soothing gesture. "What about the Eyrefield? Can't we try them again? It'd be fun to rule over those girls who raised us."

And settle a few old wounds.

"No. Ever since the last skirmish the Solo male has taken them across the Sand River and into the Londolozi. He doesn't want to face us for the control of the Mala Mala."

"I don't blame him."

"You know," ventured Shaka, hesitant, "Makhulu and the others still hold the Londolozi with the Ottawa pride. If we chase after the Eyrefield and coordinate with them, we could run a pincer on those girls and trap them like a herd of buffalo. They would have nowhere to go."

"No. Absolutely not. I'm not going back there to ask the others for help."

"I understand, but if we bring them a whole pride I'm sure that the Big Mak will forgive–"

"I said no!" He jumped on his feet, his heart beating wild, his self-confidence gone. "I'm staying in the Mala Mala no matter what. This is our territory now. *Ours*! You can't give up on it so easily like that, Shaka. You just can't!"

Shaka heaved himself up slowly and leveled his gaze on T., his eyes deadpan. The younger lion felt his anger disappear all at once, as if blown out. The last of the burning embers quickly ceded place to a sort of cold quietness that gripped his entrails and dried his throat. He took a step backward. His claws caught onto something hidden in the ground – some weird, sprawling root maybe – and he stumbled on numb legs for a couple of steps before steadying himself.

"I'm not your enemy," said Shaka, calmly.

"I know."

"And I will never give up on this territory, or you."

"Shaka, I know. I'm sorry."

This was more tension than T. could stomach. Eager to mend the rift, he launched himself forward to give his brother a head-rub. To his stupefaction, Shaka avoided the physical contact. The subtle lurch wasn't much of a dodge at all, barely a half-step, really, but T. understood his brother's meaning plain enough. Shaka's body was stiff and withdrawn, his demeanor as hard and ungiving as those giant boulders that had thwarted their plans with the Styx.

His anger returned. Stung, he jerked his head back and broke contact, the voice in his head ready to bite. Already some dark remark plucked from the dark recesses of his mind was ready to roll off his tongue. He quickly licked his muzzle to get rid of it.

Shaka was scrutinizing him. Not with the cold arrogance of Makhulu's superiority but something softer that resembled sadness, which, in a way, was far worse. His pensive tongue darted to his rhinarium a couple of times. T. could practically hear the thoughts stampeding inside that calm, rational head of his.

Eventually, he relented and bowed his head. "Fine," he said as he leaned forward to return the head-rub, "we'll do it your way."

T. let out a sigh of relief. Shaka returned to his dozing and he ambled away along the bank of the river. Now that the issue had been settled in his favor, he was more than happy to let it rest. After a few steps, he settled on a nice spot of freshly grown grass and let his eyes wander over the sparkling water.

A small hamerkop waded in the shallows on the opposite side of the river. The brown bird was carrying a tiny bundle in his long bill, some small branches that he had snatched out of the mud. T. watched him walk gingerly back and forth, his head bobbing forward after every step, his brown crest raised high above his head. He stopped by a side puddle and dropped his branches to pick up a more promising cluster of large leaves coated in mud. Ecstatic, he raised his head high and scurried away, ready to take flight. As he extended his wings, he abruptly stopped mid-stride and turned back around while shaking his head. Back at the puddle, he dropped the leaves and regained his original cargo. Then he froze again, unable to decide.

T. smiled internally. He could relate. To do a thing, even a hard thing, you know must be done, that was easy. But to decide between two different, equally promising paths… That was the maddening part: the uncertainty before the leap that gripped the entrails and froze the limbs. Branches or leaves, choose wisely, little bird, your life might depend on it.

And once you're in the air, whatever else you do, don't look back.

The hamerkop settled on the cluster of leaves and flew upstream, all the way back to a large nest built on the fork of a tree overhanging the river a mere frog's leap above the water. In the middle of the nest, his pair was waiting for his return. After a quick greeting that reminded T. of their own head-rubs, the hamerkop cautiously lay

His pair? Presumably the author means his mate.

his leaves down and stepped back to admire his work. Good, but not perfect. He stepped forward again and adjusted the position of his cargo several more times with tiny, precise jerks of his bill. Finally, he let it rest, satisfied.

Even from afar, the humongous accretion of branches, mud, and brown leaves seemed more beehive than bird's nest. T. knew from experience – he had explored similar deserted nests in his youth – that the structure was a proper complex, complete with several hidden egg chambers and a secret exit at the bottom for cat-related emergencies. Given the bird's small size, the amount of work and energy required to build the thing and maintain it was baffling. Even if one took into consideration the bird's need to protect himself against predators, it seemed a gross overkill. While T. would probably never fully understand why the flappy ball needed to do it, he was willing to bet that it was at least in part due to the fact that he was taking pride in it, the same way that a lion takes pride in the range of his roar.

That roused him. His gloom over the Styx's temporary setback was unwarranted, he decided. The entirety of the Mala Mala was theirs, this was no small feat. And to think that there had been a time when that exact same stretch of grass had been his dread, every shadow of a leaf lurking in his nightmares like a monster on the prowl. Now it seemed flat and empty, vanquished, like a thundering rhino who had lost all his vigor once spilled open.

He yawned and licked his muzzle. A hunk of flesh ready to be consumed, that was the Mala Mala to him now. So be it. He was no cat to turn down a good meal.

He ambled back toward Shaka and let loose his roar. His brother leaped to his feet and nearly fell into the water. After steadying himself, he chuckled and added his own bellows to the chorus. Flank bumping against flank, they trotted away from the Mlowathi river and weaved themselves a path through the short grass in stops and starts, each ten steps interrupted by the need to answer the other lion's last roar, outdo it, find strength in it.

Their casual meandering slowly took them back to the only two Styx lionesses who had not run.

Tsavie raised herself up and went to greet them with a wary head-rub. With her belly held close to the ground and her ears flattened against the back of her head, her attitude guarded and submissive, she reminded T. of a cheetah taking a drink while keeping both eyes on some nearby crocodile.

Shaka ignored her and went straight to the other lioness, an older sister of hers named Lefu. Soon the noise of their vigorous mating rose over the hushed savannah.

"You guys raised quite a racket," Tsavie said with a flattering voice that was too high and loud, a poor imitation of cheerfulness. She was careful to keep her back turned to her sister's fate, T. noticed.

He stretched and laid himself down. "Just a bit of fun, really."

"Victorious fun?"

He rotated his head and scanned her demeanor for any trace of smugness. All he could see was meek humility. "No," he finally growled, "the remainder of your pride has escaped into the Djuma."

"I told you they would."

"They'll be back soon enough," he said blankly while repressing a sudden need to lurch for her throat. "The Djuma cannot sustain them indefinitely, most of the herds are still in the Mala Mala. And they have cubs to feed."

As soon as he heard the words escape his throat out loud, he realized that he had made a mistake.

"They saved the cubs too?! All of them?"

"Yes. They used the koppies for cover and fought us off before escaping into the night, like hyenas."

He found solace in the fact that she would have learned the truth one way or the other anyway. No point in lying, it would have been perceived as a sign of weakness.

Still, Tsavi's all-too-visible elation grated against his temper. It awoke confused feelings inside him. A small part of him could not help but be touched by the relief he saw spreading on her muzzle, as if some internal warmth had suddenly arisen in her belly and melted away the anxiety. For some reason, it brought him back to old memories and he caught a glimpse of his younger self reflected in the glint of her eyes. He promptly chased the disturbing thought away.

Unable to contain herself any longer, Tsavie giggled loudly. She seemed ready to break into a caper. He growled internally, his body tense, and swore to himself that, should she dare try it, he would strangle her where she stood.

Luckily for the both of them, Lefu suddenly let out a fierce cry of pain, higher pitched and louder than usual. In the wake of the shriek, they both heard Shaka growl his pleasure. The exchange brought Tsavie back to the ground faster than a buffalo's blow to the stomach. She ticked and lowered her head, her demeanor cold and neutral once more.

T. pounced on the opportunity and nonchalantly sauntered toward her two cubs romping in the short grass. His long shadow fell on them and he savored the way they wilted and shrunk at his approach. In a heartbeat, Tsavie was standing in front of him again.

"Cute little balls of fur," he whispered. "They seem well-fed."

She drew herself up and kept quiet. He lowered his muzzle and took a whiff of their scent. A tiny, brazen paw awkwardly lunged at his whiskers; he felt the small claws grate against his rhinarium. He raised his head back up, eyes gleaming, and said in the most casual way possible: "Whose are they anyway? Mine or Dread's?"

"There's really no way to tell. They could be Shaka's for all I know."

T. wrinkled his muzzle. He had not thought of that. It was true that ever since their coming to the Mala Mala the two of them had made a point of sharing just about everything they had conquered, amicably, for the most part. He took a second glance at the cubs. He had to admit, that little wild kitten looked as much like a diminutive Shaka as any ball of fur had any right to. Funny how he had never even contemplated that eventuality.

"What does it matter if their yours or Shaka's or Dreadlocks' anyway?" said Tsavie, her voice quivering slightly. "Isn't it enough to know that they've been fathered by a Mapogo?"

"Yes yes, of course. We'll protect them. With our life if needs be."

Upon hearing his words, she shivered and tensed up. This time he found no pleasure in her reaction. Only a sad lassitude. "Tsavie," he sighed, "why did you stay here with us when the rest of your pride ran?"

"My cubs are Mapogos, I didn't have a choice."

"The Shaw male doesn't know that. He would have accepted them as if they were his own."

"Even then, I can't raise such a young litter on the run. Either the pride would have left me behind and they would have starved, or you would have caught me and I would have found myself right back where I started. Either way, it made no sense for me to try to flee."

"One of the other Styx girls had young cubs too."

"Yes, but they were Shaws so she really didn't have a choice. Quite frankly, I am amazed that she made it. I never thought that the Styx pride would be able to successfully fend off two of the mighty Mapogos."

T. laughed heartily at that last swipe. "The split is what you didn't anticipate. You thought that the six of us would move-in on the Mala Mala together." He leaned toward the cubs. "And I bet that you had planned for Dreadlocks to be the one watching over these two, not me."

"T., they could just as easily be yours, I swear. They *really* could."

"Maybe," he said, unconvinced.

He suddenly became aware of the silence behind him. A warm pull awoke in his midsection. He turned himself around and leaped away, Tsavie and the cubs already forgotten.

Shaka ambled back on faint legs, his eyes satiated. "She's all yours, brother," he breathed out as they brushed flank.

He found Lefu sprawled behind a nearby tree. Judging by the tracks on the ground, she had dragged herself there, perhaps in a vain attempt to escape his notice. He shook his head derisively. Even without the help of the obvious trail of crushed grass, he could have zeroed-in on her fast panting from half a horizon away.

He rounded the tree and took a long, pensive look at her.

Back when they had first met her, the elder lioness had been one of the Styx's lead killer. Not just another rump-grabber, sink-your-teeth-where-you-can-and-hang-on-for-dear-life kind of huntress, but an actual point-cat, a horn tickler with a thick neck, bulging shoulders, and powerful jaws that were used to deliver the kiss of death to even the strongest of buffaloes. A lioness after T.'s own heart.

Now, less than a moon since their arrival, she seemed but a scrawny approximation of her former self. The fur on the back of her head had grown thin and fallen in patches, revealing spots of raw, pink flesh underneath; her neck was a ruin of scars; her emaciated core little more than a carcass of jagged ribs and vertebras. At one point, some unknown lion had broken the tip of her tail and bent it at an angle. T. suspected Shaka.

As he looked closer, he realized that fresh blood was now coating the right side of her neck as well. In the fast-falling twilight, it glistened black and blue, like a mamba's scales.

His urge deepened. He stalked forward.

She raised her head and scrambled to find her legs. After a couple of pitiful, teetering steps, she flopped back down abruptly, betrayed by the putrefying wound that was still eating at the muscles and tendons of her left back thigh. T. stopped and took the time to try and remember what had happened. He was fairly certain that the bite had occurred during some feeding frenzy, but which one? Probably the big buffalo they had brought down a couple of dawns ago. Yes, now that he thought back on it, he could remember him and Shaka ganging up on her and forcing her away. Still, for the life of him, he could not figure out which one of them had delivered the actual bite. Nor why.

He shrugged it off. It didn't really matter anyway. What was done, was done. Cold blood and all that.

After another failed attempt at getting up, Lefu let out an angry growl and swiped the ground at her feet with her still-powerful front paws.

She's not used to being so weak. She doesn't know how to deal with it.

Although he was standing in plain sight, he still made a point of walking slowly as if she were an antelope he had to surprise, savoring the foreplay for all its worth. The anticipation before the strike, he had learned a long time ago, was half the pleasure. Already he could picture in his head all the things that he would do to her.

The grass tickled his paws and sent a thousand delicious ants crawling up inside his limbs, all the way to his neither region where they converged. His chest contracted spasmodically and a half-strangled roar escaped his throat. Gasping, unable to contain himself any longer, he charged through the last few steps.

"Please," Lefu whimpered, her voice hoarse and supplicant, "please, not now. Not again. Please. *Please!*"

He laughed at the absurdity of her plea and fell on her like the proverbial bird of prey. Her front paws scuffed the dirt as she backtracked frantically in a vain attempt to bring her rear flat against the tree. He easily flanked her and ruefully pushed her off the protection of the trunk.

Then he straddled her.

With his two front legs firmly planted on either side of her body, he lowered his head forward and tightened his jaws around her neck. Flecks of caked blood came undone and tickled his palate. He sucked them in and let the tip of his tongue play with the remnants of Shaka's work.

She shrieked and bawled and twisted in place hysterically. He let go of her neck, brought his weight forward, forced her head down. The cutting edge of his fangs scraped over her right ear and eye, all the way to the sensitive parts of her muzzle. His tongue played with her whiskers. She jerked her head to the side and tried to squirm out from under him. He tightened his grip with his thighs and squeezed her in place. Her hips pushed up against his belly, hard. To his surprise, he felt himself being slowly lifted off the ground. Malnourished as she may be, she sure had some spunk left in her; she seemed ready to leap straight up to the rising moon and back.

No, no, no! Cats don't do cartwheels in the air. Everyone knows that.

The mating bite is gentle and never breaks skin

Laughing, he adjusted his position and used the full force of his pelvis to shove her hips back down. Her legs buckled and he heard something snap. A tendon, maybe. He bit down on a flap of skin near the back of her head and felt his fangs pierce cleanly through the fold. She screamed in pain.

His claws protracted as he entered her. Lost to his excitement, his muzzle let go of her neck and he had to flatten himself against her back to keep her locked in place. His wet rhinarium wandered up the back of her head, drinking-in her scent. He let his saliva slather her fur even as his busy tongue cleared a new patch of raw skin behind her left ear. Then his jaws closed in on her skull and he pulled back as hard as he could, arching her neck backward.

He felt the panic travel through her in one big tremor. Her eyes rolled inside their orbits. Her groans of pain dissolved into half-choked hysterical hisses. As her flesh contracted in revolt, her body thrashed in spastic bursts like a snake contorting itself under the steady foot of a secretary bird.

"Don't!" she shrieked. "Don't! PLEASE, DON'T!"

He tuned her voice out, closed his eyes, tightened his hold. Her head became a fixed point in space, independent from the jerks of her shoulders. As a lioness, she had quite simply ceased to exist. She was Makhulu sitting in judgment; Skoro mocking him; Dreadlocks making him feel small and insignificant. She was Shaka and his sad eyes. She was his mother dying.

The pumping of his hips took on a life of its own. The barbs of his penis raked her insides. As he focused his attention inward, he gorged himself on the desperate grinding of her helpless body and stole his pleasure out of her suffering. His forwardmost left fang punctured her skull. His lungs emptied themselves in a warm guttural groan. A white light exploded inside his mind. He jerked his head to the side and twisted her neck sharply. Locked in a spasm, he kept pulling as hard as he could, hoping for some mad reason to extend his orgasm by stretching her vertebras.

In a heartbeat, it was all over.

His penis retracted back inside his body like a timid turtle. He relinquished his grip and stumbled away on cold, bloodless paws. Suddenly, it felt as though something vital had just been yanked out of his lower belly. The pain was not entirely unwelcomed. He roared and stomped the ground in an effort to compensate for the numbness of his claws and the sudden emptiness that gripped his entrails.

By the grass, he was feeling strong!

He broke into an easy laughter and turned to face Lefu, hoping to see her share in his excitement. This was a good rumble they had enjoyed together after all.

Her expression cut his giddiness short. A new wound at the top of her skull was bleeding steadily all over her muzzle; with every one of her deep exhales, he could see the flow being blown slightly outward. Fat drops showered the dirt at her paws in steady *plops*. Shocked, she lowered her head and tried to blink some of the blood away from her eye before running a delicate tongue over her lacerated rhinarium.

Had he really done this? That seemed excessive. He had only meant to play the game a bit harder than usual. Have some fun. He did not recollect being so violent. Well, maybe the wound looked far worse than it actually was. The scalp always tended to bleed fairly easily after all. Any small cut could be responsible for this amount of blood. Maybe she was the one who had reopened an old wound, what with all her reckless thrashing around. He could not be blamed for that. She should have been more careful.

The root of his forwardmost left fang throbbed inside his mouth. Perplexed, he ran a delicate tongue over it and felt the tooth wobble slightly. There was no rationalizing this part away; his body remembered the bite.

He leaned forward and went to give her an apologetic head-rub. “Ya’kay?” he asked, instinctively putting on a bit of a tough show so as to hide his misgivings. “Bit o’ rough ride, eh? Sorry’bout that.”

She recoiled in fear and disgust. “Don’t touch me!” she screamed. “Get away from me!”

She pushed away and retreated toward the tree with both her eyes trained on him.

He sprang into action and matched her retreat, refusing to let any kind of gap widen between them. “Com’on! A wa’ jus’ playin’ is’ all. Neve’ meant to really hur’ ya.”

“Yes, you did. You meant to do everything you just did.”

“Alrigh’, alrigh’. My bad. A’ll be moar careful nex’time. Promise.”

“This isn’t even about getting the cubs for you, is it? There is something else crawling inside you, struggling to get out. Something dead. The mange’s got you, T.! The mange’s got you on the inside!”

He sighed and dug deep into his reserve of patience. The mange? Really? That putrefying disease that ate at a lion’s skin?

The whiny cat was not being reasonable. He rolled his shoulders and strut in front of her with his tail raised high, a half-snarl fixed on his muzzle. “I have no idea what you are talking about,” he said coldly, each one of his words carefully articulated, “but maybe you ought to take a long, hard look at yourself before you go on spitting big words like that. I’ve seen the way you move, huntress. In your state, I don’t think you’d be able to catch water if the rain were pouring down upon you. We hold you by the stomach, don’t you ever forget that. And don’t think that you can bite the fangs that feed you and get away with it either. No such thing as a free meal this side of grass. If I share my buffalo with you, you can bet your sweet bottom fur that I’m going to collect myself some tender meat in return. You’re tracking?”

A wet, blood-soaked cackle dodged Lefu's guard and escaped her throat. "Yeah, I track you alright big lion. Tender meat. Like a hippo. I heard the story, T. I know all about how Makhulu made you feed last like some second-rate, gimpy cat. How the reason why you're in the Mala Mala in the first place is because you ran in fear of him. You're no true independent lion. You're a cat stuck in a tree who's afraid to climb down because his brother is waiting for him at the bottom."

T jerked his head back, stung. "I'll kill you for this," he low-growled, his tough act suddenly gone the way of spilled blood. "I'll fuck you straight down the underside of grass, watch me if I don't."

She stood her ground and held his gaze but was smart enough to bite down whatever remark she might have had burning at the tip of her tongue.

He considered leaping at her throat for another bout; teach her a lesson and break her spirit for good, somehow. But after going through a number of scenarios in his head, he found that he no longer was in the mood. The spite and anger had deserted him, only the emptiness remained. He walked away.

As the night darkened, he hastened to find Shaka.

TWENTY

ANOTHER CUT

"Where have you been? I was looking for you."

Stretched out on a cushion of green grass with her limbs tucked-in underneath her body and her head resting on her front paws, Defiant kept her eyes shut and let a soft grunt out. "I've been here."

Not needed

"Your sister said that you might have gone looking for the herd."

"Nope, stopped right here."

"I checked for your trail by the river."

"No point, since I was here."

"I couldn't find any paw prints…"

She replied that, once again, it was because she had been, in fact, here.

Makhulu laid himself down next to the uncooperative cat and gave her rump a light nibble. "Fancy a rumble?"

Lions do not mate wherever they fancy. They mate only when a female's in season.

stocky

She opened her eyes and scratched her muzzle with her left paw, yawned, raised herself on her front legs slowly. After taking stoke of the bright sun, she thought better of it and fell back on her flank. "Not right now," she said, her eyes shut once more. "Too hot."

"That never stopped you before."

She did not dignify his comment with an answer.

Makhulu found his legs and stood to better contemplate the open veld in front of him. It was, truly, a beautiful morning. The recently rejuvenated grass was growing bright green, the soft soil felt moist under his paws and, despite what some lazy cat might say, with the light breeze blowing through the land and ruffling his mane, the temperature was quite agreeable. He let out a soft, satiated bellow.

"Please don't," groaned Defiant, half-asleep.

He turned to face her. "A lion ought to have a right to roar whenever he wants. Especially when he is inside his own territory."

"With such a big domain to his mane, a lion ought to be able to raise a racket somewhere else. Don't you have a far border to patrol somewhere? I'm sure that if you look hard enough, you can find a tree that you haven't marked yet."

He laughed and quietly laid himself back down next to her. "You're leading a hunting party tonight?"

She answered with a grunt and a nod.

"Any chance you might find a buffalo?"

"Sure. Any chance you might join us? The pride could use that big weight of yours."

"Don't you worry about that. Once that buffalo is dead, you'll see plenty of my big weight." She swatted his rump with her tail and he laughed some more. "The Ottawa girls are restless," he continued, more seriously. "They're eager for a challenge."

"They're young."

"They're Mapogos."

"Is that what you think?"

"Well, are they not our daughters?"

She raised her head to face him, her eyes sparkling darkly, her sleep gone. "Regardless of which coalition fathered her, a huntress belongs to her pride. Those girls are Ottawa, not Mapogo."

"True as that may be, they are still a part of our legacy."

"Lions have no legacy."

"Huh?"

"Male lions have no legacy, that is why we suffer them. Even their so-called territories are not really their own. The land belongs to the pride, the huntresses who will still be prowling it long after the old male is dead and gone and another young cat is strutting in his place, secure in his confidence that he owns the grass. Just another fool."

Makhulu grunted at the suddenness of the blow. One thing he liked about the lead huntress, she sure knew how to deliver a bite. "What about his brothers?" he countered, somewhat weakly. "A lion can always count on his brothers."

"Really? You still believe that after everything that has happened?"

"Our bounds might be strained but we're still a coalition. We'll come together should the need arise."

"You tell yourself that."

"You're going to pretend that you girls never have any quarrel among yourselves?" Makhulu said, his voice sharper than intended.

"Of course not. But a lioness is a member of a far more tight-knit community. We're all mothers and sisters linked by blood and a hundred shared hunts. A unit. When I train those huntresses, I make sure that they understand that they are part of a greater whole, the pride, which they serve. By comparison, your loose coalition's only purpose is to serve your individual needs. Sooner or later, you always end up fighting among yourselves for something you cannot share. If you ask me, you big manes don't live together so much as use one another. All that talk of brotherly love is quite pathetic."

"I don't suppose that I can really blame you for thinking that. After everything that has happened, I guess you have a right to hate us."

"I don't hate you, Mak. I pity you."

"Pity? Us?"

"Yes. For all his roaring and scent-marking, a lion lives an empty life. He has no true attachment to any pride or territory; no real bounds to his brothers; no certitude as to what the next dawn might bring, or whether the fight that will break his spine is waiting for him around the next thornbush. He comes and goes as if blown by the wind, with nothing to his mane."

Makhulu mulled on it for a bit. To his surprise, he found that he did not hate the idea. Not anymore. "Nothing but the ground on which he stands and the meat inside his belly," he whispered, his voice soft.

"Now you're just being poetic."

"You know, Shaka would disagree with you."

"Yeah?"

"Yes. Before he left, I tried to convince him to stay, briefly. I pointed out our prides and territory to entice him but he rejected me."

"Smart cat. He knew that those things were not truly yours to give."

"That's not what he said, though. He said: 'The only thing a lion ever truly has, are the things he's done'."

She laughed at that.

"You don't agree?"

"Let's just say that it's quite a lofty way of seeing things. Coming from the Lionheart, I guess I shouldn't really be surprised. Me, I'm more of a claws-deep-down-into-the-ground kind of cat. If I can see it or smell it, it's real. Everything else's just noise."

Makhulu cocked his head in puzzlement. "The Lionheart?"

"Just a nickname some of the Ottawa girls came up with for your brother."

"A compliment, I am sure."

A short, derisive snort escaped the lioness' muzzle. "Speaking of those two, any news of the breakaway degenerate and his favorite enabler recently?"

"Sort of. Last I heard they were still wreaking havoc among the Eyrefield and the Styx in and out of the Mala Mala. Their chase appears to be…relentless."

"They'll tire soon enough. The Mala Mala is too big for them."

"Shaka maybe, but not T."

Secretly, he was proud of his younger brother's accomplishments. When he had watched him go, so small and vulnerable compared to that enormous horizon that had swallowed him whole, he had fully expected to hear the news of his demise within a few moons. Even with Shaka with him it had seemed an overly long leap for the two of them.

He had made his peace with it. Told himself that not all cats were meant to last.

Now entire seasons had come and gone and the two lions were still going strong. 'The Mlowathi males' he had heard them being called a couple of times by some wandering lionesses without pride, usually in a hushed tone of repressed terror. With the last of the Shaw male rumored dead, the entirety of the Mala Mala had become their domain, a territory nearly as big as the one the other four Mapogos controlled. What a feat!

Sometimes, in the dead of night, he would go to the edge of the Londolozi and wait by the shore of the Sand River in hope of catching one of their roars from across the vast stretch of grass that separated them. He would never answer, of course, but sit quietly and listen to their proud back and forth, a soft gleam in his eyes, his mind reminiscing back to simpler times when the coalition was young and the whole horizon seemed ready to buckle under their weight. In those moments, he found that he almost missed T. and his senseless, ear-grating, temper-rattling mumbles. Whatever it was that the impetuous cat was chasing after, he truly hoped that he would one day catch it.

"There's a rumor going around," Defiant said, interrupting his reverie, "that Dreadlocks and the twins have been seen crossing the Sand River a couple of times, presumably to help the other two submit some of the Eyrefield girls. Is that true?"

"I don't know. Could be."

"Doesn't that bother you?"

"Unlike your precious little tight-knit unit, I don't pretend to rule over my brothers' every moves. They're free to come and go as they wish."

"Provided that the degenerate doesn't try to come back here, right?"

"Yes, of course."

Their eyes crossed. Defiant appeared unconvinced.

"You have my word," Makhulu said. For some reason, he felt that he owed her the reassurance. "I won't let him cross the Sand River again."

"The other three, they're in the Mala Mala right now?"

"Dreadlocks and the twins? No, they're with the Ximhungwe pride, I think."

The lioness lay back down with a groan. “Talk about cats without shame. Those girls want to exploit the vacuum left by the Sand River pride. They’re eager for a taste of those Singita herds.”

“Little do they know, the Ottawa girls have long beaten them to the leap.”

“Yeah, well, sometimes a cat has to be opportunistic. Those hunting grounds don’t grow on trees. Nothing wrong with trying to be the first one to the meat.”

“I’m pretty sure that I heard a vulture say something similar once.”

“The day you want to start feeding on grass, you make sure to let me know.”

They frittered much of the morning away in that fashion, Defiant increasingly eager to sink her teeth in that elusive sleep, Makhulu determined not to let her.

Around the change of sun-arc, her faint snores informed him that he had lost the battle. He moved off the spot and indulged an inner urge to scent-mark a couple of bushes and rub his face against the foliage. He stumbled upon the twins’ faint scent – they had been here no later than a couple of dawns ago, probably on their way to subdue the Ximhungwe – then Dreadlocks’.

He pushed a couple of calling roars out and let the vibrating bellows wash his mind off of Defiant’s nonsense. The answer did not take long to reach him. Leonides, he judged. He growled happily. He wasn’t alone after all. His brothers were still here for him. Most of them, anyway.

The lion was a half day of lazy meandering away, at most. This meant that the Ximhungwe was close by too. Now that could be trouble. He wouldn’t be surprised if the coalition were to end up in the middle of a full-scale pride war soon. Huntresses were not known for their instinct to share their precious territory with other prides, and for all her talks of being decent, Defiant could be quite cold and relentless in her insistence to dispatch any foreign lion that might hinder the livelihood of her precious unit. When one thought about it, she wasn’t unlike T. in that regard.

He chuckled internally as he tried to picture her reaction if he were to ever tell her as much. Maybe it was best not to yank on that particular tail.

He played with the idea of rejoining his brothers for a short while then decided to circle back toward the Ottawa instead. He wanted to catch a glimpse of his daughters as they prepared themselves for the night's hunt. Maybe he would join them. He could use the excitement.

By late afternoon, a commotion attracted his attention. He rounded a thornbush and found Defiant and her three daughters gathered in a semi-circle and gingerly swatting at something he could not see. As he walked-in to investigate, one of the daughters peeled off the group, her young predator gaze trained on her quarry, and tried a flanking maneuver. A burst of snarls erupted amid a cloud of kicked up dirt. The young huntress growled and hurried to rejoin the protection of her sisters, a fresh cut on her muzzle.

Makhulu picked up his pace and went around the group. Judging by the furiousness of the angry snarls, he was willing to bet that the girls had trapped a honey badger. Good for learning, that. Nothing like a tiny mouth filled with teeth lunging at your whiskers to teach you the art of the dodge. Too many young huntresses tended to think themselves invincible as soon as they had started to develop some muscles around the shoulders.

Intent on watching them tear the honey badger apart and perhaps volunteer a few hindsight, he trotted closer. As soon as he laid eyes on their quarry, he stopped in his track. This was no training session, he realized belatedly. The Ottawa pride had trapped a young male lion.

"What's this?" he bellowed.

The three young huntresses jumped away and closed rank to face him. In their eyes, he saw no recognition or warmth of any kind. No shame either. Only a cold, calculating, guarded hostility that made him feel estranged for some reason, as if he did not really belong here with them.

"We found him shambling around inside our territory," said Defiant. "He's practically starved to death already."

"A wander-male?"

That did not seem right. With barely any hair to his nascent belly-mane, the juvenile looked little more than a stretched-out cub; far too young to have left the protection of his pride voluntarily.

The older lioness flashed that amused snarl of hers. “You don’t recognize him, do you?”

“What do you mean?”

“He’s one of yours, from the Sand River pride. He’s part of your precious Mapogo legacy.”

Makhulu wrinkled his muzzle. Try as he might, he could not see any resemblance between him and that scrawny, half-dead thing. “Are you sure? That doesn’t seem possible. The Sand River girls disappeared seasons ago.”

“Looks like this one survived whatever happened to them and managed to find his way back, somehow.”

“Must be some kind of super-cub,” muttered one of the daughters, not without some small measure of respect.

“Has he talked to you at all? Told you what happened?”

“No. We tried to ask but got nothing. Only snarls and whimpers. I think he’s gone mute.”

“He must be in shock.”

Defiant licked her muzzle as she pondered that possibility. “Whatever happened to him, all of his sufferings are about to be over.”

She went to grab him by the spine.

“Let him go!”

Makhulu leaped forward and Defiant retreated with a surprised shriek. The three young huntresses scrambled to take position on his right flank, ready to lunge, but hesitated at the last instant. A single low-growl quieted them.

Defiant drew herself up and regained her composure. “Well, well, well,” she cackled, “look who’s decided to care about his cubs all of a sudden.”

“There is no need to kill him,” Makhulu said in a tone that he hoped sounded calm and reasonable. He made sure to cover the cub’s body with his own. “He’s no threat.”

“How noble of you. If only you had shown nearly as much backbone with your first litter.”

“This is different.”

“Yes, it is. This one’s most likely not even yours.”

“What do you want me to say? That I’m sorry about what happened before? Because I am. You know that I am.”

She sucked in her breath, tried to hold it, failed. "Then acknowledge it!" she barked.

"Acknowledge what?"

"That you killed those cubs! Not just your brothers. *You.* I want you to look me in the eye and acknowledge that you murdered your own small ones! Murdered them with your withdrawn placidity, your blind ignorance, your… your… YOUR FUCKING LACK OF CARE!"

The outburst tore right through Makhulu's defenses. "Alright, I did!" he screamed back, his temper and insecurities spilling out. "I killed them! Me! Here, you're happy? I'm sorry, Defiant. For everything. We Mapogos turned out to be failures, me first of all. After taking over so much of the Sabi Sands and killing so many young cats, we should have been more focused on protecting our prides and help you raise the next litters in order to make up for the losses. The six of us together, with so many huntresses under our rule, there is so much that we could have accomplished. And you know what? For just a moment, I really thought that we would.

"Instead… I don't know. We were supposed to be more than just killers but it seems that the only thing we are really good at is spilling blood." He stopped. Under his laborious breathing, the grass had suddenly grown really quiet. "So here you have it, my confession. But whatever you might think of the Mapogos, or me, that young cub has nothing to do with any of it. Don't take your revenge out on him."

"Saving him won't be enough to redeem yourself, Mak. It's far too little, far too late."

"Maybe you're right, but that's the only thing I can do right now."

The lioness' eyes went from Makhulu to the young male's exposed belly, then back. She seemed caught off guard by his acknowledgement of the facts. She had lost her footing. Finally, she turned around and trotted away with her three daughters in tow. "If he's not Ottawa, he doesn't feed at our kills," she bit out from over her shoulder.

Makhulu watched her disappear behind a thicket of trees. Once she was clear and gone, he stepped away from the young male.

"You have a name?" he asked, his voice gruff.

No reply, only two yellow eyes fixed on the ground, seemingly intent on ignoring his very presence.

"Where is your pride? Do you know? The Sand River girls. Can you tell me what happened to them? Are they still alive?"

Still no reaction.

"Some other cat got your tongue, eh?"

Makhulu sighed. There was no point pushing the young lion around, he would only retract inside himself even further. Maybe Defiant was right. Maybe it was too late.

He ambled away with his head bowed and his eyes downcast. As soon as he rounded a low thornbush and cut the line of sight, a short yelp arose, followed by a frantic scrambling of paws. He stopped and turned around. The young male froze a half-dozen paces behind him. He smiled internally. The fits and stops repeated themselves a couple of times and the distance shrunk progressively until, finally, the last of the young male's reserve broke and he rushed to the level of his flank. Soon they were walking side by side comfortably.

They reached an overflowing water hole. Makhulu went to lap a drink out of a nearby puddle and a flock of white birds scattered at his approach. Once he had decided that it was safe enough, the young male followed his example, his eyes held high, his posture a perfect imitation of Makhulu's own stance.

"You don't have to talk if you don't want to," Makhulu said. "I know how it is. Some things, you just can't put words on them. That's alright, I can talk for the both of us."

The young male shuffled his paws and wriggled his rump, his attention entirely focused on his drinking and the puddle in front of him.

"You remind me of one of my brothers. He went through some trauma himself when he was roughly your size; had a hard time adjusting to it too. The sharp edge of grass gets to everyone sooner or later, of course, but for those few cats who are touched too early… Well, I guess it cuts a bit deeper. You'll get over it eventually, don't worry about that. Just like he did. He was very reserved for a long while. Not mute like you, not quite, but shy and soft-spoken. And precise. Yes, very precise in his speech, as though he needed to think every syllable seven times over before uttering it out loud. Once he found his confidence however… By the grass, there was no shutting him up any longer. Sometimes I wonder if that's not the real reason why I pushed him away."

The young lion raised his head, his eyes wide and interrogative.

"Don't worry, I'm not going to do that to you. As far as I'm concerned you belong with us. I guess what I'm trying to say is that, even though I don't know exactly what you've been through, I know that there is still a way forward for you. Just take it slow, one meal at a time."

Makhulu pricked up his ears, suddenly aware of a cacophony of growls, curses, and desperate grunts he recognized quite well reaching him from half a horizon away. The sharp taste of freshly spilled impala blood tickled his palate.

"Speaking of meals," he said as he pounced forward, "follow me."

Defiant had not waited for nightfall after all. He wondered if this was an opportunistic kill or something a little less innocent. Maybe the proud lioness had been eager to sink her teeth into something warm after their last encounter. He chuckled internally. Funny how he could have that effect on lionesses these days.

He reached them shortly after it was all over. Already the huntresses were ripping the impala apart. Upon seeing him, Defiant raised her blood-soaked muzzle. "Oh no you don't! Not ag—"

His bellows drowned her voice out. He fell into a fast camper and barged through their clumsy scrum like an elephant through green foliage. One of the younger huntresses lunged at him and tried something brave. He brushed her off and swiped her on the muzzle, not maliciously but hard enough to drive his intent through her thick skull. She leaped away with an outraged growl and the rest of the group adopted a more respectful distance.

Defiant fell quiet and stared at him with hollow eyes. As she padded back and forth restlessly between the carcass and the group, unable to decide on a course of action, he saw in her fast breathing how the hunt had left her drained and weak. The proximity of the meat, so tantalizingly close and yet out of her reach, was chafing at the back of her throat, driving her insane. He could almost taste her vexation on his palate.

So much for making amends.

Well, he had other priorities.

He turned his back on her and used the left side of his jaw to gnaw at a protruding rib. The timid male made his entrance from under the cover of a thick bush and after having given the girls a wide berth moved toward the carcass slowly.

His progress was excruciatingly meticulous. With every one of Makhulu's abrupt jerks and pulls on the carcass, he would freeze and sometimes even retreat. Makhulu paid him no mind. He knew that the young cat's stomach would do the work for him, eventually. The temptation was simply too great, as evidenced by the ceaseless darting of his tongue on his rhinarium.

He focused his attention on a recalcitrant piece of meat stuck in-between the base of a rib and a stubborn patch of hard leather. After having peeled most of the skin off — not so easy a task: every time he pulled on the tricky edge, the whole carcass seemed to go along with it — he lowered himself and extended his raspy tongue to try and lick the morsel off the bone. He closed his eyes. He could feel the tasty bit jiggle from side to side, tied down by one last nerve. He cursed and leaned forward. His muzzle peeled back in a greasy half-snarl and his upper left fang groped for a way inside the tiny crevasse his tongue had created. Finally, he felt the canine slide in. The point pierced through the flesh and he slowly pulled back, at first tentatively, so as to test the strength of the anchorage, then, once he realized that the morsel would not rip apart, more eagerly.

Victory! The last nerve gave up and the morsel popped inside his mouth. He swallowed it down with a satiated groan and savored the way it went through his esophagus before settling nice and heavy inside his stomach, where it belonged.

He licked the grease off his muzzle. Now, all he had to do was to repeat the same process all over again. He shook his head and repressed a dispirited sigh. Was there any creature above grass whose life was more miserable than that of lion? All that work and effort for a single bite.... It was enough to sap all the strength out of a proud cat.

A soft crunching reached his ears. He raised his head and saw the young male munching on one of the impala's back thighs, half-hidden behind the shaky limb.

"Nice of you to join me at last."

The young lion stopped mid-bite, ready to bolt. Once he realized that the big dark-maned was not about to lunge at him and break his spine, he returned to his feeding.

Together, they assaulted the impala from opposite ends.

Another dozen bites later and Makhulu felt full. He stepped away and lay down in front of the carcass so as to keep the increasingly impatient huntresses away. The young lion was still going at it eagerly, his big belly protruding grotesquely out from under his emaciated frame.

"Well, you're strong-headed, that much is clear. If I remember correctly so were your older brothers. Skoro and Leonides were always going on and on about how the overconfident belly-manes were standing up to them to defend their pride's kills, only to be chased away every single time." He stopped, hesitant to pursue the river of his thoughts any further. He did not want to spoil the bit of rapport he had managed to build. But he needed to be sure. Finally, he let it out as plainly as he could: "Any chance they might still be alive?"

The Sand River male stopped eating. The way he lowered his head told Makhulu everything he needed to know.

"And the lionesses?"

The young lion shrugged.

"You ran, didn't you?"

Once again, that eloquent silence. Trapped by the memory, the young male began to fidget his paws irresistibly in front of him, ready to flee. Makhulu jumped to his paws and hastened to give him a head-rub that embraced the entirety of his body. "Easy there. It's alright. You did what you had to do. You're a survivor."

The shaking stopped and the young male appeared to calm down a little.

"This reminds me of a male I once met. Dzunani, he was called. He had the unfortunate reputation of being quite the mellow cat because he would keep to his own small territory without trying to expand, seldom roared, and would always let his females, the Ximhungwe pride, eat first after a kill. At the time we were still a young coalition. We had just taken over the Ottawa girls and were expanding toward, well, your pride actually. The Sand River girls. Now in all honesty, in those days, we were crazy cats. Hungry and wild and vicious, happy to give chase to any four-legged thing just for the sake of the adrenalin. I've personally lost count of the number of leopards I've chased up a tree, to say nothing of the hyenas I've killed.

"One morning, I struck out on my own for a little while. I didn't think anything of it at the time, I just wanted a bit of quiet for myself. I had no idea that another pride was nearby. That is, of course, until this Dzunani fellow came bursting out from the tall grass right in front of me. Oh how I wish you could have been there to see him with me. A huge, bloated mane far too big for his face; a scrawny, bended neck, like the small trunk of a baby elephant; stick-thin ankles seemingly too weak for his enormous flat paws; and, to top it all, a blank expression on his muzzle, like a void that would have made a retarded hippo appear like the smartest cat you've ever seen in comparison. Truly, he was a comical apparition. Disheveled like a thornbush. A laughable excuse of a lion. Except for the eyes. By the grass, I still remember how those pupils bore right through me at the time, as if I weren't even there at all. You see, that one morning, perhaps for the first time in his entire life, Dzunani had found his courage and decided to lay it all down on the dirt in front of him, no matter the cost. And... Well, would you believe it? That was actually enough to undo me. Yes. Me. I honestly don't know what happened. All I remember is that something inside me lost its footing and the next thing I knew, I had turned around and begun running. I did not stop until after I was safe and sound with my brothers. Afterward, we heard Dzunani roar his victory for all he was worth."

He chuckled warmly as he relived the event. Although he had been deeply embarrassed at the time, he now found that he cherished the memory all the more for its unique peculiarity. He had not meant to go on and on like that but now that the words were out he was glad that he had. It felt good to talk about these things to someone who was not his brother.

"So you see, even proud cats can sometimes be gripped by fear. It doesn't mean anything other than the fact that you have a strong and healthy survival instinct. You shouldn't feel any shame but rather try to embrace it. If you can use the fear to your advantage, you will go far. And don't ever waste a single heartbeat of your life worrying about what others might think of you. To ignore your own safety for the sake of appearances is not only dangerous, it is a show of weakness. Only the fools and the insecure do that."

The young male nodded his head gravely. He had lapped every single word out of the story as if they were so many bites out of another, sweeter meal. Now he seemed more relaxed, perhaps even at peace.

Makhulu yawned and stretched. His legs were sore, he needed to walk some of that new weight off. As soon as the two of them ambled away at a relaxed pace, the huntresses eagerly pounced forward and ripped through what few greasy bones were left.

"We did go back to finish him off, eventually," continued Makhulu, oblivious to the cries of rage and consternation echoing behind him. "We ripped Dzunani apart without so much as a second thought. When the Ximhungwe girls saw what we had done they fled and swore to protect their cubs and never submit. All lionesses always say the same thing at first, you'll get used to that. Now most of them are dead, killed by the hardships of a life on the run, and the few who are left have finally swallowed their stubborn pride and accepted to join the protection of my brothers. And the only thing that is left to prove that Dzunani ever existed is that memory I have of him."

His voice trailed off. He fell into a morose silence. The memory was not so warm anymore. Just another lion they had murdered. Try as he might, he could not remember the particulars of the actual fight.

"I guess I should have gone back to kill him on my own," he whispered to himself. "Single combat. I owed him that much."

He pushed the thought away and broke into a brisk camper across the plain.

A few days came and went in a similar manner. The Sand River male kept mimicking Makhulu's every move while eagerly lapping up his stories. His mental health and confidence seemed to improve greatly, but the dark-maned was still worried about his stubborn refusal to speak. Once he thought that he had heard him chuckle briefly after having listened to one of Dreadlocks' funnier mishap — a sorry tale of sheer stupidity involving the big lion's overeager stomach, the slippery banks of a muddy river, and a very irate porcupine — but he could not be certain it had not simply been a throat clearing.

Also of concern was the fact that his frail body did not seem to gain any muscle. After every meal, his belly would hang down almost all the way to the ground like an obscene pregnancy, ready to burst, but his chest and hips still remained as emaciated as the first day he had seen them. He put it down to the trauma his digestive system had probably gone through during his long days of wandering alone. Soon everything would be back to normal, he told himself. The young male just needed a bit more time to adjust.

One afternoon, they shared a giraffe and went to sleep.

When Makhulu woke up, he found the young male still laid down in the exact same position he had left him. His heart skipped a beat inside the emptiness of his chest. He did not need to lower his muzzle to know that the young cat's scent was gone.

Defiant walked past him. Upon noticing the small corpse, she stopped abruptly. Her eyes grew wide.

"Did you do this?" he asked.

"No," she said, her voice flat.

His scent wouldn't be gone, but it would tell him he was dead.

"What about the other girls? They're always eager for blood." Although there was no visible wound on the body, that did not prove anything. A hard shake could split a spine just as easily as any puncture wound.

"It wasn't any of us, Mak, you have to believe me. We all knew how much you cared about him. We would never have done something like that to you."

"Then what?"

She let out a measured sigh. "There is no way to know for sure, but it appears that his body was not receiving enough energy. I guess his heart just gave up."

"I gave him enough meat to feed three lions five times his size."

"I've heard of cases like this. Maybe he stumbled upon the wrong carcass when he was struggling out on his own and caught the taste."

"The taste?"

"It's something you get from bad buffalo meat. Something to do with white flakes in the tissue, although there is no way to tell at first. We call it that because, apparently, it feels like some thin layer of fat is clinging to the back of your throat. Long after your meal has been digested and forgotten, you still have the taste of the buffalo inside your mouth. Once you catch the taste, the grass has you by the stomach. You're done. You might think that you can fight it but no matter how much you eat, you're going to starve."

Makhulu closed his eyes. He had never heard of such a horrifying death before but he had to admit that it sounded eerily like something the veld might throw at a living lion. Were it not for the grief and despair that gripped his entrails, he might actually burst out in a mad laughter at the sheer irony of the thing. Meat that kills you by starving you. One had to admire the grass' sharp sense of humor.

"For what it's worth, I'm sorry," said Defiant. "I didn't like him being here but the young cat was clearly a survivor like you, as strong as old wood. He didn't deserve this."

Nobody ever does, that sure don't stop the grass from growing.

"I know how it feels to lose a cub," she continued. "It's like a cut on the heart. Like you've been clawed from the inside."

"So?"

"So if you want to talk about it, I'm here."

He tore himself away from the sight. "There is nothing to say."

The memory of Dzunani barreled through his mind, unwanted. He had begged around the end, but not for himself. "Take the territory but spare the cubs," he had said. "Please! You don't need to kill the cubs!" The others had laughed at his plea. What was it that T, had said? He could not remember the exact words. Some clever little remark about the cat's line ending along with his life. Dzunani had ignored them all as if they didn't even exist. Spilled wet all over the grass, every single one of his limbs broken multiple times, he had dismissed the tremors of the lions eating him from behind and kept his cool gaze on him, Makhulu, while waiting for an answer from one dark-maned to another. Makhulu had only averted his eyes and walked away. Extremely unusual behaviour.

He pushed the memory out of his mind. "It's not my first cut," he said out loud. "Won't be the last either. Cubs die, that's just the way it is. Especially Mapogo cubs, it would seem."

"Not your daughters," he heard Defiant say behind him as he ambled away. "I'll see to it that your daughters live. On this, you have my word."

TWENTY-ONE

NKORHO

She's dead!

The sudden realization slapped Shaka's mind like an elephant's trunk to the face. He snapped his head up and took a step back, away from Lefu's fast-glazing, accusing eyes. The coldness of her deflated body lingered on the tip of his muzzle. He shuddered and hastened to lick it off.

They had killed her. She had done everything they had expected of her, submitted in every way imaginable, and still they had killed her.

Why?

How?

Even as he stared at the ruin of her neck and the fresh bite marks on the back of her spine, near her tail, he failed to comprehend how she had come into such wounds. A feeding frenzy, maybe? Surely their mating could not have been that rough.

His eyes zeroed-in on the half-congealed blood that was still seeping slowly out of the old puncture wound on the back of her skull. T. had done that, he knew. One mating session after the next, he had taken pleasure in reopening the wound again and again and again so as to prevent the bone and flesh from ever healing properly. “Sliding-in from both ends,” he had taken to calling it, and joked that the increasingly reeking and swollen crater was his “personal hold on her”.

Shaka growled at his own abject stupidity. Here he was, standing by her corpse, as shocked as some wide-eyed cub smelling blood for the first time, wondering how she could possibly have died, when the true mystery was in fact how she had been able to endure that obscene treatment for so long. The fester on the back of her head alone would have burned at her brain like nothing he could possibly imagine. And to think that she had endured it all stoically while knowing perfectly well that the wound would never heal, that T. would never *let* it heal…

He had known all of this. He had known and done nothing. She was sworn to his protection, same as any other female, and he had let it happen right under his muzzle without so much as a word of protest. Worse, he had let himself being carried away by his brother’s wild exuberances and played along with some rough mating of his own.

The guilt struck him in the gut, hard enough to empty his legs and make him stumble. What kind of a sick, cowardly cat was he? How could ever hope to look at his own reflection in the river and call himself lionlike ever again? He was nothing but a mindless killer with all the honor of cold-blooded reptile.

As if on cue, a large crocodile slowly emerged out of the placidity of the shallow river where Lefu had gone to take her last drink. His powerful body easily swam the distance to the carcass and stopped at the edge of the shore to gauge Shaka’s intention. Once he had decided that the big lion was no threat, the crocodile delicately grabbed Lefu’s head and gently pulled her down the depth of the river.

Shaka felt a wave of nausea surge inside his throat and promptly turned away. He came face to face with Tsavie.

"She only stayed because of me," said the lioness, her voice blank, her eyes two slit trained on the glaring spot where Lefu's last bubbles were disappearing quickly. "She could have easily fled into the Djuma with the rest of the pride, but she knew that I could not follow. She stayed behind to help me raise my litter. I killed her, Shaka. I killed her with my cubs."

He brushed past her. He had no word of comfort to offer her. All he knew was that he needed to put as much distance between himself and that river as possible. Fast.

He broke into a gallop and strived to outrun his own shadow.

Once it felt like his heart was about to burst, he eased down and savored the surge of happy blood bathing his mind in a much-needed numbness. His solitude suddenly became unbearable. He pushed out a couple of calling roars and picked the pace up again as he zeroed-in on T.'s answer.

"Where have you been?" his brother asked. "I was about to call you."

"Lefu's dead. I found her body by the river."

At least T. had the good grace to appear somewhat concerned by the news. "Who killed her?" he asked, genuinely surprised.

"We did. She succumbed from her old injuries."

All trace of concern disappeared from his brother's muzzle, replaced by an abject expression of mock sorrow. After having considered the issue for all of a half heartbeat, he simply nodded his head. "A small matter, considering the greater scale of things in the Mala Mala."

In that moment, for a single poignant heartbeat, Shaka found himself hating his brother in a way that he had never thought possible. "You're the one who killed her, T.! You *tortured* her to death!"

"Bah, she was already dead weight when we met her. Far too weak to hunt. If you ask me, I don't think I really had anything to do with her death at all. She may have been walking around and all, but there wasn't much of her old self left inside that depleted fur of hers. She wasn't even cleaning her paws anymore. No, trust me, she's the one who decided to stop swimming. And that's why she sunk. Nothing anyone could have done to save her."

"You punctured her skull! Broke her spine! She didn't 'stop swimming', T. You're the one who pushed her under." He sucked in a shaky breath, feeling the rage cede place to that enormous, guilty weight inside his guts once more. "And I helped you do it. That's the golden sun honest truth of it. By the grass, she was ours and I helped you kill her."

T. growled and swiped the ground with his front paw. "It doesn't matter Shaka! *She* doesn't matter. Just let it go already."

Both cats fell into a sullen silence that seemed to stretch on without end.

"I have a surprise for you," the unapologetic lion finally broke in, his tone carefully conciliatory. "I stumbled upon it a couple of dawns ago. That's why I was about to call you."

Shaka sighed and closed his eyes. Now that he had emptied his chest and heard his own words spoken out loud, he found that the whole thing seemed rather pointless. Good or bad, what was done was done. No amount of arguing would undo it. And whatever else he might be at times, T. was still, for better or worse, his brother.

"What is it?" he asked.

The dangerous half-snarl made its appearance and chased the sullenness away, as if the previous exchange had never happened at all. "Oh trust me, you're going to love this. That's about as lionlike as it gets!"

Without waiting, T. fell into a bouncing trot and moved away from the Mlowathi river, deeper into the veld, toward the edge of the Mala Mala.

Shaka watched him go and felt his anger flare up again. More than anything else, he hated the easiness with which his brother had dismissed his accusations and run a circle around his temper as though he did not matter at all. Well, he didn't have to follow him if he didn't want to. He was a free lion after all. He could just as easily go back to the river and fritter the afternoon away with Tsavie and her cubs. Maybe go on a hunt later. Nothing wrong with that. Nothing wrong at all.

T. disappeared behind a thicket of trees.

Cursing softly, he pounced forward and hurried to catch up.

After a short run, they stopped by the side of a seemingly ordinary tree. Shaka already had some idea as to what they were about to find. The breeze was blowing their way. "How many?" he asked.

"Have a sniff."

He lowered his muzzle toward the base of the trunk and peeled his lips back to expose his palate. The strong scent of foreign males immediately assaulted his mind. He recoiled in disgust. "Are those the same manes we've been trading roars with over the last few days? The so-called Majingilanes?"

"Yesssss. I guess they got tired of playing the loud game, the young fools. Now they're making a move. They've marked the tree to test our defenses and prove a point before retreating back inside the Nkorho. I've already had a quick look around, their tracks are easy to follow."

"Wait, you mean to engage them?"

"Of course. We're going to have to fight them sooner or later, we might as well take the initiative."

"T…This is far too dangerous."

"What do you mean? We've killed intruders before."

"Not like this we haven't. This isn't like falling on a trio of Toulon males in the dead of night while they're asleep, or murder a couple of isolated belly-manes who don't know any better. This is an actual standing coalition. You've heard their roars. You know perfectly well that there could be as many as four lions waiting for us at the end of those tracks."

"More like five, I would say. So what?"

"So what? What do you mean: 'So what?' We should retreat back across the Sand River and warn the others, that's what! The six of us together, we can engage them."

"And give up the cubs? Are you crazy?"

"They're five strong lions, T.! *Five*. Can you still count? There is only two of us."

"Tell me, which group is larger, the herd of buffaloes or the squad of lion going after them?"

Shaka clenched his jaws and shook his head. He knew that he should not indulge his brother's madness a heartbeat longer, but a part of him could not help it. T.'s high spirit was contagious. "The herd," he said coldly, knowing full well that he was walking into a trap.

"Exactly. And yet, time and time again the smaller squad triumph over the bigger herd. Why? Because they are *organized*, that's why. That's the secret! Numbers alone are meaningless, purpose and strength of will is everything. Give me a small, determined minority

Buffalo are anything but placid!

over a large, placid majority any time of the day, and I'll give you more grass than you can possibly dream of."

"T., those are not placid grazers we are talking about but actual fighting cats…."

"We can do it Shaka! By the grass, I know we can. So long that we're smart about it. See, we don't call them out and wait for all five of them to come to us. Rather, we take the fight to them. We move quietly through the grass and ambush them one by one when they least expect it. Once we've taught a couple of those pretentious, inexperienced belly-manes what the wrong side of a fang feels like, I guarantee you that the others will lose all taste for further bloodshed right quick. They'll run back where they came from and we won't ever have to worry about them setting foot inside the Mala Mala and catching us unaware ever again. And, as an added bonus, the Nkorho will be ours."

Shaka jerked his head back, confused. He had to admit, the idea was starting to grow on him. It didn't sound nearly as crazy as what he had expected. With a bit of planning, and a healthy dose of luck, they might be able to pull it off. But they would have to be very, very careful.

"We'll have to move extremely quietly," he heard himself whisper. "No roars or scent-markings of any kind."

"Yes, yes, absolutely."

"And we'll have to make sure that any Majingilane we ambush is isolated. We can't afford to have the others attack us from behind."

"We'll make sure."

"They'll have to spread out at some point, right? They can't always stay together."

"Not if they want to cover any kind of ground, no. Besides, you've heard the way they roar. They're young and full of themselves. They don't know anything about anything."

"This is what's best for the cubs. We have to protect the cubs."

"Yes of course, the cubs," said T., jubilant, "and think about the reputation too. Think about Makhulu's face once he learns that we've defeated a coalition of *five* lions."

He leaped forward, ready to break into a gallop.

Shaka remained where he stood, his front legs suddenly cold and weak. "You–you really think that we can pull this off? I mean, how can you be so sure?"

T. turned around and went to give him a reassuring head-rub. "Come on, bro, trust me. When have I ever steered you wrong?"

They entered the Nkorho at night and moved under the canopy of low bushes on soft feather-paws, their shadows gingerly skirting the rays of moonlight shining through the thin branches. Out in the distance, they could hear the five Majingilanes roar at the top of their lungs. Shaka caught a whiff of freshly-spilled buffalo blood. "They're absolutely not afraid of us," he muttered under his breath. "It's like they think they already own the place."

"They're persuaded that we'll cower in fear and keep to the Mala Mala,"

"They're about to learn better."

They found the carcass at dawn. As they left the cover of the low trees, they spread out and slunk through the yellow grass with twitching ears, their muzzle on high alert for any foreign scent. Once they had ascertained that the area was clear, they stood up and converged on the pile of greasy brown bones. The usual signs of trampled grass, spilled blood, and fresh scats were everywhere to be seen. T. circled the carcass a couple of times, in search of a trail. "Some of those scats are still soft," he pointed out. "They can't have been gone for very long."

"They must have left shortly before sunrise. They'll be looking for some shade to digest in peace."

T. nodded his head quietly while staring at the landscape in front of them. A good dozen islands of green acacias could be seen rising out of the dry, sunbaked grass in every direction, anyone of them large enough to hide a full coalition under their low, sprawled-out canopy. He went back to studying the hard-packed dirt. "That way," he decided.

They kept their belly low and shoulders hunched even as their legs hurriedly ate the ground with small, eager strides. Already Shaka could feel the brightness of the sun hammer at his mane, firing up his blood. Stalks of hardened grass grazed his fur and pricked the underside of his paws. Bits of vegetation invaded his airways and stuck to the back of his throat. He found himself salivating profusely.

Truly, it was a beautiful day. A Sabi Sands day. He had forgotten how good it felt to be on the prowl again.

No hunt like a lion hunt.

T. stopped and abruptly turned around with gleaming eyes, his half-snarl threatening to rupture the corner of his muzzle. "They've split," he whispered while pointing at the trail in front of him. "Four of them went that way but, for some reason, the fifth one chose to strike out on his own, that way." with what?

Shaka licked his rhinarium, feeling the last of his misgivings evaporate. "Let's do it."

Even at a fast trot, it took them the better part of the morning to follow the tracks. Shaka didn't mind. In fact, it seemed too good to be true. With every new step they were getting further away from the rest of the Majingilane coalition and closer to finding the fifth lion alone and vulnerable. Judging by the careless, meandering tracks he had left behind, it was clear that the young cat had allowed himself to drift away from his brothers without a thought in his head. Shaka swallowed down an angry growl. How could any lion be so oblivious?

They're young. They've just killed a big buffalo. They think that they're safe inside the Nkorho, that they can't be touched.

T. was right. Numbers alone could not make up for the sheer stupidity and arrogance of a bunch of belly-manes who were persuaded that they had it all figured out already. The two of them would tear through their coalition like a herd of antelopes and send the survivors running all the way to the far side of grass and beyond. Same as they had done with all the other males.

He stopped to sniff the air. They were close, he could smell it. All around him, the Sabi Sands had fallen quiet, as if holding its breath. "T.," he whispered.

His brother froze. After sucking in a breath, he nodded his understanding and began to investigate the ground to his right.

Shaka stalked forward and scanned the bushes ahead. With the glare of the sun shrinking his pupils, his eyes could not penetrate the shadows of the undergrowth. He had to get closer. The soft breeze ruffled his mane.

He knows we're here.

Something predatory growled inside his chest. He checked a low bush, turned to the left, peered inside a tangle of vines.

Two yellow eyes stared back at him.

"Over here, T.! Over here!"

The young Majingilane exploded out of the cover of the creepers and raced across the scrubs.

In a heartbeat, Shaka and T. were in hot pursuit.

They skimmed the edge of a flat dirt lane and flashed by a slow-moving rumbler before cutting back into the grass. T.'s muzzle seemed stuck to the Majingilane's tail but Shaka had fallen behind a bit. Feeling his heart leap inside his chest, he sped up to close the gap. The young lion came face to face with an impenetrable thornbush and precipitously veered to the left. T. leaped forward and cut him off. He jumped to the side and tried to speed up again. Shaka sliced into his rebound trajectory and impacted his body at full speed. The two lions went rolling in the dry grass.

The overturned Majingilane growled his outrage at the top of his lungs and erupted in a frenzy of blind swipes and lunges. Slightly dazed by the impact, Shaka kept his hold on the overturned rump despite the storm of claws raking his mane. Something sharp pierced through his front paw. He hollered in pain and jerked his head back before mindlessly biting down on the hind leg helplessly kicking through the air in front of him. As he clenched his jaws and pulled back as hard as he could, he felt the bone snap in his mouth.

The chorus of roars redoubled.

T. jumped in and grabbed the Majingilane by the back of the head. "Go for the groin!" he screamed while pulling the muzzle as far away from Shaka as possible. "Go for the groin!"

Maddened by fear, the young lion ripped himself free of T.'s hold and lunged at his head. Before T. had time to recoil, the Majingilane's fangs had closed on his muzzle and sliced through his rhinarium.

Shaka used the distraction to dive on the exposed scrotum. His fangs ripped through the tender flesh, pierced the exposed testicles, tore a gash into the lion's lower belly. Unable to contain himself any longer, he stepped back to roar his pleasure and swallow the mouthful of flesh he had ripped off. Blood and saliva splattered the grass at his paws. An insane need overcame him. Lunging forward again, he buried his muzzle deep inside the wound he had created and closed his jaws around the retracted penis. With a vicious jerk, he ripped it off.

The Majingilane shrieked and relinquished his grip on T.'s muzzle. In shock and reeling with pain, he lay his head down slowly, gasping for a breath, the claws of one front paw still awkwardly stuck inside T.'s right ear. Bleeding profusely from several cuts, T. groaned and bit down on the offending limb.

All the way from where he was lying with his head in-between the Majingilane's hind legs, Shaka heard the wrist snap. He sniggered briefly before going back to his task of shattering the pelvis.

The remainder of the fight was mostly a formality.

Exhausted, they took turn holding the Majingilane's head down while the other lion furrowed his midsection. At one point, the young cat managed to break free and rolled onto his stomach. Half-snarling and half-growling, he tried to raise himself up while Shaka and T. remained at the edge of his reach, their own roars drowning out his frantic protest.

His hind legs could not support his weight any longer and he had to drag himself forward slowly.

After granting themselves a couple of heartbeats to catch their breath, they rolled him one last time and fell on the muscle of the upper right thigh, oblivious to the ever-weaker swats of his front paws. Soon the last of the fight had leaked out of him and he lay his upper body back down, quietly.

Shaka stumbled away, drained. The world danced in front of his eyes for a brief instant. He put his right paw down to steady himself and winced at the pain. He looked at the wound and realized that the fang had pierced clean through the bone. It would heal eventually, he judged, but right now he could not put any kind of weight on it.

T. went to give him a head-rub.

"You alright?" Shaka asked, suddenly worried. It seemed to him that he hadn't seen his brother in ages.

T.'s right ear looked like it had been chewed out. A deep gash now disfigured his right nostril. Another cut, above his right eye, was bleeding all over the side of his muzzle. Despite this, the young lion appeared in good spirt. "You want to finish him off?" he said, his eyes gleaming.

Shivering and in shock, his fast-heaving flanks gasping for a breath, the Majingilane lay prostrated with his eyes closed and his broken limbs tucked against his belly in one last, pathetic, self-soothing hug. The ruin of his pelvis was still bleeding freely all over the scuffed-up dirt. They could hear small, high-pitched whimpers escape his throat after every deep inhalation, like a cub.

"No need," spat Shaka. "He's already dead."

They moved off the spot of their killing and found some shade to tend to their wounds and restore some of their strength back. As the afternoon turned to dusk, they roused themselves again and quietly made for the Mala Mala.

Shaka groaned at the slowness of his limp. As long as he was careful, his front paw did not hurt much, but his muscles were sore and stiff, awkward, as if the entirety of his body had been carved out of a single block of rigid wood. He could not trot and had to stop frequently to lick his throbbing paw. Eventually, T. picked up the pace and went ahead to scout a safe path forward.

Night fell.

Laughing softly at his weakened state, Shaka stopped one more time to catch his breath and allow some blood to flow back to his extremities. At this miserable pace, it would take him the whole night to leave the Nkorho. It did not matter. Once safely back inside the Mala Mala, they could take all the time they wanted to rest and heal. Then they would come back and chase the last of the arrogant fools away. Perhaps even kill another one, just for the fun of it. Probably not. Truth be told, after what they had done to their brother, Shaka seriously doubted that the young Majingilanes would have the stomach to tarry in the Nkorho much longer.

He sucked in the fresh air of the night, pricked his ears up, and took the time to savor the rising cacophony of nocturnal frogs preparing themselves for their regularly-scheduled orgy. Those sounds had accompanied many of his nights ever since his infancy and they made him feel at home in this foreign part of the veld he had just invaded. When one thought about it, it was funny to consider that at the exact same time when he and T. were intent on killing off their rivals, a different species sharing the same patch of grass had an entirely different idea in its head. As far as the frogs were concerned, a lion's roar was probably akin to distant thunder. Something they had no control over and cared little about.

A branch cracked in the darkness ahead of him.

"T.?"

No answer.

A mild shudder traveled down his spine. He rotated his ears to scan his surroundings. It sounded as though he was alone but with the incessant frogging going on around him, he could not be completely sure. Something in his gut was not at ease. He should get going, he decided. He had already stopped for far too long.

He heaved himself up and filtered the air through his palate.

The strong smell of the Majingilanes slapped his muzzle. Two pairs of eyes shone green through the silver grass in front of him.

"You!" he growled.

His heart leaped inside his chest. He bounced forward and gave chase, his wound suddenly forgotten. The cocky fools had dare sneak up on him! Him! By the grass, who did they think they were?!

As he expected, the two Majingilanes immediately fled at his approach. That infuriated him even further. The cowards did not even have the guts to stand their ground like proper cats! He would teach them to try and ambush him!

"T!" he roared while speeding up. "Come quick! I've got two more over here!"

As soon as he said the words, a fast pounding of scrambled paws answered him from behind. He smiled internally. It seemed that his brother had not been nearly as far ahead as he had thought after all. Good. By sunrise, the so-called Majingilane coalition would be reduced to a single pair of dumbstruck cats trying to find their way out of the Nkorho with their tails tucked between their legs. As far as Shaka was concerned, this was just fine. Oh yes, just fine.

Something wasn't right.

He could discern two lions gaining on him from behind, not just one. He came to a skidding stop, the taste of bile bitter in his throat.

To his astonishment, the last two Majingilanes slowly emerged out of the grass behind him. The leading pair promptly turned around and closed the trap on the other side, a contemptuous snarl baring their fangs.

"Fuck you!" screamed Shaka, his mind suddenly blank.

He charged the nearest Majingilane and impacted him at full speed, hard enough to send him rolling head over paws in the grass.

The other three rushed his backside, toppled his legs, threw him to the ground. His head impacted the hard-packed dirt with a soft thud. He breathed in dirt and coughed as he tried to get his bearing in the dark. He had lost sight of his attackers but he could still feel their combined weight pressing down on his rear, pinning him in place. Their bellows, above all else, were deafening.

He snarled and tried to twist around. He had to protect his spine. His spine was exposed!

Without ever fully relinquishing their grip, they danced at the edge of his reach and jostled him around for a bit while nipping at his rump, their fangs slicing through the flesh with every bite.

A dozen fires erupted all over his backside. He screamed in pain. "T! They got me, T! I can't get up! I can't get up!"

Yes, he could. He had to. A burst of adrenalin fired up his spirit. Roaring at the top of his lungs, he rotated himself and lashed out blindly ahead, his front paws extended in front of him. His claws caught onto a muzzle. He pulled down with all the might of his shoulders and lunged forward with his jaws, rejoicing as he felt his fangs cut through a rhinarium. The Majingilane tore himself free and leaped backward with an angry yelp.

Shaka laughed.

Got you, you piece of sh—

Someone grabbed him by the back of the mane and slammed his head down. A fang punctured his skull above his eye socket and crushed his cheek. The left side of his face collapsed, as if pushed inward. His lungs emptied themselves in one big whoosh.

He felt his back legs being forced apart. A warm breeze tickled his genitalia.

"NO!" he shrieked. "NO! NONONONONO!"

The Majingilane's fangs ripped through his groin and his words turned into a mindless, incoherent cry of pain. The agony was worse than anything he had ever imagined; he thought he might actually die from it.

Brushing away the spasmodic beating of his right leg, another Majingilane joined his brother. Together, they pulled his midsection apart and burrowed into his lower belly, ravaging him.

Cold shock washed over him and dulled the pain.

For the first time since the fight had begun, he noticed that a rumbler had appeared a few steps away from them. The other-worldly beam of light emanating out of its broad muzzle – like a small, cold sun – jumped around in the darkness before settling on their little group. As it glanced over Shaka's pupils, blinding him for an instant, it shocked some small measure of sanity back into his mind.

Still growling faintly, half-crazed by fear and pain, he raised himself on his front paws and bended his neck toward his rear... just in time to see a big chunk of something grey disappear down the gullet of one the Majingilane.

"T.," he sobbed hysterically as he sagged back down, his courage gone. "They're *eating* me, T..."

He sucked in his breath, forced the sobs out of his mind. He would have to get it all back one way or the other once the fight was done, he decided. Put it back in, somehow. But first, he had to get out of here.

How? He could not get up. He was too weak to fight back. And the pain...By the grass, the pain was coming back.

He raised his head and roared his desperation as hard as he could.

A commotion arose in the nearby grass. All the weight suddenly disappeared from his body as a clash of snarls and roars erupted to his left.

A mad laughter briefly escaped his lungs. One of those roars, he could have recognized anywhere.

Through half glazed eyes, he caught a glimpse of T, facing off with the four Majingilanes amid the frenetic glare of the rumbler's light ricocheting off their fur and liquid eyes. For a half-heartbeat it seemed as though his brother might be able to break through and join him, then the Majingilanes tightened their ranks and unleashed a four-pronged attack that mauled him from every side and threatened to roll him over.

T. took a step back, then another. From above the Majingilanes' manes, their eyes crossed.

"Please, T! I'm begging you, please. Don't leave... Don't. DON'T!"

T. turned tail and disappeared into the darkness.

Shaka collapsed back down, as if undone by a vicious blow. He tried to crawl forward, toward the high grass, but his shoulders were made of soft mud, he did not have the strength. He retched and gasped in agony. His lower half was like a molten rock of pain anchoring him down.

The Majingilanes moseyed back toward him, flank bumping against flank, their eyes gleaming green in the rumbler's light. He could hear them sniggering softly as they circled his body and returned their attention to the sprawled-out ruin of his neither region. Soon their insistent pulls began to rock him in place again.

He let it happen stoically. It didn't matter anymore. Nothing mattered. T. had left him.

One of the Majingilane straddled his spine. A heartbeat later, he heard a sharp *crack,* like the noise of a lion biting through a thick branch.

Funny, that. Why would any cat want to bite through a branch at a time like this?

Blessed relief washed over him as the molten rock suddenly disappeared. His front paws turned fuzzy, almost ticklish; his mind grew heavy and dull, as if he had fallen into a warm river, or maybe a very thick morning fog. The kind of fog he and T. liked to play in, back when they were young cubs and even the most mundane dead bough looked like a monstrous buffalo they had to assault. "Steady paws, brother! The safety of the pride depends on us!"

From far, far away, he could still hear some faint munching noises. Resisting the urge to fall asleep, he heaved himself up on his front paws and looked down at his rear.

He frowned his groggy muzzle, perplexed.

Crouched on either side of him, the four lions were busy masticating some kind of juicy meat. That was fine by him — after such exertions, the young cats deserved a proper meal — but what troubled him was the strange parasite that seemed to have landed on his rump. Like some kind of giant white spider.

He leaned forward and squinted his eyes against the rumbler's intermittent glare, striving to make sense of what he was seeing.

By the time of his last heartbeat, he finally realized that he was staring at the bones of his own hips and spine.

"Oh," he blurted out as he died.

TWENTY-TWO

THE FRONT END OF FEAR

"FUUUUUUCCCCCCKKKKKK!!!!"

T. leaped forward, whirled around, turned back again. "Fuck!" he roared, gasping. "Fuck! Fuck! Fuuuuuuck!!"

He had to go back. He had to help Shaka.

He closed his eyes and made a conscious, bone-jarring effort to try and stop the quivering in his limbs. He was struggling to get a breath through his tight chest. With every slow, purposeful inhale he could feel the open cut burn through the split skin of his right nostril.

There was no point, he knew. Shaka was gone. He had circled back shortly after dawn, once the Majingilanes had moved on, and seen it with his own two eyes, that nothingness left amid a crater of trampled grass where his brother had once stood.

And the jackal… By the grass, he had seen the jackal too.

You did not see that! That was not real.

Yes, it was. And he *had* seen it. As real as the crimson dirt and the claw marks; as undeniable as a helpless lioness cartwheeling in the air. A small jackal, barely the size of cub, strutting around victoriously with a large chunk of Shaka's mane inside his mouth. The only thing left of that cat who had been his breathing, loving brother only a dawn ago.

He froze in his tracks, roared, and cursed some more. A small voice inside his head, ever cold and rational, cheerfully pointed out that his distress was not solely in the name of Shaka's blood. Much of it was, in fact, self-pity. Disgusting, abject, and utterly self-centered; a fitting emotion, for a lion who runs.

He shook his head and roared his protest. The voice was right, of course. In the shadow of his grief, he could sense the bitter fear running circles around his mind, hidden behind every thornbush and blade of grass, waiting to pounce and turn into a full-blown panic. Shaka's death had shaken his grip off of the hindquarter side of the beast. He was alone and vulnerable again, at the mercy of the horns.

His eyes rolled inward. His stomach constricted. Folded in half, he retched and vomited. Half-digested chunks of the Majingilane burned through his throat and came spilling out in front of him. He jerked his head back and turned away from the accusing puddle, a weak whimper on his muzzle.

A soft rustle in the trees cut his mewling short. Suddenly alert, he pricked his ears up and frenetically scanned his surroundings for any trace of the Majingilanes.

Nothing.

But how could he be certain? Every shadow seemed a crouched lion ready to pounce, every ominous murmur of the grass a soft paw sneaking up on him. He whirled in place and aggressively sniffed the air.

He should never have roared like that! Of course! What was he thinking?

A cold shudder traveled down the length of his exposed spine and bounced back to his mind. Still half-roaring through his teeth, he bolted forward and melted himself in the tall grass, his belly low, his shoulders hunched.

He reached the Tsalala pride by mid-afternoon.

Tailless pounced forward and rushed to meet him. “Is it true? Is he down?”

“Huh?”

“Shaka. Is it true that the Majingilanes have killed him?”

He stared at her with wide, incredulous eyes. For the life of him, he could not understand what she was talking about. Then, it came back to him. “Yes,” he rasped. “They, huh, they were gone, but then they came back and… I wasn’t there, I didn’t see… I mean I came back for him of course. As soon as I heard. I tried to help, I tried to… It was too late, he was already… They *ate* him, Tailless. They ravaged his mid-section and groin! And his mane… Afterward his mane was… stolen.” He fell quiet and began to retreat, his head held low.

Tailless cut him off. Her gaze, usually hard and withdrawn whenever she was standing in his presence, now seemed soft and compassionate. This had a chilling effect on him. It was as if suddenly, for the first time since he had met her, she was seeing him as a lion.

“You have to stay and stand your ground,” she said. “If the Majingilanes get to us, they will murder every single one of the cubs. You know perfectly well how these things are done. Now more than ever, the pride needs you, T. *I* need you.”

T recoiled in horror at the preposterous demand. The lioness was mad. Stand and fight? One against four? She had no idea what she was asking. “I can’t,” he blurted out. “I’m sorry, I just *can’t*.”

He brushed past her and broke into a gallop. Tailless chased after him. He sped up.

“T! Don’t do this! You have to defend the pride!”

“I’ll get the others,” he screamed from over his shoulder. “Just try to hold on for a little while. Hide the cubs. I’ll come back, I swear!”

“T! Those cubs are all what’s left of Shaka!”

He pretended not to hear the lie.

The sun turned orange and plummeted in front of him. Darkness found him lost in the endless expanse of the Mala Mala, alone. He stopped and lay down with his back awkwardly pushed against a tree. The trunk was too thin, he could feel his rump overflow on either side, but the feeling of the hard bark pressed tight against his tail and spine helped calm his mind a bit.

Despite his need to keep a low profile, he began to push out a series of calling roars. Partly because he missed Shaka, and partly because he could not bear the oppressing silence of the surrounding night. After every unanswered bellow, he could feel his heart sink a little bit lower inside his chest. Eventually, exhaustion snuck up on him and he fell into a restless sleep.

He resumed his trek by the first lights of next dawn. The Majingilanes, he realized, would probably not pursue him any longer. Not until after they had submitted the Tsalala and Styx prides. He had escaped. dominated

His mind turned blank, his paws grew numb. He punched through one horizon after the next at a slow, automatic pace that cared little for the change of scenery or the terrain that it was striding. A water hole found him thirsty, he went to lap a drink out of the muddy water. Through the ripples, a disheveled, haggard lion gazed back at him. He tore himself away.

Not needed He reached the Sand River by mid-afternoon of the next day. Under the overcast sky, the grey water looked calm and tepid. He waded-in slowly, careful not to trip on the slippery bottom, and pushed through with clenched jaws. Fortunately for him, this was still only the beginning of the rainy season and even at its highest point the river was only about shoulder high. He kept his head high and crossed the last of the shallows before rounding a thicket of reeds growing on the opposite shore.

That's when he saw them waiting for him from the vantage point of an elevated position.

He stopped at the foot of the muddy bluff, his dripping legs suddenly weak. Although, of course, he had known that such a moment was coming, he now realized that he had unconsciously repressed it. With his mind entirely focused on what he was leaving behind, he had allowed himself to ignore what he was running toward and was now completely unprepared. Not needed

The four cats, for their part, could not seem to be less concerned if they tried. Spread out in-between two rumblers with their bodies nonchalantly sprawled across the grass, it seemed as though they had simply been waiting for him to catch up after a short patrol. As if he had never really left at all.

The twins were clustered together. Laid down behind them, Dreadlocks was quietly suffering through the indignity of their tail tails swapping against his muzzle. Seated on his haunches a bit to their left, near a rumbler, Makhulu was staring at him.

T. sucked in his breath. The first thing that struck him was how different the elder mane looked. Less imposing, somehow, as if the passing of the seasons had robbed him of some of his vigor. His tired eye above his broken cheekbone was more noticeable, his stance ever so slightly more slouched. His mane, still as black and golden and imposing as the first day T. had met him, now seemed to be hiding a much thinner body. Under his yellow, haunted eyes, his battered muzzle had greyed.

Overall, he was still the Big Mak. There just seemed to be less of him.

Caught in-between the river behind him and his brothers in front, T. stood still and waited patiently. He kept his mind blank and his eyes purposefully focused on nothing at all. He found that he did not have the courage to consider the consequences of a rejection. It was easier to just go numb, turn inanimate, and wait for it to happen. Whatever the cats' decision, he would take it in stride and deal with it one step at a time. He was far too exhausted to really be scared anyway.

Suspended heartbeats came and went inside his tight chest. After what seemed like an eternity, Makhulu finally nodded his head in that curt, almost dismissive manner of his. He licked his muzzle.

T. felt his lungs release his breath in one big, half-swallowed sigh. His front paws began to quiver uncontrollably. Unable to refrain himself any longer, he hastened to scale the bluff and after one last hesitant pause, launched himself toward Makhulu's mane. To his utter surprise, the dark-maned did not recoil.

The physical contact alone was enough to slap the tension out of his shoulders and unwind his tight belly. Without it, his legs had no more defenses against his exhaustion. He dropped down at Makhulu's paws with his eyes half-closed and strived to keep his relief from bursting out of him in the form of an uncontrollable chuckle.

Until that very instant, he had not realized how much he had needed it, this touch of another cat, the physical reassurance that he was not, in fact, alone. He still had brothers who cared. After everything that had happened, he was still, amazingly, a Mapogo.

He stood up and went to greet the others. Dreadlocks seemed genuinely happy to see him. Leonides too, although he did not show it as much. Skoro's attitude, however, was far more guarded.

"You're back, then?" he said after granting him only the most tenuous of head-rub.

"Yes."

"And Shaka?"

T. bit his tongue. Of course, they all suspected. But they needed to hear it from him. They needed him to confess. "A coalition of five lions moved-in on us."

"Those Majingilanes we've heard so much about?"

"Yes. We went to confront them in the Nkorho. We killed one, but then Shaka was ambushed at night, and killed in return."

These last few words felt like he was spitting out stones. A second wave of relief traveled through him. Now that he had found the strength to utter the facts out loud, he could face them with objective eyes. In the end, the whole story was fairly straightforward. Banal, even. One Mapogo for one Majingilane. Tit for tat. Had it happened to any other coalition of cats, he would have dismissed the whole affair as completely unremarkable, not worth a single moment of his time.

The only issue, of course, was that this time it was Shaka who had been claimed by the grass. He could see that the others had a hard time accepting the abrupt turn of events. Skoro, especially, seemed enraged. He began pacing back and forth.

"Where were you?"

"Huh?"

"Where were you when it happened? Did you see him being killed with your own two eyes?"

"I…It was all very confusing. There was a rumbler, and–"

"A rumbler?"

"Yes. Shining its light all over the place. I couldn't get a proper bearing on things. And there was so much roaring everywhere, you can't imagine what it was like. I tried to help, of course, but then the four Majingilanes jumped me and–"

"You ran." There was no hatred in the way Dreadlocks said the words, only sadness and understanding.

T. bowed his head. "Yes, I ran."

Skoro was not satisfied. He pressed his face tight against T.'s muzzle. "Did you see his body?" he hissed. "Did you see him dead?"

"I… I came back in the morning."

"And?"

"There was nothing left, Skoro. Only blood and bits of bones and a chunk of… of his… He's gone, alright. Trust me, he's gone."

Skoro tore himself away with a growl. After one last scornful look at his brother, he began to make his way down the bluff, toward the river.

"Where are you going?" Leonides called out.

"You heard the cowardly prick. He ran! He didn't see Shaka die. He didn't even see his body! For all we know, Shaka's still alive somewhere. He probably needs our help."

"Skoro!" said Makhulu. "There is no point. Shaka's dead."

"But you heard him yourself…"

"T. is many things but he would never have fled unless he was absolutely sure that Shaka was gone. Besides, the Majingilanes are not stupid. They wouldn't let a rival male escape like that. Not once they have him dead to rights."

"How can you be so sure?"

"When have we ever?"

The argument was sound, it sapped the strength out of Skoro's temper. Sullenly, he retraced his steps back to the group.

"I still can't believe it," said Leonides. "I mean, any one of us fools, yeah, sure, I can see it happen. But Shaka? He was the best of us after you, Mak. Certainly the smartest. I don't think I ever saw him take a single step forward without first having considered all the possible ramifications. How could the Majingilanes even catch him in the first place?"

"I'm sure the circumstances of his death were not entirely his doing," Skoro growled with his eyes trained on T. "After all, even the most enduring of cat can be dragged underwater by dead weight."

Before T. could think of something to retort, Dreadlocks stepped forward to interpose himself. "Did Shaka say anything before he died?"

"No. I mean… No. Even if he had, I wouldn't have been able to hear anything anyway. The roars were too loud. Too much confusion. I couldn't hear."

The rational voice inside his head began to laugh. He pushed it down and suppressed it.

"Looks like you did not escape completely unscathed either," said Makhulu, and pointed at the deep gash that cut through T.'s nostril.

"What, that? Yeah, that was the first Majingilane we caught. He fought back pretty hard. Practically tore half my rhinarium off."

"Well, it's not too bad as far as scars go. Makes you look dangerous. Makes you look like *him*."

He had meant the remark as a compliment and T. accepted it as such. "Ain't nothin' eve' been'easy 'bout bein' 'lion, eh?" he groaned through clenched teeth. Even though he had meant it more as a joke than anything else, for the first time in his life the throaty voice and accent rung hollow to his ears. It sounded fake, like a poor parody of a cat struggling to appear tough. Risible. His half-snarl turned into a fixed grimace. He fell quiet.

"So, what do we do now?" asked Leonides.

"The Majingilanes won't stop after such a victory," Makhulu declared. "Once they've rested long enough and restored their strength, they will push across the Sand River. We need to be prepared."

"You don't think that they will stop to take control of the prides first?"

Makhulu sighed. "No. They know that Shaka was just the beginning. We're still around and we still outnumber them five to four. They will want to even those odds before they allow themselves to settle anywhere. We need to make sure that we don't give them the opportunity. And that means taking the fight to them."

"Yes," Skoro agreed vigorously. "A revenge raid. For Shaka. We find these young cats and we murder them where they stand."

"For Shaka," agreed Dreadlocks.

"For Shaka," T. whispered, careful not to let his unease show. "More blood, for Shaka."

TWENTY-THREE

THE ELEPHANT PLAIN

Well, that little farce sure had not turned out like anything they had expected.

Skoro stretched his spine and cringed slightly as he felt the blood-flow return to his numb extremities. The moonless night was crisp and dry all around him; under the faint light of the bright stars, he could see his own breath smoke in front of his muzzle in tiny grey clouds. It would be another frosty morning, then a nice temperate day under a clear blue sky.

Perfect day for a hunt.

He sat on his haunches and looked up. As if on cue, another one of those peculiar tiny white dots streaked across the night sky before disappearing suddenly, as if absorbed by the meadow of stars. Chuckling softly, he craned his head up and waited for the next one, mesmerized. To his delight, another two twinkled in quick succession, a bit lower on the horizon. Not for the first time since he had begun to notice them a couple of nights ago, he wondered what they were. "Hey Leon, come over here."

"What's up?"

"Come here, there is something you need to see."

A crunching of dry leaves betrayed his brother's approach. Leonides took position next to him and he felt the tuft of his tail graze against his lower back. His warm breath tickled the inside of his left ear.

"What is it?"

"Look up and wait."

A few long heartbeats elapsed.

"Skoro, what are we looking–Oh!"

Three dots, brighter than the ones before, lit up the sky almost in unison. Then another one followed on their heels, as if trying to catch up.

"Nice, isn't it?"

"What are they? Some kind of stars?"

"I have absolutely no idea."

They shared the moment in silence. After the disheartening letdown of the failed raid, they could do with a bit of a distraction. Skoro wondered if the others would notice the dots as well, down in the Singita.

"Shouldn't we be looking for the Majingilanes?" Leonides finally asked, his head still tilted back.

"Nah, those cats are long gone."

They had crossed into the Mala Mala with the outrage of Shaka's fate still raw in the back of their mind. Clustered together in a way that had reminded Skoro of their younger days, they had scoured the grass and roared their challenge for nights on end, hoping with bitter hearts that the young fools would be arrogant enough to meet them on flat ground. Five against four. The greatest showdown the Sabi Sands would ever see.

Skoro shook his head, slightly ashamed at his own stupidity. Now with the benefit of hindsight it was obvious that their plan had been doomed from the start. The Majingilanes might be young, but they were not braindead. They would never willingly engage in a fight against older males with inferior numbers. Had the situation been reversed, Skoro had no doubt that he would have acted in the exact same way. For them to actually expect the rival coalition to be so easily manipulated… Well, that was just plain arrogance on their parts. They had let their grief blind them.

"You think they ran? You think we scared them away?"

"Maybe. Maybe they had no intention of coming here in the first place. Who knows?"

"But Makhulu said–"

"I know, I know. But you've seen it yourself, the Majingilanes were a no-show. Truth is, I'm not entirely sure that Makhulu's instincts are as sharp as they used to be. We shouldn't rely on his expertise so much anymore." Two words

Leonides took some time to digest the information. "I suppose he's grown a bit…placid recently."

"Yes, and slower too. He actually scared me during the last buffalo hunt, almost got himself trampled."

"He's still the Big Mak, though."

"Undoubtedly."

More dots streaked the sky. After a while, Skoro noticed that Leonides was giggling softly next to him.

"What's so funny?"

cubs

"We did show the young kittens what was what, though, didn't we? After such a loud show of force, do you think there is still a cat anywhere in the Sabi Sands stupid enough to challenge us here?"

"I guess not."

He frowned his muzzle. Even though they had clearly come out on top, the whole affair had shone an uncomfortable light on a truth he had never even considered before: this was the first truly large coalition they had had to face. Before the Majingilanes, they had only ever engaged lone males or, on occasions, duos. And always with clear superior force, five or six of them together. Of course everyone knew that Makhulu had been keen to seek out lone males one on one in his youth, but he had eventually outgrown that phase fairly quickly. And smartly so. Even odds were no good odds at all, as far as Skoro was concerned. Since he had come back, T. had told them stories of how he and Shaka had fought wander-males on equal footing, two against two, and even once ambushed a sleeping trio and sent them running. But that was just them and their mad tempers. Clearly one could see where that had led them.

Skoro was not overly worried. Like the Big Mak had rightly pointed out, they still outnumbered the Majingilanes five to four. And even though this did not sound anywhere near as good as six against one, it was still much better than, say, four against five. If the Majingilanes were anything like him – and after their recent refusal to show up, Skoro had good reasons to believe that they were – they would steer clear of any group of lions larger than a duo.

In theory, that meant that the Mapogos could relax.

Still, the fact that they lacked the experience to deal with such a large coalition was not something he was particularly comfortable with. It made the Majingilanes' behavior harder to predict. For the first time since Makhulu had murdered Nhlanguleni, they could not simply kill their way out of a potential threat. They had to learn to live with it, manage it. This was nerve-rattling, to say the least.

"You know," said Leonides, "when we first crossed back into the Mala Mala I was really looking forward to treading those grounds again."

"Why?"

"I don't know. I guess I was just hoping it would be like returning to the old days. Simpler times, before all the prides and the split and everything else. In the end it just felt like more empty grass and another hostile horizon. Not at all what I remembered it to be."

"Dirt's just dirt, the lions you're with are what makes the land. In the case of the Mala Mala it was the Eyrefield pride, but we've long outgrown it now."

"Have we really? Sometimes I wonder."

Skoro rolled his eyes but kept quiet. Leonides could be quite gloomy at times, it was just the way he was. It would pass with the rising of the dawn, he knew.

"It did feel good to go out there and roar at the top of our lungs, though," his brother continued. "If nothing else, at least we were all together side by side once again."

"With one exception."

"Yeah, one exception. You know, for a while, I really thought that we would see him materialize out of that horizon as if produced by the haze or something. I had it all pictured in my head: he would casually camper up to us – all torn and slashed to shit, but still alive, nonetheless – and sit down by our side with that big broad, satisfied snarl of his etched on his muzzle. And he would say: 'Boys, you won't believe the story I have for you!'"

Skoro chuckled. "That would have been epic. Shaka's level of epic."

"I guess I just couldn't admit that he was really gone for good. I'm still not sure that I can."

"Me neither, Leon. Me neither."

"It's like… I don't know. It's like there is some kind of pattern to be found."

"A pattern?"

"Yes, in death."

"What do you mean?"

"Well, the Sunset Boys all died eventually, right?"

"Yeah, so?"

"Then we've witnessed the death of countless other lions, by our fangs more often than not."

"Isolated wander-males and weaker cats, so what?"

"And now Shaka…"

"What are you trying to say?"

His twin swallowed loudly before letting it all out in one big breath: "If Shaka, of all lions, can be killed. What does that say about us?"

"Hey, hey, hey, easy there. The circumstances surrounding Shaka's death were exceptional. It doesn't apply to us."

"Why not? We can be killed too, can't we?"

"Yes, of course. The danger is always there, every cat knows that. But that doesn't mean that death is inevitable. Our life is still our own. As long as we stick together and choose our fights carefully, there is no reason why we shouldn't be able to go on indefinitely."

"I'm sure that Shaka must have believed the same thing, right up until the end."

"His death is the exception, not the rule."

"Are you sure?"

"*Yes.*"

Skoro fell into a sullen silence. The dots above had lost their appeal, he did not like the way they always seemed to blink out of existence so fast. Leonides was wrong. Heart-wrenching as it was, Shaka's death was still only a temporary setback when compared with the grander scale of things. The five of them were strong. Invincible. Together, they could take on any threat that came their way. Easy.

"Come on, let's go."

He found his paws and wandered aimlessly at a lazy pace with his muzzle low.

He let his mind being absorbed by the usual trivialities of the night. A small bird bounced through the leaves and disappeared under a thick thornbush. A slightly lethargic snake recoiled at his approach. Not entirely sure as to the species, he kept his distance and stumbled upon a small claw mark left on the trunk of a large acacia. Hopeful, he scanned the canopy above in search of the two gleaming eyes that would betray the presence of a leopard. The climb would be challenging, to be sure, but it was always fun to watch the smaller tree-hugger snarl and retreat into the thinnest branches before falling like some overripe fruit. If they worked it out right with Leonides waiting below, they could probably catch him.

Leonides caught up to him and bounced into his flank. After noticing the signs on the trunk, he tilted his head back as well. "You see him?"

"Nah. The marks must be old. Either that or he heard us and fled."

They moved on.

"I've always liked the Elephant plain," Leonides observed. "Something about the edge of a territory, I guess. We should keep going for a while, just the two of us. We could go on an adventure and see what's beyond."

"Yeah," said Skoro, perfectly aware that in two dawns time, at most, he would be back by the side of the Ximhungwe pride enjoying a nice buffalo meal. "Yeah, maybe we will."

Leonides growled happily and struck out on his own. Skoro stopped to mark a tree and scuff the dirt, then resumed his inspection of the canopies. He did not have much hope for the leopard but it was a nice way to spend the night. He could still hear his brother's footsteps ripping through dense crawlers somewhere to his left. Leonides, it seemed, was having great fun blazing himself a path through a bush of some kind. Perhaps he had stumbled upon a scrub hare or an aardvark.

Not a porcupine, Skoro hoped. He was in no mood for more drama this night.

The footsteps stopped. He froze and waited for the faint crunch of bones that would tell him if his twin had been successful in his attempt. Instead, he heard him call out his name, his voice strangely high-pitched, as if caught by surprise. "Skoro? Is that you?"

A low growl broke the silence of the night, as soft as a mother's sigh; it froze Skoro's blood inside his veins. This was no Mapogo growl, he realized instantly.

Before he had time to fully grasp what was happening, a sudden commotion tore through the dry grass and impacted the spot where he had last placed Leonides. A storm of roars erupted.

"Skoro! They're here! By the grass, they're right here!"

Skoro's heart reacted faster than his mind. He scrambled his legs and leaped blindly forward to his brother's aid. The ground heaved under his paws. Kicked-up dirt filled his nostrils. All of a sudden, it seemed as though he had stepped through a thin veil in the middle of the darkness and fallen into a world of a different chaos. The noise, especially, was like a wave breaking upon his head, every deafening roar a slap that shrunk his balls and jostled his spirit.

Just like that, he realized more astonished than scared, he had stepped into the fight of his life.

He found Leonides pinned down by the four Majingilanes pulling him in every direction. One of the attackers was holding him by the back of the neck. Another had his head in-between his rear legs. A soft crunch, strangely audible despite all the mad bellows, sent Skoro's mind into a frenzy.

"Leon!" he heard himself scream, somewhat stupidly. "Leon, get up! They're killing you!"

He threw himself against the nearest Majingilane, the neck biter, and sent him rolling. Two paws assaulted him from behind. He whirled in place and plunged into the deep, black mane that had suddenly arisen in front of him, his muzzle searching for the throat, both his paws furiously raking the exposed chest.

The opposite cat buckled and tried to disengage. Shrieking unintelligibly, he fell on him and toppled him down, a chunk of half-torn skin still stuck inside his jaws. In the confusion, he tried to get a feel for the tender belly.

Just when he was about to sink his fangs in, some kind of almighty force barreled through his hips and ripped him off his target before slapping him to the side as if he were a mere cub. His jaws snapped shut onto thin air and a searing pain shot up his brain as one of his canines pierced through his tongue. His head smashed into the hard-packed dirt.

Reeling from the shock, slightly dazed, he stumbled around and struggled to get his paws back under his body while trying to catch a glimpse of the braindead grazer who had been stupid enough to blindly charge straight down the middle of a cat fight like that.

Something was still pushing down on his rump. Too late, he noticed the hot breath tickling the middle of his spine.

"NO!"

The fangs stabbed his vertebra.

A burning *pop* traveled up his spine, then coldness. His lower midsection collapsed under him, numb and paralyzed. He whirled in place and lunged at the Majingilane's muzzle. His fangs cut into the hated flesh. The younger male jerked his head back and retreated toward his brother at a nonchalant pace, a satisfied snarl on his muzzle.

Sobbing uncontrollably, Skoro dragged himself in the opposite direction as best he could, his front legs desperately clawing for traction on the unyielding earth. He was done for, he knew. A heartbeat ago he had been standing tall, as strong as ever, secure in the fact that he had control over his own life; now, he was a hopeless cripple.

He felt the moment pass him by and disappear, so close that he could almost taste it. There would be no do-over, no second chances. In a blink, it had all been taken away from him. Forever.

The monstrous enormity of the thing gripped his entrails. He retched and nearly fainted. How could something so near in time already be so irremediably out of his reach? It wasn't fair! He hadn't been given enough time to consider things properly. He deserved another crack at it. Another chance. By the grass, his brother's life for another chance!

The Majingilane pair closed in on him.

"Get back! Get back!"

He pushed away with his forelegs and tried to backtrack as fast as he could. Suddenly, his hind legs labored the ground in a spastic motion. Taken aback, he froze and watched the tremors unfold with wide, unbelieving eyes. The Majingilanes stopped short of their assault as well, puzzled by the sudden fit of those limbs they thought they had cut off.

His legs! His legs were moving! He could not feel them any longer, but they were moving. He could still use them! He focused his mind on his left back paw and tried to move it. The appendage responded, at first tentatively, then more assertively. Choking with relief, he tried the other paw and watched his claws protract and retract in unison as if it were the greatest thing he had ever seen. His knees bent under his command, his tail slammed the ground with renewed vigor; he did not feel the impact, but that did not matter.

Just like that, his second chance was within his grasp.

He heaved himself up and roared his defiance at the top of his lungs.

"You missed!" he heard one of the Majingilane growl at his brother. "How could you fucking miss?"

The second lion shrugged and lowered his gaze toward Skoro. His tongue darted out in an obscene gesture and cleaned the fresh blood – his blood! – dripping from his muzzle. "Who cares?" he spat. "Just grab his neck, I'll finish him off."

Skoro backtracked slowly and fended off some of the Majingilane's less than eager probing assault while making sure not to let the second male outflank him. His mind was clear again. It was time to think strategically. Four against two was no kind of odds, they had to disengage.

He feinted an assault on the nearest Majingilane, leaped to the side, blew past the second one and rushed to Leonides' aid. His brother was still battling against two of the Majingilanes. He shoved them to the side and forced his twin to his feet.

"Can you move?"

Some kind of wet gurgle escaped Leonides' throat as he nodded his head vigorously. "I'm still a fucking lion," he growled while leaning heavily against Skoro's flank. His legs were quivering under his weight and something dark was gushing out of his mid-section in a steady stream, but he kept his muzzle straight and his eyes cold. "We fight?"

"No, we run."

They stumbled toward the nearest thornbush. The four Majingilanes coalesced into an impenetrable line in front of them. Bellowing insults back and forth, they backtracked slowly and scrambled toward another cluster of low trees as fast as prudence allowed.

Once again, the Majingilanes cut them off.

They tried to push through and another fight erupted. Working as a unit, the Majingilanes strived to split them apart. They almost succeeded and after Leonides came very close to being isolated and toppled down a second time, they were forced to retreat hastily.

"Now what?" his twin spat. His voice was thick with tremors. The short scuffle had sapped most of his last remaining strengths and Skoro could hear the frustration getting to him.

This could not go on. They had to figure something out. Fast.

While fending off multiple probing assaults, Skoro led his brother away, slowly, and tried to work the problem. He knew that the Majingilanes were not playing some random game of cat and mouse. This was a deliberate strategy.

They won't let us go back toward the Singita or the Londolozi. They can't risk having us rejoin with the others.

This meant that there was only one choice left for them. One direction. As much as he hated it, he could think of no other viable option. "Good news!" he exclaimed with fake cheer. "We're going exploring."

They broke away at a gallop.

Perhaps wary that they might attempt to circle back around them, the Majingilanes did not immediately give chase but fanned out on either side so as to prevent any chance of the two Mapogos breaking away unnoticed. Smiling internally, Skoro heard their calling roars dwindle behind him. This would not last, he knew. As soon as they realized their mistake, the four killers would be on their tracks again, more eager than ever. But at least now they had a head start.

He lowered his head and adopted a meandering course he hoped would prove harder to follow. Next to him, Leonides was panting hard but kept pace nonetheless, as if physically fused to his flank. Skoro did not dare push him too hard. As valiant as his brother might be, he had no idea how much more punishment his heart could take.

They settled on a more sustainable brisk trot. The distant roars were still hot on their trail but did not seem to be gaining any obvious ground. A strange calm befell them. Unseen branches came and went on either side of them, grazing their mane. Creepers gripped at their claws. Loose blade of grass clung to their blood-soaked bellies and flanks. Here and there, they had to dodge the occasional treacherous hole. Pushed beyond all ordinary limits, their body kept going through the motions steadily, one step at a time, as if carried by a volition of its own, some inner surviving instinct their rational mind knew nothing about.

Should they ever stumble and fall, however, Skoro seriously doubted that they would ever be able to get back up again. He tried not to think about it.

His back legs and tail were still numb to all sensation. With every leap forward it felt as if he were being pushed from behind by some alien force supporting his body. The experience was perplexing, to say the least, but he was not about to complain.

They had to stop when they came upon a strangely-shaped hedge with no leaves. The weird, crisscrossing, thin branches stretched in a straight line in front of them and disappeared in the darkness on either side, blocking their path forward.

Skoro had never seen such a peculiar tree.

It was not very tall as far as trees go, about as high as a small elephant, but that was still more than enough to prevent them from leaping over it. He thought about climbing the thing, but the branches seemed far too thin to support their weight. Besides, the hedge had no depth to it, no obvious point on which they could rest their paws. It was just a sheer vertical rise of thin, naked branches. Something about their flat, crisscrossing pattern reminded him of the odd shape of a rumbler's muzzle. He gave the hedge a small lick and hastily snapped his tongue back. It was cold and tasted like blood.

An outburst of roars echoed behind him, closer than before. This was no time to pause and ponder the peculiar beauty of all things above grass. They were still very much in the middle of a life and death situation.

Through the naked branches, he could see more grass stretching out under the stars, all the way to the horizon. That was all he needed to know.

"Come on, let's go."

He leaned forward and tried to shoulder himself a path through the obstacle. The hedge bent outward but did not yield. After a single step, he found that he could go no further and was forced back.

What the fuck?

He tried again, harder. The thin branches held tight and mercilessly cut into his muzzle and mane. Howling in pain, he took a couple of angry steps back and lashed out. This was beyond ridiculous. After everything they had gone through, they were being stopped by a tree. A tree!

He threw himself against the hedge with all his strength. The branches shook, briefly, but held steady. He collapsed back down, his muzzle on fire.

"What do we do?" exclaimed Leonides. "What do we do?"

Behind them, the roars were gaining fast. The Majingilanes had picked up their scent.

He wouldn't know any of these names, as they're human ones.

"Follow me."

They turned right and struck toward the Arathusa. Vaguely remembered names danced inside Skoro's mind. After the Arathusa, the Djuma then, a bit further, Chitwa Chitwa, where they had killed Blondie so many seasons ago. And beyond that, the dreaded Nkorho.

They came from there. They knew that thing was here! That's why they were in no hurry to give chase. They knew that we would be cornered anyway. They're forcing us back toward more familiar grounds.

This would not do. They could not allow the Majingilanes to turn them into frightened antelopes.

Once again, he threw himself against the hedge. To no avail. Impossibly, it was just as strong here as it had been at the first point of impact. Swallowing down a bitter roar that would betray their exact location, he continued forward. He could feel the hated thing graze against his left flank, taunting him with its unyielding rigidity.

"Over here! Look, over here!"

Leonides struck forward on his own and stopped by a spot where the base of the hedge seemed to have been uprooted. Underneath it, the earth had been upturned and reshaped into a small dome, almost like a swollen wound trying to heal. Skoro stopped just long enough to catch a whiff of the animal responsible for such a peculiarly placed burrow. He had to swallow down a small cry of relief. Of course, he should have guessed.

Sun blaze almighty, shine bright and warm for the noble stubbornness of honey badgers.

They flattened themselves atop the dome and crawled underneath the loosened base of the hedge. The sharp branches tore at their manes and fur. As they grazed against the wound on his back, Skoro felt a violent shudder jolt his body. He clenched his jaws tight and squeezed through.

Once on the other side, they broke into a gallop without so much as a glance backward.

Dawn found them trudging aimlessly through the foreign grass, one stumbling step after the next. The heat rose and hammered at their dehydrated bodies. Panting heavily, Skoro stopped and squinted his tired eyes against the unwelcome brightness of the morning sun. His shoulders and chest were one big, burning cramp. Everything under his back wound felt cold and dead. He gazed at his hind legs and realized that they were shaking uncontrollably. The underside of his paws was raw.

A thick rivulet of saliva dangled from his peeled black lips and plopped heavily on the ground at his feet; he ran his tongue across his muzzle in hope of recapturing some of the precious moisture. It was no use, they had to find some shade and let their body cool down. The grass knew they had earned it.

Halfway lost in the haze ahead of him, Leonides was still shambling forward with his head held so low, his muzzle seemed to graze the ground.

"Leon, stop! This is pointless, we have to rest."

"Not yet! We're almost there, Skoro. Almost there."

"Almost where?"

No answer. Skoro lunged forward and settled at Leonides' level.

A disquieting chill took hold of his heart.

His brother's mane had been ripped in several places, exposing the pink underneath, and his left ear was missing. Atop his mangled muzzle, his eyes were glazed and unseeing. Behind his battered neck, his left shoulder blade, broken in the fight, had turned purple and swollen to absurd proportion, afflicting him with a hunchback appearance and an ever more noticeable limp after every step. The fur of his gaunt flanks had turned dark brown, slathered with caked blood and dry saliva.

Worst of all was the wound in his midsection. The steady bleeding had covered the inside of his thighs in a gleaming coat of dark red. Skoro looked back and noticed a greasy trail that betrayed his brother's progress all the way back to the horizon; he tried not to think about the amount of blood involved. He lowered his head and stole a glance at the gash. Something grey was dangling out of it. He jerked his head back and swallowed down a sudden outburst of emotion.

"Hey, Leon, buddy, maybe you should take it easy. The Majingilanes are not after us anymore. There is no need to push yourself too hard. You really should save your strength for the way back."

"Just a bit more, Skoro, please. We're so close, we can't turn around now."

"So close? So close to what buddy?"

"The far side! Can't you see it? It's right there. By the grass, we've made it. We've... We've... Just a bit further, okay? Afterward we can... We'll have..."

His mangled words devolved into a chuckle, then a coughing fit. He winced in pain and struggled to catch his breath. It sounded as though he was breathing through a mouthful of bodily fluid.

Skoro hung back and let him proceed quietly. Although he could only see more grass stretching in every direction himself, with no end in sight, he did not have the courage to tell Leonides that.

They trudged forward quietly.

By mid-morning, Leonides collapsed. He groaned faintly and extended his front paws in front of him in a vain attempt to squeeze one last step out of his empty body, then stopped. "Did we make it?" he whimpered. His eyes were closed shut. "Did we reach the far side?"

"Yeah, we did. You were right all along. It was right there."

A happy little growl escaped his twin's lungs, like a cub who has caught his mother's tail at last. "What is it like? I can't see too good right now. Can you describe it?"

"Well, it's, huh, it's... Let me think. You know, it's so beautiful, it's actually kind of hard to put into words. But I guess you could say that it's... It's..."

He choked up. He could not think of a single convincing lie to tell Leonides. A whole life spent in snarky comments and useless witticism and now that his own twin was dying at his feet, begging him to describe something that was not there, he could not find the words to deceive him.

He swallowed down a need to roar and turned away to hide his shame.

He had to get himself back under control. Leonides needed him. The sun. He would fabricate something to do with the radiance of the sun. Something white and bright. Peaceful. Like rays of light sparkling off a clear river on a hot afternoon. Yeah, that would be alright. Better than the truth, anyway.

He ran a couple of sentences inside his head, then turned back around.

And froze.

Leonides flanks had stopped moving. Resting atop his limp forelimbs, as if sleeping, his muzzle was dry and crusty. His lax tongue, sprawled out in the dirt itself, did not seem to care.

Skoro flopped down next to his twin, his mind blank, his body dull.

So much for bright stories.

He closed his eyes and let his exhaustion blunt his pain like a protective cocoon wrapped around his heart. "I'm sorry I offered to trade your life for mine," he said as he delicately nudged Leonides' head. "I didn't really mean it."

He pressed his spine tight against Leonides' lukewarm back and collapsed into a bottomless sleep.

TWENTY-FOUR

THE THIRD STRIKE

"Hey, wake up! They're back!"

Dreadlocks' insistent voice ripped him out of his shaky slumber. He jolted up and wheeled around in panic, his mind racing to catch up with his heart. "Where? The Majingilanes? Where, Dread? *Where?*"

His brother was already halfway into the lank. "Not the Majingilanes. Skoro and Leonides! Look, they're back."

T. growled in relief. "About time those two showed their manes." He leaped forward and bumped into Dreadlocks' flank. "I wonder where they've been."

"Maybe they've found a new pride they didn't want to tell us about. Maybe it's the Sand River girls."

Dreadlocks' tail was positively wagging with excitement. After the death of Shaka and the chaotic disappointment of their short-

Canine body language, not feline.

lived venture into the Mala Mala, it seemed that the big male was in desperate need of some good news.

Although he could not really understand why, T. had a feeling that the good-natured cat had taken the loss a bit harder than the others. He could see it in the subtle changes that now affected his demeanor. Gone were the days when Dreadlocks could be counted on to follow his stomach down yet another comical blunder. He had grown more distant now, more prone to long reflective stares, almost sad, in fact, but more assertive too, in a quiet, somber sort of way. A new Makhulu.

This was more than a bit galling to T, he had to admit it. The broad-chested cat had accepted this new state of being, this new aura, with such ease. As if it were the most natural thing in the world, his due. He had no idea of the length some other lions were willing to go for a chance to look like he did. The things they were prepared to kill....

He chased the thought away.

At least the return of the twins would offer a welcome distraction. Perhaps they should go on another hunt together. Bring back the taste of the older days by taking down something truly massive. Something challenging even for the five of them. Not a hippo, of course not, but a rhino maybe, or, even better, an elephant. Now wouldn't *that* be a hunt to remember?

Smiling internally, he watched as a lone figure rounded a thicket of trees and slowly meandered its way toward them.

Dreadlocks' tail froze. The figure's head was hung low, its body rocking back and forth after every step. What had looked like a playful skip from afar now seemed far more ominous, as if the cat had lost his grip on his balance and was on the verge of toppling down.

"Is he...dancing?"

"He's limping," T. breathed out. "Look at him, he can barely walk!"

Makhulu joined them. "Any of you see Leonides?"

They scanned the horizon, to no avail. Skoro's figure was laboring its way through the grass alone. Suddenly, T. realized that his brother had yet to stop a single time to wait for his twin or throw a glance backward. In the air, his scent hung distinct, exposed, with no trace of Leonides' presence mingled in it whatsoever.

They raced to meet him.

"Skoro, you alright?"

"What happened to you?"

"Look at that bend. By the grass, his spine! How is he even walking?"

Skoro collapsed at their feet. "The Majingilanes," he croaked, his voice a hoarse whisper. "The Majingilanes ambushed us."

"Where? When?"

"Elephant plain, a couple of nights ago."

"Why didn't you call for help?"

Some kind of high-pitched, exhausted laughter escaped his brother's throat. "We had no time. It all happened so fast… The four of them fell on us in the middle of the night. We didn't stand a chance. Not a chance–"

"Skoro, look at me," said Dreadlocks, and lowered his head. "Where is Leonides?"

The lion opened his mouth, tried to say something, failed. He shook his head.

The ensuing silence hit them all like a blow to the stomach. Makhulu moaned faintly and flopped down on his haunches. T. bowed his head and closed his eyes.

From five to four. Just like that, eh?

A vile kind of pride took hold of his heart, temporarily chasing away the disquieting fear. The twins had not fared any better than he and Shaka had. Worse, in fact. With Shaka, they had at least managed to kill one of the Majingilanes. Leonides had gone down alone, like a grazer. Of course he knew that he could never share that thought out loud with the others.

He leaned forward and hurried to give Skoro a light nudge. "How's your spine?" he said. "Does it hurt?"

"It's not too bad, actually. The wound kind of throbs and I can't feel a thing below my chest anymore, but at least I can still move my legs."

"You're very lucky," said Makhulu. "The fangs must have missed some of the nerves by a hair's width."

"Yeah. Lucky. That's definitely what it feels like."

T. let loose a small appreciative chuckle and delicately ran his tongue over the grievous wound before slowly making his way back to Skoro's face, taking stoke of all the gashes and cuts his battered body had sustained along the way. When he spoke, his face was serious again, almost solemn: "For what it's worth, I'd say you've earned your nickname now, brother. You are one fine-looking scarred Pretty Boy."

Skoro raised his head in surprise. Upon realizing that there had actually been no sarcasm hidden inside T.'s voice, he swallowed down a growl and simply nodded. "Thanks," he whispered.

"What do we do now?" asked Makhulu. "About the Majingilanes, I mean."

"We need to go back and avenge Leonides, of course. We need to put an end to them before they do the same to us."

"And lose someone else in the confusion?" groaned Dreadlocks.

"Not if we catch them unaware first, we won't. We isolate them one by one and–"

"T., it's not going to happen," moaned Skoro. "Don't you see it? After what you and Shaka did, I seriously doubt that the Majingilanes will ever stray from one another ever again. You taught them too well. If we try to go after them, again, they'll simply lure us onto unfamiliar ground and ambush one of us, again."

"So what? We do nothing?"

Skoro closed his eyes and fell quiet. Makhulu turned toward Dreadlocks. "What do you think?"

"Whether we want to admit it or not, we have lost the Elephant Plain and the area of grass around it. Right now, we need to focus on protecting what we have left inside the Singita, even if it means patrolling a much smaller territory. The Ximhungwe pride will need us, they must be our priority."

"What about the Ottawa?"

Dreadlocks clenched his jaws, shook his head. "I'm sorry, Mak, but we can't afford to be overspread into the Londolozi as well. We'd be courting disaster."

"That's it then?" Skoro asked, his voice caught between pain, sorrow, and shameful relief. "With Leon gone, we give up on the first pride we ever took and accept that we've lost it all?"

"Only for now. Things can change pretty fast above grass. Who knows what the state of the Majingilanes will be a moon from now? And we haven't lost it all. We still have the Ximhungwe, and each other."

They all agreed, perhaps a bit too eagerly.

T. walked away. He had heard enough. The other three would spend the rest of the day soothing their battered temper and mourning Leonides' loss, he knew. He did not care to share in the effusions.

He sped up at a light trot and let his mind wander.

Yes, things could change pretty fast above grass, usually for the worst. That was the story of just about any cat who had ever trodden under the sun. But not for them. They were supposed to be the one constant, the rock with six heads towering over it all. Now, he wasn't so sure. Worse than the death of Leonides was the suddenness with which the blow had come. Another brother had been yanked out of his life, as if pulled underwater, and he had had no time to react. No time to see it coming and fight.

He broke into a gallop.

In his mind, the river had turned into raging rapids. He began to doubt his own ability to remain afloat. He was grasping at elusive branches, choking on fear, sinking.

Inside his head, the little voice laughed darkly.

Down and down they go, the cartwheeling cats; through the grass, they make a splash, swelled up and full of gas; and underneath the empty sky, the flies, and the glazed eyes: the snarl of a dry carcass.

So who was next?

He stopped. This was no way to live. No one was next. Certainly not him. He was still swimming. Still moving strong. All he needed to do was to get back behind the hindquarter side of the beast and be in control of his fear again. Be the thing that is feared.

His meandering course carried him through the rest of the day. At night, he stopped to rest and, as had become his custom ever since he had waded back across the Sand River, push out a couple of calling roars for Shaka.

He came across the Ximhungwe pride a few dawns later. Dread, Mak, and Skoro were not far off, he could smell their scents in the air. He marked a nearby tree and quietly stalked forward to get a better vantage point, undetected.

With everything that had been going on, he hadn't had the opportunity to meet these new females yet. Now, he could see why Dreadlocks wanted to protect them so much. The lionesses currently relaxing in the green lank in front of him looked healthy and well-fed, satiated. Proper meat-bringers. With, as far as he could see, over half a dozen cubs his brothers had fathered in his absence. The litters looked quite young, he couldn't help but notice. It would be a long while before they would be weaned from their mothers' care.

It suddenly occurred to him that he was an intruder to this touching sight. Regardless of what his brothers might say on his behalf to alleviate their doubts, the lionesses would never really see him as anything else but the cat who had come from afar after they had already surrendered to the Mapogos. The one they didn't really know. A stranger.

"Who are you?"

He looked down and, to his surprise, found himself staring into two inquisitive eyes framed by two large ears, a spotted brow, and a tiny, tightly shut, stern muzzle. The cub looked slightly older than the other romping balls of fur he had noticed earlier. Tougher too, with the fluff of his juvenile fur marred by thin, white scars and the top of his left ear missing. An appearance that contrasted sharply with the show of tranquility and prosperity displayed by the Ximhungwe girls.

"I said: 'Who *are* you?'"

He smiled at the audacity of the insistent voice. There was a roar hiding in there somewhere, striving to get out, no mistake about it.

"I'm the cat who doesn't belong," he said, slightly amused.

That did not impress the cub in the slightest. "If you're a filthy wander-male, you shouldn't stay here. The Mapogo Boys are not far. And they kill any lion who threatens our pride. They will tear you to shreds."

"Somehow, I doubt that. But you can relax, I'm not here to start trouble."

Perhaps caught off guard by the lack of effect his words had had on the intruder, the cub blinked a couple of times and remained quiet, his tiny paws firmly planted into the ground, his head tilted up, defiant. "Why are you here, then?" he finally asked.

"Good question. Truth be told, I don't really have anywhere else to go."

"Well, it doesn't matter. If the Mapogos see you, trouble is going to find you whether you want it or not."

"I take it that you're Ximhungwe yourself?"

The cub said that he was, and what was it to him anyway?

T. chuckled and laid himself down. "Which one of the Mapogo is your father?" he asked. "Do you know?"

"Not really. Skoro, I think. Maybe Leonides."

"Which one would you prefer?"

"If I had a choice, you mean?"

"Yeah. If you could pick any of the Mapogos as your direct father, which one would it be?"

The answer came without hesitation, unequivocal: "Dreadlocks."

"Really? Why?"

"He's bigger. Stronger. I want to be like him when I grow up."

"Well, what about Makhulu?"

"Makhulu's an old mane," the cub whispered after having quickly checked his surroundings, a cheeky light gleaming inside his eyes. "Besides, he looks like he's always sad."

T. bit down on his tongue and repressed a sudden laughter that would have betrayed his presence to the rest of the pride. "You know, you might just be right about that, cub," he breathed out once he was certain that he had the guffaws firmly back under control. "By the grass, you might just be right."

"What about you? If you're not a wander-male, what pride do you belong to? Do you know your own father?"

"Not really, no. I mean, there was this one male, back when I was your size. I don't know if he really was my father but I did hate him more than any of the others combined. I guess that's as good a sign as any other." Cubs love their fathers, and vice versa.

"Why did you hate him? Wasn't he there to protect you?"

"Yes, of course. And I suppose that, in his own way, he did. But he also was a really hard cat to like, trust me. Rough, uncouth, and totally unpredictable. A cub-killer. I used to be terrified of him more than anything else above grass. Every night, I would dream of killing him."

"Did you ever get the chance?"

"No. He died before I was big enough. Killed by some other wander-males. I did watch him melt away in front of my eyes, though. That was nice."

The cub nodded his head slowly. For one so young, he seemed to have a strangely strong grasp of such things. "At least you've outlived him. He's not a part of your life any longer. You're free."

"If only things were so easy."

"You still hate him? Even after he's dead?"

"No, not really." T. ran his tongue over the notch that cut through his nostril. "But I think I've become him."

There was a time when he would have beamed at the thought. Not so much anymore. The achievement felt pointless, empty, like spending an entire afternoon clambering up a grassy knoll through thick scraggle and clingy lank only to realize once at the top that it was, in fact, a very low hill to clear. A small, barren hill on which he stood, alone, with no horizons whatsoever.

"Me, it's my mother I hate," said the cub.

"Why is that?"

"She left me behind after all my siblings died. I think she just… I don't know. I think she just gave up on me! As if I was worthless. I had to keep up with the pride all by myself. Every night, I thought that I was going to die. By the grass, I was so scared."

"You shouldn't take it personally. It probably wasn't anything you had done. Lionesses can be hard mothers at times, especially if it's their first litter. She wouldn't be the first cat who felt overwhelmed and chose to walk away."

"It still feels personal when you're the one who has to suffer."

"Yeah, I guess there is no way around that."

A short silence ensued. For some strange reason T. could not begin to fathom, the cub seemed to have warmed to his presence. He took a couple of short steps and snuggled up against his mane.

"Can I ask you something?" he asked.

"Sure."

"Does it ever feel less lonely? Once you grow up, I mean. Does the grass ever feel less empty?"

T. stared at the cub, taken aback. "No," he finally growled. "No. Big or small, you stand alone."

He watched as the unease spread onto the young cub's face. For half a heartbeat, it looked as though he might be about to break down into whimpers, overcome by the harsh reality of the life awaiting him. Then his countenance hardened. He stomped his paws, nodded his head. His tiny jaws clenched, as if ready to swallow anything that might be thrown at him.

In that instant, he looked old.

And T. realized what he had to do.

The solution was so simple, it at been staring at him straight in the face, literally, ever since he had found these new huntresses. He could never live like an intruder tiptoeing on the edge of the pride as if asking for their permission to exist. Not him. Not after everything he had been through. He had to make an entrance. Introduce himself properly. And get back on the hindquarter side of fear in the process. He might not like what he had become, *who* he had become, but there was no turning back now. This was his one and only hill, and he had to make his stand on it.

As for the lonely cub, it would be a mercy. He knew this better than anyone. No deceiving warm glow for him. No witnessing his cartwheeling mother being shattered by a river of horns like some limp piece of rotten wood.

No brother to call your name and beg for your help in the middle of the night while he is being torn to pieces, and all you can do is keep your head down and run, the abject flight of a coward who has turned his back on the one and only cat who's ever–

He shut the voice down and stood himself up, brusquely.

No, there would be nothing of the sort. Far better to put an end to the misery before it even starts.

The cub took a step back. A whiff of sudden fear reached T.'s muzzle. He let it invade his mouth and slowly seep into the mucus of his palate, savoring the sweet, intoxicating flavor like a long-awaited meal. Saliva dribbled down the black corners of his lower lip. Already, he was panting slightly.

Until this very instant, he had not realized how much he had missed it.

Some lions, ya kill too, cub. This, ya'll learn soon enough.

He still hesitated and teetered on the brink for half a heartbeat. His legs, suddenly made of soft wood, seemed incapable of propelling him forward into his leap. His heart lurched inside his chest, as if to hold him back. *Think of your brothers!* it cried. *They won't forgive you a second time!*

He pushed the thought away. After everything that had happened, they could not afford to send him away. One way or the other, they would come around to the new reality.

He plunged headfirst and grabbed the cub by the neck while squeezing the air out of his windpipe. He shook, briefly, and groaned in pleasure as he felt the tiny, satisfactory snap of the spine pop inside his mouth. The body went limp. He dropped it at his paws and took a couple of steps back to better contemplate what he had done.

A second wave of barely repressed guffaws – high-pitched, like cackles – escaped his chest. He was feeling so light on his paws all of a sudden. Free once more! Free from the fear!

Free-falling, more like.

Suddenly alert, he whirled toward the rest of the Ximhungwe pride. None of the females had stirred. He remained undetected. But he could see more cubs playing amid the grass, blissfully unaware. He lowered his belly, hunched his shoulders, stalked forward.

Six little cubs, hiding in the grass,
"But where could they be?" the big lion asks.

His feverish mind lost track of time. Day turned into night, then day again. With the moon full and bright above him, his cat's eyes barely registered the changes in light. His reality had merged into one continuous, half-dreamed game of hide-and-seek.

He caught the first three easily enough before the Ximhungwe girls became aware of the threat. On the third dawn – or was it the fourth? – the pride was in turmoil. Being no virgin to the way of things, the lionesses immediately recognized the bite marks for what they were. But, to T.'s delight, they failed to comprehend how that was possible. Surely, it could not be the work of a lone wander-male. Not with the three Mapogo males so relaxed less than a few leaps away from the pride.

He stopped and watched them cry out in anguish and confusion as they stumbled upon yet another corpse. Comfortably hidden in the grass downwind from them, he refrained from popping out to take credit. Instead, he waited to see what they would do. After a brief flash of temper, two of the older lionesses set about searching for the killer – he flattened himself down a bit more as they scanned the area, just in case – while a third grabbed the last remaining cub, a small female, and hastily trotted away.

He easily bypassed the huntresses' searching party and followed the mother's trail, quietly.

To her credit, she did try to cover her tracks by adopting a meandering course full of random changes of direction. Once, he even had to precipitously dive for cover at the last instant when she suddenly doubled back to check her surroundings. Eventually, she settled on a spot and hid the cub inside a thicket of dense bushes. Then she stood still, her head on a swivel.

He laid himself down comfortably and waited. Time was on his side, he knew. Lionesses need to hunt and eat, same as any cat.

When the sun began its falling arc, she left and rejoined the others. He waited for her tail to disappear in the grass and counted another ten heartbeats before pouncing forward.

He made short work of the little female.

"That's a harsh blow to swallow, I'll grant you that," he said to her afterward while ripping a leg off from the rest of her body. "And all of it because you wouldn't let me get a few bites out of a hippo I had killed. You should have known better than to push me around. Shaka's dead now, and it's all because of you. If you hadn't pushed me away I would never have left, and he'd still be alive." The two glazed eyed looked back at him from atop the tiny, blackened muzzle. He grabbed the small carcass and swung it around, spraying the grass with fresh blood in the process. "Do you hear me?! You did all of this. You killed him. And Leonides. And the cubs too. Yes, it's all your fault. You're the greatest cat-killer of us all. You–"

T. froze. From the other side of the thicket, a tawny shape stirred. He watched, petrified, as Dreadlocks rose from his nap and stared at him through the dense foliage.

"That'sh no' wha' ya' shink," he stammered out, the cub's corpse still firmly lodged inside his jaws.

Dreadlocks said nothing. In his large, unblinking eyes, T. could see no shock or anger. Only resignation. He nodded his head and walked away.

T. broke into a gallop in the opposite direction.

That same night, Makhulu came after him.

"T.!" he heard the old cat bellow in the distance. "Where are you, T.?! I know you did this. We took you back in and this is how you thank us?!! Come and face me, T.!"

"I did what I had to," he roared back, defiant. "What any lion would have done!"

The heavy thuds of Makhulu's footsteps zeroed-in on his voice and hammered at the hard-packed dirt, closer and closer.

He fled.

He was doing this to spare the old-mane's life, he told himself. Should it come to blows, he would have no choice but to kill the weaker lion. He did not want to lose another brother. Not like this.

Makhulu was hot on his tail, he could smell his scent. He veered toward a low forest and elongated his strides while relying on his whiskers to weave himself a path through the unseen vines and thin branches whipping at his muzzle and mane. For half a heartbeat, he thought about climbing up a tree, but his pride could not accept it.

The Sand River was not far, he could smell the freshness of the water. He wondered if Makhulu would try to chase him all the way to the other side. Banish him a second time, so to speak.

He tripped over a tangle of roots and went sprawling in the dirt. He scrambled to his paws, leaped in a different direction, changed course again.

No. Regardless of whatever else that might happen, he would not go back. Not alone. Better to stand his ground against Makhulu than face the emptiness of the Mala Mala alone ever again, even if that meant killing another brother.

He began to prepare himself mentally for the coming fight.

Fortunately for him – well, for the both of them, really – Makhulu was not the lion he used to be. As the darkness of the night slowly waned and turned into a greyish twilight, the heavy footsteps gradually lost ground. Soon, they could be heard no more. "T.!" the dark-maned roared one last time, his heavy panting cutting his words short. "You're a coward, T.!"

T. slowed down to a camper and ignored him. His mind was blank. He was done feeling like he had to explain himself all the time. One way or the other, his brothers would accept him back. They had to. At dawn, he crawled under a nice bush and fell asleep.

He awoke in the middle of the afternoon. After crawling out of the bush, he yawned and stretched his sore muscles.

Dreadlocks was already waiting for him, seated on his haunches. "You had a nice sleep?"

T. went to seat by his side, his attitude carefully neutral and non-threatening. "I did, actually. First time in a long while."

Dreadlocks nodded his head curtly. His body was stiff, his eyes fixed on the horizon. As he absent-mindedly chased a fly off, the muscles of his shoulders and forelegs bulged under his skin. Although T. knew perfectly well that it was not possible, he could have sworn that the broad chest had grown in size since he had last seen it. Under the lush darkness of the disheveled locks of mane grazing the ground, the tawny fur seemed too tight, overstretched, as though the skin of the old Dreadlocks could no longer fully contain this new lion striving to get out.

"I'm guessing you haven't missed a whole lot of meals recently, have you?" said T.

The quip fell flat at the paws of the stoic lion. "The hunting's been good recently. The girls even took down a buffalo while you were asleep this morning. Me and Mak joined them."

"How is he? Still angry?"

"He's better now. I talked to him."

"Yeah? What'd you say?"

"That you were you, and that we should accept you the way you are. Because you're still our brother and we can't change you."

"I don't need you to speak on my behalf. I can stand on my own."

"I know you can. Truly, I do. But *something* has to change. We can't keep fighting among ourselves like that anymore. Not after what happened to Shaka and Leonides. And the cubs. By the grass, T., we have to stop killing our own cubs."

"I had no choice! The cubs weren't mine. If I hadn't done what I did, the Ximhungwe girls would never have accepted me. I would have been forced to live on the edge of the pride like some–"

"I know, I know. I don't blame you."

"You don't?"

"No, and neither does Skoro."

"And Mak?"

"Like I said, I talked to him. He'll come around in due time, don't worry about it. But starting now, the bloodshed has to stop. The Ximhungwe is our last pride. We need to take care of them."

T. bowed his head. "Only one pride left," he spat sullenly. "How did it ever come to that?"

"We underestimated the Majingilanes. We thought that we could push them around like any other lion, but they proved themselves to be quite resourceful, and brave."

"If I didn't know any better, I'd say you admire them."

"Of course I do. Don't you see it? They're us."

"Us? What do you mean?"

"They are young, hungry, cruel, and boisterous, just like we used to be."

"How can you even say that? We're the Mapogos! There has never been another coalition like us. There never will be! Besides, you weren't there when Shaka died. If you had, you would never call those cats brave. They tore him to pieces while he was still alive. Ate him! I heard him beg, Dread. *Beg*!"

Beg you to come back, you mean.

Dreadlocks remained unphased. "I seem to remember a few gutted cats begging for our mercy as well. Cubs too, of course. Once, I even heard the strange story of one of our own mating with a lioness he had just killed, only to eat her afterward…"

T. clenched his jaws shut. "If you like the Majingilanes so much," he muttered, "maybe you should try to join them."

"That's not the way it works, brother."

An awkward silence ensued. T. did not like where his brother's head was at. A scolding about the cubs, he could understand. Not this talk of the Majingilanes being their equal. Never.

"We really thought that we were something special, didn't we?" Dreadlocks said. "Thought that we had it all figured out. 'Here comes the mighty Mapogos, untouchable and invincible!'" He shook his head sadly. "Turns out, we were nothing special. Just the newest batch of young cats eager to leave their mark on the grass. We had our fun. Now it's the Majingilanes' turn."

"It's still four against four. We're not done yet."

"Three against four, I'd say. In his state, Skoro can barely fight. And Makhulu… Well, let's just say that the two of them together might make for one good lion now."

"You're too hard on the old mane. He might not be able to run the way he used to, but he's still a steady cat."

"Not more than Leonides or Shaka were. Not by a long leap. That's why I need you, T. I need to know that I can count on you to watch over them and the pride while I'm gone. You and I are the last of the fighting Mapogos."

"Gone? Where are you going?"

"I need to clear my mind for a little while. And there is something I want to investigate."

"Investigate? What do you need to investigate?"

Dreadlocks sighed. "Do you remember the Sand River pride?"

"Vaguely. As I recall, it was mostly the twins' pride."

"Not quite, they never really had full control. Anyway, one dawn, the whole pride vanished."

"Vanished?"

"Yes. As if they had evaporated into thin air. Leonides and Skoro went searching for them but found nothing. Then, a couple of moons later, one of the young males stumbled back inside the Ottawa territory, so shocked out of his mind that he could not utter a single word out to anyone. Makhulu tried to take care of him, but he died eventually."

"How?"

"We don't know for sure. There was no obvious wound. The Ottawa girls tried to feed Makhulu some crazy story about bad buffalo meat, but I don't believe it. I think the lead Ottawa killed him, somehow."

"That wouldn't surprise me. She's a nasty piece of work, that one."

"His death is not important. He was the youngest one, I'm surprised he made it back to us at all. But, if you recall, the Sand River pride had a total of five sub-adults: two females and three males."

"Ah yes. I remember now. I was looking forward to fighting those young belly-manes one day. Too bad some foreign cat beat us to it."

"How?"

"What do you mean?"

"How does a cat kill five sub-adult lions – not to mention two full-grown lionesses – so fast that none of us so much as hear a single roar of protest? And the youngest one walks away? It doesn't make any sense. No coalition is that powerful."

"You think something else killed them? Something other than a bunch of lions?"

"I don't know. That's why I went to investigate after Leonides and Skoro came back without an answer. Turns out, if you push far enough across the Singita, you'll eventually come face to face with some kin of weird, stretched-out hedge."

"A weird, stretched-out hedge?"

"I honestly don't know what else to call it, but it's some kind of tall, hard vine for sure. Toughest one I've ever seen. I couldn't push through, I had to crawl underneath it. But it was worth it. On the other side lies a whole different world."

"Different? How?"

"Well, for one, lots of bipeds everywhere. I think that's where they nest. More importantly, plenty of buffaloes. But they're different. Fatter and slower. Easier to take down. The meat just melts on the tongue like nothing you've ever tasted before. I tell you T., this other side of the hedge, that's the place to be."

"And you want to go back now despite the Majingilanes making moves on us from all sides?"

"Yes. Right now they're busy submitting the Eyrefield, I've heard the roars from across the river. Those girls will give them a fight – Fer most of all – but they won't last forever. If I don't leave now, I may never get another chance. Skoro told me that they bumped against that same hedge in the Elephant Plain when they were fleeing from the Majingilanes. He said that Leonides died on the other side of it. I want to have a look and see if I can find him. Him, and the slow buffaloes."

"Aren't you concerned about the bipeds? You said there was a lot of them."

were

"So what? They're just bipeds. Even when they're away from the rumblers, they don't do nothing."

anything

"I'm not so sure."

"What do you mean?"

This time, it was T.'s turn to sigh. "It was a while ago," he said, hesitant to share the story, "long before the Majingilanes. I was lying down with one of the Styx girls when a small rumbler happened by with two bipeds on it. Well, kind of inside it, actually, you know how weird they can be. Anyway, I had nothing better to do, so I went to have a look from up close. I wanted to see what those bipeds were really about. If they could feel anything at all."

"And?"

"They can feel fear, that much is clear. I smelled it on them, saw it in their eyes."

"All grazers feel fear."

"Yes, but there was something else behind the eyes, something stiffer, almost lionlike. I tell you, these two bipeds, they didn't like me being so close, but they were still in control. They didn't just run away like some mindless grass-eaters. I would have hunted them down if they had."

"What's your point?"

"I think they're killers too. I don't know what, I don't know how, but I think they're killers."

Not needed

Dreadlocks scratched his right ear, slightly non-plussed. "Even if that's true, why should we be concerned? Hyenas and leopards are killers and we don't run away from them, do we? Those bipeds are nothing without the rumblers. Barely the size of a gazelle."

T. acquiesced. Dreadlocks was right, of course. Already he regretted having shared the story. And for what? A weird feeling in his guts he had experienced many seasons ago?

"No," his brother continued, "the real challenge will be to evade the Majingilanes while I cross the Elephant Plain. Once I'm on the other side of the hedge, I should be fine." He rose and gave T. a light nudge. "When I come back, things will be different. In the meantime, the fate of the Mapogos rests on your shoulders. You're top cat in my absence, so try not do to do anything overly stupid, eh?"

T. felt his legs turn to mud. He hastened to rise and clear his throat. "What if… Dread, what if the Majingilanes show up and I'm not up to the task? What if I run?"

Again.

Dreadlocks' body was already halfway into the long grass. He turned around and shook his head, his eyes gleaming faintly. "You're a strong lion, T. Stronger than you think. And you've got a lot of bravery inside you. If only you could see it yourself."

On this, he ambled away.

T. watched his brother go with a pang in his heart.

He knew that their fragile little equilibrium of peers was at an end. Dreadlocks had become the new dominant male and that was that.

Still, he did not care.

He loved that big broad chest of a cat. After Shaka, Dreadlocks had been his closest brother. With him gone, he felt vulnerable again, deserted for the second time in as many seasons.

He licked his muzzle and stomped his paws in a vain attempt to calm his restless nerve. No sooner had the outline of the big lion sunk below the far horizon that he began to cherish the time when he would come back. nerves

But he never did.

TWENTY-FIVE

THE HEIGHT OF THE MOUNTAIN

Skoro extended his hind leg out, retracted it, extended it again. His suspended paw played with the sun and drew slim shadows on his face and neither region. He closed his eyes and wriggled his rump to try and work some warmth into his lower half. A sharp rock hidden underneath the loose sand grated against his protruding vertebra. He shuddered briefly and lay still. It was no use. The wound had healed but everything below the bend of his spine was still hopelessly numb – except, maybe, for a light tingle that sometimes reached him as though through a thick layer of mud, but then again only if he stomped his paws hard enough.

No matter how hard he tried, he could not seem to get warm. Even now, with the near-solid rays of the afternoon sun hammering at his mane and shining red through his eyelids, the lower part of his body remained stubbornly stiff and frozen, distant.

He thought he knew why. It was the chill of that night still clinging to his flesh. In his pride, he had fooled himself into thinking that he could just walk away from it, turn his back on the event and move on. But, of course, things were never so simple. A part of him had stayed behind with Leonides. That was why it was always so cold. Just like his twin, it was rotting.

He willed his tail to move and heard the satisfying swooshing of the tuft swiping through the fine, powdery dust. Even though he could not feel the movement, the sound was soothing.

Gnats bit at the side of his muzzle and assaulted his left eye. He ground his head deeper into the sand. A soft crunching sound invaded his ear and blotted out the world. He tried to focus on it. Find some respite in the silence. A thin crust formed at the corner of his nostrils and tickled the base of his whiskers. He licked at it without thinking and instantly made the whole mess worse. With the entire side of his muzzle now coated in wet, clingy sand, the moisture became a focal point for the crazed insects.

His position was untenable. He opened his eyes, shook his head, rose to his feet.

Sun blaze almighty, it was a hot day. Warped by the distant haze, the horizon appeared shut out, inaccessible. On either side of the sand lane, short stalks of yellow grass were standing as stiff as fangs. Despite the oppressive heat, they scurried with life. A few grasshoppers jumped away at the approach of his shadow. He leaned forward, vaguely curious, and noticed a large black beetle stubbornly lumbering her way through the unwieldy stems. Her body was stiff and heavy on her thin legs, made of one rigid block, like a smooth black pebble. Her long antennas were like two thin whiskers groping for the world ahead of her. He watched her as she tilted sideways and came dangerously close to being overturned. She knew what she was doing and her strong little claws never lost their grip. She reached the edge of the grass and tipped down a claw mark that was like a gulley to her. He watched her climb the opposite bluff, her legs straining to find a good grip on the loose sand. Once at the top, she stopped to clean her antennas before attempting the ascent of a mountain he had created by shifting the sand around when he had laid himself down.

She wasn't as smooth as he had first thought. Thin scratches marred her rotundity, and she had five legs not six: he could see the tiny stump on her left flank wiggle uselessly in the air along with its sister-limbs, doing its part. A battered thing she was, quiet and obstinate. Like him.

A cloud of flies broke the flow of his thoughts and assaulted the moisture of his eyes. He snorted a couple of times, turned around, yawned. The dry, clean smell of the savannah mingled with the warm bodies of his pride reached him. In the back of his palate, the clingy smell of the rumbler still idling uselessly across the sand lane a couple of leaps away left a slightly nauseating aftertaste. Panting through half-closed jaws, he let his saliva dribble out and carry the taste away.

A pair of cubs swerved around his back paws and assaulted the tuft of his tail by delivering tiny bites he could not feel. He sat down on his haunches and watched them proceed.

They were not half-bad. Awkward in their leaps, of course, and slow, but they had an instinct for teamwork. The bigger one managed to sink his claws in. He rolled himself into a ball and brought the tuft to his chest. Then, growling happily, he leaned forward and attempted to close his jaws around the tail itself. His mouth was not quite big enough and he was forced to gnaw at the sleek fur instead.

Skoro whipped his tail back up. He had not felt any of that. His appendage was like a dead branch. More flies landed on his muzzle. No longer buzzing around his head, they just sat there, as if they owned the place. He scratched his nose and sent them flying. The second cub went back to assaulting his back paw. He forced him off with a rough shake and plodded away.

The cubs gave chase.

It was his own fault, he chastised himself. He should have known that this would be a day for insects, cubs, and other boiling things. He should have kept still and play dead. Instead, his movements had sealed his fate, like a gazelle pronking straight into the unseen huntress hidden behind the bushes.

He could always flee, of course. Cut through the grass and make good his escape. Young as they were, they would never dare follow him. But that meant walking under the afternoon sun over those hard stalks and chaffing creepers, and those nasty little things that were always getting stuck inside your nostrils…

No, he had a better idea.

He angled toward the nearest lioness and casually walked by her rump. As expected, his attackers immediately peeled off his trail and veered toward the more familiar scent. The deed done, he settled back down at a respectful distance and watched the girl rouse herself slowly, the two cubs now feverishly bumping against her neck.

"You could have led them a bit further away," she growled, her eyes half closed. "Could have taken them all the way to the far side of grass, maybe."

"I figured they might be missing you. It looked like they needed a familiar scent."

The cubs rounded the lioness' body, each on one side, and assaulted her tail. She indulged them by dragging the tuft across the sand back and forth, occasionally raising it above their head whenever she felt they had her cornered, only to slam it back down moments later, to the cubs' delight.

"What they truly need is the touch of a rough cat," she said, quite serious all of a sudden. "Put some fear into them and teach them the taste of their own adrenalin in the back of their throat. Show them how to swallow it down and push through. Their life won't be a game forever."

"Maybe I should take them to my brother, then. They'd learn fast."

The tail froze. The lioness' eyes widened, suddenly alert. "Don't joke like that, Skoro. Not ever."

He bowed his head, slightly ashamed. "You know I don't mean it. Besides, you've seen him at the giraffe kill a couple of dawns back, you know he's accepted the new batch. The mini-pogs, he calls them. Don't mind his sniggering, that's just the way he is sometimes, I don't think he can really help it. He needs the posturing. Especially when he's in front of you girls. But he's got his own female and cubs to take care of now. He won't be doing it again."

"I've seen you fight, though. The three of you, you still fight all the time. For one of us, for meat, for whatever. I know big manes like to scuffle, but I've never heard of other males fight so much."

"Don't you mind that either, it's just rough playing. We've been doing it for so long, it would feel weird to stop now. Would feel like something's terribly wrong."

"With Dzunani, it was different."

"Yeah? In what way?"

"He was calm and somber, almost quiet. In fact, I don't think I ever heard a growl out of him that was out of place. But he was no push-over either, he knew where to draw the line. A good father and a good hunter, he would always pull his share with the rest of the pride."

"That's because he was alone. Lone males always let the pride absorb them. They have no coalition to fall back on, no brothers, so they find the socialization wherever they can."

The lioness let out a light chuckle. "I can still remember that one time when we saw him strut around and bellow his victory. It was right after he had sent Makhulu running. By the look of him, you would have thought that he had conquered the entirety of the Sabi Sands and brought a hundred prides under his paw. By the grass, he was so proud." The chuckles ran their course. She squinted her eyes and lowered her head. "Of course, by then, me and the other girls we already knew that it was all over. The Mapogos were coming for him. He would never be able to stand up to them a second time, not alone. But we let him have his moment. He was a good cat."

"He did stand in the end, for what it's worth. He didn't try to run away like some other males."

"Lots of good that did him."

"Yeah. I can still remember Makhulu's eyes when he asked us to follow him. Said that we had a cat to kill. I had never seen him like that before, with so much spite leaking out of the yellow in his eyes. For half a heartbeat, I actually thought that T. had done something terrible, unforgivable, and that he was the cat Makhulu wanted us to kill. All of this was long before the split, of course, but already these two had some hard times getting along. Anyway, when we came, Dzunani stood his ground and fought the six of us as best he could. It didn't last long, but he was brave. He kept saying that we should at least spare the cubs. Take the territory and spare the cubs."

"What did you reply?"

Skoro licked his nose, then his front paws. The cubs had moved off the lioness' tail and were now assaulting a stick in the grass. He noticed how they instinctively took turn shaking the branch from side to side while the other one pinned the opposite end down with his front paws. "We didn't lie," he finally said. "We're many things, but we're not liars. We told him his line would end along with his life. At the time, we thought that we would get control of your pride soon after. We didn't anticipate that you would be able to evade us for so long."

"It wasn't easy, believe me. After Dzunani died, we had to give up our territory. We tried to live off hunting smaller preys while staying on the move so as to keep the cubs out of your reach, but in the end it didn't work."

"Why not?"

"Not enough food, too much wandering around. And the fear. By the grass, you don't know what it's like to know that you're being hunted all the time. Hunted by your own kind, no less. Turns you jittery on the inside, like a hyena. We did everything we could for the little ones but their bodies could not take the pounding. It was the weirdest thing to see, really. They would be walking right behind you on moment and then *poof*, drop down. Never a sound or a squeal, just collapse straight down as if something inside them had suddenly come undone, decided that it had had enough. 'Sorry guys, I guess I just don't have another step left in me.' The first few times, I turned around and tried to help them back on their feet, thinking that maybe they had tripped over a branch or something. Then, I would realize that their eyes were distant, somehow. You know the kind: wide open, but not tracking. And I would know."

"How did your sisters take it?"

"Pretty hard, actually. Me, it was my first litter, so it wasn't too bad. You never expect your first ones to make it anyway, it's just the way it is. But a few of my sisters could not accept watching their young ones waste away like that. You see, they felt responsible. Felt like they were bad mothers because they could not provide enough meat. Had it been you guys, maybe it would have been better. A quick shake of the neck and that's it. Nothing anyone can do about that but roar and grieve and move on. But that's not the way it happened. So one by one, they stayed behind with the last of their cubs who could not keep up. They stayed behind even though they should have known better. Should have known that there was nothing they could do. I never saw them again."

"They starved themselves for cubs they knew they could not save?"

"Some of them did, yes. Another got so mad with hunger, I watched her try her luck against a bull elephant. I screamed at her not to do it, but of course she didn't listen. I'm not entirely sure she could understand me at this point. You should have seen her eyes: two ravenous pits. And her mumbling: 'Got to get me some, get me some, get me some.' Like a mad droning. It was all over in a heartbeat. The elephant didn't even slow down, like he was crushing a gnat or something. She was lucky that way. A few of the others, the ones who, like me, had decided to keep on going no matter what, not so much. They wasted away slowly, like the cubs we had abandoned."

"In the end, how many sisters did you lose?"

"Four. I am the only adult who made it. Me and three young huntresses – little more than juveniles at the time – we are all what's left of the original Ximhungwe."

Skoro jerked his head back, as if slapped. He had never heard that part before. "When we killed Dzunani," he mumbled, "I didn't anticipate that things would be so bad for your pride. It feels pointless to have wasted so many lives like that."

"Well, now that you know the other side of that story, would you do things differently if you could?"

He glanced at her but she kept her muzzle hard and expressionless. Her eyes shone through him, waiting to see if he would lie. "No," he finally said. "No, I guess not. Dzunani was in our way, we did what we had to do. Everything else that happened to your pride, that's just life on the far side of grass."

She nodded her head slowly and he relaxed a little. He felt as though he was a cub again and had just given the correct answer to one of Sifit's harder questions.

Like so many other huntresses, she was past the hate and the obfuscation, past the need to blame. She had turned into a beetle herself. Cold and stoic, she would keep on trudging through the grass no matter how high the stalks, how vicious the pain. Eyes front, one step at a time, and don't you look back, sister. No matter what you do, don't you dare look back. Save the cubs you can. Let the grass take the rest.

The only thing that mattered to her now, as far as he could tell, was honesty. To try and deny her the pain she had been through, pretend that things could have been different, had he only known of her hardship, worst of all, to try and apologize, would be tantamount to taking something out of her, something vital, buried deep inside her guts, that held the rest of her together. It would undo her. He was a monster to her, he knew, but she could accept him as such, so long as he remained an honest monster.

"You and three juveniles, that's four grown lionesses now," he said, eager to change the subject. "Who's the fifth cat?"

"A Ravenscourt girl. We took her in after you gutted her pride."

That quieted him for another few heartbeats. "Quite a thing we did to this place," he muttered again, this time more to himself than for her benefit.

"You only realize that now?"

"No. Of course not. I've always known. But when you go through it one event at a time, it feels different, more diluted, like stones scattered in the grass. Whenever you step on one, you know it's not the first, and you know it won't be the last, but at the same time, it's still just one stone. You can discard it. Shake your paw and move on. But now that I look back on things…"

"You realize that stones add up, and you can see the size of the mountain you've left behind."

"Yeah, something like that. Quite the fucking thing."

"Well, you guys sure made an impact on this veld, there is no denying that. Too bad you won't be leaving too many cubs behind, though."

He looked at her, at the casual way with which she cleaned her paws while she said the words, and realized that, in her mind, she had already moved past him. Discarded him, like a stone. Already she was getting ready for the next males who would come along. He shuddered briefly and wondered if she had looked at Dzunani the same way.

"Hey, you want to hear something weird and kind of funny?" she said.

"Yes. Please, yes."

"Do you remember Tailless from the Tsalala pride?"

"Not really. She was T. and Shaka's girl."

"But you know of her, right?"

"Of course. She's a legend. Started the whole Tsalala pride all on her own, just her and a litter of cubs. Then there is the time when she faced the hyenas and bit off her own tail."

"Right. Well, she didn't submit to the Majingilanes after your brother left."

"She didn't?"

"Nope. The rest of the pride did, but not her. She took all the small ones and left to start from scratch all over again. Word on the wind is she's doing pretty well too. The cubs are still alive and well fed."

"And the Majingilanes just left her be?"

"Guess so. They're still busy enough with the Eyrefield anyway."

That drew a small laughter out of him. "My sister Fer is lead huntress at the Eyrefield. She's probably giving them a cat fight they'll never forget."

"Wait, that's not even the weirdest part about the Tsalala. Get this: Tailless had an elder daughter – still has, I guess you could say – and that daughter just lost her own tail under the exact same circumstances."

"You're kidding!"

"I kid you not. She got set upon by hyenas too, had to stand her ground, lost the tail. From what I heard, she bit it off too. Everyone's calling her Young Tailless now."

"Wow. What did the old Tailless have to say about that? She must have been so proud."

"She probably doesn't know. She can't come back to the pride anymore, the Majingilanes would kill her. And from what I heard, the other huntresses have turned on her as well."

"Why?"

"It's strange, actually. They think she deserted them. Chose the cubs over the wellbeing of the pride. If I were her, I would watch my spine. Those girls can be quite vengeful."

"You see, that's one of the main differences between a pride and a coalition. You girls can never seem to let spilled blood grow cold. You keep grudges."

"And you guys don't?"

"Not as much. When T. came back after his split, we didn't turn him away. We accepted him back and–"

"Yes, I know all about the leeway you afforded your wayward brother, Skoro. I don't need to hear more about it."

"I guess you don't. All I'm saying is that lionesses can be pretty hard on each other at times, to say nothing of members from other prides."

"Funny you should say that. Have you heard what happened to the Ottawa recently?"

"No, what?"

"Defiant's dead."

"Really? How?"

"Buffalo kick."

"Don't tell T. that, you might actually make him happy."

He would have to break the news to Makhulu as well, he reflected. That might be a little less pleasant.

"Well," the Ximhungwe lioness continued, giddy, "for once, that would make two of us. With the lead huntress gone, the Ottawa is in turmoil. Only three young girls remain, and they can't hope to hold onto such a large territory on their own. As for the two young belly-manes, they have turned to wandering alone. They won't last long."

"Now that you mention it, I had to chase two lean cats off a kill recently. I knew that there was something familiar about their scent."

He made another mental note to warn Makhulu. The dark-maned had fathered the two young males shortly before Shaka's death and the chaos that had ensued, he knew, but even though they were related, the Ottawa Boys were still wander-males. And wander-males kill cubs.

"I don't care about the belly-manes so much as the three huntresses," the Ximhungwe lioness said. "With the Ottawa on such a precarious footing, now is the perfect time to push through the Londolozi. If we don't, some other pride will beat us to it. Good hunting grounds over there."

"What about Makhulu's daughters?"

She stifled a groan. "What about them?"

"They will never willingly let go of the Londolozi."

She bowed her head curtly, as though granting the point, and returned her attention to her front paws. Once done, she yawned and took stoke of the cubs now playing near the rumbler. They could hear the bipeds on the rumbler's back chirruping softly after every one of the cubs' awkward romps, like overgrown birds.

The lioness stood and stretched her spine. “One thing you Mapogos did get right,” she said while ambling away, “sometimes a pride got to go.”

TWENTY-SIX

ON PATROL

"Go? Go where?"

"Over beyond that low hill. I think I heard a grunt."

"A grunt? What kind of a grunt?"

"The buffalo kind. Come on, let's go."

Makhulu leaped forward and sped up to a vigorous camper, his head hung low, his jaws panting wet over the soft cushion of fat, green grass. The moist ground gave an elastic spring to his steps. He crossed a thin dirt lane and angled toward the knoll rising in front of him. T. caught up to him and lightly bumped into his flank. At the foot of the hill, they elongated their strides and pushed up the slippery bluff all the way to the narrow top where they laid low, inconspicuous.

The buffalo scent hit them immediately, carried by a sharp breeze that ruffled their mane and shielded their own presence.

Makhulu breathed-in the mix of soft leather, acidic musk, and grass-based excrements. His stomach rumbled.

Below him, the small herd, maybe two dozen pairs of horns, was enjoying a lazy afternoon by the side of a fresh water hole. Satiated grunts and a few short snorts reached his ears, along with the muffled thuds of split hooves hitting the soft grass and turning it into a desolate landscape of tortured mud. A big male raised his head toward the hill. Makhulu lowered himself and held his breath. He wasn't overly worried. Although the grass was far too short to hide them, he knew that they had the distance on their side.

As expected, the buffalo's weak eyes glanced over them, past them, unseeing. He returned to his casual grazing, ears and tail flicking absent-mindedly to ward off clouds of flies, his busy muzzle seemingly dictating the movements of his entire body.

"They're well-fed and placid, I'll give you that," whispered T. "Which one you're thinking?"

Makhulu took the time to consider the issue. He wanted to make sure that he had a good understanding of the dynamics within the herd before deciding on a target. Not just the size and position of each individual, but their likely character and ties to each other as well. He wanted to know which one had some fight in him and which one would run, which one was more likely to be helped and which one would be left behind to fend for himself, alone. This was not easy, given the big, dumb beasts' lack of expression and seemingly non-existent social cohesion, but, fortunately for him, this hunt was only for two lions. They didn't need to be overly greedy. A small target of opportunity would do just fine. Something tender that did not require too much effort.

"That one," he finally decided while pointing at a calf who had ventured away from the others and was now grazing near a thicket of thornbushes. An orphan, most likely.

T. nodded but did not rise. Ostensibly, he licked at the gash under his front left paw. The wound had stopped bleeding but was still glowing bright red. "Guess it's your turn to take the lead," the lion said. "Please, do call me when you're done."

Makhulu repressed a grumble. No point arguing, his brother had the half-snarl etched on his muzzle.

He retraced his paw prints going downhill, then cautiously rounded the knoll and made for the thornbushes. By doing so, he lost visual contact with the calf, but that did not matter much since he already knew the general direction of his quarry. He slid under the low canopy of thin green branches and tangled vines and crawled forward with his shoulder hunched and his belly almost to the ground.

A branch cracked. So near, he thought for an instant that he was the one who had stepped on it. He froze and looked down. No, his paws still knew how to thread the creepers undetected. A snort and a ripping sound reached him a bit to his left, then the soft rustle of green wood being pushed to the side. The noise of the calf's mastication, at first imperceptible, rose and rose until it seemed that nothing else in this world could be heard. A brown spot danced on the other side of the thicket, half-seen through the dense canopy.

One more half-step and he froze again, his muscles tense, his muzzle and head lined up with his spine. He kept his claws retracted for the time being. Given his current position, it was too much of a risk getting caught in the underbrush. He put all his weight on his hind legs and eyeballed his target's trajectory as best he could despite the obstruction. No need to be a perfectionist, he could correct on the bounce.

He leaped forward and exploded out of the foliage with a brusque, half-swallowed roar. The calf jerked to the right. He missed the tiny rump, rebounded, lunged for the neck. His jaws closed around the throat. With one violent twist of his body, he wrenched the calf off his hooves and slammed him down, almost hard enough to break the neck. A single, desperate bleat escaped his victim's lung. He adjusted his fangs and squeezed through the windpipe and artery. The beating of the tiny heart slammed against the roof of his palate, fast and wild. He straddled the calf's body and settled himself comfortably for the throttle. His heavy weight pressed down on the heaving flank and crushed the chest; he felt a couple of ribs snap under his belly. The calf's thin legs jerked in the air and frantically searched for a ground that was not there anymore. He kept him pinned down and watched as the tremors progressively dwindled. After a few last spams, the legs turned rigid and dead, extended out to the side like some stiff boughs out of a toppled trunk.

It wouldn't be much longer now. Already the one eye fixing him had rolled inward and turned white.

"Makhulu, watch out!"

He jerked his head up just in time to see the compact boss of the buffalo's horns barrel into his flank. No pain, amazingly, but his jaws went limp with shock and the calf's neck slipped out of his mouth. He leaped to the side and skidded wildly over the green grass. The buffalo was still on him, over him, blotting out the sun, refusing to break contact. A shove caught him on the hip and spun him around, then a second blow toppled him down. This time, he felt the pain, like a wildfire exploding inside his guts. He swallowed down a growl and scrambled to get back up. His legs could not seem to move fast enough. Two horns tickled his underbelly. Before he had time to scream, he felt himself being propelled up in the air, as light as a feather. Blue sky, green grass, blue sky again. He landed on his face, rolled to side, stumbled to his feet.

The world danced in front of his eyes and made no sense at all. In the middle of the dizzying maelstrom, a fuzzy black spot was barreling toward him, threatening to fill his vision. He could feel the heavy, turf-tearing thuds reverberating up his paws. He knew that he had to run, but his legs were temporarily disconnected from his mind. He could not move.

By the grass, he could not move!

Another fuzzy spot, this one tawny and black, leaped in front of him. A roar and a curse. The two spots danced for a few heartbeats, then the new arrival led the thunder away.

Without thinking, Makhulu turned tail and ran as fast as he could.

Moments later, T. rejoined him at the foot of the hill. "Mak! Are you alright?"

"No." He doubled over in pain and flopped down at his brother's paws. Something wet and boiling sloshed around inside him. Spikes of pain radiated out of his midsection and cut his breathing short. "Belly," he gasped, "belly's all smashed."

"Don't try to talk," T. said, his voice hushed, his muzzle and tongue frenetically going over his body, searching for a wound. "Keep your strength. No blood. I can't see any blood. Can you feel your hind legs? Your spine took a beating, that's for sure. I saw you cartwheel in the air. Two turns! Just like… Well, never mind that. You seem alright. Can you move your tail for me? Yeah, that's good. By the grass, don't you know that a cat is supposed to land on his feet? What about your ribs? How do they feel? Cracked? Don't worry about the belly. No lion this side of grass has ever died of a bellyache. None that I know of, anyway. I once met a lioness who died of a cheek-ache, but that's only because the mange had her. Got her cheek, then her head, then the rest of her, then she died. You should have seen her around the end, all leathery and red and putrefied. You would have thought that she had been turned inside out. She could hardly breathe no more. Can you breathe alright? That's important. You're lucky the horns only grazed your skin. You're not cut. No blood. I think you're good. Yeah, I think you're good. What do you think?"

Makhulu closed his eyes and let out a muffled growl. The spikes of pain progressively receded. He sucked in a breath of relief and relaxed his curled-up limbs. His claws, he realized, were still protracted.

"Talk to me Big Mak! How do you feel?"

"Better." He found his paws. "I'll be alright, I think." He checked his fangs with his tongue, gave his muzzle a lick. "Can't feel my face, though."

"That's because you've used it to shield your legs from the impact of the landing," T. laughed. He gave him a head-rub.

"How does it look? My whole muzzle feels like it's askew."

"Don't worry about it, symmetry is a highly overrated concept anyway."

They moved off the hill at a light trot, eager to put some distance between them and the herd. Makhulu began to relax. The pain was completely gone now, and the last of the adrenalin was progressively ebbing away and ceding place to the happy blood of relief – or what passed as the happy blood of relief for him these days. He slowed down to a walk. "What happened to the buffalo after I ran?"

"I led him away as far as I could until he just broke contact and trotted back to the herd. I thought about going for a leap, but I was worried about you."

"I never even saw him coming," mumbled Makhulu. "I thought I was in the clear. If you hadn't been there to save me…"

"Next time, we'll let the Ximhungwe girls do the hunting. What's the point of having a pride if we don't steal their kills, anyway?"

Makhulu groaned. The happy blood had been short-lived and now he could feel the shakes spread through his limbs and neither region, almost like an emptiness. "There used to be a time when I would have immediately gone for the biggest bull. Now, I don't know. I feel like I don't have the same juice anymore. Or maybe all the buffaloes have suddenly grown heavier."

"That must be it for sure."

They stopped by a water hole. Makhulu laid himself down and went for a few cautious laps. He was feeling so useless all of a sudden. So ashamed. Yeah, he didn't have the same juice anymore, that was an understatement. But why? Physically, he was still strong. Perhaps not as much as he used to be, but still more than enough to go by. So what was wrong with him? Why the trepidation before the leap? The second-guessing and the shuffling of feet? He never used to have so many thoughts bouncing around inside his head before. At least not in times of action. His judgment always used to be so clear and smooth, simple. Go left, go right, a lunge and a bite, the buffalo is down, the enemy cat broken. A roar. Victory.

Now? Shit, it felt as though his mind had grown too big for his heart. And the more he worried about thinking about things, the more he overthought everything. The spiral was neat and self-serving. No way out.

He noticed T. glancing at him out of the corner of his eyes while scuffing the ground. The younger lion marked a nearby bush, then pushed out a roar.

Makhulu jerked his head up. "What are you doing? We're deep in the middle of the Singita–"

Another roar. Then a third. His brother turned to face him with gleaming eyes, a cheeky half-snarl etched on his muzzle.

"T., no one can hear us here. What's the point?"

But T. was not listening. He shrugged and casually trotted away. Every third step or so, he stopped and roared. Short, senseless calls that no one else could hear.

Makhulu followed his tail and squeezed out a bellow of his own, hesitant at first, more assertive toward the end. He caught his breath and immediately pushed out another roar. The throbbing air warmed his chest, cleared his mind, brought life back to his throat. His intercoastal muscles were burning. He laughed and kept pushing, again and again and again, until it felt like his whole front had caught on fire. He sucked in a hasty gulp of air and went right back at it, louder.

"Mapogo?" T. screamed ahead of him.

"Mapogo!" Makhulu roared back.

"MAPOGO????"

"MAPOGO!!!!"

They burst into a gallop and tore through the undulating meadows at full speed. Gravity only had the most tenuous grip on their leaping strides, the grass not at all. Somewhere far behind, half-muffled by the pounding of his heart and the wind of his speed, a petty lung implored him to stop. *Can't keep up!* it moaned. *Need a break!* Of course, he knew better that to listen to the cowardly organ. He asked his legs and chest if they could keep going. They cackled briefly: *Does a hyena shit on the grass?*

He sped up.

"MAPOGO! MAPOGO! MAPOGO!" he roared, loud enough to be heard all the way to the far side of grass and back.

"MAPOGO!" T. agreed, loud enough for Shaka, Dread, and Leonides to hear him. "MAPOGOOOOOOOOOO!!!!!!"

Suddenly, he collapsed and went rolling head over paws before settling down limply on his side, as if dead. Makhulu overtook him in a blink, turned around, bumped into his rump. Although rendered temporarily deaf by the thumping of his heart and the laboring of his panting lungs, he could clearly see the younger lion's flanks heaving up and down spasmodically in front of him. His brother had fallen prey to an uncontrollable laughing fit.

He dropped down next to the grimacing head.

"Couldn't take… another step… if my life…depended…on it," his brother wheezed in between two guffaws. "By the sweet edge of sharp grass, that's the golden sun honest truth of it."

"Mapogoooo," Makhulu replied. His vocal cords failed him and the roar died the death of a strangled hen.

T.'s laughter redoubled. "Cats everywhere, beware! The Mapogo fowl is on the prowl!"

Makhulu laid his head down on the soft cushion of grass and let his own bursts of hilarity run their course. A vulture landed next to them and tip-toed his way forward, his bobbing head inquisitive and full of hope. Makhulu slammed his tail against the grass and flashed his fangs. The big bird took flight precipitously. That led them into more helpless guffaws.

"No more," implored T. "Please, my ribs gonna split."

Eventually, they quieted down.

A sweet torpor took hold of Makhulu's mind. Resisting the urge to sleep, he looked around. From up close, the three claw-marks that still disfigured T.'s brow were clearly visible. His brother, he remembered, had taken the brunt of the last enemy incursion a couple of moons ago.

"How's your face?" he asked. "How are the cuts?"

"Just scratches, really. They don't even itch anymore, so that's nice. Soon, there won't be so much as a scar left to tell the tale."

"Only memories."

T. growled happily. "Hey, you really think we fought off the three Matimbas that night?"

"Who knows? Everything was so confused."

"The one I fought was huge. Proper immense cat. I'm telling you, that was Hairy Belly Matimba for sure."

"I mean, that's entirely possible. The Matimbas are in the Londolozi now, I've heard them trading roars back and forth with the Majingilanes. Then again, it could have been three of the four Majingilanes as well. They must have grown quite a bit since we last saw them. It could also have been some other unknown trio we know nothing about."

"I sure hope not," groaned T. "Between the four Majingilanes who have taken roots in the Mala Mala, the three Matimbas who've decided, for some baffling, mysterious reason, to leave their brothers in the Manyaleti and are now trouncing through the Londolozi, and the five young Selatis breathing down on our herds this side of the Sand River, cocky as you will, the Sabi Sands is getting really crowded at the moment."

"I know. We need to be very careful. We're not the biggest coalition above grass anymore."

"Just the nastiest."

Another fit of laughter, this time not as joyous as the last. It died young.

"Next time we go on patrol, we should make sure that Skoro comes with us. Leave no cat behind to be ambushed alone."

"I agree," T. said, serious again. "Besides, it will do his lazy ass some good to get away from the lionesses for once."

"It's the mini-pogs. He wants to keep an eye on them."

"Keep an eye on his next meal, more like. His belly has grown so heavy, his spine is all bent out of shape."

Makhulu swallowed down a chuckle at the irreverent comment. "You shouldn't joke like that."

"It's alright, he can't hear me. Even if he could, he knows I don't mean it. But he sure spends far too much time with the little ones. If you ask me, that's not healthy."

"Speaking of cubs, don't you have your own ball of fur to worry about?"

A short silence that was as awkward as it was unexpected ensued. Suddenly, it felt as though an invisible gap had widened between the two of them.

Two words

"Well, actually, no," T. whispered. "Not anymore, I don't."

"What do you mean?"

A short laugh escaped his brother's nostrils, halfway between a snort and a sob. He raised his head and pretended to casually lick his muzzle, but it was obvious to Makhulu's eyes that his tongue was only making a show of going through the motions. Soon, it stopped. His neck grew stiff, his eyes, forlorn, settled on the horizon. "You remember how the Ximhungwe pride refused to accept my cub after her mother was killed and her brother snatched by a leopard? How they tried to turn on her and break her neck?"

"Yeah, I was there. I remember you jumping in and laying some paws too. You saved the cub that day." That had been an unusual sight, but one that had filled Makhulu's heart with warmth.

"Yeah, well, as it turned out, I didn't."

Makhulu clenched his jaws. "They went around your back, didn't they? Killed her in the dark?"

"No, not exactly. That afternoon, I made it perfectly clear that I would kill any cat who dared touch her. I was anxious at first, because I wasn't sure whether I would be able to keep an eye on all of them at

Lions would never do this – if a female dies, the others will raise her young.

once. Then, when I saw that they were steering clear of her, I relaxed. If you recall, all of that happened shortly before the Selatis crossed the Sand River and moved in on our herds for the first time. When you called for the patrol, I went because I thought that the issue had been settled, that the threat had worked."

"It didn't?"

A small rictus appeared at the corner of T.'s lips. On either side of his muzzle there seemed to suddenly exist an invisible force holding his head rigidly in place and floating above ground. "None of them so much as laid a claw on her, that much is true. But they also made absolutely sure not to allow her so much as a single bite out of their kills. They ostracized her. When I came back, I found her scrawny body lying down next to an old buffalo rib. In her hunger, she had tried to gnaw at the dry bone – I saw the bite marks – while, not two leaps away from her, the rest of the pride enjoyed a fat kudu." He paused and cleared his throat. "They starved her to death, Mak. Watched her waste away coldly, day after night after day. I'm sure that she must have begged them around the end, but they didn't relent. All that just to spite me."

Makhulu shook his head. He knew how vicious lionesses could be at times, but he had not expected the Ximhungwe girls to go this far.

"Well, I don't suppose that I really have much ground to complain, anyway," T. concluded. "Not after all the things that I have done."

"What was her name?" Makhulu asked softly.

"Huh?"

"Your cub, what was her name?"

"Haska. It's an anagram for…Well, you know who. She was a good cat. Not very strong, of course, still mostly just a tiny ball of fur, but she had a sharp mind and unflinching eyes. She reminded me of him at times, always curious about things, always asking questions. One morning, she asked me where it was that storks go. It was the last of the mild season, right before the first frosty mornings, when you can see the birds fly away in pointy formations. I told her that I had no idea – not in so many words of course, you know me, I could never talk to cubs properly. The next thing I know, she's running out in the open with her head tilted so far back, she's bound to fall on her ass, calling for the big birds to come down and explain themselves. *Commanding* them. Can you imagine? A tiny thing barely the size of my paw, and the first thing she does when she learns about some big, dumb birds flying off, she wants to reach out and pluck them down to give them orders. She… She…" The words caught in his throat. He sucked in his breath, exhaled slowly. "She would have made a fine huntress and that's the truth of it. Golden sun. Not just some random tail-biter but a proper horn-tickler, smart and brave, far better than any of those stuck-up Ximhungwe wannabe tough-girls."

Makhulu went to give his brother a head-rub. On the surface, the lion appeared calm and composed, but through the thickness of the mane he could feel his heart beating wildly. "For whatever it's worth, I am truly sorry," he said. "Had I known that this was happening, I would have intervened."

T. gently disengaged himself from the hug. "Thanks. It ain't nothing much anyway. Just a cub. Cubs die all the time, that's the way of things above grass. Doesn't matter. I'll put another one inside one of the Ximhungwe girl soon enough. To lose a cub is nothing. Less than nothing. The opposite of a thing. No point even talking about it. No point at all."

He rose and they ambled away together.

The patrol had lost its urgency. Makhulu was just enjoying the lazy walk now, the scents in the breeze and the feeling of grass tickling the soft cushions of his paws. Just to be standing there, in the moment, alive, with his brother, for some reason it seemed important. Precious.

"Have you heard anything about your own two boys recently?" asked T. "The belly-manes Defiant raised?"

"No. Last I heard, they had crossed the Sand River and entered the Mala Mala."

He didn't need to say more. Just to think about it made him feel sick to his stomach. Yet another pair of cats that he had failed.

"There is nothing more you could have done, Mak. They're grown, they need to find their own way."

"I could have taken them in with us. Share my kills with them. The grass knows we have enough herds."

"But not enough lionesses. Sooner or later, their urges would have led to more killing. You know how it goes. The pride could never have taken the stress. Not again."

"Maybe."

"Don't worry, I'm sure that they'll be fine. Defiant was a pain to live with, but she didn't raise no dumb cats."

"Still. Just the two of them against all those coalitions? Numbers matter, T."

"Solo made it, and that poor belly-mane was lonelier than a leopard stuck on a tree in the middle of a flooded river. I bet you, to this day, he's still boasting about how he fought me off to some gullible lioness somewhere."

"Maybe. Maybe they'll be fine. If they can cross the Mala Mala and keep going toward the sunrise, who knows?"

At least he wouldn't have to know either way. Wouldn't have to see. The grass had swallowed them whole.

"Say, I've been thinking about something recently," he said, eager to change the subject.

"What's that?"

"Your accent. It's been a while since I've heard those rough, mangled words of yours. What's going on?"

"Nothing. Just outgrew it, I guess."

"Oh, ya' outgroawn 't, did ya?"

"Huh?"

"Ya doan outgroawn my accent, cub? Iss tha' wha' ya're tellin' me? Ya've groawn all wise'up now, cub?"

T. chuckled. "You do him pretty good, I'll give you that."

"Ya kin bet yar sweet bottoam fu' A' do 'im prutty good. Doan lived wit' th' raggedy cat too, ya knoaw?"

"By the gra', an' here 'A' though' myself: M'hkulu, he ain't no sor'throat kinda cat, ain't noway he kin spea' like tha' hisself. Got toa much roar in'im."

"Ya doan groawn blind, cub? A' ain't M'hkulu no moar. A'm Br'ken Noase! A'm the topcat 'f all sor'throat. Watch me if A' ain't."

"Why, now tha' ya say it, A' see it. Ya're Br'ken Noase 'lright. Where've ya been, oald cat? A' thought ya'd be long doan and dead below the gra' by now."

"Doan't count yar buffalo doawn jus' yet, cub. A' ain't killed, killed, killed yet."

"Iss 'lright, A' outgroawn ya anyway. Outgroawn yar shadow and yar accent. 'Ven outgroawned my oawn brother, Shaka."

Just like that, the game ended abruptly. Their laughter petered out.

T kept walking steadily forward, his head hung low. “I just realized that the other dawn, actually. I’ve had more life than Shaka and Leonides ever had – even Dread, maybe, if that big oaf is actually dead and not just enjoying the time of his life in the land of the slow buffaloes somewhere. I’ve had more seasons, more sunrises, more hunts, more… everything. They all were born before me, but now it’s like I’m older than them because I’ve had more experiences. It’s so strange, when one thinks about it.”

“You still miss him as much?”

“Yes. Well, I don’t know. I don’t know what I really miss, to tell you the truth. I can’t even remember his scent anymore. I went to find a tree in the Londolozi a couple of nights ago, a beautiful bushwillow we used to mark together before… before the hippo. I wanted to see if I could find a trace of his scent again. Just to remind myself, you know?”

“And?”

“Nothing. Not so much as a hint of a whiff. It’s like he’s faded away. Like he was never there to begin with. I could try and find a cat and tell him: ‘You know this tree over there? My brother Shaka used to mark this tree. Watered it so often, he might as well have been suckling the poor thing. That’s *his* tree.’ And the cat would just shrug and say: ‘Well, prove it’, and there wouldn’t be a thing I could do to prove it. Not a thing. Which make no sense at all, because he *did* live, and he *did* piss on that bark. So how can it all be gone like that without a trace?”

“I don’t know, T. I really don’t.”

His brother shook his head briefly. “Questions without answers, I guess.” He turned and pretended to be absorbed by the sight of a couple of antelopes grazing nearby. “Want to give these grasshoppers a try?”

“We’ll never be fast enough.”

As if to demonstrate, the antelopes suddenly caught their scent and pronked away.

“Come on old cat,” T called out from over his shoulder, “there is meat for the taking today!”

He broke into a brisk camper that seemed more playful than resolute.

Makhulu sat down on his haunches and watched him go through the lush green grass, his golden shoulders rippling behind the black of his top mane, his tail swinging back and forth absent-mindedly under the bright light of the clear blue sky, like a cub. He looked so full of life all of a sudden, so carefree, as though he had somehow managed to dismiss the entire conversation, the very thought of it, out of his mind. Push it down where it could not be heard and pretend that it had never happened at all.

That was one way to do it, he supposed.

The antelopes were long gone, but T. had already moved on and was now absorbed by the task of scanning the canopies overhead. A cloud of butterflies fluttered around his muzzle. He chased after them.

Makhulu pushed out an amused roar and hastened to join him.

TWENTY-SEVEN

THE LAST DROP

Clouds came. Single ones at first, white and wispy, almost shy. They played with the blaze and threw tentative shadows on the ground before evaporating. More came in their wake, and more after them, fed, it seemed, by the ever-thicker fog rising out of the grass at dawn like water off a cat's fur after a long swim on a hot afternoon. The open sky became a cheetah, spotted white, then a giraffe, with only thin lines of the original blue still visible. Finally, it became an elephant, grey and armored, impenetrable. It stayed that way.

Rain began to fall. Occasional showers at first, then a constant drizzle. Not too bad. Nothing the mane could not handle. And the droplets felt fresh on the tongue and kept the insects low. The grass turned green and leapt up, as if desperate to reach for the source of all that moisture. A patient cat with nothing better to do could spend his days staring at it and almost see it grow in front of his eyes.

The drizzle grew in confidence, became a proper steady rain, strong enough to claw gullies out of the mud and partition the land into smaller pieces, as though appropriating it. Beaten into sullen submission, the locals sought refuge wherever they could. A nice warm burrow for the lucky ones, a tree or a shrub for the others. Meager shelters.

The wind rose. The heavy drops reached sideways, around the sprawled-out canopies, and lashed at the refugees with cold, relentless *plops*. "Stoicism is the word of the day", they seemed to snigger hilariously, drunk in the might of their power. And, of course, they were right. Nothing a cat could do now but hunker down and present a round back to the elements while trying not to think about his damp, clammy fur stretched thin over his shoulders and rump; or his drooping whiskers clinging sadly to the corner of his drenched muzzle; or, even, the rivulets of water that were pouring out of his chin like small cataracts. The soaked-out manes itched like damp grass, heavy and stifling on the tired necks.

The rain rose in intensity, became a storm. Solid blue quills pelted the saturated mud and turned the gullies into brown lakes. Some burrows caved-in, others flooded. Many died. Still stuck under his tree, a cat could now feel his bones swell, as if the rain had seeped through the taut skin and entered the marrow. Old wounds burned anew and brought forth to the mind memories best forgotten.

But that was alright. Because the storm was the last of it, the cat knew. One last furious downpour and the sky would finally crack open. He had to believe it.

The Sand River raged out of its bed and flooded the low savannah. Grassland became wetland. The tree, an island. More water came. Always more water, brown and dirty, laden with the various flotsams of a wrecked world: torn trunks and large branches, bloated bodies, and, once, a cat could have sworn, a surfing crocodile. The island shrunk. A few anxious cats looked up at the tree and pondered whether to start climbing already. Forget all dignity, play the leopard for the time being.

Those thoughts were not shared out loud.

Nor acted upon.

One morning, the downpour stopped, all at once. Of course! Who had any doubt? Not me! The grey, impenetrable cover that had seemed invincible and eternal only days ago cracked and drifted apart. The sun returned supreme amid the blue sky and hammered at the changed savannah. Where the water remained – clear, cool water that did not belong over these stretches of green grass – it reflected the sunrays and made the day feel warmer somehow, burning.

The three lions moved away from the occupied wetlands and onto drier terrain. They were weak and sore, as only cats trapped in a small place for a long time can be. Over the course of the next few days they hunted and ate and joked and did all those other things that free lions do when they're on the prowl. Then they reunited with their lionesses and cubs. Three, they counted. One missing. They thought nothing of it. They were happy, well-fed, relaxed and, most important of all, dry.

One fine morning, one of them ventured away. He walked a little bit more cautiously than the other two. The rain had laid bare a pain in the bend of his spine that was still refusing to leave, as if the bones were tearing through the skin. He was feeling damp inside, inadequate. Not weak, not really, just not as sure-footed as he used to be. For some reason, the loss of his brother was weighting a bit heavier on his mind that day.

He did not see the four tawny shapes barreling toward him at full speed through the lank. Not until after they leaped at him.

A scream: "Mak! They're here!", then an explosion of roars. He did not run. He could not run. The tawny shapes clawed at his back. He whirled and lashed out. They bit through his limbs. He roared and tried to bite back. He was too slow, too slow. He fell. Something pierced his testicles. He shrieked. He was done for, it seemed. Beaten. Overcome. Atop his prostrated body, the tawny shapes were already boiling like buzzards, eager to tear him apart.

His two brothers burst in from behind, forced the vultures away. They snarled and fought back. One brother took the brunt of it. He looked old, much older than the others, and scarred, and, as someone he loved had once so tenderly put it, somewhat asymmetrical in the muzzle. He clenched his jaws and held his ground long enough for the prostrated lion to find his paws.

The third brother was not exactly young either, but less old. He turned into a whirlwind, lashed out in all directions, charged at shadows without concern for his own safety.

The four tawny shapes relented. In twist and turns, they found the cover of a nearby thornbush. They turned back around one last time, licked their muzzle. Maybe? No. That one cat is crazy. Look at him move, it's not worth the risk. They melted back into the grass.

The three brothers walked back to their pride. Well, not Bent-Spine; he dragged himself back. They found the three females on a buffalo kill and promptly chased them off. This was no time to argue, they were not in the mood.

"Skoro, you alright?" asked T., a mouthful of buffalo meat inside his jaws.

Skoro winced and shook his head. His spinal wound was burning white hot. Inside his belly, it felt as if something vital had been yanked out, something connected deep within him, all the way to his numb scrotum. The pain was worse than anything he had ever endured before, worse than the Majingilane's bite, even. He tried to tear some meat off the carcass but found that his neck had no strength anymore. He gave up and sagged down, curled into a ball.

"Those were the Selatis," mumbled Makhulu. "They're moving-in on us."

"Why? Why now?"

"The Ximhungwe…" stammered Skoro.

"Huh?"

"The fourth Ximhungwe girl! She was in estrus. She went to mate with them, led them right to us."

"Those girls are already counting us dead under the grass, eh?" growled T. "Well, serves them right. We won that one."

"I don't think that really qualifies."

"We can't stay here any longer," said Makhulu. "Now that the Selatis have had a taste of it, they won't stop until they have control over the whole pride. We need to leave before they come back."

T. tore a string of flesh out of the open belly, swallowed it. "We've faced them before. We can do it again."

"No, we can't. Look at us. Skoro is out of the fight, I can barely stand. What are you going to do? Face them all alone?"

"No, of course not. I–"

"The only way forward for us now is to move on. Give up the Ximhungwe pride and leave the Singita. If we cross the Londolozi and keep the Sand River to our left flank without crossing it, maybe we can find a patch of grass that hasn't been claimed yet. A single tree or a bush to hide under, a couple of herds passing us by every once in a while, that would be enough. In the meantime, we'll have to stay on the move and keep a low profile, ears on alert and belly to the ground."

"Become wander-males all over again?" Skoro asked in disbelief.

"That's the only way we survive. We leave tonight."

"No," T. breathed out. The word fell out of him like something out of a vulture's grasp. He backtracked away from the carcass. "I'm sorry, Mak, but I can't do that."

"What do you mean you can't? We don't have a *choice*."

"I just can't. I... By the grass, no! Wander-males all over again?! No! No way. No, no, no, no..." He shook his head and backtracked some more. Already, he was halfway gone. His eyes were wild and crazed. "A lion's due is what he takes, Mak! No more, no less!"

"What does that even mean? The Selatis *will* take what they want, T., whether you like it or not. The shadows are all that we have left. It's the only way."

"No," he moaned. "Please, no." He ripped himself away from their gaze, turned toward a nearby thornbush.

"Don't be stupid," Skoro called out. "Come back here, we need to stick together."

But it was too late, his brother was already out of their reach. He disappeared all of a sudden, as if swallowed by the bush, and the thorns closed in the wake of his departure.

TWENTY-EIGHT

MARCH 16th, 2012

Dawn.

cold AND molten?

He stopped and raised his head. The crimson ball shone through the distant mist, its light cold and uncertain, like a giant molten eye. It rose and cleared the flat treetops on the horizon, became the sun once again. The darkness flattened and fractured at its approach, turned into thin shadows dancing precariously behind every tall tree and bush, at the feet of every low rock, beneath an awestruck cat, even.

He scuffed the ground lightly, marked a bush, stopped and laid himself down by the edge of a water hole. He leaned forward. The water was cool inside his mouth, delicious. He squinted at the reflected tongue of fire tickling his whiskers and watched it ripple quietly in front of him like a flickering flame, every bright gleam a short, powerful statement that spoke of the infinite possibilities hidden behind every new dawn.

He thought back on his life and brought forth to his mind the memories of every hunt, every fight and moment of wild triumph.

He tried to taste them all over again for the first time.

His mind kept wandering back to the quieter times, the endless afternoons frittered away, sprawled in the grass with his brothers, doing nothing. Those were the moments that had given worth to all the others, he realized now. Connected them, somehow, the same way that fur and skin connects claws and fangs and makes the body whole, turns it into a lion.

He thought about the fact that he had never apologized to any cat for the things that he had done – except, maybe, to Shaka once or twice, but never for something truly hurtful, so that didn't really count – and his heart filled with pride. His course through the grass, such as it had been, had remained his own. There was honesty in that, he decided. Perhaps even honor.

A lionlike life. Who would have thought?

He thought about the beast with horns that had chased him all night long, was still chasing him even now. He thought about what his brother had said and how he had not been able to find the words to tell him how he really felt, make him understand, make him *see.* To run and give up on the last of their territory meant letting go of the hindquarter side of fear.

And this, he could not do. Not again.

In his heart of heart, he knew that he wanted more. So much more. More hunts and fights; more females and cubs running circles around him; more lazy afternoons spent chewing the fat with his brothers. He wanted to feel the tongue of fire on his muzzle again and again and again, and savor the coolness of the night on his tongue after a long, hot day spent running under the sun.

He rose, turned his back on the water hole, weaved his way through the stiff grass with his head hung low. The heat was rising fast, already he was panting lightly.

Maybe he would rejoin the others after all. The wandering into unknown territories would be bad, but the solitude here was not much better. If he could just find the strength to tear himself away, break into a gallop and not look back, maybe he could still catch up to them. Maybe.

He slid through a thin cluster of bushwillow saplings and stopped by the edge of a twin-rutted dirt lane. He licked the notch of his nostril and glanced around.

Something in the air was wrong, he could not quite put his tongue on it. His ears twitched. The grass had grown eerily quiet all of a sudden, almost tense. A soft rustle rose out of the opposite lank. A branch cracked.

One by one, the four Selatis ambled out of the brush and stepped onto the dirt lane.

"Told you they'd still be around," said one of them, triumphantly. "I bet they thought they had us beat, the cocky cats."

They sniggered and briefly scanned the grass around them before turning their attention back to him.

"You're the big one?" a second Selati asked. He looked the youngest of the bunch, with his mane barely reaching the top of his scalp and the area behind his ears still bare. "Makhulu?"

He inhaled sharply and stood still. A small whimper of fear threatened to pass the barrier of his closed jaws but he managed to swallow it down at the last instant. Whatever else might happen today, there would be none of that. Finally, he shook his head.

"Nah," the first Selati said, "look at him. He's the younger one. The wild one."

"The crazy one."

He bowed his head at the recognition. He could not help it. A short, rough laugh spilled out of his nostrils. "I thought there were five of you guys," he heard himself say.

They ticked and drew themselves back, eyes gleaming dark.

"The Majingilanes trapped and killed our brother," the young mane spat. "Drove us right out of our birth-pride."

"Yeah, that sounds like them."

"You know these cats?"

"I met them once, briefly."

A third Selati stepped forward. "Where are your brothers, Mapogo? Where is the Big Mak?"

"He's..." He closed his eyes, opened them up again. The vast stretch of grass behind him felt cold and empty all of a sudden, a gaping void breathing down on his spine. His front right paws were quivering slightly. He swallowed down his saliva and stomped the ground. "He won't be joining us today," he finally said, and let loose his half-snarl.

That was all the Selatis needed to hear. They roared and leaped forward.

He broke right and ran away as fast as he could alongside the dirt lane, his paws frantically tearing through the soft, malleable dirt. On either side of him, the green-yellow lank was sparse and only about belly high, reinforced here and there by small clusters of young bushwillow trees that created the illusion of a thick forest. He resisted the temptation to jump behind them. The slender trunks had no depth to them and could offer no real cover, he knew. The Selatis would be on him immediately. Besides, he was faster on flat terrain.

He sped up. Small branches whizzed by his head and tore at his mane. An invading thornbush grazed his right flank. He leaped over a fallen trunk and circumvented a deeper groove.

He wasn't overly worried. So long as he managed to keep the panic at bay, he still had options. If he could just out-run them now, break the line of sight for a few precious heartbeats, then he would have a chance to lose them behind a bush somewhere. The sparse vegetation would work to his advantage, make his trail harder to follow. They would have to split and fan out in order to search for his scent. That would give him the advantage. Once rested, he could either slink away undetected, or ambush one of them.

Yes. He still had plenty of options. He was fine.

They caught up to him and slammed into his rump. The impact sent him rolling across the soft dirt. Fangs snapped at his upper thigh and under his tail. Roaring at the top of his lungs, he whirled in place and lunged for the nearest head. His fangs cut through the fur all the way to the bone and glanced off the brow, right above the eye socket. The Selati yelped and drew back. Lost to his rage, he lashed out and battered the exposed chest with his front paws while pressing forward.

Something tore at the inside of his right hind leg and stopped his momentum cold. He felt himself being dragged backward. A pair of sharp fangs grazed his spine. He wheeled about and came face to face with the other three Selatis.

"Fuck you!" he screamed.

One of them, the younger of the four cats, roared back and taunted him with his front paw extended all the way to his muzzle. His fury exploded and he charged the over-confident belly-mane. The other two sidled past his flanks and fell on his rump. Once again, he felt the nips on his spine, like birds pecking at his fur. Their awkward bills were searching for a good grip on a vertebra.

He whirled in place a third time, lunged at a cat's shoulder. His jaws almost closed-in on the top of the neck but the lion leaped to the side at the last instant and he only managed to rip a mouthful of hair out.

He spat it out and ran circles around his own tail.

They rushed him and shoved him to the ground. He roared as he rolled on his back and lashed out at the empty air. They stayed away from the reach of his fangs. His front paws caught into a thick mane and got stuck. One Selati pinned is right hind leg down while another grabbed his left ankle and twisted his limb. A third Selati stepped forward and lowered himself in-between his legs. He felt the hot breath on his scrotum, then intense pain tearing through his lower belly, like a horn piercing his insides.

He shrieked and kicked and wretched his legs free. Instinctively, he rolled back around and slammed his belly to the ground. Blood poured out of his nether region and turned the ground to sticky mud. He could feel the beating of his heart bouncing off the hard-packed dirt under his chest.

He freed his front claws, tried to get his legs back under his body.

A bite caught his right shoulder blade. He groaned and twisted his head toward the attacker, his fangs bared. The Selati jumped back in fear.

He smiled internally. He was alright. Nothing but a bunch of young, jittery, inexperienced cats after all. All he had to do was stand back up. Once on his paws, he would have options. Yes, plenty of options.

He pushed as hard as he could with his hind legs. It was no use; he could not move at all. Some kind of elephant weight was pinning his rump, immobilizing him. He tried to think of a way to crawl forward. Slide underneath the weight, maybe.

Unseen jaws grabbed his lower spine near his tail. Four canines clamped down on either side of his vertebra. Sheer terror invaded his heart. “Let go of that!” he shrieked insanely. “Let go! That’s not yours!”

The jaws squeezed and crunched the bone. A cold tremor slammed into the back of his skull. One last spike of egregious pain out of his lower half, then nothing. The bushwillows danced in front of his eyes. He whimpered and tried not to faint.

This was no glancing bite. The Selati took his time. After having crushed the bone into a pulp, he tore through the layer of muscles and excavated a small crater, like a woodpecker digging himself a home into a mass of gooey flesh.

Suddenly, the four Selatis put an end to their attack. They turned their backs on him and went to lie down in the middle of the dirt lane a half-dozen steps away, panting hard.

By the grass, this was his chance. He pushed on his front paws, tried to get up, flopped wetly back down. He winced in pain, cursed, tried again. No use. His back legs were dead, paralyzed. He dragged himself forward. One pull, then another. He stopped by the side of the dirt lane with his head facing the edge of the tantalizing grass, out of breath.

His fast panting turned into a desperate half-choked wheeze, every exhale a wet roar burning his parched throat. No matter how hard he tried, he could not seem to get his wind back. It was alright, though. He still had time. As long as the Selatis remained lying down on the dirt lane, he could still run away. Scamper under a bush somewhere and hide. Just like that one female had done to him once. By the grass, what was her name? Everything was so blurry inside his head. He could not remember. It didn’t matter. If she had escaped him that day, so could he now. He just needed his legs back. Yes, his legs and a bit of time. Once under way, he’d be alright. Plenty of options.

“Please,” he moaned while trying to shake some life back into his lower limbs. “Please.”

A rumbler came down the dirt lane and stopped a few leaps away from him. Another appeared out of the grass in front. He groaned and repressed a frantic laugh. Funny how the useless oafs always seemed to appear at the most awkward moments; as expected, they stood still and did absolutely nothing.

Time went by unnoticed. The blazing sun, now high in the sky, hammered at his face. He ran a sticky tongue over his battered muzzle. At least his wounds were not hurting anymore. Quite the opposite, in fact. All he could feel was a deep emptiness in his lower body, as if something had been yanked out. That, and a few burning cuts on his brow that had already turned to crust. Nothing to worry about, he was used to it by now.

The Selatis came back.

"NO," he roared despite himself. "NONONO!!!"

They rolled him on his back. He bended over and lashed out as best he could. Three of the lions retreated, the fourth lowered himself and clamped down on his lower belly. He watched in mild awe as his scrotum disappeared down the cat's gullet. Still no pain, amazingly, only a tear and a soft crunch.

His roars stopped abruptly. He shuddered and laid himself back down, in shock. His overturned eyes made contact with the pupils of one of the bipeds at the front of the rumbler. The creature seemed frozen in place, terror-struck, like a gazelle.

"What's the matter, little one?" he laughed shrilly. "Ain't you never seen a cat being torn to pieces before?"

The Selati stopped mid-chew, slightly non-plussed, then shook his head and leaned forward again. As he tore one last slice of flesh out of the open gash, his movements appeared delicate, almost tender, like a head-rub.

That's right, you got to be gentle when you kill another cat. After all, chances are that this is his first time.

And the truth was, they were killing him. Had already killed him. The terror came on the heels of the realization. He rolled on his stomach, resumed his crawl toward the grass. "Not yet," he breathed out. "Not yet. Not yet. Not yet."

He reached the edge of the grass, pushed a little further, stopped.

They attacked him several more times. Short bursts of vicious mauling followed by long periods of placid, almost casual, rest. He rose on his forelegs to face them every single time, but they simply circumnavigated his roars and opened him up from behind.

Finally, they moved back to the dirt lane.

He lay down, tried to crawl some more. A thin bushwillow in front of him became the sole focus of his mind. He had to reach that tree. Once there, he would think of something else to do, some other step to take, but right now he had to reach the bushwillow tree.

A storm of roars erupted behind him and slammed into his ribcage. For half a heartbeat he was persuaded that Makhulu had arrived, and his heart gladdened. Then he realized that those were not angry fighting roars but long, victorious bellows. The Selatis were celebrating.

Celebrating? Celebrating what?

Your death, big cat. Your death.

He lowered his head and pushed the roars out of his mind. They did not matter. Let the arrogant fools roar all they wanted; he had a tree to reach. By the grass, his bottom fangs for a bushwillow tree and a sip of water.

His front legs cramped up and stopped responding. He lay still for a while, panting hard, his mind blank and his numb back legs askance from his body. A puddle began to form under his groin again.

The slender trunk was now so close, he could almost reach out and lick it.

A sharp, nervous chirrup caught his ears. He glanced up. A small bird, a tit, was looking down upon him while flickering madly from one branch to the next, as if trying to deter him from coming any closer.

A raucous coughing fit that vaguely resembled a laugh cascaded harshly out of him. “You’ve got to be kidding me,” he breathed out. He sucked in his breath and tasted his own blood in the back of his throat.

He spat it out, looked back at the bushwillow tree, froze.

The beast with horns ambled out of the cover of the thin trunk, her enormous body black and ethereal, the muscles of her shoulders and neck billowing in the absent breeze like wisps of smoke. Each one of her slow, ponderous steps seemed to underline the beating of his heart; after a half dozen strides, she stopped.

She laid her fuming horns against his forehead. Sunk deep beneath the boss, he saw the two dark eyes, like bottomless abysses of nothingness.

He almost looked away but stopped himself at the last instant. It helped that his sore neck did not move so well anymore.

Two words

He drew himself up on his front legs and returned the gaze. His half-snarl made one last appearance.

"Ah, fuck it," he croaked out loud.

Then, calmly, he died.

TWENTY-NINE

THE GHOSTS IN THE DARKNESS

The impala swam to the edge of the water hole, briefly stood in the shallows, jumped back into the deeper water. As she scanned the shore for another way out, a spot where she would at least have a chance to get a head start, she arched her head back to stay above the waterline. Her nostrils flared. Water spurted out of her muzzle. After having gone around the water hole a half-dozen times, unable to make up her mind, her wild kicking became desperate, almost angry. She was reaching the end of her strength. Her head disappeared under the water, rose back up, disappeared down again. She cried weakly and redoubled her efforts. She was swimming in leaps now, her whole body bobbing up and down like some weird frantic duck, her nostrils two buffaloes pounding the surface of the water after every strong exhale.

Finally, she made for a small island in the middle of the water hole.

She scaled the steep muddy bluff and collapsed by the foot of the green bushes that covered the center of the island. Gasping for a breath, she lay there with her head bowed and her front legs stiffly extended in front of her burning chest, her lower half still crouched on the slope behind her.

The pair of wild dogs sprung into action. A quick gliding swim, like two fowls taking flight, and they reached the island on the opposite side. They used the bare, steep banks to move around the impenetrable bushes, their long, thin legs gobbling the short distance up with a few easy leaps. One last dash and they fell on their quarry. The impala bleated, once, and tried to dart back into the water again.

Not fast enough.

They grabbed her by the shoulders and neck, brought her back to the island, adjusted their hold tighter, dragged her across the narrow stretch of water.

Finally, they reached the opposite shore.

The rest of the pack jumped out of the bushes. Five dogs in total; they ate while moving. Suspended in the air, the impala watched her lower belly disappear without a sound. Her right back leg fell down. Her insides glistened in front her eyes briefly and painted the dogs' muzzle red. Not much blood on the grass below. No time.

Makhulu roared and leaped out of the lank. The wild dogs snarled. Leaping sideways, like vultures, they tried to present a united front. One of them lunged forward and clamped down on the impala's remaining hind leg. Makhulu swiped at him. The dog yelped and beat a hasty retreat. Another growl, soft and ominous, and the pack scattered for good.

Makhulu looked down at what remained of his prize and cursed. Those dogs were fast, he should have moved-in on them much sooner. Then again, he had been afraid that the impala might escape in the confusion. He had seen it happen before, once: a big, dumb, over-eager cat burst in on a bunch of lionesses and tries to steal their kill. In the middle of the ensuing flash of temper, the kill somehow comes back to life, stands up, and, before anyone has time to ask: "Who was in charge of that death-bite again?", scatters like the wind.

He smiled internally. Well, maybe he had done a bit more than just seen it happen. By the grass, he could still feel the burn of Defiant's glare on the back of his mane that day. And his half-mumbled response: "You girl should have told me that you were not done yet."

Yeah, those had been fun times indeed. Fun times under the sun.

He snapped out of it. He had to hurry. Soon the vultures would betray his presence.

He went around a patch of greasy, trampled grass and grabbed the leg that had been torn away early on. The impala raised a quivering head and looked at him with soft, imploring eyes. He paid her no mind. Once done with the leg, he turned his attention to the gaping wound in her mid-section and worked his way up from there. Not much to eat, but at least it was fresh meat.

A couple of vultures landed nearby. He raised his head. Up in the sky, more birds were circling his position, waiting. He groaned and carefully sniffed the air. His ears flickered. No trace of the last Kruger male yet – or any other male, for that matter – but that did not mean much. Those foreign cats could be sneaky. He licked his nose and considered what remained of the carcass, the small head and the slender neck. His stomach growled.

Not worth it. The birds were already here.

When the birds are here, that's when it's time to take flight.

This was something he had learned on his own over the past few moons. Funny how the grass was full of these little pieces of wisdom for the old cat who wishes to stay alive. Things that were, in hindsight, obvious, but still had to be learned the hard way. Like, for example: "Keep your roars short", "Don't tarry at the water hole", "Keep away from the open grass", and his personal favorite: "When you tell your brother to run and flee while in the middle of fight with a couple of younger, stronger males, do make sure to tell him which way to go."

He moved off the spot of the killing, swiftly crossed a small stretch of open ground, slunk underneath a thornbush. Once on the other side, he kept to the cover of the lank.

Night came, cool and silver under the full moon. He stopped and tried not to think about the hunger still nipping at his stomach. He pushed out a couple of short calling roars, cringed, did it again despite himself. He had to. This was the only way they stood a chance of finding each other over the vast expanse of grass. Even after all this time, he had to believe that Skoro was still around somewhere, that there was still hope.

He changed position after each burst and made sure to listen intently at the quiet of the night, his jittery paws ready to run away at the first sign of a foreign footstep.

"Skoro!" he called out. "Skor–"

The grass rustled softly. He froze and fell quiet.

He thought he could hear something breathe. Something big. His muscles tensed. He adjusted his stance and carefully considered the position of his exposed spine. In a trap, the second cat always come from the opposite direction, he reminded himself. He licked the stub of his fang and prepared himself to whirl.

A shy voice rose. "Mak? Mak is that really you?"

"Skoro?"

"Yes!"

They leaped forward and bumped into each other.

"By the grass, I thought you were dead. I thought the Krugers had you!"

"They almost did, but I managed to run away."

Makhulu took a long hard look at his brother. Despite the protruding ribs and spine, Skoro seemed lively enough, if a bit exhausted. His mane, although now greasy and disheveled, still framed his massive head; above the battered muzzle, a small, feverish flame was still shining strong inside his slightly haggard eyes, betraying his intact resolve; his body had leaned – around the shoulders and flanks, Makhulu could see folds of skin hanging loose where the bulging muscles used to be attached – but still appeared strong and responsive.

Only his balance was not quite right anymore. Even at rest, it seemed that Skoro could not stop himself from wobbling back and forth ever so slightly. That, and the bend in the spine that was more visible than ever, as though a rock was slowly being pushed up and out of the body, made him cringe internally. Two words

"How have you been keeping yourself all these moons?" he asked softly. "You got some hunting?"

Skoro licked his muzzle. "Not much. Just a few carcasses here and there, whatever I could steal from hyenas and leopards, mostly. I…Well, after we got separated during the fight with the Kruger males,

Lower case

I really thought that I was alone. I felt guilty, so I kept to myself, away from all the other cats."

"Guilty? Why?"

"I thought that I had abandoned you. Left you to die alone like we did T. Mak, I'm so sorry. I should never have run. It's just that when they came, I… I don't know."

"Easy there. You did the right thing. I'm the one who told you to run, remember? I did the same. They were much bigger than us, that was the only thing to do. The smart thing. And don't you dare try to put T.'s death on yourself either. You know perfectly well how it went down. He *chose* to walk away from us."

"Yeah. Yeah, I guess you're right. How did you escape those cats anyway? I thought they had you dead to rights."

"I just ran. They chased me around for a little while and at one point they came so close that I thought I was going to have to pivot and fight, but then they just gave up. I could hardly believe it, to tell you the truth."

Skoro bowed his head. "Maybe they just couldn't be bothered anymore. It's not like we're much of a threat to any of them anyway." A dark little laughter escaped his lungs.

"Hey, you want to hear something funny?" Makhulu asked.

"Always."

"One of those two Kruger males is already dead."

"Really? What happened?"

"I don't know for sure; I just found his skeleton. I think most likely the Majingilanes are making moves around here."

Skoro's good spirit melted away as fast as it had come. "The Majingilanes are in Sabi Sabi now?"

"I think so. The Selatis and the three Matimbas are pushing too. I've heard roars. And there is still that one last Kruger to contend with, of course."

"Not to mention all the other opportunistic wander-males everywhere. Mak, that's a lot of cats we need to evade. Too many. We can't stand our ground. We're getting pulled in every direction. We were lucky once, but I don't know how much longer we can last. I mean, if it had been the Majingilanes chasing after us instead of the Krugers, I really don't think that they would have given up the fight so easily."

"I know. I'm sorry. I really thought that these parts would be better, less crowded, and that we would be able to find a small patch of unclaimed grass for ourselves. Turns out there is no such thing in the Sabi Sands anymore."

"So what do we do?"

"We keep going. We leave the Sabi Sabi, push through the Lion Sands, and keep going until we finally find a place where we can rest, away from everyone else."

"That's… That's unknown grass, Mak. You really want to go exploring now? Just the two of us in our weakened state?"

"We don't have a choice. Whatever we find over there, it can't be much worse than our condition here."

That settled it.

They stuck to the darkness and rested during the days. Hidden under thornbushes, one cat always on alert, they listened as the distant roars brought to their flickering ears the back-and-forth story of the Matimbas and Majingilanes and Selatis fighting it out. The Kruger male, Makhulu was happy to notice whenever he licked his fresh scars, seemed to keep mostly quiet.

One night, they stumbled upon a litter of three cheetah cubs.

"Oh, those are rare," whispered Skoro, his eyes wide with surprise.

"They can't be much more than a few days old. Look at them, they're still blind and moist, helpless."

"Blind, moist and helpless," Skoro cackled, "I once knew a lion like that." He looked around. "Where do you suppose the mother is?"

"The moon is still big, she might have gone for a short hunt. She won't be away for long, though. She must have been really desperate to leave her young ones alone like that."

"Like us."

They ate quickly and moved off the lair. At dawn, they came upon a faint roar, then another, then another again.

"Those are not lions," Makhulu said, perplexed.

They crested a small hillock, looked down carefully.

"I knew it!" Skoro exclaimed. "I knew they were some sort of weird grazers. The ones we've been seeing all our lives must have been the stray-away, like Dagga Boys for buffaloes. We must be close to a herd now. "

Another rumbler appeared in the distance, screeched past them, disappeared as fast as it had come. The smell of its presence lingered in the air and stuck to the back of their throat. throats

"They move faster here," Makhulu observed, "much faster. And in a straight line, with purpose, like they have somewhere to go."

"It's like all grazers, their confidence grows with their numbers."

"What's with that lane of black dirt? We've never seen that before."

Skoro shrugged. "Who cares? It's just dirt."

"It doesn't look like dirt."

In truth, from afar, it looked more like a giant mamba to Makhulu's eyes. He could see the dark skin shimmering under the rising heat haze. He searched for the head but could not find it, only a giant body stretching from one horizon to the next. He shuddered briefly. A snake the size of an entire plain. Longer, even. What other absurd monstrosity did the grass have in store for them?

"Come on," said Skoro, for once the braver of the two, "let's go." He took the lead and slowly went down the slope, his rigid tail flickering giddily behind the sharp bones of his scrawny rump.

After one last hesitant yawn to filter the air – the scent of so many rumblers was overwhelming and almost made him gag – Makhulu reluctantly followed in his footsteps. It was nice to see Skoro's spirit flare up like that, if only for an instant. Despite their recent losses, the scarred cat was not so battered after all, some warm blood still remained around those ribs.

But the rumblers' sudden change of attitude was disquieting. He flinched as another one of the thunderous beast roared past him. Back when the dumb oafs had been trudging along the grass in fits and stops, their demeanor timid and somewhat silly with those absurd bipeds swaying back and forth on their backs, he had only ever considered their presence as a source of mild amusement and wonder. A pleasing spectacle for a curious cat.

Not here.

For the first time in his life, he realized just how imposing the rumblers truly were. How loud. The power hidden behind the mass. It made him feel small in comparison, vulnerable. Worse, it made him feel as though he did not know the land he was treading on anymore. As if everything that he had learned throughout his life was no longer relevant.

They came to a stop by the side of the black lane.

"See?" said Skoro. "Just dirt."

Makhulu placed a tentative paw on the glistening surface. It was warm to the touch. "And hard. Talk about hard-packed dirt. This is no ordinary dry ground, this his rock." He took a sniff, jerked his head back. "Stinks like them too."

"You think this is the edge of it?" Skoro asked, his voice suddenly breathless. "The far side of grass?"

"No. Look. Plenty more grass on the other side. A whole horizon's worth. Probably a lot more."

Three rumblers roared past them in quick succession, then another two. They dropped to the ground and flattened themselves against the edge of the black lane. Makhulu could feel the tremors travelling all the way to his muzzle.

"I wish Leon were here to see this," whispered Skoro. "He would have loved this." He raised his head. Another rumbler was speeding toward them, faster than the others. "Would have been the first one out of the trench too!" he suddenly exclaimed.

His body moved all at once, like a rock breaking free from a cliff. He jumped in front of the hulking mass and stopped, his head raised high, his paws planted squarely on either side of his open chest, a Mapogo.

The rumbler kept on charging. Makhulu screamed. Skoro stood still.

At the last instant, the rumbler swerved to the left and came to a screeching halt.

"Told ya!" Skoro exclaimed triumphantly, a shaky snarl on his muzzle. "We're still lions and they're still grazers."

More rumbler came to a halt on either side of the lane, this time at a more respectful distance.

"Come on," said Skoro, "let's go see that other side of grass."

They followed the black lane in a single file, like conquerors on the prowl. At their approach, more rumblers clustered to the side and quietly watched them go by, like birds on a branch. Makhulu could feel the wide eyes of the bipeds following his every move. He veered toward one of them and pushed out a short roar. The rumbler hastily backtracked. He chuckled and caught up with Skoro.

The vegetation called to them. They angled toward a cluster of flat-topped acacias and spread out amid the tall, green grass.

Skoro licked his muzzle and pointed toward the distant trees. "Now, were I a leopard living in these parts, that might be good place for me to keep my kills away from roaming lions."

"Worth a try, I guess."

They broke into a trot and swerved around the low thornbushes. This new land was not so unfamiliar after all. The grass sure smelled the same and, imbedded deep into the moist ground, Makhulu could make out all kinds of spoor he recognized quite well: the light brush of a water-monitor's tail, the two sharp grooves left by a gnu's hooves, a small, half-faded, flat indentation that may or may not have been left by a baboon. Perhaps he should not be so surprised. What else did he expect? Grass was grass.

They reached the acacias and scanned the canopies above.

"Any luck?"

"Nope."

Makhulu inspected a small sapling, then froze. "Skoro, come have a look at this."

"What is it? Oh! Oh, shit."

The ground near the base of the young tree had been scuffed. On the trunk, they could smell the urine, potent and acidic on the palate.

"How many do you think?"

Makhulu took a closer sniff. "At least two. Probably three. They were here no more than two dawns ago. At least one of them is black-maned, and big."

"How can you tell?"

Makhulu pointed at a tuft of black hair trapped underneath a piece of bark, higher than any point their own mane could reach.

"Maybe he's not so big. Maybe he was just standing on his hind legs to look for something in the tree."

"Maybe."

"But you don't really believe that, do you?"

"No."

Skoro's body shivered violently. All his resolve and strength of will suddenly seemed to leak out of him, as though he had just been kicked in the head by a zebra while in the middle of a leap. "Three big males," he whispered, "it's the Sabi Sands all over again. We're right back where we started. By the grass, all this walking, and we're right back where we started." His eyes welled up. In the scintillating yellow, Makhulu saw the depth of his despair flashing bright. "I–I don't know if I can go on like that much longer, Mak," he moaned.

Makhulu drew himself up and took a couple of steps back. He kept his gaze straight and distant. Should he give-in and try to comfort his brother with a head-rub, he knew that he would break too. And then they would both be lost. "We'll find food," he said sternly. "We'll keep to the shadows, keep quiet, and forage for whatever we can find. A cat can live like that, as long as he's not too picky. Trust me, I know."

Skoro shook his head. "It's not just the hunger though," he gasped. "I feel empty. Empty in my bones. Drained. The wound in my spine is burning all the time and won't let me sleep, my back legs are cold and numb, dead, it's…it's like I got no strength anywhere left in me no more! Like I'm just an empty fur rattling along the grass for no reason at all."

"Now, you stop that…"

"Why? What kind of a life are you talking about anyway? Keep to the shadows?! Keep quiet?! Like we're some kind of brown hyenas? We used to own it all, Mak! As far as our eyes could see and beyond! Now just look at us. Everywhere we go is claimed land. It's like we have to steal the very steps we take!"

Makhulu growled and swiped him on the muzzle, hard.

Skoro yelped and jumped away, ready to bolt. He caught himself at the last instant and stood his ground, his head bowed, his paws quivering. Finally, he sucked in his breath and let it out slowly. "Sorry," he said. "You're right of course. Life's still life. We'll do it your way."

They moved off the trees and slunk underneath the brush.

Days came and went. A new dry season settled in. Their demeanor changed, became more reserved, quiet, like snakes. A simple look and a brush of the tail, a quick exchange of whispers, now that was a whole conversation.

During daylight they learned to sidle through the tall grass with one eye on the sky looking for vultures and the promise of a carrion. Their ears were constantly flickering, ready to jump at the first sign of a heavy breath. At night, they would relax a little and keep prowling while taking reassurance in the thick darkness that protected them. Unless it was a full moon. Then, they would act as if it were still daylight.

They seldom rested anymore. They could not afford to waste the time as they had to forage constantly just to stay one half-step ahead of their hunger. No small amount of meat was too small to investigate.

What's that smell? Mongoose? Yes, but old, at least three dawns faded. Well, you best go and have a look just in case, what do you have to lose anyway? Wait! Not so fast. That's a perfectly good tree you just walked by. Look up, a cat can easily find himself a leopard's kill in such a tree. Now, you don't want to miss out on that, do you? Alright, the tree is barren, the mongoose is long gone. No worries, look over there, that's a water hole. Could be a turtle hiding in the mud. Could be a baby crocodile in the reeds. Could be all kinds of wonderful things. You won't know for sure until you've checked, old cat.

After several days and nights of relentless patrol, sleep would find them still standing. Half-delirious from exhaustion, they would stumble around and wrestle with the creeping grogginess while blinking fast to focus their mind. One more place to check, they would try to bargain. One more and I'm done. Can't rest now. Could be a whole buffalo lying down in that shallow valley over there. I need to check. The valley first, then the acacia over there, then I'm done, promise.

Eventually, the slumber would sneak up from behind and smack them in the back of the head. Their legs would take control and they would stagger toward the nearest bush, crawl underneath it, and collapse into a dead slumber that seemed to weaken the body even more.

Come dawn, the routine would start all over again.

Makhulu found that he could survive on this new regime, at least for the time being. He had grown lean, yes, but he remained vigorous, wiry. The lack of sleep was like a dull pain constantly thumping in the back of his mind but he could live with it. In a weird kind of roundabout way, it reminded him of his youth.

Skoro's state, however, was alarming.

He watched him plod by mindlessly, like a grazer, his hungry eyes relentlessly scanning the ground at his feet, a steady stream of saliva dribbling down his peeled black lips. Suddenly, he stopped for no reason, closed his eyes, and assumed a vegetative state.

Makhulu felt his heart sink. The lion he knew as Skoro had melted away. His spine was like a thin trunk running through his taut fur; trapped underneath the trunk, the all-too-visible ribcage looked like curved branches; his tail was a wispy vine; his limbs had thinned and seemed to have grown lengthwise, like roots still groping for nourishment long after the rest of the body has died. Only the mane remained, as deep and lush as the day of his first roar, like some kind of indomitable foliage.

On an impulse, Skoro resumed his trek.

They trudged on quietly for a bit, then stopped near a termite mound. Makhulu gave the structure a hopeful sniff and was rewarded with a smell of decay that betrayed the presence of the fungus the busy insects were growing inside. He immediately started digging.

"What are you looking for?"

"Eggs. Lizard eggs."

"In a termite mound?"

"Yes. The termites need to keep the inside of their colony warm to protect their precious fungus. Water-monitors know this and use it to their advantage by laying their clutch inside the mound. Then, they walk away. Since the termites can't destroy the shells, the eggs are safe, and the insects have no other choice but to repair the damage made by the big lizard and keep the clutch cozy and warm inside their colony for the duration of the incubation. Once the hatchlings are born, they just dig their way out."

"That's smart. And you gonna eat those eggs?"

"If I can find them, yes. I bet it's not so bad. When you think about it, it's still a kill."

"I don't think it counts if the thing isn't born yet."

Something in his brother's voice made Makhulu turn away from the mound. He shook the dirt out of his mane and licked the few termites that still clung to his muzzle.

Skoro's sprawled-out body seemed very flat against the ground, like some giant, desiccated leaf. Almost as if his presence were a trick of the light, as if he didn't exist at all.

"You need to eat something," Makhulu heard himself say stupidly. "Skoro, you absolutely need to eat something."

The leaf shook faintly and looked a lion again. A hoarse laughter came gushing out of the tick-covered muzzle. "Let me know when you go on the next hunt," the thing that was still Skoro said, "I'll be right with you." He marked a pause to catch a wheezing breath, winced in pain, closed his eyes. "On second thought, I think maybe I'll let you do the take-down."

At a loss for words, Makhulu went to give his brother's flank a light nudge and lick some of the dirt off his fur.

"We gave it a good try," whispered Skoro, "but I really don't think that we were meant to live like this, Mak. Like warthogs with our muzzle to the ground, burrowing for scraps. That's not us."

"I know. It's alright. Just rest for now, I'll figure something out."

"Don't beat yourself up, that's not your fault. We did everything we could."

"Does it hurt much? The hunger?"

"Yes. By the grass, yes. It used to feel like an emptiness in the stomach, but now… Now it's more like a tight little ball weighing me down, burning me from the inside." He licked his palate and swallowed his saliva. "That's the strangest thing, though. I haven't had buffalo meat since before we rejoined, but I still can't get the taste out of the back of my throat. It's like some fat is stuck down there or something."

That undid Makhulu.

Unable to control himself any longer, he bowed his head and flopped down next to his brother. An onslaught of irrepressible tremors shook his tired frame. He tried to contain them as best he could but a small whimper still escaped his jaws. He hurried to shut it out.

"Mak, you alright?"

"Yep." He cleared his throat, gave Skoro a light nudge. "Yes, of course."

He found that he didn't have the strength to return to the termite mound. It had been a stupid idea to begin with anyway. Exhausted, he just lay there and listened to his brother's breathing.

The sun slowly rose in the sky. Their shadows shortened. A pair of giraffes warily walked by them before disappearing behind a cluster of acacias, their powerful legs stomping the ground threateningly after every step, their high-perched flanks, so tentatively close, as unattainable as the moon itself.

“Mak?”

“Yes?”

“Nothing. For a moment, I thought that you were gone.”

“I’m right here Skoro. I’m not going anywhere.”

“Hey Mak?”

“Yes?”

“I, huh… I don’t think I’m gonna stand up again.”

“Sure, you will!” He tried to force some cheer into his voice but found that he could not control the quivers of his vocal cords any longer. “You’re Skoro ‘Pretty Boy’ Mapogo, the battered lion. Look at you. Even after they broke your back, you kept on fighting, kept on living. Everyone knows that you’re invincible.”

Skoro chuckled softly. “Skoro ‘Pretty Boy’ Mapogo,” he repeated slowly, savoring the words. “The battered lion. I like that.”

“I thought you might.”

The chuckles turned into a grimace. Skoro winced in pain and shuddered, then curled into a ball. “All these fights,” he breathed out, “and I’m dying a deflated death.”

Eventually, he fell into a shaky sleep. His legs quivered briefly, as if trying to run away, then stopped. A long whimper escaped his lungs. In it, Makhulu could discern the word “hurt” repeated over and over again, like some pitiful, delirious complain.

He nuzzled closer. The sharp bones dug into his back like the stubs of an old trunk. The thick mane tickled his fur. He let his weight sag down on his brother’s chest and felt the shallow breathing trying to push up weakly against his flank. He realized that he was holding his own breath. His whole body was like a block of hard wood. He exhaled slowly, relaxed his limbs, and let himself sink a bit deeper into his brother’s chest.

Skoro’s body was overcome by a few hard tremors. He kept his weight in place and focused his eyes on the clear blue sky above. Nothing on his mind but clear blue sky.

The breathing stopped.

He lay still and listened. Crickets chirped in the grass. The pair of browsing giraffes grunted softly to one another. Out in the distance, a hornbill on a branch called for a mate. A hundred sounds reached him. More. He listened to each one of them intently. Listened as the rest of the world kept on going, unperturbed, as if nothing had happened at all.

Then, he understood that it would forever be like this.

And that we are, all of us, at heart, alone.

EPILOGUE

WHAT IT ALL MEANS

The old male roused himself and blinked the memories away.

Below him, the savannah sparkled in pools and puddles under the full glare of the afternoon sun. The Dagga Boy was long gone. He licked his crusty muzzle and slowly stumbled down the hill. His gait was awkward. He moved in fits and stops with his body turned sideways from the slope and his front legs acting as a brake against the downward pull. He tried to imagine the others seeing him move like that and had to repress a short, derisive laugh. By the grass, T. would never have let him live it down.

He reached the nearest puddle and leaned forward. His position was terribly exposed, he knew, but he didn't care anymore. He was thirsty.

He stopped to lick his muzzle and looked down at his reflection. The sparkling water caught his mind.

They were all lined up by the side of a shallow stream, young and boisterous again. They had just left the Eyrefield pride and taken their first steps as a coalition. On the opposite bluff, a lone biped was standing next to a small rumbler. They paid him no mind.

"So, what does it mean?" asked Leonides.

"Huh?"

"Mapogo. The name you've chosen for our coalition. What does it mean?"

"It's from an old saying I heard when I was a wander-male. Basically, it says that a leopard can change his coat if provoked. Figuratively, of course."

T. raised a worried head. "We're going to name ourselves after a bunch of cats who spend most of their life stuck in a tree?"

"You're missing the point. The idea is that the leopard will adapt his behavior based on the threat in front of him and always try to overcome it. Meet any obstacle head-on and with absolute violence, live unapologetically, that's what Mapogo means."

"Oh," whispered T. "Oh, I like that."

"It's not true, though," groaned Skoro.

"What's that?"

"Leopards don't always face their enemies. More often than not, they run."

"By the grass, it's a *metaphor*," Dreadlocks exclaimed while rolling his eyes. "It's not meant to represent real leopards."

"How thick can a lion's skull truly be?" Shaka sniggered. "With all that extra bone-weight, it's a marvel that you are still able to keep your head above ground at all."

"He's far too ugly," Leonides said, "the grass wants nothing to do with that face."

"You all are just jealous because you know that the name I proposed was far better. We should have called ourselves 'Skoro's five', and that's that."

They shut him up with a chorus of snarls and a few rough shoves. He gave back as much as he received. Then, their tempers spent, they returned to their drinking, flank bumping against flank, and enjoyed the peace and quiet in a rare moment of unbroken harmony.

The memory rippled away from the old male's gaze. He raised his head and turned away from the puddle. For a full, gut-wrenching heartbeat, he was truly surprised not to find his brothers by his side.

He groaned softly, lowered his dripping muzzle, made for a patch of tall grass.

One last look at the open savannah behind.

He tore himself away from the tantalizing view and slowly plodded into the lank. The vegetation wrapped itself quietly around his flanks and swallowed his body whole. The tuft of his tail tarried behind for a brief instant, disconnected and suspended in the air, it seemed, as if hesitant to join the rest of him and share in his fate.

Finally, it followed in the lion's wake, never to be seen again.

THE END

A WORD ABOUT *THE FAR SIDE OF GRASS*

Although this story is based on real events, *The Far Side of Grass* remains, first and foremost, a work of fiction.

While the Mapogo coalition was a real coalition of six lions whose lives in the Sabi Sands, from the early 2000s until Makhulu's final demise in 2013, have been widely documented by the wildlife guides working at the safari lodges in the area, the characters in the novel have been, quite obviously, humanized: they talk, they joke, they curse, they cry, they have personalities, ponder the meaning of things, and, when the mood strikes him, one of them even formulates bad little songs in his head. This was done in an effort to tell the story as if seen through the eyes of the lions themselves, thus creating an experience that, I hope, will prove immersive to the reader. Should any wildlife purist read this book, I hope they'll understand… and forgive.

Throughout the writing of the book, I've let myself be guided – quite shamelessly and comfortably, I should say – by the concept of verisimilitude, or the *appearance* of truth. *The Far Side of Grass* is neither a completely factually accurate account of the life of the Mapogos, nor a pure fabrication. It kind of floats in between.

Most of the facts and events presented in the story are based on actual observations made by the various people (whether guides or tourists) who had the opportunity to observe the Mapogos in the flesh. In some cases, the timeline has been altered to fit the narration. Most notably: the killing of Makhulu's cubs by the other five Mapogos occurred in 2007, before the killing of Blondie and the long chase after the Nkuhuma pride. Most of the other lions present in the story are real lions whose interactions with the Mapogos have been documented. As much as possible, I have used the names given to them by the guides (more on that in a moment), but, when sources failed me, especially for lionesses, I have also created names of my own.

The life of a lion, much like that of a human, is made of repetitions: hunt, eat, sleep, roar, repeat.... In order to create a story that was engaging and not just a long litany of similar events, I had to leave a lot of things out. Some events that lasted several months and might otherwise have filled an entire book, such as the tribulations of T. and Shaka against the Styx pride, for instance, are just mentioned in passing. All in all, I've endeavored to re-create a fair and balanced picture of the life of this coalition, without insisting too much on every hunt and fight, which would have made them appear like blood-thirsty monsters, but without shying away from the violence that defined their lives either.

Some events depicted in the book are still a matter of controversy to this day, mostly due to a lack of data. Whenever possible, I have left the story opened to interpretation by the reader – did the Mapogos really fought off the Matimbas? Who knows for sure? Not them.

However, in some cases, such as the death of Leonides for instance, I have felt that, for the sake of the story's clarity, I had to choose one version of events. In those moments, I went with the explanation that seemed to make the most sense to me given the sources available and the reputation of said sources, while steering clear of conspiracy theories as much as possible (yes, in our modern age there are conspiracy theories regarding just about anything, including the lives of lions...).

In contrast, some readers might be frustrated by the lack of clear answer regarding Dreadlocks' and the Sand River Pride's disappearance.

This is not an omission on my part, nor is it a result of a lack of information. Put simply, those events were too unlikely to have been understood by the lions themselves, and their inclusion, I felt, would have stretched the limit of verisimilitude a bit too much. I have left clues in-between the lines, a quick internet search should help the reader answer any remaining question.

Lastly, in case it needs to be said, *The Far Side of Grass* does not constitute in any way, shape, or form an endorsement – nor a condemnation, for that matter – of the South African vigilante group known as Mapogo a Mathamaga.

A WORD ABOUT THE NAMES

Ridiculous. 'Dreadlocks' and 'T.' are far too human - lions don't know what these things are.

Upon perusing this book, the reader already familiar with the Mapogo story might raise an eyebrow, and possibly bare a fang, at the choices I have made when naming his or her favorite lions.

Once again, the concept of verisimilitude has been my guiding principle. I wanted to create the impression that the lions themselves had come up with those names. In order to do that, I had to steer clear of monikers I felt were too cliché, too human-sounding, or too descriptive. After all, it makes little sense for a cub to be named Scar Hip if that scar is still a long time coming in his future.

Luckily for me, the Mapogos were quite infamous throughout their lives, and each of them received several monikers from the different wildlife guides who had the opportunity to observe them. While this gave me a wide array of names to choose from, it can also add to the confusion. So, let's break it down one by one while I explain some of the choices I have made.

Makhulu – also sometimes seen spelled as Makulu – was the elder Mapogo. No confusion possible there: Makhulu is Makhulu. His origin is not clearly known, but it is believed that he was born to a different pride than the five other Mapogos, although his father would most likely have been a member of the same coalition that fathered the others, thus making him a half-brother of sort. He lived the longest of all the Mapogos and was last sighted, to the best of my knowledge, in Mala Mala in January 2013.

Then come two of the Mapogos commonly referred to as 'the twins.' In *The Far Side of Grass,* they are known as Skoro and Leonides.

Skoro was mostly known as Pretty Boy by the local guides, and also Bent-Spine toward the end of his life. I found that these two names were too human-sounding and descriptive, so when I read about one guide referring to him as Skoro, I jumped on the opportunity. The other nicknames, Pretty Boy and Bent-Spine, remain present in the story, after a fashion. Skoro lived the second longest of the Mapogos and was last seen in December 2012 while moving into the Kruger National Park along with Makhulu.

Leonides was known by a multitude of other names: Red, Scar, and Rasta to list only a few, with perhaps Rasta being the most common one. I felt that that last moniker would lead to some confusion with his brother Dreadlocks, so I went with the name I thought was the less cliché or human-sounding. Leonides died in 2010. He was the second Mapogo to die. The exact circumstances of his death are not known for certain. The version depicted in the book is based on an audio recording of a lion fight occurring at night at the Elephant Plain, and the fact that Leonides' body was never recovered.

Then comes the Mapogo commonly known as Dreadlocks. While this name might stretch the boundaries of verisimilitude – what could a lion possibly know about hairstyle? – the only other monikers I could find for him were Snip Tail and Scar Hip, which, I felt, were too descriptive. Since I did not want to create some confusion by making a name out of thin air, I kept the common name and tried to come up with a short explanation that might be satisfactory for the sake of the story. Dreadlocks died in 2010, he was the third Mapogo to be killed that fateful year. He was last seen alive while leaving the northern parts of the Sabi Sands reserve.

Lastly, the two younger Mapogos. In *The Far Side of Grass,* they are known as Shaka and T.

Shaka was more commonly known as Kinky Tail. Just like for Skoro/Pretty Boy, I went with the less descriptive name, Shaka, and only alluded to the other moniker as a nickname of sort. Shaka died in 2010, killed by the up-and-coming Majingilane coalition. He was the first Mapogo to be killed. His death was filmed by local guides and is well documented.

This brings us to T, perhaps the most infamous of all the Mapogos. Throughout his life, he was known by the local guides as Mr. T, although some also called him Mohawk or SaTan, due to his peculiar mane and his behavior that was considered, at times, extreme, even for a lion. Try as I might, I could not reconcile the idea of a lion living in South Africa being named after a human actor/wrestler from the United-States with my concept of verisimilitude. The other names were also a no-go: too descriptive, too human-sounding, too morally charged. In the end, I decided to simply drop the “Mister” out of the name and came up with a fictitious explanation for this uncommon, one-letter moniker. T. died in 2012, killed by another up-and-coming coalition known as the Selatis. The fourth Mapogo to die, just like Shaka’s, his death was filmed and is well documented.

The same loose principle of verisimilitude was used for the naming of the various coalitions and prides.

The fathers of the Mapogos, known in *The far side of grass* as the Sunset Boys, were actually called the West Street Males by the local guides. Since I could not accept the idea of a lion knowing about the cardinal points or what a street was, I had to improvise. Their individual names are left unchanged, it being understood that by the time of the story, they are already old and have earned their nicknames.

The Eyrefield pride, the birth pride of the Mapogos, was also known as the Sparta Pride by some lodges, while the Shaw males were also known as the Rollercoaster Males. In both cases I went with the less human-sounding names.

ACKNOWLEDGMENTS

The resources I have used throughout the writing of this book are too numerous to be listed completely here, but a few deserve to be mentioned.

The 2015 documentary: *Brothers in blood, the lions of Sabi Sands,* directed by Daniel Huertas and written by Craig Garner. This is the compelling summary of the lives of the Mapogos that sparked my interest for this coalition in the first place.

The Wildfact forum, accessible at this address: http://wildfact.com/forum. On this forum, a large community of internauts from all over the world share their enthusiasm for cats big and small, including the Mapogos. You guys have helped me make sense of the timeline and provided me with a trove of photos and first-hand reports from local wildlife professionals I would never have been able to find on my own. This book could not have been written without all of you.

The Rob The Ranger Wildlife Videos YouTube channel, accessible at https://www.youtube.com/robthe rangerwildlifevideos. The seemingly never-ending stream of high-quality videos Rob posts on his channel on a regular basis has allowed me to get a great, down-to-earth, unedited view of the Sabi Sands as seen through his lens – not just the Mapogos but also the greater wildlife of the area. And all of that without leaving the comfort of my chair! Rob can also be followed on Instagram at: https://www.instagram.com /robtheranger

The WildEarth website, accessible here: https://wildearth.tv. This website has allowed me to gain a better understanding of the various prides' dynamic throughout the Sabi Sands at the time of the Mapogos, thus adding some much-needed background information to the story. Many of those prides still exist today. Some even have their own Facebook page (!).

Cry of the Kalahari, written by zoologists Delia and Mark Owens. Their study of the behavior of large carnivores (especially lions and brown hyenas) living in the Kalahari desert constitutes a fantastic read for anyone interested by the African fauna.

A big thank you to Colleen Holland and Karen Gilliam for the huge summary of the Mapogos' life they have posted on a now defunct Facebook group. You guys helped my research a great deal.

Last but most certainly not least, I would like to express my deepest gratitude to all the wildlife professionals working in the Sabi Sands and greater Kruger National Park reserve and without whom the story of the Mapogos would probably have remained, like the story of all the other lions who came before them, untold.

Printed in Great Britain
by Amazon

85976567R00222